SWIFT
the
STORM,
FIERCE
the
FLAME

Swift the Storm, Fierce the Flame

A Novel

MEG LONG

WEDNESDAY BOOKS
NEW YORK

First published in the United States by Wednesday Books,
an imprint of St. Martin's Publishing Group

SWIFT THE STORM, FIERCE THE FLAME. Copyright © 2023 by Meg Long.
All rights reserved. Printed in the United States of America.
For information, address St. Martin's Publishing Group,
120 Broadway, New York, NY 10271.

www.wednesdaybooks.com

Designed by Michelle McMillian

Library of Congress Cataloging-in-Publication Data:

Names: Long, Meg, author.
Title: Swift the Storm, Fierce the Flame: A Novel / Meg Long.
Description: First edition. | New York : Wednesday Books, 2023. | Audience:
    Ages 12–18. |
Identifiers: LCCN 2022043586 | ISBN 9781250785121 (hardcover) |
    ISBN 9781250785138 (ebook)
Subjects: CYAC: Missing persons—Fiction. | Revolutions—Fiction. | Science
    fiction. | LCGFT: Science fiction. | Novels.
Classification: LCC PZ7.1.L6653 Sw 2023 | DDC [Fic]—dc23
LC record available at https://lccn.loc.gov/2022043586

Our books may be purchased in bulk for promotional, educational, or business use.
Please contact your local bookseller or the Macmillan Corporate and Premium Sales
Department at 1-800-221-7945, extension 5442, or by email at
MacmillanSpecialMarkets@macmillan.com.

First Edition: 2023

10 9 8 7 6 5 4 3 2 1

For Vanessa, whose friendship always saves me, no matter how thick the jungle or strong the storm.

CHAPTER 1

Swift is the storm that rages
Yet
Fierce is the flame that shatters the dark

I'm not usually one to push every limit around me, I swear. Being engineered to follow orders, fighting back against authority doesn't exactly come naturally to me. But when every onboard warning light is flashing and my flyer is heading straight for the eye of a giant storm, I will push against the very laws of physics if it keeps this ship from crashing into the planet's surface below.

It's a simple fight to see who yields first—me or gravity.

And I wasn't engineered to lose.

I shove the controls forward again, trying to get a grip on the flyer's descent as we plummet toward the planet and the storm that covers an entire third of it. But the ship's steering is not responding like it should. I growl in frustration because it's technically not my fault we got shot at by both syndicate bounty hunters and the jump gate authority when we tried to leave the Tundar jump station.

It's partially Jens's and Jori's fault. My former genopath squad-mates, who were posing on Tundar as low-level syndicate bosses, surprised me on the ice planet's jump station and offered me the intel I'd been searching for, specifically the location of my ex-partner I've been chasing across worlds. But anything to do with the twins comes with a price. If my genetics are designed so I can blend in anywhere, these two are engineered to make a profit out of any situation and by any means possible. They're not the most physically imposing of the genopaths from my former squad, but they are the most devious.

And I was desperate. So, the twins gave me the intel I needed, intel that's led me through two jump gates and across the charted systems. But the price I paid was steep; they reported me to Nova, the shadowy organization that genetically engineered me and the rest of my squadmates to serve corpo needs. I escaped from their grasp two years ago but the execs and lab hacks at Nova really don't like it when we disobey orders, let alone disappear and pre-tend to be dead. And since they have agents all over the charted systems — Edge Worlds and Corporate Assembly planets alike — it wasn't a surprise when the authorities tried to stop us from leaving the Tundar jump station. So, it's mostly the twins' and Nova's fault my poor ship is malfunctioning.

The rest of the fault belongs to the bounty hunters. They weren't there for me, though. They were there for the girl and wolf running through the station with me. Sena and Iska. The two of them are the only reason I survived my time on Tundar at all. Even though Sena helped me and another scientist get through the infamous sled race across Tundar's icy wastelands, she and her wolf, Iska, still killed a syndicate den boss at the race's end.

And while Boss Kalba certainly deserved his fate for murdering Sena's mothers, the syndicates don't really care about those backstory details. Take out one of their bosses without permission and there are consequences.

Consequences that included a buttload of bounty hunters shooting at my flyer while we were fleeing the jump gate commandos. And that is the reason why the steering currently isn't working and why we're pointed not at the portions of the planet below us covered by lush green, but directly at the vortex of the dark swirling mass of clouds gaping like a giant hole.

The infamous hellstorm of Maraas.

The most expansive storm system among all the charted worlds. A weather event so big it makes the blizzards on Tundar look tame. And since the ship's auto-descent protocols seem to be malfunctioning, too, it looks like we're going to crash our flyer right in the middle of it. No one's coming to our rescue, and there's no way we can make it to the Maraas jump station for repairs. Nope. There's no choice but imminent disaster and the giant storm currently looming below our broken ship.

But I didn't survive that damn sled race or a mauling by a demonic bear to just crash into a hellstorm over a godforsaken jungle. I will not let bloody syndicates or Nova agents or even gravity win this round. I smash a few more controls in an attempt to push anything out of the ship's onboard systems. The flyer's thrusters fire momentarily but then whine and sputter out; someone must've shot through the engine's fuel lines during our escape.

Looks like we're going down right into the eye of the storm. That might make it harder for me but not impossible. Nova engineered and programmed me to do the impossible on a regular basis.

"I hope you two are strapped into something!" I yell to Sena back in the common area. I get a curse and a crashing sound in response.

"Remy, what the hell is going on?!" Sena shouts as the banging sounds continue. We didn't exactly have time to review on-ship safety protocols, so Sena and Iska might not be secured back there. Not to mention everything else I left lying around the common space.

"We're entering Maraas's atmosphere," I answer. "But we're not exactly slowing down like we should be."

And our steering is also malfunctioning, but I leave that part out.

"What?" Sena's shout is followed by some equally angry-sounding barks from Iska. But I don't answer. Instead, I slow my breathing and tell my body to release more adrenaline into my veins. I'll need all the extra focus and awareness I can get, and thankfully, with my genetic alterations, adjusting specific hormone levels is as easy as flexing a muscle.

Right as my sensory perception amplifies, we hit the upper layer of the atmosphere, the planet's gravity latching onto the ship with a yank.

And we plummet down, down, down into the sky.

I try to slow us down by adjusting the ship's flaps, but everything is shaking and bouncing as we hit the first pockets of wind and air. The sky darkens around us, gray clouds filling the viewports.

Out of nowhere, a low-orbit substation looms directly in our path. I yank the flaps hard to avoid smashing into it, jerking the entire ship to the side as my adrenaline spikes automatically. More crashes and very angry cursing echo from the common area behind me, but all I can see is a giant name filling the viewport: *ARC1*. The words painted across the substation are close enough to reach out and touch. A familiar green corporate logo follows the name and then disappears into nothing but a blip in our wake as the danger passes.

"Remy! What the hell was that?!" Sena shouts.

"Just a low-orbit satellite, no big deal!" I yell back as I force open all the flaps the ship has in an attempt to slow us down before we get below the clouds. The flyer slows slightly and I'm able to level us out for a moment. I quickly check the emergency systems, scanning the main holoscreen for our parachute status.

But instead of a status report, everything is red and flashing and really unhelpful. Eyes back on the sky, I try again to steer us out of the storm, but the clouds have taken on a life of their own. Strong winds snag the flyer and draw us into the vortex.

There's nothing to do now but react.

The gray sky shifts to total black, and I've got only a split second to decide what's more important: getting us through the storm or hacking a way to open our chute. Calculations fly through my head.

Storm first. Chute after.

Using the flaps as makeshift steering, I force the flyer east, toward the edges of the storm. Then a gust shoves the ship forward, tipping its nose straight down. My ponytail whips around, dark hair filling my vision while my stomach punches into my throat as we go completely vertical.

"Remy!" Sena shrieks from the back.

"Got it!" I level out the flyer as best I can, but the wind pushes us nearly sideways next. Iska starts to bark and I can't really blame her. Flying under normal conditions can be hard for first-time offworlders. And these conditions are not what I would call ideal. But Sena and Iska are tougher than they look. They survived a thousand-mile sled race across the most dangerous landscape of any of the Edge Worlds. What's a bumpy landing compared to blizzards, ice goblins, and giant osak bears?

But the way we're falling, this landing is going to be a lot more than bumpy. Only one way to get through the storm. I have to kill the flaps. We'll have absolutely no drag to slow us down, but if we keep getting blown around, we're going to crash for sure.

Decision made, I punch the controls for the flaps and we streak through the sky like lightning, the flyer cutting across the wind. Rain pelts the exterior like thousands of bullets finding their mark as we fall into the heaviest part of the storm.

My eyes jump between the weather outside and the holoscreen that's attempting to read the planet's surface through the tempest. I grip the controls tighter, waiting for some sign of an exit. My body moves with the ship instinctually, reacting to the eddies and currents in the storm. I know my opening is coming; I just have to time it.

Blip. A dot appears on the holoscreen along with the faintest sound, the ship's programming finally registering a settlement or a large building. A few more dots appear as the holo warns of elevation rising up to meet us. Getting closer now.

The flyer has two chutes. Only two shots to use them. But not in this wind. We'll get swept away, back into the vortex. The blips get louder.

Almost there.

Ten thousand feet.

The whole flyer shakes violently as the storm rages around us.

Five thousand feet.

A particularly strong gust of wind pushes against the ship, knocking us off trajectory and spinning the flyer around in an arc. Iska howls in the back and I think Sena is screaming at me.

A thousand feet.

But then there's a break in the clouds, and we're bursting free from the dark mass into calmer skies, just like I knew we would.

"Hold on!" I shout.

I release the first chute.

The flyer jerks upward and I'm flung against my seat, but we're still careening toward the treetops. The jungle rushes up at us, and I release the second chute and open all the flaps at once. Again, the ship lifts up from its dive and we sail over branches, bouncing on top of treetops like a stone skipping across water. Each jump, my stomach jerks up to my throat, then back into my feet. Each impact, the safety belt snaps across my barely healed ribs before I slam back into the chair. Each tree trunk we crash into might as well be a mountain. But I don't puke or lose my cool. I was engineered better than that.

Finally, we hit earth and slide through the overgrowth, knocking down a few trees and barreling through underbrush. My viewport is now nothing but vines and leaves and limbs as we bump and bounce across the ground. Then the ship snags on something; the flyer tilts up, precariously balancing on a wing tip. The world is stuck vertical for one frozen moment.

And I can't help but grin. We're all in one piece.

Bloody brilliant.

Then we crash down to the planet in a sudden drop. The ship slams into the ground, jerking me hard enough to leave bruises in the exact shape of the harness across my shoulders and chest. The lights flicker and the ship's power sputters out. I suck in a breath listening; thankfully, I can hear Sena's and Iska's heartbeats, erratic but strong.

The smile is still stuck on my face; I kept us from crashing. Gravity didn't win.

A piece of the ceiling crashes next to my chair.

Mostly.

I unclick the safety harness, chuckling to myself.

"We made it!" I shout to Sena and Iska in the common room.

Then I take in the jungle outside, and my breath hitches as old memories threaten to resurface. Memories of a broken girl, bleeding and lost amid the endless expanse of the jungle wilds. A tall waif of a girl with freckled skin, wispy blond hair, and piercing blue eyes.

A girl who saved my life. And who I failed to save when it mattered most. My elated confidence turns into a bitter whisper.

"Welcome to Maraas."

CHAPTER 2

Pushing the memories away like I push the dark, errant strands of my now-mussed hair away from my face, I peel myself out of the pilot's seat just as there's another crash, this one back in the engine room. Tentatively standing and testing my weight, I take a breath, sniffing for odors of leaking fuel, but nothing dangerously flammable hits my nose. Mostly just burned plastic and seared metal. I don't catch even a hint of the tangy scent of iron. No one is bleeding; that's a relief.

"You two still in one piece?" Ignoring the jungle outside and shaking off the dregs of the memory triggers, I slowly shimmy past the seat and poke my head into the common room. Debris is everywhere. Datapads, utensils, boxes of clothes and accessories. Sena knocks over a small crate next to her as she unhooks her seat harness. Her black curls have sprung loose from her braid, her hair as messy as mine. Her pale-ashen face is wan from the ship's thrashing, but her gray eyes hold a storm of their own.

"I swear I left my stomach somewhere in atmo," she responds after a beat, her voice low but unwavering as blood slowly returns to her cheeks. "I don't think I like flying much."

"I promise it's not usually that bad." Sena's first cross-systems flight and we get tangled up in a dogfight against a dozen ships and then fly through a storm as big as a moon. I quickly scan her as she stands, looking for visible injuries my nose might've missed. Sena catches my look.

"Nothing but bruises," she says, nudging the crate farther out of her way, clearing a path out from the row of passenger seats in the corner. Iska's white-tipped red ears poke up from behind another box in the kitchen area, followed by the rest of her russet fur. Somehow, she's also unscathed from the landing.

The wolf picks her way over to us, knocking over some small crates that must've flown out of the cargo hold when the storm was whipping us around. I hold out a hand toward her snout and she huffs before licking my palm. At least she's not too mad about the bumpy flight.

"So, what do we do now?" Sena asks, coming close and checking over Iska herself.

My stomach growls.

"Food first. Burning that much adrenaline always makes me hungry." Ignoring Sena's side-eyed look, I inhale deep again, this time sniffing for something edible in the flotsam around us. Wading through the mess as I follow the scent of food, I finally find what I need in one of the smaller crates; dry nutrition bars and commando-issue meal packs stare up at me in the dim light. Yum. I tear open one of the protein bars and wolf it down in two bites, then hand some to Sena while stuffing a few in my pockets. I tear open another crate as I munch on a second bar.

"Now that's settled, we need to change into clothes better suited for the jungle and rain," I say as I sift through the pile of random clothing inside the open crate. "We'll overheat if we wear any of these layers outside."

Not finding what I need, I open a few of the lockers built into the far wall and dig around in at least three of them before spotting something more appropriate for Maraas near the bottom of a drawer. I pull out the sweat-wicking attire and toss it toward Sena.

"Are these all your disguises and stuff for blending in?" Sena asks, fingering a few of the dressier items from the crate. "Like you had in the warehouse on Tundar?"

My heart skips a beat. "Most of it is."

What isn't mine belonged to someone else. The same someone I let down in this stupid jungle. Someone I've been trying to find ever since. I quickly swallow past the reminder of my failure and push on. Now's really not the time for triggers and memories.

"You're taller than me, but there's still some things that will fit you." I soften my voice as I point at her. "It's going to be too hot here for your cloak. And the jungle tends to destroy things with the mud and heat. We'll have to leave it on the ship."

She gently fingers the edges of her newly patched cloak. I know how hard it is for her to part with it. After we were rescued from certain death along the sled trail and Bakir returned with Sena and Iska both nearly dead from exposure and their wounds, Pana and I had done our best to ensure her cloak was salvaged. Sena saved both our lives more than once over the course of the sled race; it was the very least the doctor and I could do for her. So, Pana and I pieced together the missing parts of Sena's life while her physical wounds healed. Bit by bit, and with the scavvers' help, we repaired the cloak and finally were able to return it to her. Now she's going to be parted from it again.

"We'll keep it locked in here while we're on this world." I gesture at the wall behind her. "There are smuggling holes all over the ship that no one knows about. It'll be safe."

We lock eyes and a moment of understanding passes between us. She slowly nods, accepting my unspoken promise. I hand her some clothes to try on and point her up to the bathroom to change. Iska lies down at the bottom of the short ladder leading to the living quarters and waits sullenly, watching as I pick through more clothes.

I find what I need, and I quickly slip into my own thinner, sweat-wicking layers. Layers made for the jungle. Bottoms that are lightweight and sturdy and won't rip on trees or branches. A thin, fitted top to keep the moisture and bugs off my skin. Waterproof boots that can tromp through mud and swamp alike. I even dig out a brush and, using a tiny hanging mirror in the locker, get my mass of long dark hair off my face and neck. I ignore the faint scars from the osak bear still crossing my cheeks. The lack of sun and moisture on Tundar has left my complexion blanched and pallid. But the sun is much stronger in this world, and my skin won't stay sallow for long, especially with my genetics. The scars will fade soon enough, too.

I throw the rest of the odd clothing and accessories back toward a crate. I won't need any of them on this planet. Not the colored lenses to change my brown eyes. Not the UV hair dye to erase my brown locks. No, I won't use any disguises here since my ex-partner will see right through them. Stretching out my stiff limbs, I feel like I can finally breathe, better than I ever could trapped in the multi-layers needed to survive the Tundar cold.

I might've been engineered to survive almost anything, but the long exposure to the ice was pushing even my limits. I was built for cities, for infiltration. Nova, the organization that not-so-secretly builds genetically engineered agents, designed and trained me to blend in anywhere, with anyone. To read body language and visual cues, to detect what people want in seconds and use that to my advantage. To be a perfect spy. And while my senses are enhanced with the DNA of deadly predators from all kinds of worlds and I can control my body's reactions to stress and stimuli, the tundra wasn't exactly on the short list of places Nova needed a spy to thrive in. I was made for crowds and chaos, not for blizzards and desolate wilds. Being off that world is a true relief. Though this planet is not much safer.

Sena returns similarly dressed, holding her cloak neatly folded in her arms. That cloak is the only thing she has of her mothers, and I'll be damned if I let something happen to it. I asked Sena to come here with me. And while I'm not entirely sure if it was because I wanted to or if my programmed instincts thought she'd be useful, I owe her this much at least.

"The clothes look like they fit okay," I say, awkwardly breaking the silence that has descended in the space.

"They're good." She smiles faintly. "Feels strange not to pack on more layers, though. I can't even imagine a world with no ice."

"No ice and no wolves. But there's plenty of other preds to keep you busy, both human and animal." I point to her cloak. "Let's put that somewhere safe."

I lead Sena to an innocuous-looking part of the wall situated above the passenger seat she was in earlier. Standing on the seat cushion, I press on one of the panel corners with the chit chip in my wrist. A hidden lock activates and the panel pops open to reveal a large empty space behind it.

"There are hidden compartments all over the ship that open with my chit chip alone," I explain as I gingerly take her cloak and place it on a shelf in the compartment. I see the emotion in her eyes as I lock the panel again.

"It will be safe here," I repeat. "I promise."

The last promise I made jumps into my mind unbidden. A promise to be better than what Nova programmed me to be. The promise I made to my only friend, then promptly broke when I failed to save her. I've spent the last two years running from world to world, trying to atone for that failure while tracking the one person who knows what happened to her. And now I'm back here. Where it all started. Where I'll finally catch up to the snake that betrayed me.

Kiran.

My ex-partner, another former squadmate of mine, the reason I failed my friend in the first place. He was always too good at keeping secrets and I know he knows where she is. Now he's somewhere on this world, and once I catch up to him, I'll get the answers I need to save my friend at last.

Until then, I don't plan on breaking any more promises, especially this one to Sena. I double-check the lock on the panel and then make my way through the mess toward the engine room so I can get a handle on the ship's damage.

"What can I do?" Sena's voice follows me as I flip on a few emergency lights. The copious contents of the ship whizz through my mind while I consider Sena's skills.

"You can load up on weapons. We'll need to be prepared for anything out here. Guns, knives, explosives. Whatever you can find and want, it's yours. There's even some arken blades in one of the lockers, next to the kitchen sink, I think."

Sena makes a nearly inaudible noise in response that's somewhere between a grunt and a squeal as I climb down the ladder to the engine room. Sounds of opening and shutting locker doors follow shortly afterward. Even though our upbringings couldn't have been more different, I understand her excitement. While I don't know exact details of Sena's life before the race, it's easy to guess it was sparse, like everything else on Tundar.

Like my own childhood was.

Nova doesn't let its homegrown genopaths have personal items. Our illegal existence might be a well-known secret, but most of the rumors about us add to the mystery of our abilities. Nova probably spreads those rumors itself. But what is never talked about is how we're treated. How we're trained. Nova birthed me and raised me in a highly controlled lab that was more a military institution than anything else. We weren't allowed belongings, and displaying any kind of ownership at all was promptly punished. One of the reasons I hoard all the junk on this ship is simply because I can. No lab coat is going to show up and confiscate a damn thing. And I'm happy to share it with Sena. Everyone deserves to have their own things.

A few minutes later, Sena peeks into the engine bay, a long arken blade strapped to one thigh, her trusty ax on the other.

"How does it look down there?"

"We burned through most of the fuel getting away from the syndicate chumps shooting at us. The engine's blown more than a few valves from when I pushed it too hard so we could get to the jump gate. And the gravity pull from the jump we hijacked completely overstressed the thermal reactors."

Sena blinks at me. "And that means what, Remy?"

I sigh. "It means we're not moving the ship anytime soon. I need a lot of parts and a lot of time to fix it. Too much time." Leaving the smell of engine oil and burned electronics behind, I slowly climb the ladder back to the communal space, my mind whirring.

"So, we're supposed to be looking for your ex-partner, who the twins said was somewhere on this world helping some syndicate," Sena says on my heels. "But we also need parts for the ship. I'm guessing you have a plan for all of those things, though, right? You always have a plan."

"Making one as we speak," I reply, stopping at the still-open weapons locker to get my own supplies. I shove a serrated knife deep in my boot for emergencies, then grab for the flash bombs on the bottom shelf, my favorite weapon of choice. I didn't pack any for the race when we were on Tundar, and I regretted it the entire time. They're small, but their weight is reassuring. Big enough to fit in my palm, each one is capable of large-scale fiery destruction. Perfect in a pinch. I stuff a handful in various pockets as I turn back to Sena and explain our next move.

"Based on the feeds before we crashed, we're somewhere in the jungle. Luckily, we crashed inside the mag zone." At her confused look, I grab some discarded utensils and lay them out on top a nearby crate, making a line of dull knives and chipped spoons across the surface. I should've explained this before, but it's been nonstop running since we left Tundar.

"The only habitable place on Maraas is a long strip of land along the maglev train rail." I trace the line of utensils. "This train track sits above the tree canopy and runs from the eastern plateau here"—I point to the right side of the crate—"travels over the lowlands of swampy jungle, and ends in the western mountains at the mines." I finish my path at the other end of the crate.

"The magnetic pulse that the rail line emits produces a low-frequency hum which doesn't really bother humans." I glance at

Iska, calculating the auditory range of her ears. "Or vonenwolves, probably. But it does keep a lot of hearing-sensitive preds, especially the swarms of anacrocs or batimalu apes, far away. So, the magnetic zone that exists around this rail line is essentially the safest area on the planet."

Going back to the right side of the crate, I continue. "There's a small corpo city, Verem, at the top of the plateau here. And a syndicate outpost tucked into the caves underneath it. Those are the only places we'll be able to find parts for the ship. Everything else is a mess of crowded slums or endless jungle. And based on what I saw on the holofeeds, we're not near the plateau or the sprawl, what they call the slums under the mag tracks. We're somewhere to the south."

Sena studies the utensils, then looks up at me.

"So, are we going after your ex-partner or are we chasing down the parts first? Either way is a trek, right? At least we crossed worse terrain on foot on Tundar."

"They really don't teach much about the other worlds on Tundar, do they?" I hold in a chuckle. Tundar may be one of the most trying worlds I've ever been on. Below-freezing temperatures, predators in every shadow, and an endless white tundra under constant threat of blizzards and ion storms. But every Edge World has its own dangers. Maraas is no exception. I cross the communal space to the airlock door. I need fresh air at this point, even if it's wet, sticky jungle air full of memories. Sena follows me, the wolf on her tail.

"The problem isn't the terrain. It's the storm," I say, punching in the activation code and holding my breath until the closed system whirs back to life. At least the crash didn't knock out all the onboard feeds.

"The storm? You say that like . . . it's just one storm?"

"It is. One giant storm. The hellstorm." The holoscreen controls flicker on as I explain. "It covers a third of this entire world. It circles around the whole planet and hits the livable areas every twelve days or so, grinding everything to a halt and changing the entire landscape of the jungle. What was solid ground before turns into rivers or lakes or swamps and then is gone the next cycle."

Iska sniffs at the edges of the door and paws the ground. She's ready for fresh air, too. The holoscreen dies and I smack the side of the panel hard enough that it comes back on.

A long breath escapes Sena's lips. "So, you're saying we'll have to find some way to get to this Verem place and back in less than two weeks or the ship gets blown away?"

"Or flooded or pushed farther into the swamp. You get the basic idea, but yeah." I nod and swipe at the holoscreen to open the airlock door. With a beep, the system starts the routine atmosphere checks needed before deactivating the lock. Finally.

"On your world," I continue, "no one had flyers because the ion storms knocked them out of the sky. On this world, no one outside of Verem can afford flyers, let alone maintain them, because there's nowhere to keep the ships safe from the storm except in the one hangar that's built into the side of the plateau."

"We have no choice but to head for the city then," she says. "And we'll have to get there fast."

"Verem isn't exactly like the Ket, though." I think back to the frozen city held together by syndicate gangs and desperation. "While there's a heavier corpo presence here, the syndicates hold the true power on this world, just like on Tundar."

The substation in orbit we almost collided with pops into my head, as well as the corpo logo that was plastered across it. "Or at least that's how it was two years ago. Things might've changed. But it doesn't matter; I'll figure out a cover story that explains us and the ship. Hopefully, we can get the parts we need and track down my ex-partner Kiran's location without too much trouble."

I can't help but smile at the excitement humming through my veins. It's not only the anticipation of finally catching up with Kiran; it's the complexity of our situation. A dozen moving parts that could change in an instant. The test of my skills and reactions. The whisper of chaos and trouble. All things I was engineered to excel at.

The door beeps, finished with its scan of atmo conditions. The airlock clicks and the door panel opens with a whoosh. An immediate blast of hot air hits me in the face, but that isn't what causes me to take a step back in hesitation.

Half a dozen commandos are positioned around the door, automatic guns pointed right at us. I was so focused on our own problems I forgot to listen before opening the door, and now we're completely surrounded by bloody commandos. My ears pick up the hum of flyer engines, too. I let some adrenaline flow into my blood, but my smile doesn't dim. This is just another moving part for me to maneuver.

"Tell me you've already solved that cover story problem," Sena whispers as she scans the troops around us. I square my shoulders, hoping she catches the movement and understands that we're going to be fine.

"Hands up where I can see them," a broad commando shouts. Another flyer, larger than mine and with mounted guns, hovers into view behind him. That same corpo logo is marked on both wings of the ship. The green, leafy outline I saw in orbit. My mind whirs through facts as I raise my arms. TerraCo. Third-largest corpo on the Assembly worlds. Biggest corpo presence on Maraas. Specializes in energy and resource development. Which is basically corpo-speak for resource plundering to fuel the Assembly worlds' power. Guess things aren't exactly the way they were two years ago if the commandos greeting us are TerraCo chumps instead of syndicates.

Pulses and heartbeats fill my ears as I bring the commandos into focus over the usual sounds of the jungle. I don't have to see them all to know that twelve commandos and now two flyers face us down, everyone armed to the teeth.

I keep my palms open and facing the man who spoke. Sena follows suit next to me, whispering to Iska, but my focus is on the broad commando now stepping forward. His ruddy white face is peppered with scars, much like how his roughed-up armor is covered in scratches. Unlike the others, his buzzed head of straw-colored hair isn't hidden under a helmet. Must be up the chain of command high enough to not bother with protocol. His beady green eyes look me up and down.

"What are you doing flying in restricted airspace and landing without a permit?"

I shrug, keeping my movements slow. "Didn't know we needed a permit for crashing."

The commando stares dead at me, his eyes devoid of any emotion. "We've shot people for less."

The words, meant to intimidate and scare, only serve to ratchet up my adrenaline while a distant part of my brain is calculating just how much the power dynamics on Maraas have changed in two years.

The leader nods to a few of the commandos on our right, who begin to move closer to us. I hatch a dozen escape plans as I watch them, searching for an option that doesn't end with us getting shot at. My fingers itch to reach for one of the flash bombs in my pockets, but instinct tells me to wait for a better opening.

"What's your business on Maraas?"

My eyes jump back to the commando in charge, and the plans in my head shift as an idea for a cover story suddenly snaps into place.

"We work for Dekkard Shaw," I say.

A few of the commandos exchange a glance, though their pulses remain steady. No signs of fear or uncertainty. Guess a syndicate head boss's name doesn't hold as much weight around here as it used to. Which means the power has truly tipped in favor of the corpos. Doesn't matter. I've got their attention.

The lead commando taps his ear as a message relays over his comms. I zero my focus in on filtering out all other sounds so I can clearly hear the feminine voice crackling into his earpiece.

"Interesting," the voice says. There's a pause.

"Bring them to me."

CHAPTER 3

The ride in the TerraCo flyer is a breeze compared to our earlier landing, even if we are forced into the cargo bay at gunpoint. At least they let us keep our weapons. Guess they're not worried about two girls with arken blades and a half-feral wolf.

Their mistake.

The heat from the jungle and the ship engines is a blanket of sweat and stale air around us as the flyer glides over the treetops. After the dry chill of Tundar and the recycled air on my own flyer, it's like trying to breathe in hot soup. The sharp edges of the hard metal seat cut into my thighs, and sweat pools under my legs despite the moisture-wicking layers.

Next to me, Sena's leaned up close to one of the tiny windows, peering down on the jungle below. Her eyes dart up from the canopy to check our captors every few seconds. As we boarded the flyer, I told her in a whisper to follow my lead. She gave me a look somewhere between a glare and an eye roll. By her feet, Iska is quietly panting through the heat, muscles tense as we fly. Her eyes, like mine, watch everything. No sign of the predator wolf she can be. Yet.

Like me, she's waiting.

Just as Iska was designed to fight, this is what I was made for—improvising chaos in scenarios like this. It's not anxiety or nerves pooling in the pit of my stomach; it's the buzz I was engineered to get from high stakes and unknown outcomes.

I glance out the window to check on the tow ship in our wake, currently dragging my poor broken flyer in its mag field. The lead commando—I heard the others call him Taggert—insisted they board my ship to search it for contraband, whatever that means. Probably looking for things they can claim and confiscate. As if the corpo chumps don't take enough from the rest of us. Good thing Sena and I locked up the valuables and left the rest of the mess out in the open. I hope they had fun sorting through the piles of mildewy clothes.

The flyer dips suddenly and Sena's hand jumps to her stomach. The lower angle gives me a better view of the plateau we're approaching, and the city spread out across it. A city I learned like the back of my hand for my last mission under Nova's control. My orders were to pose as a bodyguard to infiltrate a syndicate and help engineer a coup to replace its leadership. The syndicates on this world are more organized than on Tundar. There, the bosses come into power on their own and then claim loyalty to one group or another. But here on Maraas, there was only ever one syndicate.

The Vega.

As the ship circles the city to approach the hangar on the far side of the plateau, any sense of my familiarity with the cityscape dissipates. Two years ago, Verem belonged to the Vega. The city was small but growing, a mix of corpo offices and syndicate strongholds. TerraCo controlled a few buildings, just like the other corpos that had enough balls to brave the hellstorm and attempt business on-world. But TerraCo and the other corporations were limited in their power.

But seeing the city now, it would appear that Dekkard Shaw — the Vega lieutenant I helped put into power — has abandoned Verem entirely.

We fly lower, closer to the more populated districts, and the green of the TerraCo logo flashes across buildings and transpo trucks alike. Only the corpo district looks pristine; the rest of the city is nothing but run-down warehouses or offices along with decrepit lodging on stilts. On the plateau's edge, right in the center of the corpo district, a new tower, tall and pristine, looms over the low-lying buildings. The green logo on its side a reminder of who watches over the city. I try to remember the Verem I knew from before, but there's just no trace of the place that lives in my memories. I spot none of the Vega complexes or even the red-light district. It's like the city has been reduced to TerraCo's holdings surrounded by slums.

The sight sits heavy in my stomach. I could've prevented all this had I not failed that night. Had I not been betrayed by Kiran.

Just as my anger rises, Verem disappears and the flyer dips below the plateau's surface, revealing a large cavern in the rock. The only on-world ship hangar, hidden under the belly of the sprawling city above. Our flyer sails through the opening, vast enough to accommodate ships three times as big. We head to the end of the long runway and set down with a bump on one of the landing markers.

The hangar is bigger than I remember; the corpos expanded on what the syndicates started. Before, there were only a handful of flyers that parked here. Now there's a heavily armed fleet of a dozen or so ships. Whatever TerraCo needs so many ships for can't be good.

Not everything has changed, though; beyond the ships tucked into the rock wall, I spy doors that I know lead to tunnels carved into the rock of the plateau. They used to run all the way to the Vega headquarters. Now the entrances are sealed tight as if TerraCo wants to cut off all paths, all reminders of the Vega.

Sena and I file out between commandos. The jungle heat continues to crawl up my skin even in the depth of the cave. Sweat drips down my spine; my very bones ache from the oppressive warmth.

A scraping sound catches my attention. Behind us, the tow ship has dragged my dangling flyer right across the rocky bottom of the cavern entrance. It flies precariously down the runway, then releases the mag field. With a bang, my flyer drops roughly onto the cracked pavement. My jaw clenches as I turn to the lead commando.

"Was that really necessary? You've damaged it even more."

The commando, Taggert, shrugs, again with a total lack of emotion. "The tow ship pilot must be new. I'm sure you can ask your boss, Dekkard, to fix it for you." He puts extra emphasis on Dekkard's name, and I know something's up. As the Vega boss, Dekkard should be respected and not mocked. Rather than say anything that could potentially expose our flimsy cover, I settle for glaring at Taggert as he points to a large elevator at the back of the cavern.

"You two, walk. The dog stays here."

Sena glares at him. "Not a chance. Where I go, the wolf goes."

A growl rumbles low in Iska's throat as the commando considers the wolf. After a beat, he rolls his dull green eyes and jerks his chin toward the lift. "Whatever, we don't have all day."

"Where exactly are we going?" I ask, not expecting answers but watching his body language instead. "I have my own people to check in with. Syndicate protocols. You've heard of them, right?"

"You and your friend"—Taggert glances down at Iska, ignoring my sarcasm—"and dog are going to check in with the director first." He pauses right in front of me, forcing me to stop midstep or plow into him. It's a childish attempt at a power play, but I let him have it. Let him think he's got the upper hand for now. He's making his role as the head enforcer of all things corpo so transparent I almost laugh.

The goon leers closer, forcing the stench of stale breath and sweat up my nose.

"Everyone sees the director first."

I already knew they were taking us to see the corpo boss. Now I know that they're ignoring syndicate-corpo protocol, too. Taggert's beady eyes bore into mine, but I don't flinch or blink. If he thinks he can intimidate me with size or threats, he's very wrong. Though the smell might make me take a step back. Sometimes my enhanced senses are not an advantage.

"Fine." I step around him and his odor toward the lift doors. "I'll make sure we have a little chat about compensation for ship damages while we're there."

Taggert barks out a laugh as he lumbers behind me. "Oh, that'll be fun. For me."

Sena gives me a look as she follows, but I nod reassuringly. Iska hovers close, panting from the heat, her eyes taking in the tiny space. Sena places a protective arm on the wolf's side as the three of us step into the open lift. The wolf whines almost inaudibly, but my ears still pick it up. Iska doesn't like elevators much. Considering they were all she saw before being forced to fight, I can't blame her.

Taggert files in with us and scans his chit chip on the operating panel. The numbers light up. All the way to the top. And now I know where we are, directly under the tower. A fitting location for the director of a corpo office. I've met a few director-level executives in the past. None of them were what I'd call helpful. Mostly they were giant pains in the ass and had a knack for making whatever my mission was at the time more difficult.

Up and up the lift climbs, six stories in total. Not high at all compared to buildings on the Assembly worlds but stupidly tall on a planet with a revolving hellstorm. The elevator slows to a stop as we reach the top. Next to me, Sena's jaw tenses as she waits for whatever's going to be on the other side of the lift doors. But neither of us is prepared when they open directly into one of the most ostentatious rooms I've ever seen.

The office is massive, big enough to fit three of my ships inside. Icy air hits us with a blast as we're pushed out of the elevator, goose bumps prickling as the cold hits the sweat on the back of my neck. Dense white fur that looks suspiciously like osak bear hide covers the floor. Nothing on this world has fur that thick. Either the director cares more about aesthetics than functionality or every part of the decor is an intimidation technique.

Sena and I exchange a glance, her gray eyes spelling out her surprise. I know she notices the fur. Taggert presses the three of us forward, past a small lounge area with sleek chaises and tables so low they're practically useless. Everything is done in bright, piercing white. Not a speck of mud or dirt from the jungle to be seen, like the rest of the world can't touch this place. True corporate opulence at its most obscene. A giant white desk, the entire top a holoscreen, sits at the apex of the office. The walls behind it are made of floor-to-ceiling windows that meet at a point, like the tip of a triangle.

As we stop in front of the desk, I blink in surprise at the glass windows, pointing like an arrow out into the wilderness. Glass is a stupid luxury on Maraas since the hellstorm will generally destroy anything not properly reinforced or too rigid to survive the wind speeds. Most of the buildings on the plateau use composite plastics for windows. But these are true glass, not a composite. The cost to keep them intact every storm cycle must be astronomical.

Beyond the glass, the jungle stretches across the view. A story or so below us and just above the canopy sits the maglev rail line, snaking across the valley to the distant mountains. A high-backed chair behind the desk, also white, swivels around, revealing a tall, lithe woman with shock-white hair shorn close to her head. I now see where the decorating theme comes from.

The woman's thin lips spread into a smile as she folds bony fingers over the holoscreen, her eyes studying us. She's dressed in tailored, light layers that probably cost more than my flyer. Not a trace of sun across her pale cheeks, her skin almost as white as her hair. Expensive gold jewelry coils tightly around her neck and bare arms, like snakes slithering up her limbs. The whole picture is dramatic, calculated. Even the sunlight frames her figure in the window.

This director is definitely going to be a huge pain in my ass.

"Welcome." Her smooth tone of voice is as deliberate as everything else. "I'm Director Weiland. Have a seat." She gestures at two chairs in front of the desk as Taggert takes up post behind her. The chairs are low enough to the floor that anyone trying to get in and out of them would look like a fool. Which is no doubt the point.

"We'd rather stand, if it's all the same to you," I say. "It was a long, rather cramped flight getting here."

Her amber eyes narrow a fraction.

"Of course. As long as you're comfortable," she says nonchalantly. "Tell me your names."

"I'm Remy Castell. And this is Sena Korhosen." I don't bother with fake identities. Even though Nova assigned me and my squadmates each of our names, it's still mine. And it will check out in corpo databases. Since the director has far more resources than I currently do, she would no doubt easily uncover any false aliases. Besides, the bounty on Sena and Iska is more convincing that we're syndicates than any lie I could fabricate. The director stares at each of us in turn, her upper lip twitching slightly as her eyes land on Iska, who's decided to lie comfortably on the soft carpet and sniff the edges of the desk. Not an animal fan, this director.

"We work for the Vega syndicate," I add, pulling her attention from the wolf.

"Taggert mentioned you worked for the Vega," she practically sneers. "You'll have to forgive me but I'm very busy and I haven't got all day, so let's skip past the niceties and protocol."

Now I know Dekkard's name holds no power since even she has no problem ignoring typical syndicate-corpo relations. Throughout the charted systems, the syndicates may appear to be the underlings of the corporations, but the one wouldn't exist without the other to do their dirty work. Respect between corpo directors and syndicate bosses is a touchy subject. One that is usually handled with caution to avoid misunderstandings, assassinations, or all-out wars.

The director's gaze bores into me; she clearly doesn't care if I challenge her lack of protocol toward the Vega boss I supposedly work for. "You landed on my planet without a permit, and I need to know what your business is here."

"Like I told your commando, we're here for our boss, Dekkard Shaw," I say. "We're supposed to report to him first for further orders."

Though her face remains impassive, the director's pulse jumps slightly at Dekkard's name; it's not erratic or fearful but something else. . . .

She's excited.

"What are you reporting? And what further orders?" Her voice drips like honey. Excited because she clearly wants something.

I shrug and say nothing. A syndicate doesn't have to explain their orders to a corpo. I may not be a real syndicate, but I know how to act like one. We stare at each other for a beat. Her amber eyes jump from me to Sena, still judging, still assessing.

"And you? Do you speak?"

Sena steals a glance at me. "I'm working on talking less," she drawls. I manage not to laugh. We both have been in trouble enough to know it's best to wait before offering up excuses and lies that might bite us in the ass. Weiland wants something and wants it bad. Her breath hitches before we answer her questions. Her heartbeat races when she hears Dekkard's name. And something predatory lurks in those amber eyes.

The director rises, walks around the giant desk, and perches on the edge farthest from Iska and closest to Taggert. The commando stands at attention behind her like a good little soldier.

"Taggert reported that he found no identifying markers on your ship. No sign of any Vega insignia. Nothing."

"Part of the job," I reply, not missing a beat. My mind whizzes through the possibilities of what she's looking for. Something related to Dekkard and the Vega, that much is obvious.

Weiland leans closer. "And what exactly is your job?"

An idea hits as pieces of information begin to connect in my head. And I smile.

"We're trackers. We find things . . . things that don't want to be found."

Her pupils dilate almost imperceptibly as her eyes widen, and I know she's taking the bait. I may hate where I come from, but Nova's programmed instincts and designer genes are very good at reading people. Especially people who are threats.

"Isn't that interesting?" Weiland leans back, running one bony finger across her lips as she pretends to think. "Shouldn't part of your job also entail staying up-to-date with changes within your organization?"

She says "organization" like it's something unfortunate stuck to the bottom of her boot, but it doesn't matter because I can see the small, satisfied smile tugging at the corner of her lips. She thinks she's got us where she wants us. So, instead of asking what she means like I know she wants me to, I simply stare and wait for her to explain.

She presses again. "It's obvious you don't have an inkling as to what's going on, do you?"

I cross my arms and raise an eyebrow. "Why don't you explain it to us?"

Something flashes in her eyes, but she presses her lips into a line, walking back to her chair and letting the moment drag out as much as possible before gracefully sitting and steepling her fingers, again pausing to make us squirm.

Sena and I don't budge. We've been through much worse.

"Dekkard's yielded Maraas as his seat of power. His operations run exclusively on Abydos now," Weiland finally drawls.

I don't outwardly react but I'm more than a little shocked. The Vega no longer controls Maraas and Dekkard's on a different Edge World? After we helped him take over the Vega two years ago? Nova has to be responsible for this. Which means Kiran must be involved somehow, otherwise why would he be on this planet?

Weiland looks at me like a cat who's caught a mouse. "It's been months since we took control of this world. I'm surprised you didn't know."

"We were on Tundar." Sena speaks up, thinking nearly as fast as me. "In the sled race," she continues. "We've been stuck in the wilderness for months. No comms and no messages." I watch her out of the corner of my eye as she talks. There's no fear on her features at all. Hard to be scared when you've already faced your worst nightmare.

Weiland looks down her nose at us. "And yet, you still didn't know which world your boss was on?"

"I never said we came here to see him," I jump in. "Only that we're here on orders for him and to report to him." I keep my voice level and bored. As if I'm not at all bothered by her line of questioning. Which I'm not. The change in planetary power dynamics doesn't affect my goals. But I am curious as to the whys and hows. Everything on this planet is out of whack. Corpos having full power here, it's unheard of. Syndicates rule the Edge Worlds. It's that way on Tundar, on Abydos, on others.

"Tell me then, what exactly are your orders?" Weiland asks.

I don't answer. Regardless of Dekkard's position, I don't answer to her.

Weiland smiles that catlike smile again. "If you're planning on running some sort of syndicate-led mission on my world, I'll need to know the details so I can approve it. Otherwise, you can fly right back off-world again. I don't allow syndicates to run wild on my planet."

And just like that, everything clicks. I know what Weiland wants even if I'm not aware of all the specifics.

"Actually, Dekkard sent us to assist you with your little problem."

She sneers. "I don't hire syndicates in any capacity. And you know nothing of my problems."

I smile as I recall the conversation I had with the twins before leaving Tundar. That Kiran was on Maraas helping a syndicate boss named Revas. If Kiran is here helping a syndicate and Dekkard's abandoned this world, it can only mean one thing. Someone's paying for a revolution. It's how the corpos and syndicates restructure power, through proxy wars and secretly funded coups. Which means her problems overlap with mine since I'm after Kiran, who's probably organizing this new coup.

"We were sent to find Revas," I say, taking a final gamble.

Weiland's pulse skips and I know I've got her. It was the only logical conclusion. Kiran is helping Revas and not the director, therefore the director must want to stop the syndicate. Weiland stews in silence for a few beats before finally speaking.

"My own commandos can't track Revas down, not in the city nor in the outpost. What makes you think you can find her?"

"I told you. We find things that don't want to be found. And we're the best. That's why Dekkard sent us. It takes a syndicate to find a syndicate. He doesn't want Revas taking any power either."

"And why didn't Dekkard inform me of this directly?" she says, her voice measured and even. Not a hint of the rage I suspect is simmering below the surface.

I shrug. "It's not my job to ask those questions. Seemed like he wanted to repay you a favor." I'm guessing, but my guesses are always dead-on. By the way Weiland's gaze grows distant, I'm right about this, too. It's not hard to figure out that however Weiland came into power, Dekkard had a hand in it. He always was a snake, serving his own interests more than the Vega's, and I wouldn't be surprised if Weiland paid him off to look the other way while she took over this planet.

"And that favor is you, here to solve this little Revas problem. How convenient," Weiland muses, considering the two of us again before speaking. "You find her for me, and I'll let this in discretion pass and waive all fees and punishments for your illegal flight path and landing on my planet without a permit."

She's offering a lot more than I expected her to. The only way we're getting out of this room is if we agree to be her new gofers. But that doesn't mean I have to pretend to accept her first offer. I need her to remember that we're supposed to be syndicate thugs, through and through. Nothing else, no ulterior motives. I smile. Convincing people I don't have ulterior motives is second nature for me.

"And what about our ship?" I demand, leaning forward over the desk. "Your tow crew damaged it on the flight over here."

While Weiland's heartbeat quickens, her face grows hard, losing all hint of warmth and the thin veneer of politeness she's worn the whole meeting. Oh, she's full of rage, this one. The director rises, meeting me eye to eye.

"I don't think you understand. My offer is as is. No negotiations or add-ons are possible. You violated my airspace. You landed without a permit. You are on my planet."

But I refuse to budge. "We're supposed to bring Revas to Dekkard, but I'm guessing you'd rather her come here first. You want us to follow your orders over our boss's? That's the price. Nothing taken, nothing given."

She glares at me, her pulse pounding in my ears loud and steady. She really doesn't like being challenged. But it would be too suspicious if we just took the deal. Syndicates don't ever do something without a benefit. It's the way of the Edge Worlds, the way of the entire charted systems.

"You're lucky I don't have Taggert shoot you where you stand," Weiland practically growls. Then she sighs and stares at us for another silent moment. "But I can be reasonable. Benevolent even. We'll repair your ship in exchange for you tracking down this nuisance and bringing her directly to me. No amendments. Are we in agreement?"

I let her stew for a beat, then I nod. "Consider it done."

She agreed far too easily. Which means she knows something, something she's not saying. But it doesn't really matter now. I got what I wanted; I'll find Kiran, get the info I need, and be off-world before the director's any the wiser.

"Fabulous," Weiland says, her stormy expression unchanging. "I expect results before the next cycle of the hellstorm hits the city. For your sake, I hope you can deliver in time. No results and I'll have to treat you as the common criminals you are in violation of corporate law. I'm sure you know what punishments would follow. Now, I've got more important things to handle. Taggert will show you out."

As Taggert shuffles toward us, Weiland levels her gaze directly at me once more.

"Happy hunting, Remy Castell."

Something about the way she says my name makes my spine stiffen. She says it with ownership, like she's said it before. Like she knows exactly who—and what—I am. My focus narrows onto her and her alone. But before I can analyze it further, the look is gone, and she flippantly waves Sena and me away.

Taggert steps forward, ushering us menacingly toward the elevator. I can still feel her amber eyes boring under my skin. The director's hiding a lot more than she's letting on, and I suspect this won't be the last we see of her. It doesn't matter, though; I won't be around long enough for her to pull out all the hidden secrets up her sleeve.

Besides, I've got my own tricks to play.

CHAPTER 4

Taggert's glassy green eyes glare at us the entire ride down in the lift. I can't help but give him a little smile just to get under his skin.

"Make sure your people start working on those ship repairs. We're going to be ready to leave before you know it."

"I'll believe that when I see it," the commando snaps. "You should worry less about your ship and more about finding your target. The director has no patience for failure."

The oppressive heat blankets us as the elevator drops from Weiland's office, and sweat trickles down my spine once again. My moisture-wicking layers can't even attempt to keep up, especially in here; it's basically an oven of magnified heat and humidity. I don't know how the commando can stand wearing full body armor.

The doors finally open and Taggert steps out of the lift, motioning for us to follow. Gone is the long runway of the hangar cavern; we're on a different level, this one not underground. An airy breeze tickles my neck, bringing slight relief from the elevator's confines and, with it, familiar smells. Rusted metal, burning meat, a hint of rain. The smell of Verem. We walk down a short hallway and then through another set of doors that Taggert opens with his chit chip.

The space opens up into the city's main train station. Not fifty feet away from us, the mag rail tracks divide the terminal into two platforms, each with dozens of people scattered around. Some, dressed in TerraCo uniforms made of simple layers, are glued to datapads. Others are outfitted in commando or jungle gear, engineers and security guards probably heading for the mines. I spy a few indents moving around in the in-between spaces, remaining inconspicuous in their colorless uniforms. The overwhelming TerraCo presence has transformed the station into a hub for corpo activity and not much else. No miners or traders heading out to the sprawl that I can spot. No syndicates running security. No sign of the train either, but I can hear its approaching rumble just under the ambient noise.

"You just going to stand there and gawk or are you going to actually get to work?" Taggert's stopped just in front of Sena and me, his arms crossed as he stares at us.

"Just waiting for you to leave," I shoot back.

The commando tilts his meaty head to one side. "Consider me your escort."

I try not to roll my eyes. I shouldn't be surprised Weiland assigned Taggert to babysit. The director is far too obsessive about keeping things under her thumb. I wonder if she even really wants us to find Revas or if we're pawns in some larger game she's crafting. Doesn't matter either way. My first move is to get rid of this dead weight. Luckily, I spy a group of commandos walking just close enough to us as they head for the train tracks.

"So," Taggert drawls. "What do the expert trackers have planned first?"

The mag rail vibrates slightly, signaling the approaching train. Perfect timing. I glance at Sena and raise an eyebrow. She inclines her head once. Ready.

"Funny you should ask," I say, reaching an arm forward and slapping Taggert hard on the shoulder like we're friends. He sneers and takes a step back, just like I knew he would.

And bumps right into one of the commandos behind him.

There's a shout and shove as the offended man reacts, pushing Taggert away from him.

"Watch where you're going, you chump!" the commando hollers. Taggert quickly regains his balance, though I can almost see smoke coming out of his ears as he flips around to the group. Passersby stop in surprise at the sharp shout. I nudge Sena with my elbow, and she folds herself into the growing crowd, Iska disappearing with her.

"You should watch who you yell at, boot!" Taggert spits in the guy's face, shoving him back a step in return. The group realizes who he is, but it's too late for them. Taggert's been embarrassed and he won't let any of them off the hook. Just like I suspected. Commandos with egos are so predictable.

More people stop to stare, giving me just enough crowd cover. With Taggert's full attention on the other commandos, I take one slow step back, then another.

Just as the train begins to glide into the station, I take off at a sprint. I spot Sena three strides ahead, moving toward the edge of the platform. I catch up, steering us right toward the train tracks while checking behind us once more. Taggert's realized we've given him the slip. He's moving our way and bringing the commando group with him. The train pulls up closer and closer, nearly cutting off our exit, but Sena and I are faster.

I point to the tracks in our path, and without changing pace, Sena leaps down, followed by Iska, then both clamber up to the opposite platform. I steal one more glance, grinning at Taggert's red, angry face before I jump down onto the tracks. The train is barreling forward, but in two strides and a quick jump, I'm up on the far platform just before the train slides home.

With a solid barrier keeping Taggert from catching up, I take the lead and head for the exit. We step out of the domed station and onto the street, a dozen or so other scents attacking my nose as we carve a path through food stalls, servo bikes, and foot traffic. Underneath it all is another scent, moist and sweet. Of fresh rain and thick heat.

The scent of the jungle.

And even though I'm still walking, still dodging the crowds, the smells act like a catalyst, memories rushing to the surface of my mind unbidden, and then the street fades and I'm back in one specific moment, reliving my worst nightmare.

The memory takes over my senses completely, and in a blink, the city is gone and I'm opening my eyes to see Kiran, my supposed partner, at the helm of a drop ship, lifting off, stranding me on the jungle floor. The heat from the engines blasts me in the face as the ship clears the bushy treetops. I try to shout, but I'm sluggish from whatever chems he knocked me out with. I can just make out his face, set in a frown, but he keeps his dark eyes far from mine as the ship ascends into the sky. As if refusing to look at me while he abandons me in the wilds will somehow lessen his traitorous actions.

When he said he had urgent orders from Nova, I trusted him, like I always did, and he used that against me, knowing my guard would be down around him. Then he stuck me with a needle and now I'm waking up here, in the jungle on the sidelines while he takes control over the entire mission. I should've seen this coming. He never could stand it when I wasn't under his thumb.

My fists clench. I know he's going straight back to the plateau.

Going to finish the coup we started. To get rid of the only friend I ever made. A friend who saved my life. Who showed me the truth about Nova. About all of it. And now she's back in the city. Injured. Alone. With Kiran and his uprising heading straight for her.

Ferns brush my skin as I manage to stand and take in the small muddy clearing. The jungle marsh surrounds me on all sides; the sickly sweet smell of vines and leaves and wet mud fills my senses. No people. No metal. No signs of humanity.

I, too, am alone.

But my internal compass knows the direction back to the plateau, and as I step that way, I spot a discarded arken blade nearby. Kiran must have left it as a tease. To give me some sort of twisted amount of hope. As if one arken blade will help me get back in time to save my friend.

I'm going to kill him when I find him.

More memories of being alone out in the wilds, searching for a way back to the friend I lost, crowd my mind. My muscles tense, automatically preparing to react. To run or fight like I did then. Before my body can keep reliving them, I quickly force the memories down the way Nova trained us to and focus on the city currently around me.

Genopath training and our genetic memory means that anything I've experienced before is logged in my head, ready to replay in case I need to reuse any learned skills. The lab hacks officially called them genetic echoes. But my squadmates and I called them replays, because they felt just like we were reliving the real thing, not some echo of a distant memory.

The ability is certainly useful for memorizing how to run an exocarbon drill or how to pick a lock in one sitting. But it's very unhelpful when the memories trigger like a glitch and my body isn't sure if I'm still in danger or not. The fear and anxiety that come with the triggers and replays don't help either. If I were still under Nova's control, my hesitation and confusion would be seen as a sign of weakness, a signal that it was time to take me to reconditioning.

I blink that thought far, far away, telling my body to remember where we actually are. To focus on the smells of burning meat and not jungle foliage. We're at an intersection a few blocks from the station. Beside me, Sena has paused. Her eyes jump from me to the streets and back again.

"We shouldn't stay here," she says with a glance toward the station. Her gray eyes hold worry as she looks back at me.

Right, Taggert. I zero in my focus on a memory of the city's layout rather than anything else and glance down one of the side streets. We need a destination. I could start by sniffing out Kiran, following the trail of genopath pheromones to find him. The sooner I catch him, the sooner I get answers. I hesitate, though. I don't know if it's the memories still simmering at the surface or if I'm being driven by some other instinct. But there's somewhere I need to go first.

The place where it all began.

The Vega headquarters in the southern part of the city. The compound where Kiran and I planned the manufactured coup to put Dekkard Shaw in charge, the coup ordered by Nova. Where I met a girl who didn't care what I was, only that I was her friend.

Alora.

After Kiran dumped me in the jungle, he helped Dekkard murder her father. And I couldn't stop it. By the time I made my way back to the city, both Kiran and Alora were completely gone, disappeared somewhere off-world. She's the one I made a promise to, the one I have to save. And while I know Kiran knows where she is, I still need to see the Vega headquarters for myself to be sure there's no sign of her left.

I clear my throat. "This way," I say, pointing south. "Let's go."

CHAPTER 5

With every step forward, I let the replays fade into the background, let my body's movements take precedence in my mind. Let the city fill my senses as much as possible. Getting caught up in the memories and echoes now won't help me find Alora.

We weave through the tightly packed buildings of the corpo district. It's starkly obvious that this is where the money is on this world. Buildings aren't wooden or on stilts but are made of concrete and steel imported from off-world. Most of the dwellings on Maraas are built up above the ground to allow for the movement of water when the storm hits. While Verem here on the plateau doesn't flood as much as the sprawl of slums in the jungle below, flash floods are always a threat. Hence why most of the planet's structures are built on stilts and platforms, above the mud and earth.

Except for in this district apparently. They have the money to reinforce walls and insulation, to maintain an extensive draining system, to keep the water out and make constant repairs every time the storm hits. The streets around us are dense and busy; corpo workers and indents alike zip about with purpose. There are surprisingly more of the indentured workers in this district alone than I saw on all of Tundar, another sign of the growing corpo strength.

But once we're out of the corporate district, the city shifts into something different entirely and even the Verem from my memories is gone.

Here the stilted, wooden buildings return but are more dilapidated and worn down from the constant heat and rain than they were two years ago. Back then, the Vega leader, Rixus Vega, put effort into keeping the city clean and polished. Verem had been more crowded, more alive. But now, all signs of his work have been washed away. Muddy puddles from the recent storm fill potholes and dips in the roads. The jungle creeps in closer than ever with spider vines and giant ferns growing out of the cracked sidewalks and up rickety walls. The spider vines are notorious across the planet for being near impossible to cut with any metal blade. They grow incessantly, twisting and knotting around anything in their path, like snakes slithering in undetected to strangle their prey.

Next to me, Sena takes it all in cautiously. Her eyes roam from the street to the rooftops not too high overhead; no doubt she's planning potential escape routes in case Taggert catches up. Iska trots alongside us, her nose constantly following the scents of smoked meat and fried oil. With no protection from the jungle canopy, the sun beats down on us. The reflective heat crawls up my skin as sweat drips down my limbs.

"Well, this part reminds me of the Ket," Sena says as we slosh through a particularly large puddle. "Equally dirty. Just less frozen."

I turn us down an intersection, moving away from the city center as I follow my internal compass.

"So, where are we headed?" she asks. "The twins told you Kiran was on this world. Did they mention where? How do we know he's even still here and they're not lying?"

"There's definitely a possibility they're lying," I reply. "But they said he was helping Revas. And now Weiland is also after the same Revas. Which means Kiran is definitely here in the thick of it."

"Does that mean your old organization is here, too?" Her voice is steady, but I can hear the undercurrent of worry. The care in Sena's voice makes my chest ache because I'm still unsure if I brought her here out of friendship or out of necessity, like Nova programmed me to. I was designed to see other people as tools, as means to an end and nothing more. Two years free from the organization's influence and I'm still not sure if my actions are my own . . . or Nova's.

Maybe I can never truly escape what they made me to be.

"Nova has eyes everywhere. On every world," I say through gritted teeth. "Not just illegal genopaths like me, but other agents with gene mods and lots of greedy folks in their pockets. And now, because of the twins, they know I'm not dead. But don't worry," I reassure her and myself. "Doesn't matter if they're looking for me or not. They don't know I'm here and they're not going to catch me. Besides, I'm just a small fish compared to whatever it is they're cooking up with Revas and the Vega and TerraCo."

Sena is quiet for a moment as we walk. Then: "But if TerraCo is already the main power here, why would Nova stage some sort of new syndicate coup now with Revas?"

I shrug as we weave through a small, somewhat crowded food court. My stomach rumbles at the smell of fried meat. My body still needs fuel after all the adrenaline dumping during the crash, but I've got more important things on my mind.

"Nova stages coups all the time," I explain. "That's how the corpos fight each other. Not directly but through proxies like the syndicates or even the scavvers sometimes. They'll do whatever it takes to get what they want, and they don't give a shit about everyone underneath them. Nova thrives on that."

I lead us down another street, the crowds around us growing thinner as we move closer to where the Vega headquarters is. Or was. The buildings have an air of familiarity, but the shops and lodgings in them are all different. It takes my mind a moment to meld the current landscape with the one in my memory. This area of Verem used to be busier, used to be thriving. Used to be the center of the Vega empire. It was all an extension of Alora's father's power. Now it's partially deserted, the jungle wrapping itself around the places the humans have vacated.

A familiar blue sign catches my eye. It's the Vega logo, smeared across an old piece of metal hanging from a tall gate. A gate that used to lead to the Vega headquarters but now leads to an empty, dilapidated building. It was one of the few in this district that wasn't up on stilts but rather built partially into the rock itself. The Vega had more than enough funds to upkeep the building during the storms. But now the sides are crumbling; the roof is half gone. The color on the walls is faded, as if no one has set foot here for a long, long time. As if the paint, and the purpose of the building itself, has been washed away more and more with each storm.

I pause in front of the gate, trying to ignore the rush of feelings that come bubbling up at the familiar sight. This is where I met Alora. This is where she gave me a taste of a life beyond missions and labs. The memories surface again, good ones this time, and I can see her sneaking through this very gate, blond hair falling out of her messy braid, whispering for me to follow while she snuck past her father's lieutenants so we could go eat street food in the middle of the night. I'd never disobeyed an order in my life, but she bent and broke her father's rules simply because she had a craving for bush meat and insisted she was going with or without me.

This echo I'd rather not shrug off. It was the beginning of a friendship even if I didn't understand it at the time. I stare at the building, willing it to tell me its secrets. Willing it to reveal what I don't know. What Kiran did with Alora the night of the coup when I was stuck in the jungle. I doubt there's anything here that will give me answers; there's not even a trace of a human scent. No heartbeats that I can hear. But I need to go in and see for myself.

"I'm going in to have a look around," I say to Sena, who's been patiently watching me case the building. I swallow past a small lump in my throat. "Do you mind being lookout in case someone tries to follow me in?"

Sena studies me for a moment. I can see her piecing things together. Finally, she nods.

"Remember the birdcalls I taught you on Tundar? I'll signal if anyone shows up."

"Thank you." My voice nearly cracks as I thank her for more than just playing lookout. Even if it was my programming and instincts that had me asking Sena to come, I'm glad she's here with me.

Taking a deep breath and making sure the sidewalk around us is clear of passersby, I duck under the broken perimeter fencing and step into the compound. Following the side of the building, I walk until I find an entry door. It takes only a few kicks with my boot before the lock snaps and the door swings open. Nothing is built to outlast this storm. Not even autolocks cased in exocarbon. The humidity and rain beat all.

I pause in the shadowed doorway, listening, feeling further for signs of life. Rapid, faint heartbeats reach my ears. Not human, probably rats or other small animals.

How far the Vega has fallen.

I pass door after door of nothing. No people. No life. Nova's coup was devastatingly complete. Kiran and I did our jobs too well. I round a corner and pause. These are the old offices. Barracks and living quarters are just ahead. Beside me is a door that leads down, down into the basement of the building, carved out of the rock below.

There are more rooms down there, for more sinister purposes.

Kiran and I would meet there to discuss our orders, plan our movements. But there were also rooms where Dekkard would interrogate traitors, syndicates he claimed were moving against Alora's father. Really, they were moving against Dekkard, and he used the opportunity to get the Vega loyalists out of his way. He twisted everything to suit his purpose, to claw his way to power.

Power granted by Nova, the true puppeteer behind all of this.

The thought makes my stomach churn as I stare at the door, now sealed and welded shut so tightly I couldn't look down the staircase and hallway beyond even if I wanted to. And I don't want to.

I promised Alora that I would be better. But I couldn't stop Kiran from manipulating everything, and I still wasn't strong enough to cross the jungle in time to halt the chaos crumbling down. I made my friend a promise and then promptly broke it. I turn away from the door and quickly move past the memory of that night.

But soon my footsteps slow again, this time at the threshold of the living quarters. Alora's room is right down the hall. As her bodyguard, I had the room next to hers. But that was just the cover story Nova gave me: outside protection for a syndicate boss's daughter in a time of inner-gang turmoil. It wasn't the first time I'd posed as the help. But like all my missions, the real assignment was to get close to my mark and, in turn, close to her father so I could report on his movements, his morale, anything that Kiran could use to spur dissent against him. But getting close for that intel meant getting close to Alora.

And somewhere along the way, she stopped being a mission and became something more. Something real.

I take another grounding breath and step forward, making my way down the familiar path to our rooms. Alora's father brought me straight here after I flew in two years ago. Their last bodyguard had mysteriously disappeared, and with the growing unrest among the Vega ranks, Rixus wanted someone not connected to the syndicate to protect his precious daughter. Nova engineered the entire thing of course. The compound was a buzz of activity my first day here, and my senses were on fire keeping up with all the stimuli and people as Rixus led me through the building.

Now trash and debris litter the floor. Walls and windows are broken or crumbling. The smell of mildew and moisture is almost overwhelming. The door to Alora's room is missing completely. I stand and stare into the empty space. Everything has been cleaned out. The walls, once covered in her personal items, are now nothing but jungle grime and tendrils of reaching spider vines. Broken pieces of discarded wood lie in a corner, and there's a consistent drip, drip, drip near the back wall.

But as I move across the threshold, my memories trigger, beginning the replay, and all I see is the way it was before, the way it was the first time I stepped inside this room two years ago.

Alora is sprawled across a bed in the center of the room, her father beside me as we enter.

"Alora." The Rixus in my memory interlaces his hands behind his back. He's tall, imposing but quietly so, with ice-blue eyes and blond hair that match his daughter's. I knew, as soon as I arrived and met with him, he was not a man to underestimate.

"This is Remy Castell," he continues as the scene in my mind takes over all my senses in the present. "She'll be your new pro-tection detail."

Even though a distant part of me knows the room is empty now, in the memory I take in the walls, observing as many details as I can to form an opinion on this girl before she even says a word. Despite the authority in her father's voice, the girl doesn't look up from her spot on the bed. Messy blond hair falls across her pale face, blocking her expression from my line of sight. I listen to her pulse; it's faster than normal. I try to discern if it's because of her anticipation . . . or anger.

"I don't need a bodyguard," Alora's triggered ghost grumbles from the bed.

Anger then; she's just a typical angry girl. In the replay, I wave Alora's father back. The anger is for him and not for me. She doesn't even know me. I step closer, both in my memory and in the present.

"Maybe we can start over," I say, my voice full of quiet confi-dence meant to soothe, a technique drilled into me by Nova.

"I'm Remy," I continue. "Perhaps you can think of me as a friend. Not as a guard. Just someone else who will look out for you. Who'll be there when you need it."

My words have her blue eyes peering at me through her fallen hair. She then glances at her father behind me and sighs.

"Fine. I love being best friends with my father's lackeys." I remember noting her sarcasm; I'd been taught it was a defense mechanism. Kiran had started using it more a few missions prior and it drove me crazy.

"I don't work for your father," I correct her sharply. Her blue eyes meet mine again, both curious and suspicious. "I work for you."

She studies me for a beat, then brushes her blond hair back, revealing light freckles across her nose and a gaze that's surprisingly sharp.

"We'll see."

For the first time I hear steel in her soft voice. My opinion of her shifts; maybe she's more than just an angry girl. I don't know what other sides of herself she could be hiding.

But suddenly I want to find out.

The replay stops, the memory dissipating as I shake off the trigger, and I'm back standing in an empty building devoid of life. There isn't anything left of Alora in this room. There's no sign of her bed where we later sat and talked. No trace of the datapads she used to scan for off-world gossip. No scraps of clothing she would insist I borrow. None of the things she made a part of her life. I can't even catch the scent of her on the walls. There's just . . . nothing but moist mildew and rain puddles. It's like she's been erased.

Rage claws up my insides, a force as strong as the heat around me.

I couldn't get to her the night of the coup, couldn't save her because of one person and one person only. This is Kiran's fault. He was the one pulling the strings to destabilize the Vega. Reporting our movements and my intel to Nova. Plotting the murder of Alora's father with Dekkard. Dumping me in the jungle, where I was powerless to stop any of it.

And he should pay for that.

I stand only a second longer in the doorway. I don't head to my old room. I know what awaits me there. More, infinite nothing.

I breathe in a long breath, trying to center myself. To plan out the next move.

Something tickles my senses underneath the mildew and rain. I didn't notice it before, but now it's crawling up my nose. Something acidic. Something antiseptic.

Something chemical.

Other triggers begin to fill my mind. Memories of white rooms and endless testing, of reconditioning and reprogramming. They threaten to push away the echoes of my friend. I don't know why the smell is here, but it brings back different replays, images of Nova lab hacks messing with my brain and poking at my body. Things I don't want to remember. Things I'd do anything to forget. Everything else vanishes from my head, leaving my instincts screaming only one thing.

Run.

So, I quickly turn away from the room, from the ghosts, from the memories haunting my mind.

And I run.

CHAPTER 6

"Hey." Sena's familiar voice brings me further out of the past as I push my way through the fence and back onto the street. "Find anything?" Again, her eyes watch me with unspoken worry. I brush off her concerns and shake my head.

Nothing but cobwebs and memories.

Breathing in the fresh air helps cleanse my palate of the despair and dust. I let the city scents cloud my senses, pushing the rest of the triggered memories back where they belong. Time to focus on why I'm here. Time to find Kiran.

Odors of rusted metal, stale booze, and muddy water fill my nose. But I don't catch a whiff of any genopath pheromones. I haven't smelled or seen a hint of Kiran anywhere in Verem so far, and I'm really not in the mood to traipse around the entire city trying to sniff him out when he could already be down in the outpost or lost in the sprawl. I need a better way to pinpoint his location.

Sena studies me in silence for a moment but must read something in my expression because she points down the block.

"There's a bar farther down the road. I overheard some people who sounded like syndicates talking about it. Maybe we can pick up some information there."

A bar would explain the scent of stale booze. Possibilities zip through my thoughts. Syndicates would be a better place to start than searching the city block by block. I nod to Sena.

"Good idea. Let's go see what we can find out."

Sena falls into step beside me while Iska trots up along my other side, tongue out, panting in the heat. The wolf stalks close, her presence steady and reassuring. Iska will do anything to protect Sena, just like I would for Alora. The wolf is a true friend despite her feral upbringing and hybrid DNA.

Maybe there's hope for me to make good on my promises yet.

At the end of the block lies a decrepit old bar up on stilts. The mud underneath the building reeks of more than just stale booze. A few people lurk outside on a rickety porch while others come and go on the road around us. It's late afternoon, but I'm still picking up a couple dozen heartbeats inside alone. Probably people looking to escape the sun's sharp rays and heavy heat.

As we climb the steps to the entrance, the bouncer pays us no mind, not even Iska. The space inside is dark and densely crowded with patrons. Across one wall is a long wooden bar lined with makeshift stools, most of them occupied. Tables dot the open floor with people around them in small groups. Others mingle about, filling the spaces in between. It will be easy for us to move around unnoticed in a crowd this size.

"We should split up." Sena keeps her voice low, pausing at

the entrance to let her eyes adjust. Mine have already adapted to the low light; the enhancements encoded in my genes let me see clearly even in the darkest, dank corners of the bar. My ears pick up snippets of conversation, the creaks of tables and chairs, even the low hum of a flyer approaching somewhere beyond the Vega compound behind us. My other senses and enhancements aren't as much of an asset in places like this. Especially my nose.

"How about circling a few rounds?" I say to Sena. "And then we'll meet in the back corner by the bar in ten minutes?"

Sena nods and slips into the crowd, Iska prowling alongside her. The giant wolf doesn't seem to alarm people as she stalks around the tables. They're used to wildlife encroaching into their space here. Besides, Iska isn't one of the predators of this world that would be instantly recognizable or feared; she's not a giant anacroc or an aggressive batimalu ape. And vonenwolves are often exported from Tundar as exotic pets, so she gets a few curious and wary glances, but not much else. Guess they don't see her as enough of a threat to warrant a bigger reaction. Which definitely works in our favor.

I move in the opposite direction, weaving around people, keeping my gaze low to avoid eye contact while relying on my enhanced hearing to pick up bits of conversation here and there.

"They docked my wages again." The man complaining at the table nearest me is wearing frayed outer layers with the TerraCo logo stamped on his shoulders. The others sitting around him murmur in solidarity. They must all work for TerraCo.

"I heard they axed more miners before the storm hit. I wonder how long they'll keep us around."

The grumblings of disgruntled TerraCo employees aren't what I came to hear, so I move farther into the space, my eyes and ears peeled for syndicates rather than corpos.

"Did you hear the batimalu apes attacked another person down in the jungle?" a woman wearing thin layers and a long arken blade across her back says in hushed tones. She's standing in the corner with a few others. No TerraCo logo on her clothes. She might be a syndicate. Her companions lean forward as she lowers her voice. "They said his blood was totally drained. Nothing but a shell covered in bite marks found near the outpost."

"Damn," one replies. "Glad we're not stuck down in the outpost then."

My pulse jumps at the words. The outpost is the syndicate stronghold down by the sprawl, situated in caves underneath the plateau. Which means these three are Vega syndicates. Finally, something useful.

The woman scoffs. "Like sitting around up here is any better. We're glorified babysitters to these corpo slugs. No action, no purpose. Such a waste of time."

"I'd rather be whining about boredom than getting chased by killer ape-bats," someone says.

"Suit yourself." The woman rolls her eyes. "I'm here for one more storm cycle. Then I'm getting the hell off this planet."

"I'll drink to that." One of them loudly empties his glass, effectively ending the conversation just when it got relevant. I consider ways I could bring it back up to try to get information, but the odds are slim they'll talk to me without good reason. I don't have any openings to play.

A yell draws my attention; three TerraCo commandos near the bar are gambling on a dice game. Bored syndicates and worried corpo workers aren't exactly helpful, but a few drunk commandos might be useful later. Weiland said she had commandos looking for Revas. Might as well eavesdrop on these chumps.

"I'll take your bet and raise you triple," one of them drunkenly shouts as he shakes the cup of dice. I move a little closer, weaving between two tables.

His friend waves him off. "I already put too much money down at the bar, forget it."

I keep walking, potential scenarios buzzing through my head. But not wanting to stand out, I continue past their table, making my way to the meeting spot at the back of the bar, where I find Sena chomping on a stick of unidentifiable meat and sharing bites with Iska.

I slide onto an empty stool next to her. "Find anything?"

"Yeah, people here are way easier to pickpocket than anyone in the Ket."

I laugh. "I thought you were done with your life of crime?"

She shrugs. "We were hungry."

"If you want more chits, just let me know. We can get something better to eat than fried bush meat."

"Later." She takes another bite and nods toward the crowded bar. "The bartender takes bets on just about everything, and I heard someone lay down chits about Revas's whereabouts."

That explains the commando's lack of funds. And finally gives me the opening I need.

"I'll go have a quick chat with the bartender then."

"Have fun," Sena says in between bites.

I head to the bar and perch on an empty stool. After a few minutes, the bartender, a meaty guy with sunburned white skin, crooked teeth, and a distinct lack of hair despite his overlarge eyebrows, makes his way to where I sit.

"What can I get ya?"

I lean forward, lowering my voice and adding a bit of a lilt to my tone so I sound like I just landed from an Assembly world.

"I heard you take bets. I've got chits ready to burn if you're paying good odds. Especially if they concern the ongoing dispute between the Vega and the TerraCo director."

He looks me over once and shrugs. "I don't know what you mean."

I smile like we share a secret and scoot closer. "I know all about the search for Revas. I was discussing it with Weiland herself not two hours ago." His eyes widen slightly at the mention of Weiland's name. What an easy mark.

"So . . . you got the line on the action or not?" I ask impatiently, looking him up and down. He studies me, his eyes jumping to the outline of the chit chip in my wrist. I can practically see the wheels turning in his head as he decides that I'm the easy mark.

"We're paying high chits that Revas bites the bullet," he says in a low voice. "Ten to one odds that Weiland finds her by the next storm cycle. Twenty to one if Revas ends up dead by someone else's gun before then. It seems Dekkard didn't send her here, so she's fair game."

I pretend to consider it.

"I've got a hundred chits that Revas will be found in the next few days," I say.

The bartender's pupils dilate at the promise of easy money. He raises a bushy eyebrow and leans closer, his sweat and body odor wafting up my nose. "You know something?"

I drum my fingers on the bar top. "Potentially. I could tell you what I know . . . in exchange for more information." The man grabs a glass and starts cleaning vigorously. As if the movement would hide his excitement from me. I can hear his elevated pulse and hitched breathing as if they were shouting at me.

"I'm looking for someone." I hesitate for a flash, deciding which name to say: Alora or Kiran. But instincts and common sense override my desire to find my friend, so I choose the name that will attract less attention than the daughter of the former Vega boss.

"Kiran Lore," I say, his name like ash on my lips. "Heard of him?"

Both of the bartender's bushy brown eyebrows go up. "That grifter? What do you want from him?"

I shrug, wondering what game Kiran is playing if the bartender thinks he's a con artist. It's a fitting cover for him, someone always working an angle to trick others. Someone no one should trust.

"What I want with him is my own business," I continue. "Do you know where to find him? Or should I take my chits somewhere else?"

He jerks his chin at me. "What have you got on Revas?"

I lower my voice to a near whisper. "Insider information. Extremely fresh."

The bartender considers me again, this time with a bit more caution. With my accent, most likely he thinks I work up in the corpo hierarchy. But he's curious why I would be slumming for information in a low-rent bar like his, wearing clothes that don't match the rest of the TerraCo chumps. But I already know his greed for my info and chits will win out over his curiosity. He might ask around about me after I leave, but Sena and I will be long gone by then.

He finally sets the glass down. "Kiran was here before the last storm cycle, but last I heard, he was headed down to the outpost. Probably you can find him peddling cons in any bar from there to the mountain mines, so no promises that's where he is."

I consider the implications of the bartender's words. Kiran's not exactly hiding his movements, which means he could be up to anything, including laying a trap for me. What he's doing in the syndicate outpost is a mystery. Maybe spinning unrest to further Revas's cause against Dekkard or secretly helping Weiland with some other endgame.

The bartender wiggles his fingers in my direction, breaking into my thoughts.

"Nothing taken, nothing given," he says, his voice laced with impatience.

An idea crosses my mind and I suddenly glance around the bar suspiciously, making a show of looking for anyone trying to eavesdrop. Then I lean all the way across the bar.

"Word is that Weiland's hired a specialized retrieval team to track Revas down."

The bartender huffs in my face. His breath reeks of stale booze and rotten meat. "That's not news. Everyone knows Weiland's looking for Revas." His eyes jump momentarily to the commandos behind me. "Her goons are all over the city and outpost. Damn nuisance."

"Oh, I'm not talking about commandos. I'm talking about the genopath she hired."

His pulse jumps and I know I've got his attention.

"A genopath? Can you prove it?"

I roll my eyes. "What do you want, a DNA sample? Trust me, it's on the level." I push away from the bar, back out into the crowd. "Thanks for the tip."

He points a massive finger at me. "Hey, we're not done! What about your bet?"

Shrugging, I take two steps backward—right into the group of commandos still rolling their dice—and bump the chair of the guy with the cup in his hand. Dice and chits spill across the table.

"Hey, watch it, you punk!" one of them shouts. The bartender scoots out from behind the bar, heading my way, probably to shake me down and force me to feed him more info. Not today. With a hidden grin, I turn to the commandos and raise my voice as I point at one of them across the table. "Wait, did he just hide a die in his lap?"

"What?!" A dark-skinned female commando nearest me jerks up, tipping her chair over behind her as I dance out of the way. She points at a thin, bearded white man across the table. "I knew you were cheating, Graves! You're dead!"

Someone yells about the chair just as Graves stands to protest his innocence. More people crowd around to see the impending fight, blocking the bartender's path toward me. I duck under someone's raised arm and weave my way to Sena, who's already up and pointing at a back door. Maneuvering through the crowd, we easily slip outside, the chaos in the bar erupting behind us as we disappear down an alley.

CHAPTER 7

"Don't you know any other way to cause a distraction?" Sena laughs as we cut down another side street, putting more distance between us and the bar.

"Sure, I know plenty," I reply with a grin. "But fights and explosions work best. Especially with commandos. It's human nature."

Sena shakes her head. "You're certainly good at setting off both of those things."

I shrug. "It's also a part of my nature, how I was trained. Getting lowlifes to fight among themselves is easier than crafting some other elaborate plan. And the percentage of success is always high when people react emotionally."

"I saw fights in the Ket over less, that's for sure," Sena agrees. I lead us down another street, heading back toward the opposite side of the city. Now that I know where Kiran might be, I know exactly where we need to go.

"So, what did you say to the bartender?" Sena asks as we slow to a brisk walk.

"I asked him where Kiran was and, in exchange, told him Weiland sent a genopath to track down Revas."

She raises an eyebrow. "I thought your existence was illegal? And not something to share with strangers?"

"Oh, it is, but I didn't mention who the genopath was. People don't usually react well to meeting one in person. Most people think we're evil, robotic soldiers or some sort of all-powerful genetic boogeyman." Sena and Pana were the exceptions to that rule. And Alora. She knew what I was from that first moment in her bedroom and decided it made us kindred on account that she was genetically enhanced as well. Though her enhancements were the legal kind, her own genes altered before birth instead of the human and nonhuman gene-spliced cocktail they used to create me.

"I said it because using a genopath will make Weiland look a lot worse. People don't like the idea of someone like me sniffing around. It'll stir up more resentment against her, even if it's just minor grumblings or distrust. But might come in handy for us down the line."

"Won't it also alert Kiran that you're here?"

"Are you sure you're not a genopath?" I slide my eyes over to her. "You sure do think like one."

"I don't know if you mean that as a compliment or an insult." She gives me a side look.

"Compliment, obviously. Despite our origins and reputations, we are genetically superior thinkers."

Sena rolls her eyes. "My skills are all from surviving, not genetics. And you didn't answer my question, Remy. What about Kiran?"

I huff. "Kiran will probably find out I'm here one way or another if he doesn't already know. We were forced to play games like this all the time growing up, to try and outsmart one another. Now, since I baited him with that little tidbit, he'll probably come looking for me. Or change his tactics, making it easier to find him. Both of which are better options than me following him from bar to bar. That place reeked and so will all the other holes he likes to frequent."

Sena nearly skips a step. "You gave up the element of surprise because of smell?"

"If you had olfactory senses as strong as mine, you'd agree."

She shakes her head at me. "So, now we go to the outpost to find him, right? The one underneath the plateau."

"Exactly. I'd rather us get out of Verem anyway, especially since Taggert is probably still on our tails. Kiran's down there somewhere and we'll be out of Weiland's orbit. It's the most logical step."

I pause midstride, suddenly thinking about Alora dragging me all over this city two years ago. She always made it perfectly clear it was my choice whether to stay with her or stay behind. Though, I didn't really have a choice since my mission for the coup was to stick close to her and report back intel, but it felt nice that someone wanted to give me an option and not just orders. I look at Sena.

"Sena, if you don't want to come, you don't have to. I can find you somewhere to hole up where it's safe if you want. It's your choice." It's eerily strange to hear Alora's words coming from my lips. But it feels right. I promised her I would be better. Giving Sena an out is the right thing to do.

But she shakes her head. "No way. You're stuck with me, Remy. You helped me save Iska from Kalba. You kept me going on the race trail. You offered me a way off Tundar." Her voice grows fierce. "I didn't even ask for help then. So, yeah . . ." She coughs, clearing her throat, and then continues. "Iska and I, we've got your back."

I meet her eyes, my throat suddenly dry from the jungle heat or something. With a small smile, I turn and head toward the end of the block.

"Besides," Sena continues, falling back in step next to me, "I do not like Weiland. Or Taggert." She presses her lips into a line. "You saw her office floor lined with osak bear fur, right?"

I nod. "I thought that's what that was. Not that I particularly like osak bears after the one that almost ate us."

A small laugh escapes her lips. "No one likes them." She pauses for a beat. "But Kalba had osak bear fur in his office, too. To show he was bigger and stronger than any of the preds out on the tundra. People like him, people like Weiland, they take whatever they want however they can. Those are not people I want to be around."

I nod, wondering how much the dead boss lives on in Sena's mind, haunting her in the quiet moments. He tried to murder her. And Iska. She killed him to save herself and to avenge her mothers. I know what it's like to have ghosts following in your wake because of your own choices. The decisions we have to make never get easier.

And neither do the repercussions.

"Then we'll keep going," I say. "There's a platform lift not far from here that runs down to the syndicate outpost on the plateau's edge. We'll find somewhere to lay low down there, away from Weiland and Taggert, while we look for Kiran."

Sena smiles tightly. "You promised me some better food, too."

I almost laugh out loud. "That I did. They've got a lot more than protein bars or rënedeer sausage around here. Though the bush meat doesn't taste that much better, at least they drown it in tasty spices." That gets a lighter smile out of her, and we take off again.

Keeping to the edges of town to avoid any run-ins with Taggert, we head the few blocks over to the lift. Out here in the city's outskirts, there's little sign of TerraCo's influence. But even as we cut down alleys and intersections, the pointed white tower above the train station still peeks over the rooftops. A silent reminder that no matter where we are, Weiland is watching. A few times, I spot the flyer I heard earlier hovering near the Vega compound. Another sign that Taggert and Weiland probably aren't far behind us.

I keep us off the main streets and in the shadows as we trek. By the time we make it to the syndicate-run platform lift, the sun is sinking below the mountains on the horizon. Despite the ever constant humidity, a slight chill rides along with the breeze that rushes up from the jungle. The plateau we're on towers above the jungle canopy below. The lift that travels down to the syndicate outpost and the sprawl is built right on the side of the massive rock wall, nothing more than a rickety caged platform attached to the mountainside with some cables.

As we walk up, very few people mill about, and only one person is waiting outside the lift for passengers, slumped in a chair, her fair-skinned face covered by a hat. Two years ago, the lift was always crowded with people transiting up or down, busy with syndicates who worked in the city alongside the corpos, or even on the mag train, providing security as it traversed the valley. This platform was a bustle of activity day or night. But now the area is nearly deserted. No crowds coming or going. Makes me curious how many syndicates have been replaced with Weiland's lackeys.

I see no sign of commandos around, though. No scent of the

plastic composite of their armor or sounds of shuffling boots. I motion to Sena and Iska to follow me up to the platform, keeping my focus wide, scanning for potential threats or a trap. Absorbing everything from the sounds of the jungle below to the cadence of the lift operator's breathing. This would be the perfect place for Taggert to sneak up on us. But nothing jumps out at me. At least the girl in the chair isn't wearing any TerraCo branded layers. A syndicate, hopefully.

"What's the lift cost?" I ask her. She's half asleep, the cap covering her short and choppy red-orange hair. She peeks open one dark hazel eye that roves from me to Sena to the wolf and then back to me again. Something about her expression—a sharpness hidden under the obvious boredom—catches my attention as her eyes land on me. She's around my age, but her demeanor has me wondering if she got assigned this position as a punishment for something.

"The lift is thirty chits each," she mutters, tugging her hat down farther over her heavily freckled face and slumping in the chair, clearly not wanting to be bothered by us.

"How much?" Sena's mouth drops.

"Plus ten extra for the wolf. The fur makes me sneeze."

I shake my head. "Come on, there's no way it's that high. It used to be five chits a person."

But the girl doesn't so much as twitch. "Used to be five chits. Now it's not." I tune into her pulse but find it slow and unbothered. She's not lying or hiding anything or trying to rip us off. She must work for the Vega after all.

The girl shrugs. "Cost of doing business. Look, I don't make the rules. You wanna go down? That's the price."

Now I know why the lift is deserted. TerraCo must've jacked

up the cost of operating it and the syndicates had to raise the lift prices in turn. Most syndicates can't afford to take the lift daily at that price. What the hell was Dekkard doing as boss if he wasn't keeping Weiland in check?

"Fine," I grumble, and scan my chit chip across the holoscreen beside her. I ignore the numbers running through my head and the quickly depleting chits in my account. I've got enough. And if I need to, I'll find ways to get more. I always do.

The girl slowly stands, taller than I guessed, and stretches her arms and back before ambling over to the lift. I expect her to wait for others also going down, but apparently we're the only ones. A giant elevator designed to hold well over fifty people being used for just the three of us. What a waste.

She pauses at the step up into the lift, looking over her shoulder, cap still covering most of her face.

"Well, you three coming or not?"

Sena and I exchange a look and follow her onto the platform. Iska pauses at the threshold, sniffing the edges and glancing around cautiously. The platform resembles a giant elevator car, except the walls are made of fencing to better handle the ever-present heat. But to Iska, it probably looks like a cage.

Sena crouches down and calls softly to her. After a moment more of hesitation, Iska's trust of Sena overrides her fear and the wolf paces warily inside. Thankfully, the syndicate doesn't say anything before turning back to the control panel. She smashes a button, and the motor slowly whirs to life.

With so much open space in the lift, a soft breeze easily filters through the fence, cooling the sweat dripping down the back of my neck and my spine. The sunset in the distance casts the sky in an array of pinks and blues, contrasting with the deep, dark green of the jungle below. The mag rail curves out of the tower just down the plateau from us, its tracks snaking across the valley right above the treetops. Far over the distant mountains, I can still make out the tendrils of dark clouds as the storm cycle continues on its path around the planet. It may be a beautiful scene, but it won't last. The threat of the storm is never far from the horizon.

The platform jerks and creaks as the syndicate shoves a lever forward and activates the lift. Still sniffing over by the fence, Iska whines. She takes one glance through the caged wall and promptly shuffles away from the edge and crouches by Sena's feet. Guess the wolf doesn't much like heights.

The descent is choppy as the lift scoots and slides down the side of the plateau. It doesn't seem to have been repaired much over the last two years. Every few minutes, we jerk to a halt before plummeting a few more feet. Iska whines softly the entire time, readjusting her footing with each bump while the rest of us grip the fencing to keep our balance.

We inch toward the caves below as the sun sinks fully behind the mountains, leaving us in the fading light of dusk. As the darkness grows, the jungle begins to sing, insects and birds and all sorts of creatures coming alive. Cries and screeches alike sound from the jungle canopy. The lift hits the treetops and the temperature drops as we get closer to the ground. Without the sun's rays beating down, the weather of the planet shifts. It's still humid and wet but with a sticky chill underneath that nips at my exposed skin. Like a mist that never evaporates. At least in the caves, we'll be dry.

The syndicates claimed these caverns when Maraas was still being settled and have held on to the prime spot ever since. Alora's father was the first one to see opportunities beyond the caves; he built his headquarters above on the plateau to be on par with the corpos. Maybe that's why they were so threatened by him. Maybe that's why Nova sent Kiran and me here in the first place. To ensure that no one could stand against corpo might. To ensure the rest of us stay in our place where we belong.

Before I can analyze that further, the lift hits the ground with a jerking thud. We're at the edge of the giant cave opening, the syndicate outpost spilling out around us on the hard earth at the cavern's entrance. Food carts and hawkers have set up shop on the landing, assaulting anyone headed in or out of the caves. Dozens of heartbeats, the whir of servo bikes, and the hum of movement overwhelm my ears. Farther beyond the rock, the ground dips into a slick, muddy decline, and at the bottom of the hill, right under the mag rail tracks, the sprawl begins.

The syndicate yanks open the sliding door and then flips a switch as we step out. The lights in the lift go dark.

"You're done for the night?" I ask in surprise as Iska dashes away from the lift. What sort of transpo shuts down at dark?

The girl adjusts her cap as she watches the wolf dive into a fresh patch of mud just beyond the cave. Sena rolls her eyes at Iska's obvious joy at being out of the lift but makes no move to stop her. With a half smile on her face, the syndicate finally answers my question. "We don't do night runs. Again, not my rules. Weiland's."

My thoughts jump to the white corpo tower far above our heads, out of sight but not out of mind. I suppose Weiland doesn't want any of her employees coming down for the nightly entertainment that the syndicates provide throughout these caves. Another possibility hits me: maybe she doesn't want any syndicates creeping up in the dead of night. My mind wants to run through all the options and figure out exactly what Weiland is up to, but I ignore it for now. I need to focus on Kiran. Whatever power play he's involved with here doesn't matter. I only need him to find out what happened to Alora.

The girl locks up the cage door and then turns to leave.

"Hey." I grab her attention. If the bartender knew who Kiran was, it stands to assume the girl operating the only lift up or down has probably had run-ins with him, too. Maybe she can shed some light on his movements. "Do you happen to know a guy named Kiran Lore?"

The girl rolls her eyes. "That jerk? I hope he doesn't owe you money."

"Something like that," I say. He certainly owes me. "Do you know where we could find him?"

The tall girl shrugs. "If he's not at Arun's den, he's slinking around somewhere. You should stay away from him, though. Trouble follows that guy."

"Thanks," I say, ignoring her warning. Trouble's practically my shadow at this point. My curiosity about Kiran's motivations grows. Arun is a den boss who we recruited for our coup two years ago. I'm not surprised he's still around; Arun was always more interested in profit than politics and would do whatever it took to keep his den open and operational.

With a dismissive wave, the girl disappears into the small crowd of food stalls and hawkers trying to ply their wares to anyone who'll listen. Directly behind the clutter is the outpost, nothing more than a series of large caverns that the syndicates have made their own.

Sena eyes the entrance and the crowd skeptically. I point and we head for the cave's interior. Thankfully, it doesn't look like much has changed down here. Though, like Verem, it wasn't this cluttered or run-down two years ago. I glance down a familiar alley and see an open-air restaurant poised just near the cave entrance. The layout is the same, down to the cracked tables and plastic chairs. The giant stewpot still sits in the middle of the space, trails of dark soup bubbling over the edge. I can smell the spices of the stew even from a block away, the fragrant scent triggering more echoes of memories.

On my third night posing as her bodyguard, Alora snuck down here to eat those stewed noodles without her father knowing. In my mind, the replay simmers to life and I let it blanket me, the memory warm and comforting. I can see Alora slurping her soup at the table in the corner. I'd tailed her across Verem and down the lift, but when I sat down to confront her, she was the one to surprise me.

The rest of the memory triggers, pulling me fully into the replay, and I'm no longer standing by the alleyway but walking through the restaurant.

In my mind, I sink down on the stool across from Alora. Her blue eyes sparkle when she looks up at me. Not from surprise to see me, but from mischief. She was testing me with this little outing. I open my mouth to say something, but she speaks first.

"I know what you are."

I study her, thinking of a dozen ways this conversation could go, and then settle on answering her statement with a question.

"And what exactly am I?"

"Genopath," she whispers, loud enough for me alone to hear. I blink in surprise. I've been on this mission for three days and I've already botched it. Kiran's going to be pissed.

"It's okay," she continues. "I know because I'm altered, too." She taps her nose. "I can sense you."

"Why tell me that you know?" I ask, more curious than threatened. I never had a chance to talk to someone who had senses like me, other than my squadmates. And none of the other chumps with gene mods I've encountered had olfactory senses strong enough to sniff out my genopathic-specific pheromones.

Alora twirls the spoon in her soup. "Because you understand what it's like not to have a choice. To have your life predetermined for you."

"My life isn't predetermined," I answer automatically. My life is missions. My life is Nova. It's what I was built for; choice never once came into it. I never needed it to.

But Alora shakes her head at me. "You and I both were designed for a specific purpose. You to do . . . whatever it is you do. Me, to take over for my father. That's the path and there is no other choice. I'll never get a chance to find out who I could've been on my own. Same as you."

She leans closer, blue eyes locking onto mine as errant blond hairs nearly dip into her soup bowl.

"Doesn't that bother you?"

I shrug. "Never really thought about it much."

"You never even had the chance, did you?" She keeps her voice neutral, but there's an undercurrent of sadness to it.

I don't have an answer to her question or her tone. Pity isn't something that's ever been directed at me because there's nothing to pity. This is the way I was made. Instead of answering, I reach over and take a bite of her stew. It tastes like spice and jungle dirt.

"It doesn't matter," I finally say. "It is what it is, and we are who we are. Why dwell on things we can't change?"

"But . . . come on, what if you could be anything?" She folds her hands on the table and rests her chin on them. "Go anywhere in the charted systems, any planet. What would you do? Where would you go?"

I meet her eyes and suddenly a chasm opens up somewhere in my chest. I wasn't lying when I said I'd never thought about it. Nova never lets any of us think about life beyond our squad and our missions. If any of us shows an inkling of disobedience, we're sent off to reprogramming, reconditioning. I went through it once when I was eleven. The pain of being tortured physically and psychologically is a constant reminder to not slip up. To not let any stray thoughts enter my head. But here I am on a different planet, far from needles and dark rooms.

Maybe I can have this thought, this one time, and then suppress it all again. Nova would never have to know. So, I swallow down the spicy taste of the stew and my fear and allow myself to dream, if only for a second.

"I'd go to Abydos," I say with a shrug.

Alora's eyebrows shoot up. "Never-ending desert and lava fields? Really?"

"It's harsh, but still, it's more beautiful than it sounds. . . . What about you?" I ask, suddenly wanting to know her answer more than anything I've ever wanted to know before.

"Ceren," Alora says immediately, as if she'd been waiting for me to ask her this exact question the entire time. "A planet-sized city where no one knows me, and I can get lost for years. Where I could be anyone I want one day, and someone else the next."

I smile and find myself telling her about a mission I ran on Ceren that involved me doing almost exactly that. She laughs when I finish and then, to my surprise, I laugh in return. Something loosens in my chest, and I feel lighter than I ever have before.

The laugh brings me out of the replay, stops the trigger.

I think that was the first time I ever laughed naturally. With no ulterior motive or false intentions behind it. Just . . . a laugh.

The memory fades as I turn away from the alley and the restaurant. It makes my heart ache in a way that I've been able to ignore for the last two years on the run. But now, coming here and watching her ghost live on in my head, it's like I'm losing her all over again.

"You okay?" Sena asks next to me. I'm not sure how long I've been standing on this street corner. A few minutes probably. Feels like years. I shake the dregs of the echo out of my head. I can't let myself keep getting caught up in the replays. Alora, the real Alora, is out there somewhere. I need to focus on finding her, not get triggered by the memory of her every five minutes.

"I'm fine," I say, willing it to be true and getting my head back in the game. "I'm just running through some potential places Kiran might be hiding if he's not at the den. There are cheap rooms for rent around Arun's place, too. Good spot for him to hide or for us to lay low for the night and plan our next move if we don't find him."

"All right," Sena says with a nod. "Let's do that."

"Arun's den is in the deepest part of the cave. It won't take long to get there." A two-wheeled servo bike zooms by us and we both take a step back. Iska has already bounded across the narrow street, dodging the bike and passersby alike, leaving a trail of mud in her wake.

"This place reminds me a lot more of the Ket than Verem did," Sena says, waving the exhaust smoke away from her face. Iska barks at us from the other side of the road.

I nod as we cross more carefully. "Not as cold, but just as messy." Everything in this outpost, on this whole planet, is built up and latched onto something else like an afterthought.

As we walk, Iska darts from hawker cart to cart, weaving between more of the two-wheeled servo bikes that zoom down the roads. She frantically follows the plethora of scents while still staying close. I can't blame her. Everything smells down here, from the food to the exhaust smoke to the people themselves. I try to ignore the various scents assaulting my own nose, especially the ones that smell like sweat or something worse.

"What's this den like?" Sena asks as we head down a crowded road.

"Imagine Kalba's den but twice the size and louder. More gambling, more booze."

Sena wrinkles her nose. "Oh boy. I'm going to love this place, aren't I?"

I laugh. "If you are looking to get back into your life of petty crime, it would be the place."

"I know better than to steal from an entire outpost of syndicates. Being wanted on one world is quite enough."

"Don't worry. I know how to work Arun. We won't get into any trouble. Probably."

Sena grimaces at my response while swatting at the mosquitoes buzzing around her face. Since we left the plateau, we're no longer safe from the onslaught of insects that swarm in the jungle. Up there, the animals and the bugs are fewer, kept at bay by the altitude and whatever chems the corpos spray around the city. Down here, we're basically in the midst of the jungle swamp. Though at least in the caves, the ground is solid rock and not ever-shifting mud.

Sena and Iska stay tight on my trail as we weave through the maze of buildings. Voices holler and shout all around us. It's impossible for me to discern heartbeats from one another in these cramped blocks. We pass small-scale arms shops and hole-in-the-wall restaurants, laundry services and plenty of dens offering one vice or another. Servo bikes buzz down roads and alleyways alike, their engines adding to the ever-present noise, amplified by the cave's ceiling. They're not supposed to run the bikes this deep because of the stench of the exhaust, but no one seems to care. They've got worse problems than pollution.

We've been walking ten minutes when I catch an undercurrent of one particular scent underneath all the dirt and grime and sweaty bodies. A scent of specific pheromones that is leading toward the den.

Kiran. It's definitely him.

The anticipation of finally meeting him face-to-face after two years tingles under my skin, the promise of the coming challenge. When we were partners, dealing with Kiran was always a pain in my ass. Even when we were following orders, things always had to be his way. He'd pull all kinds of crap when we were on missions. Moving me away from the action and making my job harder, switching up my assignments at the last minute—anything he didn't like, he'd adjust. I doubt he's changed much over the last two years, so I know he's not going to make this easy on me.

We turn down a back lane, and the dull beat of a low bass starts to reverberate up my spine. Getting closer.

Another turn and we're on a wide road that runs parallel to the cave's back wall. Nothing but sheer rock all the way up to the stalactites dripping down from the ceiling far above. On the opposite side of the street, a concrete building runs right into the stone, jutting out from the cave wall itself.

Arun's den.

It's one of the larger buildings that litter the outpost—some of the rooms inside the den are cut into the cave itself. Balconies made from fencing and spare wood have been added to both levels, all full of people moving to the beat. Music pours out onto the lane, as do drunken revelers and paid entertainers. This is a club where anything can be bought, maybe even anyone.

Exactly the type of place Kiran likes to haunt, looking for marks to manipulate, pawns to move around on his board as he and Nova see fit.

Finding Kiran in this mess is going to be like finding a flash bomb in a minefield that's on fire. Keeping an eye out for traps from him or from Nova is going to make it even more impossible.

Good thing I love a challenge.

CHAPTER 8

So, this is the den, huh?" Sena eyes the rickety balconies overstuffed with bodies. "Doesn't look like the people are much different than those in the Ket, at least."

I shrug. "Syndicates are pretty much the same everywhere."

Her gaze jumps from the balconies to the people loitering around the entrance.

"This is a big building. It'd be a good place for a trap." Her gray eyes slide over to me. "Just saying."

"The thought occurred to me," I agree with a nod. "If Nova's around, there's always a possibility of a trap." But my previous conversation with the twins echoes in my head. They thought I was dead because apparently Kiran was the one who told Nova I died on this planet two years ago. He wouldn't have any reason to set a trap with them now, would he? Though his history of betrayal doesn't exactly set a good precedent. We ran dozens of missions together and I still don't know what makes him tick. He always seemed driven by some force beyond our orders. A force I never really understood.

I sigh internally. I haven't even found him yet and he's already frustrating me. But even without him and his weird unpredictability, it's still likely that Nova could have other agents inside. Agents I want to steer clear of.

I lock eyes with Sena and raise an eyebrow. "Trap or no, I'm still going in." No matter how much he pisses me off, I still have to find Kiran and get my answers.

Sena's gaze sharpens. "Don't worry. We got you, Remy." She scratches between Iska's ears. "We won't let any Nova hacks drag you back to their lab and put you in a cage."

I smile tightly; it's good to have someone that I trust, but guilt still stabs at me for dragging her into this mess in the first place. Am I simply being her friend or am I using her the way Nova programmed me to? Gaining Alora's trust was also a part of my mission and programming, and I messed that up royally. I don't want to let Sena down the way I failed Alora, and I don't want her to feel like I'm just using her either.

"I won't let anything get that far with Kiran or with Nova," I promise her. "I'm not going to let them hurt any more of my friends," I add quietly. Sena's eyes meet mine, but I don't let myself get lost in the undercurrent of emotions in them. Time to focus on the task at hand. I move toward the entrance, toward Kiran's trail.

"So, anything in particular I should know about this Arun guy?" Sena asks as we head up the steps.

"He's not power hungry like Kalba was. With Arun, profit is what matters above all."

"I'll keep that in mind."

Together, we weave through the revelers littering the entrance, me leading with Sena and Iska just behind. A bouncer stands in the doorframe, demanding chits to get inside. I ignore the diminishing amount of money in my account as I scan my wrist again. If I get the answers I need, the chits are worth it. I steal a quick glance up at the camera drone hovering above our heads. Won't be long before Arun comes and finds me.

The entrance hall leading deeper into the den is lined with neon. Pinks and yellows reflect across mirrored surfaces, casting the hall in an eerie glow. Music pulses around a hundred heartbeats, but I do my best to shut out the noise for now. If the bass bothers Sena or Iska, neither of them show it. Iska's probably used to the discord after all her fights in Kalba's den. She stalks silently behind me, just in front of Sena, her own canine bodyguard. The wolf's ears are perked forward, and I know she's listening for potential threats.

We're not so different, Iska and I.

We pass the doors that head upstairs to private rooms without stopping. Kiran's scent doesn't lead that way. The pheromones are getting harder for me to follow as the den grows more packed. The trail is still faint, and it's getting mixed in with all the bodies and mess. Pushing past a few stragglers in the hall, I follow what's left of it to the main dance room.

The club is packed. There are camera drones floating above the crowds, but there's no way to tell who's who with this many people pressed together so tightly. The center of the room is a large circular bar with its own second level for professional dancers to wow onlookers from a safe distance. The den walls around us go all the way up to the rock far above our heads. The ceiling itself is the actual cave top, complete with neon-lit stalactites throwing sharp shadows on the crowd below. A caged balcony wraps around the walls, forming a makeshift mezzanine.

As we pause on the threshold of the madness, my nose is accosted by the smell of sweat and bodies and booze. In this mess, it's nearly impossible even for me to follow Kiran on scent alone. Too many smells to sift through. If I'm lucky, I might catch a whiff if I get close to him. But I have to somehow narrow down the search area first.

"How are we going to find anyone in here?" Sena shouts behind me over the noise.

"We're going to have to split up again."

"Yeah, except I have no idea what Kiran even looks like."

I almost laugh that I forgot to describe him, though Sena and I haven't exactly had time to sit and talk about anything in a calm manner since we left Tundar. I've barely managed to relay pieces of my story in between emergencies.

"He's tall, taller than you," I say over my shoulder. "Black hair, bronze skin, and deep brown eyes so dark they look black and they're usually gleaming with the promise of violence or deceit."

Sena rolls her eyes. "Anything else that might actually be helpful, Remy?"

"Oh, he has a scar." I point to my cheek and trace a line down to my chin. "It starts underneath his left cheekbone and runs below his jaw. You can't miss it."

She nods. "If we see him, we'll come get you."

I almost ask how she would find me in this massive crowd, but her eyes dart to Iska standing close and I don't have to ask. The wolf could sniff me out anywhere, her nose better than mine, even in the packed den. I rub her head affectionately, and then, with a final look, Sena folds herself into the packed bodies around us, Iska on her tail. I guess neither of them needs a splinter wood or endless ice to disappear. After a minute, I can barely track their movements through the bodies.

Turning, I head up to the makeshift balcony so I can better scan the room, snatching a half-empty glass from a table as I go. I spotted a small corner where the rock wall meets the concrete one when we came in. The little alcove is private enough but has a decent view over the dance floor, so I can keep an eye out for Kiran.

Once I make my way there, I fake a drunken stumble close to the couple currently occupying the alcove. I run into one of the boys, bumping against his shoulder and sloshing my drink everywhere. They quickly scurry away after I spill what's left of the liquor in an attempt to cheers with their empty hands.

Claiming the spot as my own, I take a deep breath to center myself, then I let my focus go wide. It's hard to hear beyond the pulsing beat of the bass, but once I ignore it, other sounds filter in. Snippets of conversations, snatches of a booming voice or a squeal, the pounding of hundreds of feet tapping and stomping to the music. I scan the movements of the crowds around me, listening for useful tidbits, waiting for something offbeat to catch my eye. Searching for a genopath who won't move like the rest of the clubgoers.

A voice floats into my attention. ". . . my last night in this hellhole! Tomorrow, I'm out."

"Put in a good word for me when you get to Abydos!" another replies. It's a small group of syndicates. Supportive shouts echo around the cluster but no sign of Kiran. My focus jumps as a small commotion forms in another corner. A man wearing TerraCo layers is being pushed by a woman and a group of angry syndicates.

"Get the hell out of our space, corpo chump!"

I try to catch more of the conversation, but a fight is already breaking out between Weiland's employees and the syndicates. Tensions are even higher than I suspected. Security begins to wade toward them, but still no Kiran.

My fingers itch as someone walks by with a cigarette. I haven't smoked in over two years and the smoke is already making me nauseous. Alora hated the smell, so I quit. But having one during surveillance always helped take the edge off the constant stimulation. Though I claimed it helped me blend in, I picked up the habit as a small act of pissing off Nova. The scientists hated it when any of us did anything to mess up their perfect genes. Surprisingly, Kiran smoked, too, out of solidarity I guess; there were only so many ways we could push back before we got sent to reprogramming.

I rub the tips of my fingers together to keep them occupied, all the while still looking for Kiran's figure, still scanning faces for that familiar smug expression. For the scar I gave him.

It was right before we came here. I think back to the moment without letting the replay or the triggers fully take over.

We were training with long arken blades in front of the Nova execs who had flown in for a demonstration of our progress. Our squad leaders were thrilled. Take out the genopaths, parade them around, see how they've grown. See how we've molded them into perfect puppets and spies for the corporate fat cats.

Kiran and I were chosen to demonstrate the advanced reflexes and instincts Nova embedded in even its noncombat assets. That's what the Nova execs called us. Their assets. Didn't matter whether we were assassins or soldiers, spies or master manipulators. To them, we were all just property. And they could use us however they saw fit.

So, Kiran and I fought with blades. It was ridiculous. Neither of us would ever choose hand-to-hand combat. We weren't built for that, and the odds of success are too finicky. Much better to avoid the violence entirely and leave the actual fighting to those we were supposed to be manipulating or even to the combat geno-paths that Nova created specifically for physical engagements. But still, we were forced to train hand-to-hand combat because those scientists and corpo chumps have a hard-on for anything violent.

In the middle of our fight, Kiran hesitated. He had a perfectly aimed blow at my armor-plated chest that would've ended the fight and put me on the ground, but something stopped him. I don't know what made him pause; with Kiran it was probably a scheme or an angle, something to one-up me or throw me off my game. I barely caught the strange look in his eyes before I swung my own arken blade back at him. He dodged, but my blade still caught his face, the laser slicing open his bronze skin from cheek to jaw. I was silently horrified watching the blood drip down his face.

But the execs cheered, and we were ushered away. We left for Maraas the next day. They didn't even bother to accelerate his healing. Our superiors thought that Kiran's wound would help him fit in among the syndicate ranks. They were right. It did.

But we never talked about that fight, Kiran and I. Neither of us would risk blowing our cover even though I thought about bring-ing it up. Every time the light hit the scar, I wanted to say . . . something. But I didn't trust him not to use it against me somehow. To be sarcastic and blow me off. So, I swallowed the thoughts; the mission came first anyway. Or at least it did until Alora came into the picture.

And now here I am, close to finding out what happened to her, what Kiran did with her. Awful scenarios of ruthless commandos or forced indentured servitude or even worse flash through my head while I scan the people around me. I have to find her and make sure she's okay. I have to make up for my failure two years ago.

I survey the crowd again and again, looking for that scar.

"You got a lot of nerve coming in here," a deep voice resonates loudly, even over the bass. My head whips to the left, surprised that Arun, despite his height, has managed to sneak up on me in the alcove. He always moved quietly for someone so tall.

"Arun, so nice to see you again." I raise my voice just loud enough to be heard. The sharply dressed den boss towers over me. His lean figure hasn't changed much in two years, though his onyx-black hair is longer now, tied in a loose braid that trails down the exposed rich brown skin of his shoulders. The expression on his face hasn't changed much either. Calculating disdain and judgment directed right at me.

"Is it nice?" Arun raises a tailored eyebrow. The two bodyguards flanking him shift almost imperceptibly, waiting for me to try something. They'll be waiting for a good long while; I don't have a death wish. The den boss is known for carrying an exorbitant number of hidden knives. Fighting is never my first choice for a reason.

"The last time you were here on my world"—he looks down his nose at me—"you caused a ruckus. Such was the mess you and your partner made that I really don't consider it nice to see either of you again. I preferred it when the rumors said you were dead."

I raise an eyebrow. So, he has seen Kiran. Perfect.

"What are you doing in my bar, Remy?" he finishes.

I smile, nice and slow. "Actually, I'm looking for that former partner of mine. Is he here?"

Arun's eyes narrow, seeing right through my smile. "You didn't come with him? How the plot thickens. When did you get here?"

"Landed this afternoon, right after crashing through the storm. I met Weiland. That was fun." I drop her name solely to judge his reaction.

But Arun rolls his eyes and waves his hand in a dramatic gesture. "Our own personal queen. Did she send you down here?"

"Not after you specifically, so you can stop worrying." He doesn't seem threatened by her, but he knows she might be a threat to him. Interesting.

"Oh, I'm not the one who should be worried," Arun replies. "No, dear, that should be you. You were the one that upended the balance of the Vega and put far too much power in her hands. You think she won't use that power against you?" He leans closer, his breath holding hints of smoke and dark corners. "Weiland's tightening grip is your fault. You were the one responsible for Rixus's downfall. You think I won't hold you accountable?"

My spine stiffens at the name of Alora's father. It seems Arun knows far more about me than he ever let on two years ago. I wonder if Kiran told him our plans or if he figured it out on his own.

"You're right," I finally reply through gritted teeth. "I know it's all my fault. Though you weren't complaining about the power imbalance this much two years ago when we made sure your pockets were lined." I take a breath, not wanting to piss him off. "Look, I'd like to help fix things, but for that I need Kiran. Are you going to tell me where he is or not?"

His piercing eyes study me for a beat and I try to contain my impatience. Finally, Arun shrugs. "I think not. No good can come of the two of you together. Now get out of my den before I have you thrown out."

I glare at him as he straightens to his full height. His eyes, as dark as Kiran's but full of conviction, don't leave my face as he stares me down, daring me to challenge him in his own space.

"Excuse me. Did you lose something?" A familiar voice interrupts us. I lean to look around Arun's guard and spy Sena behind the chump, Iska at her side. Looks like Arun's not the only one who can sneak up on his marks. The guards immediately flank the two of them, whipping out handguns aimed to kill. But Sena doesn't flinch. Nor does she back down.

"Who's this?" Arun's eyes slide to her and then the wolf. He must not have noticed me talking to her on his camera feeds. "I don't lose things in my own den, and I'm certainly not in the mood for humor."

She holds up a small set of keys, the old-fashioned kind that turn locks rather than activate them. "It's not a joke. These are yours, right?"

I have to cough into my hand to cover my smile. Sena must've picked his pocket while the guards were focused on me. She may not have engineered genes, but her quick reactions never cease to impress me.

"I think I saw you drop them over by the staircase." She holds them out to Arun, surprise written all over his features. But she pulls back just as he's about to wrap his fingers around the ring of keys.

"Nothing taken, nothing given."

Arun growls. "And what is it you want?"

Sena releases the keys into his outstretched hand and gestures to me with a nod.

"I want what Remy wants. To know where Kiran is."

Arun glares at her for a beat. Then, to my utter shock and Sena's as well, a loud laugh rumbles out of Arun's throat.

"Not every day I get fleeced by a girl and a wolf. You've got guts, kid. I can respect that."

He pockets the keys and looks at me.

"Remy, it's never dull with you around, I'll give you that." He raises an arm and points down below, to a darkened hallway off the main floor leading to a side exit. "Now, seeing as I'm done with him anyway, why don't all three of you chumps get out of my den before I lose my patience."

I follow the line of his arm, searching the dark just as a familiar figure steps out from a corner and stands underneath the single hanging light in the hallway. Even with his features half hidden in sharp shadows, I'd recognize him anywhere.

Kiran.

Anger twists in my gut at the sight of him. He turns away from us, but I'm already taking a step toward the stairs without a second thought. Sena catches up to me as Arun and his bodyguards melt back into the throng.

"We should flank him," I say, keeping an eye on Kiran's figure. "He'll probably leave out of the side exit. I'll follow and lead him around back to the front of the den."

"Then Iska and I will go out the front and wait," she says with a nod. "The odds are better when it's three to one."

I'm about to warn her but she waves me off. "Stop worrying, we'll be as sneaky as a taikat in the shadows. He won't see us until it's too late. And if you're not back out front in five minutes, we'll come find you."

And then she's gone, and my focus is entirely on the boy disappearing farther down the hall. It takes me less than ten seconds to move through the crowd and get to the hall, but Kiran's still ahead of me, still partially hidden in shadow. My eyes adjust as I step into the hallway cautiously. His head tilts slightly to the side and I can just make out his smirk.

He was waiting for me to find him this whole time, the jerk.

Then he inclines his head toward the other end of the hallway. An invitation to follow. It's too planned, too calculated. A beat passes between us as I weigh the odds. Kiran betrayed me before; who's to say he won't again? Weiland could be waiting outside or agents from Nova. With Kiran, I never know how many sides he's playing against each other. The last time he tricked me like this, I ended up alone in the middle of the jungle.

My ex-partner waits another long beat and then with a shrug slips right out the exit door at the end of the hall. Trap or no, he still knows how to piss me off. I grit my teeth and storm after him. I didn't come this far to be a pawn in whatever game he's playing. But I don't slink out the door like he did. Pulling a flash bomb out of my pocket, I kick the door open. It slams into the wall behind, revealing a small, dirty alley where Kiran leans nonchalantly on one shoulder against the cave wall opposite the door.

My eyes want to go straight to him, red seeping into my vision, but I keep my focus and scan the alley with all I've got instead—looking, listening, sniffing for anyone suspicious or out of place. But there are no balconies on this side of the club. No people either. No goons rushing to get me. Just a small dirt pathway full of trash that dead-ends into a wall of rock.

"No one's waiting in the wings," Kiran's deep voice rumbles, somehow echoing even in the confined space. I finally let myself glare at him even though his body is angled away from me. I want nothing more than to shout at him, demand answers, but I keep my composure as I speak. Mostly.

"Not even Nova?" I ask.

"They're not coming either," he replies, a surprising amount of venom in his words. "Not anytime soon. That, I promise you."

"Don't make promises you can't keep, Kiran." I slip the flash bomb back into my pocket for now. "Especially ones where you ask me to trust you. You're a liar and traitor."

He turns, taking a drag on a smoke I didn't notice. Deep brown hair brushes his shoulders and falls in his face, partially covering his bronze skin and dark eyes. His scar peeks out from under the long hair strands. He's dressed in a sweat-wicking top, cargo pants, and heavy duty boots. Simple layers that hug his lean, athletic frame, which just makes it easy for me to spot the low-level tension in his muscles. Two years and he hasn't changed a bit.

"Me, the traitor? I think we both know that's not true. Besides, I thought you were the one designed for lies and subterfuge," he says, his eyes locking onto mine. "And I was made to make sure you got to use them." His familiar smirk grows. "Come on Rem, if you can't trust your own partner, who can you trust?"

"Certainly not you—you're not my partner anymore." I step down into the alley, approaching him slowly, trying to keep my racing pulse under control since I know he can hear it as well as I can hear his. Of course, his heartbeat sounds clear and calm.

"Ouch, that hurts." He flicks the cigarette away. "I know you didn't come all this way to give me a hard time about what happened before." Something flickers in his eyes as he speaks, but then it's gone and he's looking me up and down, assessing.

"You mean how you dumped me in the jungle and—"

"Come on. Don't be mad," he cuts me off. "You look good, Remy." He runs a finger across the bridge of his nose, mimicking the marks still noticeable on my own face from my encounter with the osak bear on Tundar. "I dig your new scars."

I close the distance between us in a flash, moving without thinking, and slam my fist into his nose. His head snaps back with the force and he yields a step.

"Shut up," I growl as he wipes a trickle of blood with the back of his hand. I don't know if he brought up the scars to compare them to the scar I gave him or if he purposefully said it to get a rise out of me. "They're practically your fault since it was you I was hunting on Tundar. The same you who left me in the freaking jungle and disappeared with my only friend. Where is she, Kiran?"

He rubs his nose and looks at me with an unreadable expression. I can't tell if he's angry or disappointed, but I'm not sorry I hit him. It felt good.

"I could tell you, sure," he says nonchalantly, as if I didn't just clock him in the face. "But what are you going to give me in return? I can't give you something for nothing. Them's the rules."

I grit my teeth. "Don't give me that crap. You owe me this. You sped up the coup and messed up everything. You left me for dead. You stole my friend. I don't have to give you squat."

Wiping the rest of the smeared blood off his face, he laughs.

"I wish it were that simple. Come on. Let's go negotiate the terms of our new partnership."

He strides past me, but I move quickly, blocking his path. "I'm not going anywhere with you, nor are we negotiating. Tell me where Alora is."

I catch a flash of a flinch on his face at my friend's name and then it's gone. With a small sigh, Kiran casually steps around me like I'm nothing more than an obstacle to be ignored.

"There's more going on than you could possibly know, Remy. Now, I'm not going to get into it with you in a side alley next to broken beer bottles and week-old piss. I'm hungry and I know you probably are, too. So, whether you want that information or you just want to punch me again, I don't care. But I'm not doing either here."

He looks at me, expression flat, but I can see some sort of emotion simmering in his eyes, feel it in his now slightly elevated pulse. But before I can analyze it further, he ambles toward the main street, throwing a final question over his shoulder.

"You coming or what?"

CHAPTER 9

Part of me really wants to stay in this alleyway just to annoy Kiran. But the rest of me wants answers and knows he's too stubborn to yield. And he's right. It does stink of beer and piss out here.

Reluctantly, I follow as he lumbers down the alley and turns onto the main road. He's heading back the way we came, toward the lift and the outpost entrance. I let him get a small lead as we walk past the front of the club, giving me a chance to spot Sena, who's leaning against the wall with Iska lying next to her, both of them doing a great job at appearing bored. Sena's eyes are lazily scanning the crowd, but they keep bouncing back to me. I know she's waiting for a decent cover before following us.

"Hurry up, Remy," Kiran's voice calls from a few yards ahead of me. He glances over his shoulder. "If I didn't know any better, I'd say you were stalling. Or maybe you're still too slow to keep up with me."

I glare at him, but I don't rush to catch up. Not yet. I need to give Sena an opening. Just ahead, a hawker cart sits on the sidewalk, perched on the edge of the curb. A few customers linger around, in line for some kind of skewered mushrooms. I wait until Kiran turns forward, and as I weave through the hawker's line, I pick an easy mark standing closest to the cart. With a quick sweep of the man's ankle and a shove to his shoulder, I send him toppling over, right into the cart. The cart's wheels get pushed off the edge of the sidewalk, and both it and the man go crashing into the street. In my periphery, Kiran looks back but I'm pretending to dodge the mess. I turn my attention to him and shrug. He rolls his eyes and continues his walk.

I glance back to Sena's spot, but she's already gone. I catch movement and a red blur as she and Iska cross the street behind us. Hopefully she stays far enough away to not be seen, though I don't let myself worry too much. She was a thief for years. She knows how to track a target unnoticed even though we're here and not in the familiar alleyways of the Ket.

"Having fun?" Kiran says as I finally catch up, falling in step beside him.

"I wouldn't call being back on this planet fun," I reply coldly. I don't want to engage him in a conversation, but I can't seem to help myself. Even though we haven't seen each other in two years, he's still the annoying partner who wouldn't miss a chance to get under my skin. And while I know I can't trust him and I should just keep my mouth shut, it doesn't stop me from clapping back at his digs.

"Oh, come on. Maraas is a great place," he drolls, pausing on a corner to let a few servo bikes pass. "We had some good times here."

"Good times?" I snap. "Being left in the jungle wasn't a good time for me."

He rolls his eyes. "You're like a broken record, Remy. Are you really going to keep holding that against me? It was for your own protection; I saved your life."

I try to hold in my exasperation. "I didn't need you to protect me."

Kiran laughs but there's no humor in it. "We both know you were going to try to stop the coup because you developed feelings for your mark. Which would've ended up with Nova sending you to reconditioning, or something worse. It's my job to look out for you, even if that means saving you from yourself."

I clench my jaw to stop from punching him again.

"Making decisions for me is not your job," I spit out, working to keep my pulse calm.

"It becomes my job when you go off-mission. Nova gives us orders and we execute. That's what we do. Just because you . . . became friends with the target didn't change our purpose."

I ignore his last comment and the way he hesitated on the word "friends," like he was going to say something else. Instead, I swallow the fire in my veins. He doesn't know anything about feelings or friends or what Alora means to me, so there's no point in arguing with him. He's not a person; he's a heartless genopath engineered to serve corporate greed. And since he has no intention of telling me where Alora is until we eat, I am simply not going to engage with him anymore. Thankfully, he falls into silence over the next few blocks, and I don't have to say a word.

As we head closer and closer to the cave entrance, I begin to suspect where Kiran is leading us. The suspicion quickly turns to a knot in my stomach when he stops a few streets later, right where

I expect him to. The cramped buildings open up to the restaurant we passed earlier. The same restaurant where I sat with Alora. The memory replay threatens to take over my present again, but I push it back.

Alora is not here.

Kiran leads me through the tables to a small one near the back. The same table Alora chose, perfectly picked because of the multiple escape routes readily available from this spot in case any of her father's friends spotted us. The fact that he knows where to sit tells me he was spying on me and Alora from the very beginning.

"Looks exactly the same, right?" Kiran plops down on a stool and promptly holds up two fingers. A server rushes off toward the stewpot. I glare at Kiran sitting so nonchalantly in Alora's chair.

Fine. He wants to play dirty. So will I.

I turn the glare into an eye roll, using the moment to scan the restaurant. There are a few patrons scattered about the tables. A familiar hat with choppy red hair underneath catches my eye not far from us; it's the syndicate girl from the elevator. She takes one look at me and Kiran, gets up, and moves to the far side of the restaurant. I don't blame her. I spot Sena in the opposite corner, sitting at a table half hidden by the chef's area. Smart. It will be hard for Kiran to see her from where he's sitting. I finally let myself sink down onto the stool opposite him.

Two steaming bowls of swamp meat stew are brought over by the server, and Kiran immediately starts digging into his.

He points to my bowl with his spoon. "If you're done surveilling, you should eat."

I hold back a sigh. Why is he always so frustrating? If I hadn't checked out the restaurant, he probably would've accused me of being too lax. I can never win with him.

His eyes study me as he shovels down spoonfuls of stew. His motion triggers another replay, not of Alora this time, but of us — Kiran and me — from before.

At Nova.

The memory takes over too fast for me to stop it, and then all at once, I'm no longer in the restaurant; I'm sitting in the canteen on one of Nova's training ships, trying to force down my dinner, when Kiran strides into the room. My breath catches at the sight of his disheveled hair and sallow skin. His cheekbones more prominent from weight loss.

He was held in reconditioning for five days after snapping at one of our trainers during a drill when they told me my response time was too slow. Five days hooked to tubes, chained to the bottom of a water tank, holding his breath until he passed out. Only then would the lab hacks revive him with a bit of air, and only enough for him to repeat the process all over again.

Nova uses reconditioning to keep us pliant but also to make sure we're always pushing the abilities of our genes. Everything is a training exercise in one way or another. Even punishments.

But in the replay, Kiran slides onto the bench across from me like he didn't just come from endless torture. Without a word, he grabs my bowl of protein mush and starts gulping down spoonfuls while I stare.

"What?" he says, not looking up from the bowl.

I hesitate. We don't really talk about anything except training. We're not allowed to discuss anything else. And especially not feelings. We're not supposed to have any of those either. But none of our squadmates would ever wish reconditioning on each other. And he went through it because of me. Even though in the end, his protest had been pointless; I was still forced to run the drill for another four hours until my response time was satisfactory.

But, looking at him now, I can't suppress the feelings, this need to ask him.

"Are you . . . okay?" My voice is barely above a whisper, loud enough for him to hear but not the ears listening through the walls and hidden mics around the tables.

He looks up from the tasteless food, his eyes fixing on mine. Something loosens in his shoulders as he looks at me, only me. As if just seeing me is enough for him to unwind the tension from the last five days.

"I'll always be okay," he says.

And then he goes right back to eating my food.

"You've been going nonstop since you landed, right?" the present Kiran suddenly says in between bites of stew, his voice jarring me out of the memory. I quickly blink the replay far away. I don't want to remember my time at Nova, not even through an echo. I don't want to remember him.

"I know you could probably use some protein," he continues.

"Don't act like you know me," I snap, mad at myself for letting the replay win and mad at him for triggering it in the first place.

"Know you like I know myself. It's how our genes work. Come on, we both know how hard it is for me to think straight on an empty stomach. You're exactly the same." His expression is hard but his eyes betray an undercurrent of worry. "Please eat."

I ignore his concern. He's clearly not going to listen to a damn word I say anyway. I pick up the spoon and scoop up a large chunk of meat. Could be anacroc or iguana. It tastes exactly like it did two years ago. Chewy and gamey. It was this spicy flavor that Alora snuck down here for. But the spice is more than just heat on my tongue. The familiarity of it helps push the echoes of the past away from my mind. Nothing tasted like this on any of Nova's ships. This spice was also one thing absent from all the food on Tundar. I didn't realize how much I missed it.

As if he can read my thoughts, Kiran glances up from his bowl and asks, "So, how was the sled race across the icy tundra? As dangerous as they say?"

"I'm not going to talk about the race with you."

He levels his gaze at me again, something now simmering there that I can't pinpoint. "I still can't believe you went out on the ice. You should've stayed in the Ket."

He's angry? Because I did the race? Then I realize he's just mad that I did something he didn't approve of. I roll my eyes yet again.

"You don't get to tell me what to do anymore. And you definitely don't get to make me feel bad for making decisions that had nothing to do with you."

"I thought you were on Tundar to track me down? Pretty sure your racing had something to do with that."

I make a face and try not to throw my bowl of soup at him. Yet again, he makes everything about himself. Even though I was on Tundar tracking him and I'd wanted to sabotage Boss Kalba and whatever deal they were making, I chose to race for one reason—so I could keep my promise to Alora to be better by helping Sena.

Kiran flags down the server and points across the restaurant. "Two bowls for the girl and the wolf, too." They nod and shuffle away.

Now he's just showing off. He already knew I came here with Sena. He probably knows everything that's happened from the moment we crashed. Another sign that he's scheming. Since he won't come out and tell me what I want to know, I'm going to have to fish for it. To try and trick him into admitting something useful. Play along with his mind games until I get what I want.

"What are you actually doing here, Kiran?" I ask instead of commenting on his noticing Sena. "Are you on a mission for Nova? The twins said you're helping Revas stage a revolution against Dekkard. Or are you actually working a job for Weiland?"

"The twins don't know everything."

"They knew that you were the one who told Nova I was dead."

Kiran shrugs, a smile playing on his lips. "So, what if I told them? I would think you'd be a little more grateful to me for help-ing you escape Nova's clutches. But, of course, you don't seem happy about that either. It's fine, I won't take it personally."

I want to strangle him, but he keeps talking. "Thankfully, I've made sure Nova's in the dark about your current location. They don't know my exact plans either. They think I'm here for Weiland, to help TerraCo, but I'm doing a gig for a much smaller outfit. Sim-pler job, easier outcomes." His eyes cut from his half-empty bowl to me. "I could use some backup."

This is what he wanted the whole time. My help. The sinking feeling in my stomach tells me that he won't reveal any informa-tion about Alora unless I agree to help him. He takes the phrase "nothing taken, nothing given" to extremes.

"What job?" I ask point-blank. Might as well get everything out in the open.

"Take back the planet from Weiland."

A laugh escapes my lips at that, the total opposite of a simple, easy job. The pieces fall into place in my head, but they're still not making much sense.

"So, you're working with Revas for the Vega syndicate? After we helped destroy their stronghold here two years ago?"

He smirks. "What can I say? I am a born opportunist after all. Just like you were born to gather intel."

I shake my head, ignoring his comment about my genetics. "I'm not here to get involved in any job of yours. You obviously know I'm here for one thing and that's Alora."

"All right." His near-onyx eyes lock on mine, a hint of excitement dancing in them. "Let's negotiate."

My anger sparks and I slam my fist on the table. "No negotiations. You tell me what the hell you did with my friend two years ago and where she is, and I'll leave you in one piece."

He leans back, crossing his arms behind his head, pretending to consider my words. He's not bothered by my threat. He knows I don't really want to fight him. But that doesn't mean I won't throw one of my flash bombs in his stew and run the other way.

"I'd like to tell you, Remy. Really. But you know I can't give you information for nothing in return. That's not how we're wired."

"Tell me where she is, Kiran, or I'll run to Weiland and tell her what you're up to. How's that for a negotiation?"

"Eh." He waves his hand like I'm offering him a bowl of cold soup. Then he leans forward across the table, right into my space. "Counteroffer. You help me with this job, and I'll take you straight to Alora when we finish."

My breath catches in my throat as I blink in surprise. But I hold back my hope. Kiran's not above stretching the truth in whatever way will get him what he wants.

"How do I know you're on the level?"

"You're not the only one who's changed over the last two years.

You used to trust me as your partner—trust me this time. So, you going to help or not?" His expression gives away nothing.

Trust him? After he ruined everything? I shouldn't be surprised he's acting like this. Lording Alora's life over me like it's nothing to him but a pawn on the playing board. He's always been this way, and he'll never change, no matter what he claims. He's too stubborn and too arrogant. The anger inside me ignites at what I can't control, and I make a decision right then. I won't use him to find Alora. I don't need him or his stupid games.

"Help you?" I finally say. "Never. I'll never help you or anyone from Nova ever again. I'll find Alora on my own."

Kiran sets his soup spoon down as his eyes drift away from mine. There's a quick flash of emotion on his face, I can't quite get a fix on it before it's gone, but it looks like disappointment.

"I'm sorry you feel that way. I really hoped that you could overlook our past."

"Why would I do that? Once a snake, always a snake."

Kiran wrinkles his nose. "For the record, I don't think I have any snake in my DNA. Though your comment makes me only about thirty percent sorry for what's about to happen."

Too late, I notice the movement of bodies on the outskirts of the restaurant.

"I swear to you it wasn't my original plan," he says with a dramatic sigh. "But you haven't exactly left me with many options."

Too late, I realize that Kiran is betraying me. Again. I was too caught up in my anger, and he goaded me into keeping my focus front and center. I fell right into the same patterns that Nova conditioned into us. As if, in the last two years on my own, I learned nothing.

Because, too late, I notice the commandos now surrounding the restaurant, cutting us off at every possible exit. Each of them armed to the teeth, weapons drawn. And there's nowhere for me to go.

Then, from behind the impenetrable line of commandos, out steps Weiland herself.

CHAPTER 10

The director stalks across the space toward our table. I was wondering when she was going to show up again. I'm not exactly in the most defendable position, but I've been in worse spots.

Out of the corner of my eye, I catch Sena ducking lower in her chair, her fingers knotted up in Iska's fur to keep her close. To keep her from rushing over to protect me from the threat. I glare at Kiran, who's still got his head practically in his bowl, slurping up the final dregs of stew.

"Unbelievable," I mutter.

"Told you you weren't going to like it," he mumbles between bites with his mouth full. "You should've just agreed to help me."

"I thought you wanted to overthrow the director," I say under my breath.

I get nothing from Kiran but a grin.

I grit my teeth. He's such a liar. Even if I had agreed, I know it wouldn't have stopped Weiland from showing up. I can tell by her posture that she thinks she's snagged a win. Taggert is close in her wake, his gun pointed at the floor as he trails behind the director like the loyal dog he is.

"There you are." Weiland stops in front of our table, her pale skin gleaming. "We've been looking for you. You know, I really hate it when people try to take advantage of me." She puts the hint of a pout on her lips, but it's almost laughable how fake the expression looks on her face.

I set my spoon down and put on my own mask, one of confusion and surprise. "I feel like that's directed at me, but I really don't know what you're talking about."

The director's fake pout fades, the lines of her face growing hard and unyielding.

"I'm going to let you in on a little insider information. Most people think I got to where I am because of connections or money, like so many undeserving fools sitting idly at the top of our system. But the truth is, I clawed my way here. You think you're smart. It's cute. I have years of experience dealing with little insolent peons like you."

I meet the ice in her stare with my own and say nothing. Syndicates or corpos, doesn't matter who—the ones at the top are all the same. Bullies and chumps. They love making dumb speeches about how incredible or how tough they are. I've heard it all before, and nothing incites them more than nonchalance. So, I yawn and rub my eyes like I'm bored and tired. Meanwhile, a plan is already taking shape in the back of my mind. It's going to be messy, but I know it'll work.

Weiland practically growls as I give her nothing. "So far since you've left my office, you've traipsed around my city and made no attempt at all to do the task I set for you, have you? Instead, you gave Taggert the slip and proceeded to mess with my citizens."

Is she talking about the commandos at the bar? This obsessive ownership of her employees is on another level.

"It's called recon." I wave a hand at the restaurant around us and use the moment to calculate angles and odds while my other hand slips unnoticed into my pocket. "I assume you've heard of it."

"Oh, I have," the director laughs. "And I've even done some of my own. You see, I pulled the latest Vega personnel records, but I couldn't find your name anywhere in them, Remy Castell."

I'm not surprised my name wasn't there. Nova might've purged it for any number of reasons. What bothers me is the way Weiland says my full name—like she knows every hidden part of me, like she owns me. But she knows absolutely nothing about what I'm capable of.

Time to give her a taste.

I still my body, as if her words have finally grabbed me. Ignoring Kiran's growing smirk, I let silence and discomfort build before I speak, making sure my voice carries across the open-air restaurant, making sure that the syndicates hear me loud and clear.

"And just how did you get access to those personnel files? That's a violation of the Corporate Assembly code. Personnel records belong to the Vega syndicate, not TerraCo. And even you can't go poking around in syndicate business without following the rules."

The corner of Weiland's lip lifts in obvious disgust as she speaks. "I make the rules on this planet, and you'll do well to remember that I hold the power here, not the Vega. And certainly not some distant Assembly code."

A man a few tables over sets his spoon down with enough force to shake the table. Taggert raises his gun slightly, jerking it at the man, the commando's threat clear. But the syndicate's fists are clenched, his jaw set. More people at the restaurant have turned in their seats, others who appear to be at their limit with TerraCo's blatant disregard for syndicate authority. Weiland ignores their stares and leans forward, placing a hand on the table in front of me. She can't even imagine a world where she's not in full control.

She's really not going to like where this ends.

"Now," she sneers. "You will tell me exactly what you're actually doing on my planet, and maybe I'll consider sending you somewhere bearable for the rest of your miserable life as an indent rather than killing you where you sit."

I slowly rise, bringing my nose within inches of Weiland's face.

"First you violate Vega protocols," I say, letting all my pent-up anger fill my voice. "And now you insult me and accuse me of not delivering on my promise. You know, it used to be that if you insulted one of the Vega, you insulted the entire syndicate. I may not be a boss, but I'm still a member in the Vega ranks. You don't respect me, you don't respect any of us. And I think you forgot what that means."

I pause and glance around the restaurant, where now the other patrons are reaching under tables as they glare at Weiland.

"In fact, I think you're trying to erase us from this world entirely. But the Vega isn't some small, useless organization for you to use and abuse. We are one of the largest syndicate groups in the charted systems and we won't stand for your corpo bullshit."

My enhanced ears pick up the quiet clicking of several guns across the restaurant as safeties are turned off and chambers are loaded. Right now, it doesn't even bother me that my speech is for show and I don't really belong to the syndicate. I'm just glad to have the backup. I smile at Weiland even as Kiran puts his stew down. I know he hears the movements, too, but he's probably waiting to see which side will come out on top before he makes his move, the predictable snake.

Weiland chuckles humorlessly. "Are you threatening me? On my own planet?"

I point my finger directly at her chest. "Maraas does not belong to you. And it's not a threat—it's the truth. Not one soul in this outpost is going to stand by and let you grind us down. Each one of us would fight to the death for our syndicate. Especially Revas. You want to know where she is?"

A heavy silence descends on the restaurant.

"Right in front of you. Here I am."

Weiland's eyes go wide in confusion, in surprise. I hear a strangled cough from Sena's direction and catch a laugh growing across Kiran's face.

I smile wide myself.

"You want me? Come and get me."

I yank the flash bomb out of my pocket, hurling it at the cave ceiling high above.

And then the top of the cave explodes into fire and rock.

Everything happens at once. I dive to the floor, away from the flames, just as people duck or are thrown behind tables from the force of the blast. Burning debris and thick flames rain down on us. The director stumbles back as a stalactite crashes to the floor next to her, spilling stew and rubble alike across her pristine white suit. Smoke clouds the space as more debris falls. With nothing but rock to burn, the flames dissipate, and there's a quiet moment where everyone is recovering from the blast.

Gunfire erupts across the restaurant, syndicates drawing on the commandos and vice versa. Iska flies out of nowhere and leaps at Taggert, knocking him to the ground and snapping at his face as he tries to get her off. More rocks plummet down from the ceiling, and I throw myself sideways as another giant stalactite crashes into the table where Kiran and I were eating.

What a glorious mess. I can't help but grin as I roll away from the destruction and keep low behind tables, making my way to Sena.

"This is your plan?!" she shouts when I crawl up next to her.

"Hey, it's working so far!"

She whistles for Iska, the sound sharp even over the cacophony of shouts and gunfire.

"We need to make for the sprawl," I shout. "They probably won't follow us there." I peek over the table and watch as commandos fall. But more troops seem to be rushing in from all sides. Kiran's nowhere to be seen, of course. Taggert's dragging a now-raging Weiland away from the firefight. The crazed director picks up a discarded gun and starts firing in my direction. I duck back down and push Sena toward the next table.

Iska bounds up to us as we crawl, then the wolf growls as her gaze locks onto someone behind us. I spin around, ready to fight, but it's the girl from the elevator. Her hat's covered in cave dust, and her face is a combination of pissed and impressed.

"You are truly unhinged! I warned you to stay away from Kiran!" She points to the chef's table, which is somehow still intact. "There's a trapdoor under Marty's stewpot and a tunnel below that leads to the sprawl. If you don't get shot, he's gonna kill you for blowing up his restaurant. So, you'd better hurry your ass up and get out of here."

"Why should we trust you?" I shout back.

"Do you have much of a choice?" she snaps, her hazel eyes flashing. "Besides, do I really look like I work for that corpo hack?"

The girl doesn't wait for an answer; she turns and army-crawls toward the stewpot. Sena and I exchange a look, but Iska has already made up her mind and is following the girl. Crazy wolf. I steal another glance over the tabletop.

The restaurant is in chaos. On one side, the syndicates have created a barricade out of fallen rocks and tables to use as cover as they shoot at the growing number of commandos. More troops are closing in; I spy a commando with his gun pointed our way. But then he gets jerked to the ground and disappears under a table. A few seconds later, another one goes flying, knocking over three other commandos. Guess Kiran finally picked a side. Though it doesn't seem like it's going to be the winning one for once.

"Come on!" Sena tugs on my shirt. "Let's get out of here before we get shot!"

I dive back down and follow her to the chef's table. The red-haired girl has pushed the giant pot of stew to the side, hot liquid oozing out from bullet holes and puddling on the floor. She kneels in the mess, uncaring, and jerks open a small door cut into the cave floor. She eyes the wolf.

"There's a ladder, but it's about a five-foot drop the rest of the way. I don't know if the wolf—"

"My wolf will be fine," Sena shouts, slipping into the opening and disappearing into the darkness. Iska paws the ground and then jumps into the hole after her. Even over the din, I can hear a thud followed by Sena grunting.

"After you." The girl motions to the door.

"No, you first." Just because I'm going along with her doesn't mean I trust her. The door could lead to a pit and we'd be trapped. The girl shakes her head, then folds her legs over the side and slips down the ladder. After she's gone, I steal one more glance over the stewpot.

The syndicates are pinned down, but I see no sign of Kiran. It hits me then that I've destroyed Alora's favorite restaurant. Now this place is nothing more than another memory haunting my head.

Shit.

Someone shouts, "Flash bomb!" and I don't have time to mourn another mistake.

I instantly drop through the trapdoor and yank it shut against the earth angrily exploding around us.

CHAPTER 11

The stench of the tunnel jams straight up my nose as I slide down the ladder and hit solid rock. My eyes adjust to the dim light almost immediately, making me wish my sense of smell was as adjustable. Sena's pinching her own nose as she gets to her feet. The syndicate girl is farther down, cracking open a chem-light so we can see. I sigh as I realize this isn't exactly a tunnel built for escape.

"Back in the sewers again," I mumble.

Sena makes a face, still holding her nose shut. "At least the ones in the Ket didn't reek this bad. Makes me almost miss the snow and ice."

Practically nothing could make me miss that hellhole of a planet, but the smell here is truly awful. Stagnant mud and sour excrement along with a handful of other scents I choose not to identify. The other girl holds the chem-light up higher, the eerie glow illuminating the dark walls around us.

"I told you not to bother with Kiran," she says, covering her own nose. "Now look at the mess you two made." She turns away from us.

Sena's eyes slide over to me with a similar look.

I shrug. "I've been in bigger messes."

"You told her you were Revas?!" Sena hisses in response.

"Hey, it worked, didn't it?"

She gives me a glare. "I don't know if I'd call this"—she gestures to the sticky sewer walls with her free hand—"working."

"You all coming or what?" the syndicate girl calls back to us from deeper in the tunnel before she disappears around a bend. With a huff, Sena follows, ducking her head low as the tunnel shrinks around us.

Iska prowls just behind her and I bring up the rear, keeping my focus on the sounds echoing through the stone corridor and not on Sena's frustration. The last thing we need is for some commandos to sneak up on us, but a part of me knows that Sena is right. That I've made a bigger mess by involving the rest of the Vega. I was acting on instinct and my training, playing the role of a dedicated syndicate; I didn't exactly intend to incite the entire outpost into a fight. With Weiland there, I just reacted.

My mind jumps to my flyer, held hostage up on the plateau. Hopefully, Weiland doesn't decide to turn it into scrap metal just to spite me. Probably she's forgotten that little detail, and I'll have time to find my way back to my ship and Sena's cloak so I don't ruin her life entirely.

I also try not to think of the destroyed restaurant in our wake. One of the problems with having razor-focus instincts and senses is that I tend to forget about collateral damage in the heat of things. I've barely been back on this planet for half a day, and I've already destroyed one of Alora's most cherished places.

The ground squelches around us, stone transforming into muddy earth, the scent a mix of rotten food and much, much worse. After nearly ten minutes of trudging around twists and turns and scraping my head across the stone ceiling, I find myself agreeing with Sena. The sewers in the Ket were freezing and full of buried bodies, but at least they didn't smell. Maybe this wasn't my best plan. Thick sewage and mud cake my boots, as moisture begins to climb up the bottom of my pants. Gross.

Thankfully, there's still no sign of pursuit. And finally, the syndicate girl slows down after one last turn. A hint of fresher, cooler air tickles my cheeks.

There's a large round opening that leads outside, covered by a grate. I see glimpses of jungle downhill and hear sounds of civilization not far off. I run through the distance in my head. Between the syndicate outpost and the sprawl is a small series of hills that gradually flatten out into the lowlands. No one builds anything on the hills because as soon as the storm hits, they become instant landslides of debris and mud. At the bottom of the final hill before the sprawl, there's a barricade made of tree limbs and trash and all sorts of junk. The sewer we're about to pop out of must deposit right above the barricade.

The girl sticks her cheek right up close to the grating, checking to make sure the coast is clear of commandos. It should be. They rarely venture down here. The sprawl residents don't have much and aren't worth the corpos' time. But not-so-distant shouts reach my enhanced hearing and I realize that, yet again, nothing is the same as it was two years ago.

The syndicate turns to us. "Sounds like they're farther uphill. If we stay low and hurry, they won't be able to find us once we get to the sprawl." She pulls a latch on the upper part of the grating, and it swings open. The air outside is cooler than the stale heat of the tunnels, but the smell lingers. Even with my engineered genes, I'm going to lose my stomach if we don't get out of this stench soon.

The red-haired girl cautiously steps out, surveying the area before waving us forward. She moves well for a low-level syndicate assigned to be a lift operator. Whatever her actual position is, she's had training. Sena, Iska, and I follow her, sliding and practically scooting down the hill, trying not to slip on the mud. Above our heads, the mag rail tracks cast a long shadow across the earth. Just beyond, the jungle presses in ever nearer, a cool breeze wafting away the stench of the sewers.

Sounds of frogs and insects buzz low in my ears along with the occasional call of a lone bird. The tundra was silent with snowfall and ice. But the wilds on Maraas teem with life and noise and movement. Here, the jungle is its own entity, alive and waiting for prey to get lost within its vines. But beginning at the bottom of the hill and sitting right under the long stretch of rail tracks, humanity ekes out an existence.

The sprawl.

A living, winding system of tree house–like structures, where every repair, every addition revolves around surviving the hellstorm. Constant replacements and rebuilding after each storm cycle, along with the ever-changing jungle floor, have made a stretch of city slums like no other. As I skid down the hill, I take in the long strip of multi-level makeshift buildings, some lifted on stilts, some hanging off the giant support beams, some even attached under the tracks themselves. Ladders and bridges of metal or rope crisscross every which way between the buildings with no logic or reason. It's like a construction site that exploded, but people still made houses and shops right in the broken rubble.

"This is disgusting," Sena says as we slide down a particularly muddy portion of the hill. Iska's body is so caked with mud her red fur has turned brown. The ground finally levels out as we hit the base of the barricade. Sena eyes the mountain of mud and debris as her nose wrinkles.

"Do we really need to crawl over that?"

"Not if you're me." The syndicate girl points to a large oval-shaped piece of metal. At first glance, it just looks like another bit of flotsam. But the girl clambers up to it and yanks on the side, revealing a small tunnel carved through the barricade. It's still muddy, but at least we won't have to crawl over the mess on our hands and knees. And it's not as bad as the sewers.

"Who are you?" I ask, more curious than ever about what her role is within the syndicate.

"I'm Lyria," she says with a shrug, as if her name is nothing important at all.

"What is it you do for the Vega, Lyria?" I press.

She cocks her head slightly as she studies me. Something about her gaze unnerves me. Alora used to look at me with a similar sort of sharpness whenever I avoided answering her constant barrage of questions. But this girl is nothing like Alora. She's too callous. Too much mistrust in her hazel eyes. This girl is a jaded syndicate through and through.

"I guess you're not really Revas, then, if you don't know what I do," Lyria says, shaking her head.

"Sorry to disappoint." I admit the lie because it was meant for Weiland, not for the syndicates. I was playing a part in the heat of the moment; I don't actually want to be confused with their leader.

Lyria shrugs. "I should've known you weren't her anyway. If you were Revas, you would've come with more reinforcements.

And you'd know that me and the others, we're all part of the Vega resistance."

"Resistance to what?" Sena asks.

Lyria laughs. "To Dekkard. Obviously. We're trying to overthrow him and TerraCo, the chumps trying to take over the entire planet. I'm sure you noticed them. What else would we be resisting?" With another laugh, she ducks into the tunnel. I make a face. It seems we're going to get drawn into this conflict whether I want us to or not.

Sena notices my expression. "When you invited me to come with you on Tundar, you said you wanted to fight against the corpos," she says with a raised eyebrow.

"This isn't exactly what I had in mind," I grumble as she disappears after Lyria. I steal a final glance over my shoulder. The glow from the lights of the outpost is just visible beyond the hills. The shouts of the commandos are moving closer. There's no sign of Kiran, nothing to indicate whether he's actually on Weiland's side or not. But he said he was trying to stop the director, and the twins told me he was working with Revas, who is apparently at the heart of all this. He'll probably pop back up sooner or later. We'll stick with Lyria for now; getting away from Weiland is as good a plan as any.

So, I follow Sena into the sprawl.

At least the other side of the barricade smells a whole lot better when I pop my head out of the far opening. Still not great; it is a muddy swamp after all. Just beyond the tunnel, the sprawl rises out of the muck, a maze of beams and bridges, rickety shacks and crumbling life pods stacked on top of each other, a mess of rope and neon and errant spider vines.

Part of me wants to go back to the outpost, where I'm more

familiar with the crowded streets. Here, nothing is familiar or recognizable. And the jungle presses in ever closer, vines and ferns growing amid pipes and wires. But I don't have a choice. So, I focus instead on the potential threats that might come from anywhere as I jump from the tunnel's ledge to the ground below. Sena is introducing herself to Lyria as I stand upright.

"I'm Sena. This is Iska."

Lyria tentatively stretches out a hand for Iska to sniff. The wolf takes a whiff but doesn't step any closer. Now that there aren't a ton of people shooting at us, the wolf is suspicious of our savior. *Me too, girl.*

"And that's Remy," Sena finishes.

"Remy." Lyria eyes me suspiciously. "Definitely not Revas. I heard she's tall and commanding. You're not exactly what I'd call tall." Lyria is taller than both me and Sena, so of course she wouldn't consider me tall. I wasn't engineered to be tall and conspicuous. Smaller is better for sneaking into and out of places without being noticed.

"No, I'm not really Revas," I repeat. "I just said that to get us out of the mess with Weiland."

"Your little speech was pretty good, though," Lyria says as she heads up one of the ramps leading from the mud to the first level of structures. "You got everyone in the restaurant riled up." She pauses on a platform and peers down at me, judgment clear in her eyes. "Are you really a Vega?"

I shrug, keeping my posture and face nonchalant as I construct my lies with half-truths. "I was once before. But I've been . . . away for a few years."

Lyria blinks at me, something flashing in her hazel eyes. "I get that. I had to lay low myself once." She turns and scrambles up a rope bridge, leading us to another ramp and across the porch of a building on stilts. Sena's eyeing the levels, a small crease in her brow. She's probably trying to discern how they all fit together or where one level ends and another begins, but it's impossible to tell.

On Tundar, the Ket was a hodgepodge of old life pods, falling-apart buildings, and abandoned ships. If the Ket was a maze, then the sprawl here is a labyrinth. Homes sit on top of shops. Hawker stands selling meat or grilled vegetables or some other bush food pop up wherever possible, on any platform that can hold them. Every deck or stoop is connected by ladders, bridges, ramps. Forgotten ropes hang down from above, connected to who knows what. Spider vines crawl over anything in their path, twisting around beams and bridges alike.

"Every time the storm rolls around, buildings and homes get destroyed or blown away or sunk into a new river that forms," I say to Sena, trying to explain the mess. "They just keep rebuilding things wherever they can with whatever they've got handy."

Sena hops down from the ramp to the porch stoop. Iska lands softly beside her and sniffs at a row of foxbats hanging upside down from a railing.

"How many days till the storm hits again?" Sena asks as she tugs Iska away from the creatures. Good thinking—their teeth are tiny but very, very sharp.

From up ahead, Lyria answers her. "Used to be nearly twelve days between storm cycles. But for whatever reason, in the last eight months, the storm cycle has sped up, slicing the time in half. We've got about five days from now before it comes back around. It's getting harder and harder to rebuild anything in such a short time."

The rest of what she's implying goes without saying. That in another eight months, the storm might be permanent, and then no one in the sprawl will have a chance to hack it out here. The people eke out a life by mining in the mountains or foraging from the jungle. All the businesses in the sprawl support those two ways of life as best they can. As we pass over the ramps and bridges, I can't help but notice the shabby condition of people's clothes and shoes. The missing windows in dilapidated life pods. Broken roofs and cracked walls on the bigger buildings, their stilts reinforced over and over again with whatever materials are handy.

As we head down another ramp, Lyria calls over her shoulder. "Almost there."

"Where are you taking us?" I ask, still looking for potential escape routes as we walk.

"A boardinghouse run by some Vega officers for syndicates in the resistance who need to lay low. It's one of the few places left on Maraas for us to recover since TerraCo generally won't send commandos into the sprawl."

She jumps down to a lower level and weaves around one of the giant support beams for the mag rail overhead. On the opposite side of the beam, a large building on metal pilings sits about five feet off the jungle floor. There's a wooden sign above the door with the Vega logo carved haphazardly into it.

And there, on one side of the doorframe, leans a familiar figure that makes my pulse jump and my rage return.

"Congratulations on a daring escape," Kiran's voice rumbles as we step onto the platform leading to the boardinghouse. He's grinning, his eyes watching me as we walk up the steps. "I especially liked the speech followed by the flash bomb. Very inspiring."

It takes a lot of my self-control not to punch the dumb smile off his face again. But I don't know how many allies he has out here, and the last thing I need to do is piss more people off.

So instead, I jab my finger in his chest. Hard. "No thanks to you. You snitched on us and were the whole reason Weiland showed up at all!"

Kiran raises his arms in mock defeat as he eyes my finger, still stabbing the soft spot right beneath his collarbone.

"My hands were tied. Weiland put an alert out on the feeds for you. If I hadn't turned you in, someone else would have. And they certainly wouldn't have led you to an easily escapable spot full of friendly syndicates, now, would they?"

Is he lying to get me on his side or telling the truth? I can feel Sena glaring behind me, so I know where she stands. Lyria is off to the side, watching both Kiran and me. Her pulse is slightly elevated. Is she in league with Kiran or is he using her, too? I'm more curious than ever how deep in this whole resistance thing they both are, but I keep my focus on Kiran. For now.

He's not wrong about the restaurant having multiple escape routes. Still, I can't trust him. He works for Nova. He left me in the jungle. He helped Dekkard murder Alora's father. So, I narrow my eyes and poke him again.

"You're probably lying."

He brushes my hand away. "Say what you want, Rem, but deep down, you know I did you a favor. And you'll be happy to know my offer still stands. Help us out with our little coup and I'll take you straight to your long-lost friend." His voice picks up a bite when he says "friend." He never did like my relationship with Alora. Nova didn't engineer us to have feelings, let alone friends. He always took that too seriously.

I glare at him. "Deep down we both know your offer isn't on the level," I say as Lyria slips behind him through the door. "You'll use me like you use everyone else. And it certainly won't end up as a favor to me."

I push past him and follow the syndicate into the main room of the boardinghouse. "I'll find my friend myself, thanks."

There's a small counter over to the left with a few sparse tables set up. Off to one side, stairs lead up to what must be bedrooms. Kiran easily catches up to me, invading my space by standing too close.

"Let me know when you change your mind." He steps in front of me and nods to Lyria. "Ready when you are." He slides his eyes back to me. "Now if you'll excuse us, we have a hostile takeover to plan that involves actual people with real problems and not just one girl hell-bent on misguided redemption."

His words are meant to cut, to piss me off, and they do. But I clench my fingers into fists and stare daggers at him while Lyria walks past us to the counter, keeping her eyes ahead and her hat covering most of her face.

I guess that answers my question. She's in the thick of it with him and has been the whole time. She probably knew what Kiran was planning as soon as we sat down at the restaurant. Or worse, she intentionally sent us right to him at Arun's after the elevator ride. No wonder she's hiding her gaze from me. I glare at her, too, but her back is turned as she speaks to the man behind the bar.

"Give these three a clean room on me."

Without another word, she follows my ex-partner toward the stairs. Kiran can't resist looking over his shoulder and taunting me further with a last smirk, leaving me with nothing but a wish that I'd punched him a second time.

CHAPTER 12

The shower water is nearly as hot as the temperature inside the stuffy boardinghouse. Makes me almost miss the cold chill of Tundar.

Almost.

I let the water wash off the dirt of the day, my mind running through the whirlwind of events that led us here. It's an old Nova habit. We were forced to constantly reevaluate our behaviors and missions, and even if we'd been successful, we'd still have to analyze and estimate a dozen other ways to improve. And though I've been free of Nova's claws for two years, my mind can't help but look for potential angles I might've missed. Did I read Weiland right? I make a mental note to keep an eye out for Taggert; his loyalty to Weiland runs deep, and he's quiet in a way that's dangerous.

Lyria seems to be a bit of a wild card. Her behavior feels familiar, a reminder of what my life was like living among the Vega.

Even though I spent most of my time with Alora, I fell in easily enough with the syndicates working for her father. Lyria moves like them, talks like them. I'm not sure if she's going to be someone helpful or another obstacle in my way.

Kiran pops into my head next, but I quickly push him out. I don't have the energy to get pissed at him all over again, and the heat makes me tired enough as it is.

Though the temperature drops at night in the jungle, the sticky warmth in the tightly packed buildings never seems to fully dissipate, even with multiple open-air windows. I rinse off some of my layers while I'm in the shower and hang them to dry on the windowsill, but they probably won't stay clean for long. Even as I turn off the shower, sweat starts trickling into every crevice again.

In just my under layers, I lie on the old mattress, still mulling over the day as I wait for Sena to finish getting cleaned up. She somehow managed to drag Iska into the bathroom with her, so I think she's attempting to clean the mud off the wolf. An impossible task. The mud here is thick and viscous. Once it dries, the cakey substance gets stuck under fingernails and sucked into skin like a virus. Even after the shower, I can feel it between my toes, under my nails, in my hair. It's worse than the ice on Tundar or the sand on Abydos.

Just like the mud sinking into my skin, the memories of this place are hard to shake. They're pressing at my edges, threatening me with perfect replays of my failures at every turn. The restaurant I destroyed a few hours ago. The Vega headquarters that's been empty for years. All reminders that even my genes weren't good enough to stop any of it from happening, not then or now. No matter how I try to be better, I fall into the same habits, the same choices. All dominated by my genetics and training and instincts, not really by me or by what I want.

Sena and Iska's return mercifully interrupts my thoughts. Sena has managed to get a good amount of Iska clean, though brown still cakes the wolf's underside and legs. Iska paces to the center of the small room and promptly shakes her fur, flinging water and mud in every direction. I cover my face with my arm but not fast enough to avoid the drops. So much for being clean. It's impossible in this place anyway.

"Sorry about that." Sena perches on the mattress across from me. Ambient light from the slums around us along with a small chem-lamp on the floor illuminate the room. Other than that, there's no additional furniture, nothing beyond the very basic requirements of a crappy room in a run-down boardinghouse.

I shrug the shoulder that I'm not lying on. "Doesn't matter how many showers we take; the mud will come right back."

She sinks farther down onto the bed and stares at the small open window. Soft green and blue light from the neon outside illuminates her skin. We're both silent for a minute, and the sounds of jungle frogs and muffled voices of sprawl residents fill the air in our stuffy room.

"How does anyone manage to sleep in this heat?" Sena asks, rolling onto her side. She's in only her under layers like me, but we could be naked and still feel suffocated in this heat. Iska's curled up on the floor beside the mattress, panting softly, and Sena lets her fingers drape over the side, lightly stroking the wolf's red fur.

"People just get used to it, I guess. Like the cold."

She hums a soft response. A breeze finally finds its way through the window, cooling the sweat on my face momentarily.

"What's the deal with Kiran?" she asks quietly, glancing at me. She must read something in my expression because she quickly adds, "You don't have to tell me."

"No, it's fine," I say, keeping my sigh to myself. "It's just complicated. Kiran and I grew up in the same squad along with Jens and Jori, your favorite twin bosses from Tundar. We all were engineered with human and nonhuman DNA to be Nova's little agent lapdogs." I glance at Iska. "No offense, girl." The wolf huffs.

"My specialty is infiltration," I continue. "I use my senses to read people's emotions and physical reactions and body language to better get in with them so I can send back intel from deep undercover. Kiran and I have similar abilities, but what he does with them is different. He manipulates more than just one or two people. He's the mastermind behind the missions. He can plan moves and traps far faster and further ahead than anyone else and always thinks he's in the right. It mostly just makes him a huge pain in my ass."

"I picked up on that," Sena says under her breath.

"Because our abilities were complementary, we were assigned to be partners on all our missions. But no matter what my role was, he always found little ways to screw with me. Either moving me away from the action or inserting himself where I could've easily handled things. He's a control freak, but Nova never really cared as long as we got the job done. Though a few times when he really overstepped, he got in trouble."

And got sent to reprogramming.

But I don't say that part out loud. I don't have the energy to talk about the physical and mental torture that the Nova hacks would put us through if they thought we were slipping in any way. A chill runs up my arms despite the heat and sweat. More replays of dark rooms, isolation tanks, and lab coats standing over me while I'm strapped to a table all flash through my mind. I don't let the triggers build, though; I swallow them down. They're the nightmares that haunt my memories, and I can't let those echoes come to life. The terror is so real and thick I might get stuck re-playing them over and over if I do.

I think about Sena's question instead. Think about Kiran and let my anger at him fill the space in my head. Let it push the fear back into the farthest corners of my mind. Kiran went through reconditioning more than any of us. And somehow, it didn't break him. Somehow, he remained the same. I never could understand why he didn't yield to Nova. Why he still would disobey orders if he felt like it. Why he kept pushing, despite the reconditioning and torture.

I find my voice and continue. "Getting in trouble never changed Kiran's actions or made him any different toward me. It doesn't matter that it's been two years—he's still exactly the same. Moving all the parts in ways he sees fit, using whoever it takes to get the job done. And pushing me around like I'm a useless pawn."

Sena laughs humorlessly. "He did turn you in to Weiland to-night and then saved you, all at the same time."

"Exactly. He's always playing every angle."

"What about two years ago, when you were both here before?"

I sigh, the familiar ache of my failure returning to the pit of my stomach.

"Two years ago, Nova sent Kiran and me here to engineer a coup so Dekkard Shaw could take over the Vega from Alora's father, Rixus. They planted me as a bodyguard for Alora so I could get close to her father and send back intel about his habits and move-ments. Which I did, at first. But then Alora and I . . . grew close.

She knew what I was and it didn't bother her. She had genetic modifications, too, though not as comprehensive as mine. She decided that made us kindred and eventually we became friends, real friends." I pause and sort through the mess of thoughts in my head, trying to untangle my emotions from facts so Sena can see the truth of what happened.

"After an incident where she almost died in the jungle, I wanted to stop the coup. Or help her escape it somehow. After seeing her hurt, I couldn't just watch her family be torn apart by Nova anymore. And Kiran knew that somehow. He was always good at reading me. So, he changed the game. Moved up his plans and jump-started the coup early. But before I could do anything to stop it, he tricked me. Then dumped me in the middle of the jungle with no way to make it back in time to stop anything."

The chirps and cries of the wildlife outside seep into the room as I fall silent for a moment.

"I utterly failed my friend, failed to keep the promise I made to her. To be better. By the time I clawed my way back to the plateau, her father was killed and she was gone. Taken somewhere by Kiran."

I chew on my lip as the familiar anger rises again under my skin.

"He kept me in the dark, like he always did, making decisions for me. I finally chose for myself, to help Alora, but he took even that away from me. No matter what, he's engineered to weigh his own interests, which are Nova's interests, above everything else. That's just the way he's made. It may seem like he's offering us a deal now, but it's going to work out in his favor and no one else's."

Sena's quiet for a minute. "How does that work, being engineered? Most people instinctively look out only for themselves, and no one else. I watched Nok choose his own interests over

Kalba's back on Tundar. How can you be sure that Kiran's interests are the same as Nova's and not his own?"

I shift on the mattress. "We're conditioned through training and other psychological methods to see Nova's orders as our own needs. They start when we're kids. If someone slips up, they're basically punished over and over again until the conditioning sticks." I keep my gaze on the ceiling, forcing myself to see only the cracked concrete and not the stark shadows pressing against my mind again. I will them far away and switch topics.

"Kiran hasn't turned me in to Nova, which means he's got a specific reason to keep me around. Probably for whatever his mission is with Revas. He'll use whoever and whatever it takes to get the job done. After it's finished, he'll toss me aside like before. That's why I can't take his deal. He can't be trusted."

Sena watches me silently, her arm draped over the side of the bed, playing absentmindedly with Iska's fur. I let my eyes drift closed. Sharing this much about my past is exhausting. I need to be sleeping, need to be prepping for whatever tomorrow brings.

"Look, I know I don't know him, Remy," Sena says, her voice soft. "But I do know that hard experiences usually make people more understanding of each other. Look at me and Iska. We hated each other in the beginning, but I know now why she lashed out at me then. Because now I understand her. I'm not saying Kiran's going to suddenly become your friend or anything. But maybe there was a reason he left you in the jungle, a reason why he did what he did. Something you don't fully understand yet."

It's the most I've heard her say since we landed. I consider her words, but in the end, Kiran and I aren't like other people or like Iska.

"I wish it were that simple," I reply softly. "But it's nearly impossible to break patterns and behaviors that are set in our genes and conditioned through years of training. The only reason I got out of that pattern was because I learned how from someone else."

"From Alora," she finishes my thought.

"Yes." I nod, my voice a little fiercer. I owe her everything.

"What was she to you, your Alora?" Sena asks, her eyes now scanning my face.

I hesitate for a moment, then say, "She's my friend. My first friend." I take a breath, whispering more to myself than to Sena. "Doesn't that make her everything?"

Sena chews on the side of her lip, looking like she wants to say something more, but with a glance at Iska, she finally nods.

"That's why I'll do anything to get her back," I continue. "Kiran has no idea what that's like. He may act like he's got feelings, but he's not capable of anything beyond his conditioning. Beyond what Nova made him to be. Whatever reason he had for taking Alora, it serves only his own interests."

Again, silence spreads across the room, this time a little heavier. After a few minutes, Sena sits up and turns off the chem-lamp. A darkness edged with a soft glow from the lights outside blankets the room. I shut my eyes against it and all the painful memories.

It's impossible for Kiran to change. Sena may have grown to understand Iska, but she was raised with her mothers' love before they died. Kiran and I were raised in a lab by doctors and psychologists and soldiers. We were tested and sent on missions and trained to feel only what would help us succeed. And it wasn't love. Nothing even close. I was lucky that someone showed me a different path.

But some people never get that chance. And even if they do, that doesn't mean they'll change for the better. Especially someone like Kiran.

※

The next morning, I wake up sweaty but somewhat rested. Usually after a few short hours of sleep, my body recharges no matter how exhausted I might've felt. On Tundar, the cold and my injuries kept me from ever fully reenergizing. Here, the ghosts in my dreams make it hard for me to rest. Nothing like being haunted by the friend you failed and the boy who helped.

Sena's nowhere to be seen, but she won't have gone too far. As I head out of the room, my senses stretch, searching for my friend and her wolf while sifting through the world around the boarding-house. The smells of burning meat and morning dew penetrate the thin metal walls; the damp air presses against my skin. It's barely after sunup and already the heat has teeth. Ramps creak and echo as people move across them, calling out to each other. Softer voices filter through the boardinghouse, a few hushed conversations here and there. I pick up a half dozen heartbeats but nothing out of place or urgent. No threats anywhere to be heard.

Until a familiar scent hits my nose, followed immediately by my annoyance rising up to meet it. I round the small twisted stair-case and unsurprisingly find Kiran on the bottom step.

"You're awake early. Is it wise to destroy lives before the sun's fully up?" I say, unable to stop myself from baiting him. I wasn't exaggerating when I told Sena how he always had to control my actions in every mission, but I might've failed to mention that I goaded him every chance I got as a way to push back against the power imbalance he liked to lord over me.

Kiran raises an eyebrow. "You look like you didn't sleep much. Like always when you have too much on your mind."

"Ignoring my questions as usual. Good to know you haven't changed at all over the last two years or even over the last twelve hours."

He puts on a fake wounded face. "I don't know what you mean. I always take your questions into great consideration."

"Okay, then what did you do with Alora?"

"How exactly do you know I did anything at all?"

I roll my eyes. Verbal sparring with him is impossible and not advisable this early. "I know because I know you. You and Alora were gone by the time I made it back to Verem. It doesn't take my engineered genes to put two and two together. That you had something to do with it. But maybe it wasn't you after all. Maybe Nova sent her somewhere. If that's the case, I'll just have to ask the execs at Nova myself."

His eyes jerk to mine, a hint of fear in them. "You wouldn't dare."

I smile, having finally gotten a reaction out of him. "Extreme situations call for extreme measures. I think you said that to me once or twice before."

"Remy, you know how stupid that would be. Whatever you're planning, they'll catch you and send you straight to reconditioning." Something beyond his expression catches my attention. His pulse is slightly elevated. His fists are clenched. I stare at him, surprised I've suddenly gotten this deep under his skin. I've struck a nerve somewhere, so I press harder.

"And why do you care so much about what happens to me? You left me to die in the jungle, remember?"

"No, I removed you from the equation. The jungle didn't pose as much of a threat to you as everywhere else. It was the only place where you would be safe. I also left you there with weapons, so I don't know why you're complaining. But if you think you're going to go toe-to-toe with Nova, I'll put you right back out there in the wilds again."

Before I can goad him further, a throat clears behind me.

"I hope I'm not interrupting but . . . clearly, I am." Lyria stands at the top of the stairs, her gaze jumping from me to Kiran, then finally narrowing in on him. Her pulse is slightly elevated; her red hair's damp from recently showering, and I can smell the remains of soap still on her freckled skin.

"We need to get going, Kiran." Her voice is harder than I expect, her words sounding more like an order than a request. It makes me reevaluate Lyria's role in all this if she's the one bossing Kiran around.

With a huff, my ex-partner steps away from me but his smirk returns.

"Don't get in too much trouble today, Rem," he says lightly. "You know you hate it when I have to rush in and save you."

I hiss, ready to smack him again, but he's already striding toward a room behind the bar. Lyria hovers for a beat, though, watching me.

"I know you two have a history," she says quietly. "But I need him. We need him to take this planet back for Revas and for the Vega. So, maybe stay away from him if you're not going to help. Though I know he'd appreciate it if you did decide to join our cause, even if he'd never say it out loud."

"I'm not getting involved with him again. I'm not here for your cause either." I realize belatedly how rude that sounds. "Sorry," I add, though I'm not sure why I want to soften my words for this syndicate girl. Better she knows who I am up front.

Something flashes across her expression as her gaze wanders away. But then she nods, her voice going hard again. "I understand. I know you're looking for someone and Kiran is your lead." She shrugs. "But maybe we could help. The Vega has a long reach across lots of worlds. And Revas, I've heard she's quite good at finding what wants to stay hidden." She fixes her stare on me again. "Something to consider."

Then she's gone, through the door after Kiran, and I'm left standing on the stairs stewing. Kiran must've told her something about me, which just adds to my annoyance. Of course, he wouldn't bother keeping my business to himself. And what game is Lyria playing, trying to bait me with an offer like that? It may sound like a perfect solution, but she'll want my help with their coup before they'll help me find Alora, just like Kiran. Nothing taken, nothing given.

How would Lyria feel knowing that I'm looking for the daughter of their former boss? Would Alora even want me to involve the Vega? All she ever wanted was to live her own life rather than be forced to follow in her father's shadow.

Ugh, there are too many variables and not enough data for me to plot a way forward. No clear path and no easy answers. The frustration mounts, so I head out and trek aimlessly through the sprawl for a solid ten minutes, giving myself space to let my emotions sink back down, far under my skin where they won't get in the way. I need to keep my head clear and sort through all this.

My stomach growls, reminding me that I can't hyperfocus

for much longer without repercussions. Food will also help my decision making, so I point myself in the direction of wet fur and the hint of snow. Somehow, I can still sniff out the touch of Tundar on Sena and Iska.

I find Sena perched on a lower ramp not far from the boardinghouse. Iska's below her on the jungle floor, her paws freshly muddy. They must've been romping around in the swamp this morning. I climb down to them, pushing all thoughts of Kiran and Lyria and the rest of it away as I watch the wolf chase a frog.

"She won't try to eat the thing, will she?" I say in lieu of a greeting. "I'm pretty sure most of the frogs on this planet are poisonous if consumed."

Sena tilts her head, watching her wolf. "She hasn't bit at it yet. Just chased it around like she's a puppy instead of a veteran fighter. Ridiculous wolf." We both watch as Iska pokes her nose into a large puddle, mud and dirty water coating her snout. Sena wrinkles her own nose.

"The dirt and muck is going to take some getting used to."

I smile and point to a small deck one level up where a vendor is barbecuing some skewers. "How about some breakfast to take your mind off the sludge?"

A few minutes later, we're seated on cheap plastic stools at a table made from an old flyer door panel. There's a steaming stack of grilled bush food in front of us, and despite its charred appearance, it's much tastier than protein bars.

"So," Sena says between giant bites, "what's the plan? Are we going to help Kiran or not?"

I break off a chunk of meat and toss it to Iska. I don't have a knee-jerk reaction to punch something when I hear Kiran's name, so I'd say my emotions are back where they belong.

"We're not helping him," I say, plain and simple.

She raises her eyebrows at the venom that snuck into my voice. Rather than tell her about this morning's encounter, I explain in a different way.

"Remember the promise I told you about before, the one I made to Alora? I promised her that I would stop working for Nova and be better than what they made me to be. So, I'm not going to be a pawn in their schemes, which is exactly what Kiran wants."

Sena swallows some meat and reaches for a skewer of vegetables. "So, then what's our next step?" She looks at me, waiting. I sigh internally. I hadn't gotten that far when I stormed out of the boardinghouse earlier. Now that I'm not seeing red or being annoyed, I realize there aren't that many other options.

Only one actually.

"Lyria told me that Revas is good at finding people. Maybe if we find Revas first, we can ask her for help."

"In exchange for what, though? Because the only thing we could offer would be to help with their resistance against Weiland." Sena shakes her head as she echoes my exact thoughts from earlier. "Which puts us right back where we started, helping Kiran."

I frown at her and bite off some more meat. I know she's being logical. I just don't like it.

"A few months ago, you gave me some advice when I didn't know what to do," she says, picking a giant mushroom off the skewer. "Now it's my turn. You told me we would probably be fighting against corpos when you offered me a place on your ship. And this whole resistance thing is for the Vegas to get their power back from those very corpos. Wouldn't your Alora want you to help? From what you told me, I think she would."

She scarfs down most of the mushroom before pointing the

skewer at me. "If Alora chose you the way Iska chose me, she would understand. She wouldn't think you're breaking your promise."

"You're not wrong," I mumble.

Sena takes the last skewer, peels off the meat, and tosses it to Iska.

"And if we're going to chase after a syndicate ghost," she continues, "then we should probably just follow Lyria. She's a Vega member who's tied up pretty tight in the resistance. Stands to reason Revas will probably cross paths with Lyria at some point if she hasn't already."

Sena's quiet for a beat, watching me. She's a lot more observant than I give her credit for. Others might mistake her silence for ignorance, her prickliness for disinterest, but toughing it out alone in the Ket gave her more than just physical survival skills. She's as shrewd as me, and maybe I should start considering her opinions instead of barreling headfirst into what are now our problems. Maybe I could use her help on this world as much as she needed mine on Tundar. She hasn't led me astray yet.

"What do you think we should do?" I ask her.

"Why don't we split up?" she suggests. "You follow Lyria. I'll tail Kiran."

It's a solid plan. Two of us and two leads to follow. I eye her for a heartbeat. Her pulse is slightly elevated, she's tapping a single finger on her thigh, and I can tell by her posture she's ready to spring into action. She wants to do this instead of just following me around. I can't blame her. I took her away from her planet, where she knew every nook and cranny, every threat and foe. And then I dragged her here. She hasn't really had a chance to stretch her legs or to be alone. Both of which she's probably craving.

So, I nod, even though I don't want anything to happen to her.

I trust her. I know she won't get tricked by Kiran like I might. She's got no emotional baggage clouding her judgment with him. And she's got Iska. Who definitely won't let anyone hurt her.

Movement from the boardinghouse catches my eye.

"Well, now's our chance to do that," I say with an incline of my head. This is why I chose this table on this level. We have a perfect view of the boardinghouse entrance. And stepping out of the main door are Kiran and Lyria. They're still in conversation, still leaning close to each other.

My mind whirs at the sight of them together. Just how close are they? Are they just comrades-in-arms or something . . . more? My nose wrinkles at the thought of Kiran romantically involved with someone. Nova didn't allow entanglements of any kind and cut us off from any sort of deep emotion, so it's not like he has any idea what love is. Probably they're both just using each other.

They stand together on the platform for another minute, speaking too softly for me to hear even though I strain my ears trying to catch their conversation. Then with a wave, Lyria heads farther into the sprawl while Kiran ambles off in the opposite direction, toward the outpost. Next to me, Sena stands.

"Meet back here afterward," I say.

With a smile and the wolf by her side, she slips down the ramp back toward the boardinghouse. I turn toward the far mountains, the direction Lyria went, and head deeper into the sprawl.

CHAPTER 13

After a few minutes, I pick up Lyria's trail. I can still detect the soft scent of the soap from the boardinghouse. How, I don't know. The sweat from the jungle sun and heat has long since washed any traces of soap from my own skin.

Luckily, it takes me no time at all to catch up as she makes her way through the lower levels. I keep to the high ground, staying just above and behind her, giving me an easy view to spy from.

She's got her black cap on backward now, her short red hair peeking out underneath. She walks unhurriedly, casually but still with purpose. Here and there she waves at some people and greets others. Lyria seems to know a great number of people in the sprawl for a syndicate who works in the city. I guess she's off duty today or avoiding the outpost since she helped Sena and me escape. Or maybe . . . she wasn't the lift operator at all but just using the job as a cover. The blanks in her story certainly raise suspicion. Just what was she doing up on the plateau?

Lyria pauses at a hawker stall two levels down, and I slow to a stop before a rope bridge, letting others pass as I watch her out of the corner of my eye. She laughs, chatting with the stall keeper, listening intently to him and his patrons. Something in her relaxed posture and easy smile has me recalling Alora and her father.

Before he was killed, Alora's father wanted the Vegas to be seen as more than just syndicate bullies. He encouraged them to establish relationships across Maraas, whether it was with people in Verem or here in the slums, or even with the scavvers out in the jungle. Alora took that charge to heart even as she questioned her role and her future. Where I was engineered not to forget a face or a threat, to blend in with those around me, Alora remembered people; she knew them. Their names, details of their lives, stories about their troubles. Where I was a phony, faking my way to belong, she was the real deal. It was the one part of her future role that she didn't mind.

Something about the way Lyria charms those around her reminds me of that. And makes me question her true purpose. Is she charming these people to get them to aid her in the revolution against Weiland? Is she high enough in the syndicate hierarchy to promise them changes should the Vega come back into power? If so, Lyria is probably important enough that she's in contact with Revas. She could be doing all this directly under Revas's orders. All the more reason for me to get closer to her.

With a wave and a piece of flatbread to go, Lyria continues on her path. I stay a safe distance behind her, still sticking to the upper levels even when I lose my line of sight. There's so much clutter with ladders and ramps and ropes that even if Lyria thought she was being followed, she'd never notice me up here. As we move, I calculate the distance between us and the boardinghouse. Two miles so far.

And though the sprawl is completely different than anything I remember, there's a familiarity in the chaotic levels and hodge-podge of buildings. But even this far out of the city, signs of TerraCo's influence still appear unexpectedly. I spot the corpo's logo plastered across the side of a building with makeshift repairs underway, on an updated bridge above a large river, even on a few hawker carts, the owners wearing matching green aprons. Like TerraCo is trying to get its claws in everything.

Lyria pauses again at a small outfitter shop, disappearing inside, and I scout the area while I wait.

Despite the occasional logo, I don't see any sign of TerraCo's commandos. They never came to the sprawl before because the Vega provided security and policing. Now I see neither commandos nor Vegas positioned on any of the pathways above the swamp or down below. No Vega guards milling around looking bored. No one stopping the few fights or thieves I spot on the trek. No security anywhere.

Though, even two years ago, the security didn't do much either.

Alora once convinced me to accompany her into the sprawl. She wanted to get out of Verem, and the outpost wasn't enough for her that day. She'd been at some meeting with her father, and though I don't know what he said to her, she returned quiet and melancholy. But after brooding for a half hour, she grabbed an arken blade and proclaimed she was going to the sprawl, with or without me.

I tried to keep us in the Vega-controlled areas once we got here. But she wasn't content with sticking a toe in. She wanted to dive into deep water and left me no choice but to stick close to her as she led us deeper and deeper into the sprawl.

I fight against the memory, trying to stop the replay, but my gaze lands on a ramp half buried in the mud and the familiarity triggers the echo fully. I'm not standing on this level alone tailing Lyria anymore. I'm down on the ground, trailing behind Alora.

As the two of us cross a rope bridge, a man steps onto a partially buried ramp, blocking our path. The me from before knows immediately what's happening; I'd already caught a whiff of his two accomplices tailing us on the levels above. The man doesn't say anything, just pulls out his blade and points it right at her.

For a moment, we all stand there, waiting. I remember running through scenarios, picturing what would happen if I let him kill Alora. Her father would be distraught, distracted. He'd make rash decisions in his grief, and the coup would be so much easier to pull off. My mission would be over, and I could leave this stupid, humid jungle.

But when the man lunges at Alora with the knife, I move, too fast to think. My foot finds his chest and he goes flying off the ramp. The other two goons flank us and send a call for more, too many for me to fight and keep Alora safe at the same time.

So, I grab her hand and we run. We sprint across the levels, Alora grinning the entire way. Even as hot rain begins to fall, drenching us, she tilts her head back and laughs. At some point, I find myself smiling, too. The rush of the threat in our wake, the rain splashing across my skin, the total freedom of not caring about missions or orders. Who we are doesn't matter. In this moment, none of it matters.

We make it back to the Vega-controlled areas, and luckily the chumps don't follow us. I lead Alora to one of the mag rail stations and onto the train heading for the plateau.

We sit in silence, dripping wet in the train car, a smile still beaming on Alora's pale face.

"Thank you, Remy," she says, her voice breathless.

"It's my job to protect you." I shake my head. "Even when you make it so much harder." Now that the elation and adrenaline are gone, I'm pissed that she'd even put us in that position in the first place.

She laughs again, a spark in her clear blue eyes. "I'm not thanking you because you saved me. I'm thanking you for being there with me. For not letting me be alone. I know it was reckless. But . . . I feel more alive now than before. Don't you?"

I blink. She's not wrong. Racing with her through the sprawl made me feel different than any mission I've done before. In the heat of the moment, I ignored my protocol, my training. Kiran will be pissed when he finds out I let an opportunity go to waste. But I chose my own path. It's terrifying and exhilarating all at once.

"You're going to be the death of me," I say to her. But slowly, I match her smile with my own.

Low vibrations pull my focus out of the memory. I was hoping that with the sprawl ever changing, my genetic echoes wouldn't get triggered by the place. But I guess my drive to find Alora is stronger than the mess of the sprawl around me. I shake myself loose from the grip of her smile and the pull of her energy. Now is really not the time to get lost in the replays.

Up above, the mag tracks begin to vibrate, announcing the train rumbling through. Coming out of the shop, Lyria pauses. I step to the side of a ramp, the sun biting through my layers as the humidity rests heavily on my skin. Other movement stills, as if everyone in the sprawl is waiting for the train.

The tracks rumble, and the buildings hanging from the rail or the support beams begin to shake and shudder. Finally, the train car rushes into view. I glance around for the lifts that go to the top of the tracks, but I don't spot any nearby. I'm still looking for some sign of a station or landing when the mag train thunders by. It doesn't slow one bit, careening down the tracks and continuing its path toward the mountains.

The mag train used to stop at multiple points along the sprawl. But now that I'm thinking about it, I haven't noticed any active stations since we left the outpost. If the train is no longer picking up workers and taking them to the mountains, then who exactly is it transporting?

Or what?

But before I can steal time to speculate, motion below recaptures my full attention. Lyria's on the move and then so am I.

We're nearing a less populated area of the sprawl. Years ago, when they first built the mag rail, the only settlements were right where the stops were. Over time, the sprawl grew beyond the stations into the snaking line of continuous buildings and life pods and modified container shells it is now. But in between the more densely populated areas, there are still deserted pockets with not much beyond abandoned structures, marshy swamplands, and errant spider vines. One of these spots is where Lyria finally pauses on a makeshift dock perched on a large swath of swampy mud.

There are only a few other people passing by, not enough for me to blend in, so I duck behind an empty life pod that's half sunk in the mud. The other buildings are mostly empty; hawkers and food stalls, the lifeblood of the sprawl, are nowhere to be seen. The jungle presses in around the dock where Lyria stands, ferns and grass poking up through the cracks in the old wood.

And then, out of the shadows of the impossibly tall trees, a figure emerges from the jungle. She's muscular and tall, though not as tall as Lyria. Her dark brown skin is smooth; I'd guess she's probably a few years older than me. Her layers are thin but sturdy and made from a mix of materials. She could almost be just another denizen of the sprawl, but her expression holds something more than those of the downtrodden sprawl inhabitants. Life lights up her honey-brown eyes. And I realize what she is.

A scavver.

Lyria nods at the scavver and they begin to talk softly. I study the newcomer. The scavvers on Maraas are different from the ones on Tundar, who keep to themselves under their frozen lake away from the rest of the planet. The Scavver War that was fought between the corpos and those who wanted to live outside their influence all those years ago had different repercussions on each Edge World. Here, the scavvers live deep in the jungle, but they still trade with sprawl residents. They've even been known to raid the mag rail in the past, stopping the train and jacking corpo resources. The scavvers on Maraas have no problem making their presence known and felt.

This girl is definitely a scavver, from the mashup of her clothes to the arken blade machete strapped to her thigh. Interesting that she came to meet Lyria without any others. Lyria must be encouraging the scavvers to join in the Vega revolution then. The thought makes my stomach sink. If the scavvers are getting involved, then it's a lot more organized than I thought. Which could mean more complications for me and potentially more bloodshed for everyone else. I need to get closer, need to hear what they're saying.

I scoot around the life pod and silently drop down to a lower ramp, catching what appears to be the tail end of their conversation as I crouch behind a railing.

"Everyone's rounded up," Lyria's saying. "They're eager to hear this intel you've promised. And what your side has to offer."

"Oh, don't worry your little syndicate head about what we can offer. It's more than good enough for your mangy lot," the scavver replies. I'm close enough that I can catch the faint scent of tahuayo flowers on the scavver girl. She must've come far to still carry the fragrance with her. Only in the deepest parts of the jungle does the glowing fire-colored tahuayo blossom bloom from the spider vines once night falls. Here in the sprawl, the fragile flowers are too easily destroyed by human activity or blown away when the storm hits. Even faintly from this distance, their scent tastes like fruity, floral honey on the tip of my tongue. The scavver points a decisive finger at Lyria.

"We want your assurances that Revas is on the level." My heart races at Revas's name on the scavver's lips. "She better make it worth our while, or we'll start dumping Vegas right on top of the burning pile of TerraCo corpses in our wake. We're not here to be your cannon fodder."

If the threat unnerves Lyria, she makes no sign of it as she nods once.

"Don't worry. I can guarantee you'll get what you want from Revas. Now, what about the intel you promised me?"

The scavver cocks her head to the side and grins. "I'll do ya one better, new friend. I'll show you that and more." The scavver motions over her shoulder, then turns away. I'm about to move to a better position, but then she jumps off the dock, followed by Lyria.

Without another word, the two slip into the jungle, disappearing into the shadows between the trees.

CHAPTER 14

I wait exactly thirty seconds, and then I snake down the ramps after them. My mud-caked boots hit soft earth as I step off the platform into the jungle.

The air is still among the trees and leaves, the sun less oppressive in the shade of the canopy. I easily pick up the girls' trail by the singed leaves and spider vines from the scavver's arken blade. They've cut a small path through the brush, heading deeper into the jungle.

I steal a glance back at the sprawl peeking through the leaves. The mag rail is still visible just above the tree line. As long as I stay within the mag zone, I should be fine without any serious weapons. The more dangerous jungle preds generally keep away from the train rail, as the magnetic force messes with their senses. I trust that my own senses will keep me well away from any paka tigers or anacrocs that might be wandering nearby.

While my instincts are generally designed to deal with people, they're not totally useless in the Maraas jungle. The tundra on Tundar was a different beast. I could barely sense anything in the snow and ice.

Pushing away thoughts of predators, I follow the trail deeper into the jungle, brushing aside long hanging spider vines and stepping around mud puddles. The smells and familiar feel of leaves and tree bark threaten to trigger more memory replays, but I keep my senses fully grounded in the moment. The two are moving fast, so I pick up my pace. I can feel in my gut that I'm getting closer to Revas. All of them must be planning something together, something big if the scavvers and syndicates are cooperating with each other. And that has to lead me to Revas. I haven't decided what I'll say to the syndicate leader to get her to help me find Alora, but I'm not worried. When I find Revas, I'll read her just like I read Weiland.

As I trail through the jungle after them, movement everywhere catches my eye. A small iguana, an army of marching ants, rustling palm fronds. My senses are pushed to the max with the sounds of birdcalls and the trickle of small streams, with the scents of ferns and flowers, with the heat that presses down on my skin.

After ten minutes of hiking, I can no longer make out the low-frequency buzz of the mag tracks in the distance behind. We've crossed out of the mag zone, into the true, wild bush. My whole body is on high alert, scanning for danger, for escape routes, for anything. We're almost a mile out from the sprawl now; I can't afford any mistakes.

Then whispers and rustling up ahead have me slowing, ducking behind a tree made entirely of roots. I peek through the limbs and see a flash of color on the ground behind a bush. Lyria's discarded jacket, the blue material a dead giveaway among the greens and browns of the foliage. I press forward, darting from tree to tree, peering carefully around each one as I follow the two girls.

The sounds of movement grow louder. Shouts and whistles, machinery in motion, plus the sharp smell of burning fuel with hints of exocarbon. Commandos, most likely. Their armor is made of an exocarbon and plastic composite. But TerraCo commandos this deep in the jungle is not a good sign.

Finally, I catch up to my marks.

Ahead, Lyria and the scavver have gotten low to the soft ground, hidden behind a giant tree root. The syndicate has tucked all her hair under the black cap to stay camouflaged. Beyond them, there's a clearing past the trees, but I can't make out anything more from this position.

I circle carefully, staying downwind and working to find a better spot so I can see what they're looking at while still keeping an eye on them. I pause at the base of a tree growing out of the ground at a sloping angle and glance back in their direction, my mind calculating distances and angle measurements. Satisfied this will do, I scramble up the tree trunk and hoist myself to higher branches without disturbing the leaves or making a sound. Pushing a large orange fruit out of my line of sight, I perch on a thick tree branch.

From this vantage point, I can finally see what's captured their attention. A few commandos stand in a clearing beside an ATV with a trailer and four tall crates on the back. But finding commandos this far from the city isn't why my mouth opens in surprise.

Behind them, deeper in the clearing, appears to be a small corpo substation. Way out here in the jungle wilds. What the actual hell?

While there are no TerraCo markings, a perimeter fence surrounds a few military-standard life pods and a bunch of machinery, including four tall pipes funneling something into the air over the trees. The wind is blowing away from my position, so I can't get a beat on what the pipes could be generating. What the hell is a whole corpo substation doing in the middle of the jungle? I can sense more heartbeats actively moving around inside the fence, but a shout brings my attention back to the small group in front.

A pale, bearded commando has been stripped of his armor and is being pushed toward the edge of the clearing by none other than Taggert. He must've been standing behind the ATV's metal crates for me to have missed him. Sadly, I don't see any sign of injuries from Iska jumping on him at the outpost restaurant. Behind him, one of the crates rattles as something moves inside it, shaking the entire ATV. Another scent hits my nose and suddenly I have a really bad hunch about what's in there.

But Taggert's attention isn't on the crates. It's currently on the other commando, tripping forward in the mud. His wrists are bound with thick straps that have some sort of tech in them. I can just spy a pin-sized light on the underside. The commando starts pleading.

"Taggert, come on, man. You know these charges are bogus." From where I sit, I'm so close I don't even have to focus to hear the voices.

"I know for a fact you were cheating your own officers, Graves," Taggert replies. "The cheating alone is enough for Weiland to punish you. Then you add letting Revas get away on top of that." My mind tries to place where this commando could've encountered Revas as Taggert drawls on. Other rustling sounds try to distract me, but I don't lose focus on the commandos. Whatever this is, it's important.

"It's a wonder Weiland didn't tell me to drop you in the middle of the hellstorm," Taggert continues. "At least out here you'll have a fighting chance at some kind of survival." He chuckles and sneers. "Hell, Graves. You could even go join the scavvers, if you can find them."

Then the pieces click together. The other commando is the gambler from the bar up in Verem; he's the same one I goaded into a fight so Sena and I could escape. And Taggert isn't referring to the real Revas—he means me. The commando let me get away from that bar, not the real Revas. Weiland and Taggert must've actually believed me when I used that lie. And now this guy Graves is getting the brunt of her anger for me escaping.

At the time it was the perfect thing to say to incite the syndicates in the restaurant. Nothing more than a trick of words to get the reaction I needed, which is now condemning a man to a terrible fate. The guilt begins to chew at my insides, but I tell myself he's a commando working for a crazed megalomaniac. That he chose his side. That they wouldn't punish him without more evidence than just my flippant accusation.

"A fighting chance?" Graves's voice rises to a whiny pitch. "With my hands tied and no weapon?"

Taggert jerks his head. Another commando steps forward and cuts the ties connecting Graves's hands. The straps stay on his wrists even though the cord between them is now separated. Graves immediately lunges for the commando's gun, but Taggert's boot moves faster, connecting right with the guy's forehead. He tumbles down into the muck, looking ready to strike again. My guilt lessens slightly at the feral expression on Graves's face; he barely looks human.

"Have some dignity, Graves," Taggert spits as the man struggles in the mud. "Now, go on. I'll give you a three-minute head start if you get out of my sight in the next five seconds."

The man stares daggers at Taggert for a beat, then he's up and bounding toward the trees in my direction. I glance down to Lyria and the scavver, except they're already gone. Shit. I was so focused on the commandos' exchange I ignored them slinking off. Useless Nova lab hacks should've engineered me with an extra set of ears.

The commando stumbles through the brush below me in full panic mode. I keep close to the tree trunk, but he notices nothing over his head as he flounders past. With the amount of noise he's making, any predator in a five-mile radius will be clued in to his path.

Taggert turns back to the others as they position themselves behind the ATV trailer.

"Let them loose," he says, his sneer growing into a grin.

One of the men nods, then activates a latch on the side of the nearest crate with his datapad. The cage doors open simultaneously, and four large batimalu apes screech and claw at the metal as they escape their confines.

The apelike bats are huge, even for their species, each one about four feet tall and easily weighing a hundred pounds. Their russet-yellow fur extends to the upper part of the membraned wings on their backs, giving them an almost vulturelike appearance. They snarl at each other, scratching with the talons on the ends of their wings as they clamber to the ground. Each one is fitted with some sort of collar around its neck, the same type of material as the straps around Graves's wrists with matching blinking lights. I glance in the direction the commando went, but there's no sign of him anymore.

This is not going to end well.

"Send them out," Taggert says. The commando behind him hesitates.

"But it hasn't been three minutes, sir."

Taggert stomps over, ignoring the snarling batimalu not three feet away, and snatches the datapad. I contemplate a dozen ways to try and stop this from unfolding, but Taggert presses something on the controls, and a shrill sound echoes at the highest frequency my ears can detect. I wince, frozen in place.

The batimalu go rigid, the lights rapidly blinking on their collars, and then they snap open their arms, revealing the full width of the membranous wings they're infamous for. The beasts are something not quite entirely ape but not quite entirely giant bat either. Flying demons if you ask me. As vicious as the karakonen on Tundar, with the added ability to attack their prey from above. I had an encounter with a juvenile many years ago, and that was enough to last a lifetime.

Taggert taps the datapad again, and the batimalu apes release more earsplitting screeches.

With a fury that would counter even the hellstorm, the four lift off the ground with a few giant flaps of their wings and then spear into the trees like lightning, following the path of the desperate commando.

Which means coming right past me first.

I press my body close to the tree trunk, willing myself into stillness. The first three whiz by, too low to catch my scent.

But the fourth is flying nearly level with the limb I'm sitting on. It swoops past and then suddenly banks hard, looping around to my branch. The claws on its legs stab violently into the wood as it lands, sending splinters raining down below. This close, I can see the small active light on the collar, hear the hum of its frequency. The batimalu opens its mouth, snarling, a row of three-inch razor-sharp teeth pointed straight at me.

In one quick motion, I grab the large fruit dangling from the branch above and hurl it straight at the creature's head. The bati-malu releases its grip on the limb, diving below to dodge the fruit. Regaining its posture with two large flaps, it roars once more and then shoots after its group.

After Graves, who doesn't stand a chance. Four monsters against one man. A man I helped condemn. But other worries crowd my mind. About the implications of a corporation experimenting with predators.

When I'm sure the batimalu aren't coming back and Taggert isn't going into the jungle after them, I shimmy down the tree trunk, glad when my feet hit solid albeit mucky earth. I hurry away from the substation and its existence. Away from the commandos and the beasts they are attempting to control. They're sending batimalu after their own people. Batimalu that are bigger than normal.

And the scent . . . Underneath the fur and smell of carrion, I caught a hint of pheromones similar to the ones that genopaths emit. Which can only mean that Weiland is in league with Nova somehow. No one else would want to alter or control a deadly predator. No one other than Nova. Does Kiran know about this? My gut says he does. Which can only mean he's playing both the corpo and the syndicates for fools.

He only ever has one mission, and that's Nova's.

I'm done playing nice with everyone on this planet, including Kiran. I'm done playing his games. He is going to tell me what the hell is going on and where Alora is. Or I will beat it out of him.

I rush through the brush, tracking the scent of the tahuayo flowers and the two girls' trail while desperately straining for the retch of the sprawl, for civilization, where I really should stay from now on.

I keep quiet but I move fast, not wanting to stay outside the mag zone any longer. The mag tracks offer the only small amount of safety from the wilderness and preds. But even a magnetic field might not be enough to stop the abomination that Nova and Weiland have unleashed.

Just as I cross the invisible line and detect the low hum of the mag field, a piercing scream echoes through the trees in my wake, stabbing deeper at the guilt in my gut.

The batimalu found their prey.

Time for me to find mine and get the hell out of here.

CHAPTER 15

I waste no time darting after the rebel and the scavver. Now that I'm in the relative safety of the mag zone, it's easy to find their winding trail through the jungle back to the sprawl. Whatever intel they were after at the substation, they must've seen enough.

Popping out from trees into civilization, I take a deep inhale to catch their scent. I climb up behind an abandoned life pod and spot the two up ahead, scaling a ladder to the second level. They're heading in the direction of the boardinghouse, sticking to the higher levels where the scavver will draw less attention. I consider breaking off and looking for Kiran now, but it's probably smarter to let my anger toward him and Nova cool so I have a level head when I confront him. Plus, I'm too curious about Lyria and this scavver now.

I give them a few heartbeats to get farther on before I sneak out of my spot and keep pace on the lower levels. The smell of jungle muck combined with human waste and forgotten food assaults my nose as we trek deeper into the crowded parts of the sprawl. Thankfully, the stench helps me push the encounter in the jungle further from my mind. The push of bodies around grows denser as the heat of the morning forces people outside the confines of life pods and walls, where a lack of airflow can make the buildings feel like ovens.

Higher up, the slight breeze helped filter the smells and the heat, but down here, I might as well be wading neck-deep through the sticky waste.

About halfway back to the boardinghouse, the two girls climb down from the upper levels and head past a building that's large for the sprawl. It's positioned near one of the track support beams, pushed up against an abandoned construction area stamped with faded TerraCo logos. The metal building rises above the mud, bigger and taller than any of the life pods around but still not as big as structures in Verem or the outpost.

I realize with a start that this place is—or was—a mag rail station. The big windows in the front were once ticket counters. The size of the building allowed for people transporting goods or animals to get inspected by corpo or syndicate regulators. Beyond the building, the platform lift that carried passengers up to the rail is a few yards down, perched on the side of the support beam, partially hidden by spider vines.

I keep an eye out for threats, but while there are a ton of people moving about, I don't see any commandos or corpo chumps anywhere. Chains crisscross the building's main door, and the platform lift doesn't look like it's been operational in a long time. Burn marks scar the building at each of the windows in the front. It's obvious that the train hasn't been stopping here for a while. No one's shouting out fares or trying to poach tickets. No movement of goods and very few food stalls in the area. The terminal certainly doesn't seem to be much of anything anymore, just a burned-out shell.

As the girls walk around the building, toward the sprawl's edge, I scramble up a rope bridge to the upper levels to follow unseen. As I climb, I peer over the roof of the terminal. A small tavern sits behind it, built out of container pods. From the outside, it appears fairly deserted. But I can hear the pulse of a dozen or so heartbeats behind the thin exocarbon-lined walls as well as a few others in strategic positions around in the levels.

The smell of sweat and bodies hits my nose, but it's what I don't smell that clues me in to the origin of the crowd. No metal or fresh oil or corpo body armor. Just wafts of booze and smoke and the hum of arken blades. The Vega. I can tell by the positioning of sentinels around the building and by the low current of tension in the air that buzzes across my skin.

I snake my way closer, climbing up a short ladder to the very top level, directly under the mag rail tracks. I lose sight of my marks as the bridge I'm walking on passes over another life pod. That's when I catch a hint of pheromones. Guess following Lyria turned out to be a blessing in disguise. Now I get to confront my ex-partner about all the weird shit that's happening on this planet.

I consider staying right here and making him come to me. But Kiran's patience and drive to win are infinite. I'm sweaty and still pissed and don't feel like playing games with him. So, I shimmy down a ladder to the lower level to face my nemesis.

"And so, we meet again, partner." Kiran's arms are crossed as he leans against a railing, looking ever bored with that arrogant smirk on his stupid face. He raises an eyebrow. "If I didn't know any better, I'd say you were following me."

"We're not partners. And believe me, I wasn't," I reply, realizing that if he's here, then Sena's somewhere nearby. "I was following someone else," I say with a shrug, hoping he hasn't spotted her and Iska yet. I might need them to intervene if this confrontation turns physical. Three on one has much better odds than just me against Kiran.

"Getting rusty, then, if I found you so easily." He shakes his head, tsking as if I've failed a test. I roll my eyes and resist punching him. I'll wait for a better opening. He moves from his perch, stepping closer to me. I shift my weight onto my toes, readying myself.

"Kiran—" I open my mouth to ask him about Nova and the batimalu, but he interrupts me, leaning into my space.

"I know you have questions. I can see them spelled out across your face. Some of them I'll do my best to answer, I swear to you." The intensity in his gaze surprises me. His pulse isn't elevated; he's not smirking. He's . . . not lying for once.

"But I can't right now. Everyone's here already," he says, stepping back. "Looks like I'll get you up close and personal to your two targets by accompanying you down there." He gestures with his arm for me to go down the ramp. "Come on. They're waiting."

I know he's being vague on purpose, baiting me so that I'll ignore my anger and questions and instead wonder who else is here besides Lyria and the scavver. But if they are waiting for him, he's right; now's not the time to confront him about Nova. Something tells me he'll answer those questions even if he won't tell me where Alora is. I swallow my frustration and close the distance between us.

"It'd be so much easier if you'd just answer all my questions now," I say, and stalk past him down the ramp, making my way to

ground level and landing between an empty food stall and a forgotten life pod. Kiran follows, pointing to the tavern as we walk
across some metal planks half buried in the mud.

"Things are about to get interesting. You should—"

My glare interrupts him. "You know, you don't get to tell me
what I should and shouldn't do anymore. I'm not the girl you knew.
Not the partner you loved to control and boss around."

His dark eyes pierce mine. "You're right. You can take care of
yourself. You were brilliant with Weiland. But maybe I'm not the
boy you knew either. A lot can happen in two years." He shrugs
softly. "But it doesn't matter if you see me any differently—I'll
always look out for you anyway." I stare back at him, momentarily pinned in place. Hidden in his expression is a look that I don't
want to decipher. An intensity that I don't have time or energy to
deal with.

I break his gaze, shaking off its weight. It's nothing more than
another manipulation.

"You only look out for yourself," I say, turning away and climbing the steps to the tavern, switching my focus to the challenge in
front of me rather than the annoyance behind.

Stale booze permeates the air so thickly I can taste it on my
tongue. The building creaks with the weight of the small crowd
gathered inside. And too late, I pick up the scent of wet fur and
a hint of Tundar ice already in the building. Sena better be okay.

I push open the door with Kiran on my tail. A dozen or so people
turn to face us both. Lyria is sitting up on the edge of a wooden
bar while Sena and Iska stand in the middle of the crowd of syndicate thugs. Kiran must've caught on to her and led her here.
The scavver girl stands near Sena, giving my friend the once-over
before turning toward Kiran and me.

"Another one? Is she armed, too?" The scavver is holding the arken blade Sena took from my ship, inspecting its weight.

Next to me, Kiran shakes his head. "All good." Why is he lying now? Of course I'm armed; he knows exactly where I like to keep my spare knife and small explosives. Again, I have no idea what game he's trying to play.

"So, who are these two?" the scavver asks as I stand next to Sena. We exchange a glance, and she raises a dark eyebrow at me.

But Lyria interrupts before I can come up with an answer.

"Syndicates," she says without moving from her spot on the bar. She glances at me, and I suddenly wonder if she can see through my cover, see that I'm nothing but tricks and lies. "Or at least syndicate sympathizers. They caused a scuffle at the outpost with Weiland last night when this one"—she points at me—"pretended to be Revas."

"A risky move considering how trigger-happy Weiland is and how badly she wants Revas put down," the scavver replies, looking at me with renewed interest.

I cross my arms. I hate when people talk about me instead of to me. "How do you know I'm not really Revas sent here to test you all?"

The scavver girl steps closer to us as Lyria grins. The syndicates edge away from the scavver. She must have more power than I originally assumed. Lyria sits observing, still with her relaxed posture and messy red hair, looking exactly the same as she did yesterday on the lift, still low-key. The scavver girl, however, is the opposite. With the sides of her black hair shorn and her skull tattooed with ink darker than her rich brown skin, there's a gravitas about her. Where Lyria blends in with the background, this girl readily stands out.

I hold my ground as the scavver stalks closer, studying me from head to toe.

"You're not Revas," she says with a smirk. "We all know that already. You're just a washed-up genopath with no puppet master. Or maybe you're a spy for someone else. But you might be useful after all." Her eyes cut to Kiran momentarily. She knows what we both are. Either Lyria or Kiran himself told her. It appears he doesn't care who knows about our true identities.

I shake my head. "I already told Lyria I'm not interested in your little crusade."

The scavver shrugs, smoothing the thick, dark braid on the top of her head.

"Your friend might be, though." She turns to Sena and my heart speeds up, but the scavver doesn't step closer. Iska watches her movements, looking ready to pounce. A growl rumbles low in her throat.

"I like your wolf," the scavver says to Sena. "Would she attack me, if you told her to?"

Sena cocks her head to the side, eerily reminding me of Iska. "I wouldn't have to tell her if she thought you were threatening me."

The scavver nods like this makes perfect sense to her. "A true dara sosken, that wolf."

"Dara sosken?" Sena repeats.

"It's scavver-speak for blood kin." The girl pauses, looking Sena up and down. "I thought you'd know that, but I guess Neran didn't teach you everything about us."

At the mention of her äma's name, my heart lurches and Sena's whole body freezes, her eyes narrowing.

"What do you know about my äma?" Sena asks, her voice low and measured.

The scavver shrugs nonchalantly, as if she hasn't just dropped a bomb on Sena's world.

"Well, for starters you look just like her. I've got an old holo from when she was about your age. Before she and your grand-parents left us. Maraas may be a big planet, but we all know each other fairly well. Your äma was friends with my äma."

Sena stares at the scavver, neither her storm-gray eyes nor her body moving, still processing the potentially life-changing infor-mation about her scavver mother and where she came from. I in-stinctively take a step closer to my friend, wanting to give her the time she needs to think. Because suddenly I'm not the only one looking for something on this backwater planet.

"How do we know you're telling the truth?" I ask softly.

The girl raises one sharp eyebrow. "Stick around, you'll find out." She stalks back toward Lyria, and they exchange a glance. "I'd love to say more, but I'm sort of in the middle of something here with my syndicate friends. You'll have to wait your turn. Pref-erably outside."

"We're not going until we get answers," I reply, crossing my arms.

Lyria sighs, and when she nods, a few syndicate chumps inch closer to us, the threat obvious on their faces. While I play like I'm a syndicate, their movement is a stark reminder that I don't really belong to their crew. I'm not one of them. Next to me, Iska's growl grows louder as the hair on her back rises.

But Kiran's voice cuts through the promise of violence. "An-swers for what, Remy?" Some of the tension dissipates at his in-terruption. He may drive me crazy, but his timing is impeccable.

I raise my voice to match his and so everyone hears it loud and clear. "I'm looking for Revas. And whatever information Sena wants on her äma," I add. "Tell us and we'll leave, simple as that."

Lyria hops down off the bar and stalks closer. "And if we don't?"

I shrug. "Well, then I might be forced to let Weiland know where we are." I level my gaze at the scavver girl. "I'm not above using that corporate snake for my own needs."

I feel Sena's gaze on me along with everyone else's, but she says nothing to challenge my bluff. Kiran's half smirk has reappeared as he watches me square off with the other girls. My fingers, having found their way to my side pocket while Lyria was moving, nudge one of the flash bombs. I may be bluffing about Weiland, but I'm certainly not going to let a dozen people get the jump on me and Sena. And I'll blow up this entire tavern if it brings me one step closer to finding Alora. That part is definitely not a bluff.

The scavver girl is smiling like she's finally found something interesting. She nods to Lyria.

"Well, I like these three." She side-eyes me. "Despite the spy. So . . . your call."

Lyria stares at me; something in the intensity of her stance sets off warning bells. She's more than she's letting on, more than just some low-level lift operator or resistance organizer. She's been quiet, but now the look in her eyes speaks volumes. She is not someone to underestimate. My index finger presses into the flash bomb, ready to activate the detonation and toss it in her direction.

Then the syndicate smiles and the predatory gaze in her eyes is gone as if it was never there.

"Remy, Sena." She nods at the scavver girl. "This is Emeko. She's one of the scavver leaders working closely with us to dispose of Weiland and her ilk." She studies me for a beat, mischief dancing in her eyes where violence was promised before. I don't know what to make of her sudden switch.

"Now that you're officially on the team"—I open my mouth to argue, but she keeps talking—"I'll introduce you to the boss you're so eager to meet."

My heart skips a beat, wondering if I missed a pulse outside that could belong to the mysterious Revas. My mind sifts through possible locations and positions. But Lyria doesn't call for anyone to come forward or signal anyone.

And then it hits me.

The syndicate sketches a little flourish of a bow.

"Lyria Revas, newly minted Vega boss, at your service."

CHAPTER 16

Sena's and Emeko's mouths both drop open in surprise. Guess the scavver didn't know everything. The pieces fall into place as one thing clicks after another, and I find myself not that surprised. I knew Lyria was hiding something. Now I know what it was.

"I told you I was good at finding hidden things." Lyria—Revas— steps closer to me, lowering her voice. "Now we both know you won't call Weiland since I'm the one you're dying to talk to. But we can't exactly trust you yet, so I'm going to need you to step outside while we conduct our business. We'll be done soon, and then we can discuss those answers you want so badly and what you're willing to do for them."

My jaw sets at her words. No wonder she told me Revas could find anything. She was talking about herself.

"Well played," I say, keeping my voice calm and nonchalant. She might've been hiding this, and she might know I'm a genopath, but she truly doesn't know what I'm capable of. She will help me find Alora, even if she doesn't know it yet. She smirks and it reminds me of Kiran.

"We'll just be right outside," I finish.

Sena holds out her hand expectantly toward Emeko. The scavver narrows her honey-brown eyes but then hands over the arken blade. I turn and head out the door, ready for some kind of breeze after the oppressive humidity in this tin building. But the air outside does nothing to relieve the feverish heat sticking to my skin.

I'm vaguely aware of Sena and Iska trailing after me, but I let the heavy sounds of their footfalls become secondary. I need to improvise a better bargaining position, and that is going to take all my focus. What leverage do I have over Revas? What negotiating chips can I use in my favor?

My mind whirs, dreaming up a multitude of possibilities. Some I discard almost instantly; others have potential and I tuck them away for later. This sort of planning — manipulating favorable scenarios and pitting players against each other — is Kiran's forte. I'm the one who gets the intel, but I know I can think of a solution if I just focus hard enough.

"Rem." Kiran's voice cuts through my thoughts. I realize I've paced up ramps to the second level of the slums without being totally aware of my surroundings. Kiran's managed to get in front of me somehow. I steal a glance back over my shoulder and see Sena a level below, sitting on the edge of a bridge with Iska by her side. I wasn't even thinking about how she might be processing the information about her äma. Or the fact that she might have family left on this very world.

A frustrated sigh escapes my lips. Balancing others while the instincts and anger roar through my blood is a true test of my limits, and I'm not doing a very good job at the moment. Me leaving Sena to herself, instinctively focusing on my problems rather than helping her with hers, is further proof that my genes dominate all my decisions.

Swallowing past the lump in my throat, I turn back to Kiran. He's standing in my path, blocking my way, staring at me with his dark brown eyes, emotion swimming just below their surface. But how much is real and how much is just another manipulation?

"You knew she was Revas," I say, the accusation clear in my tone.

He shrugs. "I was under orders not to tell any outsiders." He looks me up and down. "You technically count as an outsider."

"An outsider you keep calling 'partner,' though you certainly don't act like it. Why am I not surprised, though? Our partnership was never equal, and emotions were only something you ever used, not something you actually felt."

"Take a walk with me," he says, ignoring my jabs and suddenly switching subjects. I glare at him, and to my surprise, he sighs.

"Please, Remy. Just . . . once. We'll come right back, and then you can interrogate me or Revas all you want."

I turn away from him. "I'm not leaving Sena alone."

"You already kind of did."

I whip my head back, and he raises his hands in an innocent gesture.

"She's not a child," he says. "And she's not alone anyway. She has her wolf, her dara sosken." Something bites in his words. It sounds a little like jealousy. "She needs time to process, as do you."

"You have no idea what either of us needs. The only thing you know is what you want and how to get it."

He shrugs. "Fighting against our nature is tiresome and pointless. Will you come with me already? I'm not trying to order you around, I'm asking. Please." He looks at me expectantly as he shifts back and forth on his feet. It's unlike him to seem nervous, unlike him to be aware of his controlling behavior toward me. Totally unlike him to ask nicely. Maybe I can turn this to my advantage.

I sigh overdramatically, making it seem like I'm reluctantly giving in as I gesture to the path in front of us. "I walk with you, you answer my questions."

"I'll answer one question. That's truly all we have time for anyway." Before I can counterargue, Kiran heads down the ramp, toward the terminal building. "Hurry up, partner," he calls over his shoulder.

Shaking my head, I follow the chump as he climbs the steps to the abandoned terminal. With a quick jerk, he yanks the chains off the doors, pushes them open, and heads straight into the large metal building. After a moment's hesitation, I follow.

The space is vast, empty. Lifeless. Scorch marks line the walls like giant claws scraped their rage across the metal. The remnants of a ticket counter and some crumbling benches are all that's left in the interior. The trapped heat in the building is stale and damp; sweat trickles down my neck, my spine, my calves.

I swallow past the discomfort on my tongue, past the feeling of standing in a cavernous tomb. Were there people here when this building burned? I quickly turn those thoughts off.

"What are we doing here, Kiran? And that's not my one question."

He pauses in the middle of the room. "What do you remember about the night Dekkard killed Rixus?"

Of course, he can't answer me straight.

"We're wired not to forget things, as you well know."

"Walk me through the timeline of what you recall." He catches my glare and then again adds that word: "Please."

I resist the urge to throttle him across his stupid smirky face and instead point at his chest accusingly.

"You and Dekkard started the coup a week early. You tricked me into thinking Alora was in danger. But instead of taking me to her, you drugged me and dropped me in the middle of the jungle miles away."

"And then?"

"And then Dekkard killed Alora's father and claimed the Vega crown. By the time I made it back to Verem, you and Alora were gone. And I was left alone."

He nods, something flashing in his eyes. But instead of saying anything more about Alora or her father, he says, "Do you know what was happening elsewhere that night? Down here in the sprawl? Out in the mines?"

I cross my arms. The building around us still possesses the faint scent of char underneath the old metal. "Those weren't a part of my mission parameters."

"Neither was becoming friends with your target," he rushes out. Then winces momentarily. "Sorry. I didn't come here to argue about Alora." But I ignore his apology. His dig cuts into some old part of me that still wants to obey orders. He never would've let friendship overshadow his mission. He didn't even let me, his supposed partner, get in the way of his mission.

"What's your point, Kiran?" I snap.

"Only that while we were busy doing what we were told, what Dekkard wanted, TerraCo was out here." He gestures to the skeleton of the station around us. "They burned this building and the other terminals. They replaced all of the Vega's security on the mines, taking over their positions and refusing to yield them back, even after Dekkard emerged victorious. TerraCo upset the entire balance of the system on this planet, and no one blinked an eye."

"Corpos restructure their agreements with syndicates all the time," I reply. "It's not unusual for them to claim power if they see the chance."

Kiran shakes his head. "What I'm trying to tell you is that they didn't just see the chance. They made it happen."

And suddenly, he's got my attention. My mind blinks, assimilating what he's saying with what I know. We were hired by Dekkard to take control of the Vega from Rixus. We had to make it look like an organic coup, one where Dekkard slowly grew in power and influence and where Rixus's decisions began to reflect poorly on the overall financial health of the syndicate.

I was the mole, sent to infiltrate Rixus's inner circle by acting as a new bodyguard to his daughter. I passed sensitive information along our line of command while Kiran was placed among the Vega ranks, sowing the seeds of dissent and ensuring that any moves made by Rixus ended in disaster. That was the job. We succeeded, of course. We always succeeded.

But what if . . . it wasn't the job?

If what Kiran is saying is true, then TerraCo engineered the entire thing to grab and solidify its power right under Dekkard's nose. The true coup wasn't a restructuring of Vega leadership but a rebalancing of the entire corpo ecosystem of the planet.

No matter how much I want to deny it, the pieces fit. Two years later and TerraCo's control is proof of that. Dekkard moved his seat of power off this world, and the Vegas left here have little to no real influence anymore.

I stare at Kiran while the whole puzzle of Maraas rearranges itself into a new shape in my mind.

"That can't be right," I argue, partially playing devil's advocate and partially because I don't want his words to be correct. "Nova would've told us if they were really running the job for TerraCo. They told us everything so that we could operate at maximum efficiency. So that we could act from every angle."

"Maybe," Kiran says quietly. He paces farther across the blackened metal floor, his footprints leaving a trail in the soot, a series of stark marks across the barren ground. TerraCo burned this place and abandoned it completely.

"It's possible someone high up at Nova was contracted by TerraCo secretly and they designed the entire op without informing us or our direct superiors." He pauses to glance over at me. "But isn't it more possible that Nova knew and used us as pawns in their game? You know how they operate. The lengths they'll go to achieve their goals. That's why I took you to the jungle and told them you were dead, Remy. Because we both know they'd never let you go if you tried to save Alora. We both know, no matter how ineffective you are on a mission, they don't lose their assets. They reprogram them."

Chills run down my neck at his words despite the thick heat of the building. I don't want to think about reconditioning. Even if he is explaining his actions that night, the pain of those memories is too real. The triggers are too close to the surface with Kiran here.

"So, you're saying you did me a favor by dumping me in the jungle?" I reply instead.

"I'm saying that if you get your nose out of Alora's ass, you would be able to see that there's a lot more at stake here than just you and your little friend."

His anger surprises me. Kiran rarely shows real emotions, but now his dark eyebrows are furrowed, his mouth set.

"Why do you care so much about keeping us apart?" The question slips from my lips before I can think about it. But I suddenly need to know the answer, almost as much as I need to know where Alora is.

Kiran clears his throat, his face going slack behind his mask of expressionless boredom, and any hint of emotion is gone, like it was never there.

"I care about my missions. You and she were going to mess that up two years ago. Now here I am, in the midst of a new mission, and yet again, your relationship with her is threatening to screw this one up, too."

He's lying. I don't know about which part exactly or why, but something is off. I hear it in a skip of his pulse, a tone under his words.

"There's more I haven't told you," he says, pausing to sigh. "Nova is actively operating here on Maraas. They're up to something with Weiland."

The batimalu apes flash in my mind. I was going to ask him about them, but here he is, volunteering information for once. Definitely not a coincidence.

"I'm not surprised. I am surprised that you're claiming not to be in the thick of it."

He smiles but it's not his typical smirk, nor does it reach his eyes.

"Nova knows I'm here, of course. But they don't know I'm helping Revas."

My eyebrows go up in faux shock. "You're going off-mission? After you just said how much you care about your jobs?"

He shrugs. "In order to pull off the coup successfully, I made a deal two years ago. I didn't tell you about it because it wasn't any of your business. And I didn't tell Nova about it because they never care what we do when we're on the ground as long as we get the job done. I also didn't need them attempting to reprogram me again. I'm here now because I'm fulfilling my end of the deal by helping the syndicates. Nova thinks I'm spying on them for Weiland."

I stare at him. He's running both sides, as I suspected, just not in the way I thought. And that was a lot more information than I expected him to give. Except it was full of vague references that only leave me with more questions. Who did he make a deal with? Possibilities whir through my head as I wonder why he wouldn't tell me. But those aren't the questions that matter.

"Where is Alora, Kiran?" I ask, the only question I truly care about.

"What will you do after you find her, Remy?"

My mind blanks at his change of direction. "It doesn't matter what we do afterward—"

"You haven't even thought about it, have you? You're so focused on this one thing you can't see the bigger picture, can't see how all the moving pieces connect. How your 'friend' might be affected by what happens on this planet." My fingers curl into fists as he talks, as he sneers the word "friend." He lured me into a false sense of civility by sharing all that info. Now his claws are coming back out.

"I don't care about the moving pieces," I say. "You said you would answer my question. Where is she?"

"Help me finish this and I'll take you to her. I mean that."

I shake my head. He's definitely lying now, saying whatever he thinks I want in order to get my help, distracting me with all this other information.

"I'm not here for you or this power game between the Vega and TerraCo," I say with finality. "I told you I'm not getting involved."

"You're already involved, Remy. You are the one who baited Weiland. She thinks you really are Revas now and won't stop until you're back in her custody."

"I used the name as a means of escape, nothing else."

Kiran rolls his eyes. "Please. You could've come up with a dozen other escape scenarios, but you chose that one. Why? Because you like to drive people over the edge. Especially people in power."

He stops and looks at me, his eyes piercing.

"I see you, Remy. I know who you are." He pauses and then continues in a rush before I can speak. "You're impulsive as hell and whether the limits are laid out by Nova or by the corpos, it doesn't matter, because you will go to extremes to push boundaries and piss off authority figures, Weiland included, just because you like to. Consequences be damned."

"I don't push boundaries — I follow my damn training," I argue. "The instincts and genes that Nova programmed in me. Same as you."

"We both know you go above and beyond your training whenever possible. But fine, let's put that argument aside. You know why else you baited Weiland? Because you helped me break this planet, your friend's home, and you feel guilty about it."

Anger begins to bubble up in my veins again. "I don't know what you're talking about. I just want to find her."

"Right. Then tell me you didn't notice that TerraCo is trying to cut off the outpost from Verem. Tell me you didn't see that they've disabled the train stops to choke trade in the sprawl even after they bought up stalls and buildings. Tell me why you think Ter-raCo and Nova invested in this place only to leave it to die."

Frustration has me wanting to grab him by the shoulders and shake him hard. "I don't care about all that," I grit out. "Seeing the puzzle pieces is your job."

"And gathering intel is yours. So don't try and tell me you didn't notice all those changes; I know you did." He gestures to the burned-out hull around us. "This is what's left of Alora's world and her father's legacy. You think she'd be happy to see it like this? That's why you feel guilty. That's why you can't help but get involved. You broke this planet and some part of you wants to fix it."

I swallow hard past a lump forming in my throat. His words slide beneath my skin, cutting deep because I know he's right, even though I hadn't realized it myself. Some part of me is worried that Alora will hold me responsible for ruining her world, for destroying her family. I haven't let myself think it because I don't know what I'll do if it's true. If she hates me.

But trying to fix this mess means working with Kiran again. And I just don't know if I can do that.

Kiran sees the indecision in my face. He could always read even the smallest changes in my expressions. "Would you really not help me just out of spite?" He sighs, understanding my thoughts like I'm shouting them at him. "If you really wanted to find Alora, you'd do whatever it takes, right? Including helping me."

He walks past me, brushing my shoulder. "But maybe you don't really want to find her. Maybe you're afraid that she won't forgive you for what happened."

He opens the main doors, pushing them wide and letting the sharp sunlight shine back into the building.

"Maybe Alora doesn't want to be your friend anymore. Maybe she doesn't want to be found by you. Her father was murdered after all," he says over his shoulder. His words are quiet yet still carry across the empty space. "And, like me, you helped."

The hot rays from the sun bite the skin on my cheeks almost as much as his words sting my core. The problem with getting involved with my ex-partner isn't just the eventual betrayal. It's the fact that no one knows better than him how to cut me the deepest. And, as much as I despise him, Kiran does still know me better than anyone else. Still knows what to say to make me feel hurt and helpless. Every word out of his mouth is already a small betrayal. Not just because they hurt, but because on some level, they're true.

Kiran pauses in the doorframe. He must catch the pain and anger etched across my face because something softens in his gaze. It only churns the discomfort in my gut further.

"I see you," he repeats softly. "I know you, Remy. But you're not the only one who lost something. You're not the only one who's trying to make up for past failures. So, you can keep chasing a ghost for forgiveness. Or you can actually do something about it. I know I am."

Then he slips out, the doors quietly slinking shut behind him, leaving me in the dark, alone among the scattered ash and dust.

CHAPTER 17

I don't want to waste any more time in the dead space of this forgotten building. I give Kiran a fifteen-second lead before I push my way back out into the sprawl. The air outside is just as hot, though not as stifling as the abandoned station. But even the slight breeze doesn't help me shake off Kiran's words. Just when I hoped he was going to be honest with me. Hoped he was actually going to change his behavior. He claimed he's not the same as before, but his hurtful words proved one thing for certain: I can't trust him.

I see you, Remy.

He sees what he wants to see.

And what failures is he trying to make up for? He doesn't feel anything close to remorse or regret. Another lie to manipulate me.

Though his implications about TerraCo's ambitions and Nova's involvement aren't wrong. They're problems I don't know if I can solve, more messes I don't want to get mixed up in. Messes

I didn't want to think about until he brought up Alora and the idea of what we'll do after I find her. I didn't think about it before because it didn't matter; the only thing that mattered was that she'd be safe, and we'd be together again. But now . . . there are too many questions. What would she think of this Maraas? Where her father's syndicate legacy hasn't just been stolen but nearly erased?

Would she blame me? Cast me aside?

Not wanting to think about this new potential level of failure, I stand on the steps of the former train terminal, letting the sounds and scents of the sprawl wash over me. The calls and shouts of people with their own problems, the clamor of footsteps and moving carts. The echoes of birds and rustling of leaves from the jungle. Heat radiates through it all, blanketing my skin, pressing down on my very pores. The scents of rusted metal and fresh mud mix together. If I concentrate, I can smell hints of the gathering clouds and the coming storm.

The hellstorm is still a few days off, but there's a current of something else in the air edging closer. Yet another thing that's out of my control, one more problem I can't seem to solve.

I take a breath. I truly don't know how my friend would feel about the loss of her father's empire. I don't know how his death broke or re-formed her. I don't know what we'll do afterward, what she'll want to do. Too many unknowns, so I set those concerns aside. More like force them far away from my mind. This is one part of Nova's training that doesn't unnerve me. The ability to compartmentalize. Our memory replays might be so real I feel like I'm seeing live ghosts, but if I focus hard enough, I can turn the triggers off and shut them out entirely. I will worry about what Alora wants after I find her.

Once the fears and doubts are far away, I circle back to the rest. To Kiran and Lyria and their resistance movement.

Kiran won't tell me where Alora is unless I help him. If he'll tell me at all. Lyria said we could talk, but it doesn't take my considerable genopathic brain skills to deduce that she'll make the same offer. Maybe their revolution will be successful. Probably not. It's hard to compete with the limitless money and power of the corpo machine. Even away from the Assembly worlds on extreme planets like Maraas.

Look at Tundar. The race that everyone thrives on is run by corpo greed that destroys the planet and people's lives for profit. TerraCo is no different. The corpo chumps will probably squash the Vegas like tiny insects under their polished boots. It's the way of the charted systems: the will of the corpos rules all. Syndicates may rise and fall, but corporations exist forever.

And even knowing this, Kiran is helping Lyria. There's more here at stake than what he's telling me, that's for sure. I generally hate being backed into a corner, but my training and my instincts are telling me to go along with their plot. At least until I find the info I need.

Kiran thinks he can play me, like I'm one of his marks. It's time I put all my training and genetics to use and play him back. It doesn't matter that he makes me angry at every word, or that he'll probably betray me the first chance he gets. I will just have to be smarter and faster than him. He's not the one I care about—Alora is. And this is the best way I can get to her.

Having made a decision, I head back toward the ramp where I left Sena. She must be lost in her own storm of thoughts. And I'm not going to let my instincts continue to distract me and leave her alone again.

A drop of rain hits the back of my neck and slinks down my spine. My eyes jump to the partially graying sky. Thin clouds drift overhead and a light rain begins to fall. Something about this unexpected drizzle sets my nerves on edge.

I jump down a short ladder and find Sena taking shelter underneath a bridge near the tavern. She's sitting on the ledge, letting her legs dangle down as she rebraids her dark mass of curls. Iska lies beside her, the wolf's head in Sena's lap. Her face is distant, her eyes clouded as she watches the rain.

"You okay?" I ask, sitting on the ledge next to her.

Her shoulders move slightly upward as she ties up the braid. "Define okay."

"Struggling with that myself," I mumble. "That was a big bomb of information that scavver dropped on you."

Sena nods. "My äma wasn't originally from Tundar. I knew that much. . . . But she never talked about her past. Not the scavvers under the lake. Nothing about Maraas or any other world. And I have no idea why."

I consider a few possibilities before I speak softly. "Maybe it was painful for her."

"Too painful to tell her own daughter?" Her voice is bitter. "She taught me everything she knew about Tundar, Remy. Everything I know about survival came from her and my mom. But I always assumed it wasn't just survival for her. That she was somehow at home in the splinter wood and with the vonenwolves and with us. She made it seem like a home even when we had nothing. But it wasn't where she came from. It wasn't her home."

I consider this, thinking about my own experience with Alora.

"Maybe that's why she worked so hard to make it feel like one," I say.

Sena's gaze slides over to me. I can see the hint of tears behind her normal stoicism.

"I don't know how I'm supposed to feel about that," she says, barely a whisper. "About anything."

"If it makes you feel better, I never know what I'm supposed to feel." I sigh. "I don't know which emotions I have are genuine and which ones are . . . engineered so I can get what I want from people. Maybe that's because I'm more genopath than actual human. Nova never allowed us to have feelings. They taught us we weren't even capable of such things. If any of us ever did feel anything, we hid it, never let it show. Having feelings was just asking for punishment."

She presses her lips into a tight line, blinking at me as her fingers trail through Iska's fur.

"I think not understanding feelings is more human than you realize."

"Sucks either way." I say with a humorless chuckle. "But, Sena . . . we don't know anything more than what that scavver— Emeko—said. She could be full of shit. Or maybe she can shed some light on your äma's history. We shouldn't jump to conclusions until we find out more."

Her eyes jump back to mine, searching. "We? You want to find out more?"

I nod. "If that's what you want," I say, bumping her shoulder with my own. "If you want to find out more, then of course, I'll help you. If you don't, well, I'll help you burn them all down instead."

She sighs, her arm wrapping tight around Iska as the rain continues to fall lightly around us. Iska nudges Sena's thigh with her nose, the wolf huffing her own sigh. The melody of water hitting metal fills the silence that follows, the pings and plinks of raindrops the only sound for several heartbeats.

"I don't think I know what I want," she says, a single tear slipping down her pale cheek.

I squeeze her shoulder gently, unsure of how best to comfort her. I was made for chaos and madness and don't understand my own storm of emotions most of the time. The first sixteen years of my existence, my feelings were suppressed, controlled by Nova. I didn't even understand what emotions were until I met Alora. And for the last two years that I've been on my own, it's been a struggle to figure them out, to keep them in check. I still suppress things I don't want to deal with. I still question what I'm even capable of feeling. And with Kiran around, with him dredging up our past, it's so much harder.

"I think it's okay not to know what you want," I finally say, recalling Kiran's accusations once more. I don't want to think about whether he's right or not. Whether I actually want to find Alora or if I want to assuage my guilt. Whether she might hate me.

A soft quiet surrounds us, despite the constant hum of the slums. My senses unconsciously home in on certain sounds and smells. Lyria's small crowd gathered in the tavern just beyond our location. A hawker pushing a small cart across the bridge over our heads to escape the drizzling mist. The pitter-patter of the rain falling across the valley. And then the low rumble of vibrations as the mag train approaches.

I crane my neck, trying to get a better glimpse of the tracks above, but it's hard through the bridges and life pods and ramps. Why is the train already passing overhead again? Is it coming or going? I know Kiran said it wasn't stopping in the sprawl at all, but I have to see it myself.

"I need to check something; I'll be right back," I say to Sena. She nods absentmindedly, still lost in thought as I haul myself up the nearest ladder.

The vibrations grow stronger as the train gets closer. The bridges and ropes begin to shake slightly; buildings precariously affixed to the support columns or the underside of the tracks tremble with the motion. I jump over a railing and climb to an upper level. The slums may be pieced haphazardly together, but somehow the buildings and levels continue to persevere, even with the hellstorm cycle and the intense rocking of the train tracks, a testament to the grit of the people here.

Walking along another bridge, I map out the train's distance in my head based on the intensity of the vibrations. Not far off now. It's traveling much faster than before. I find a life pod with a small platform on the side and not many people around. Perching on the edge, I lean as far as I can, finally getting a decent view of the long line of tracks. I can just make out the train cars, maybe a mile away, coming from the opposite direction than before.

The platform underneath me begins to shake violently as the train approaches. Movement across the levels has slowed as people wait for the train to pass, to make sure nothing is going to come down on their heads. It's not uncommon for fixings to loosen and cause buildings or bridges to crash to levels below.

With bated breath, I track the train's path as the hum of the mag field shifts into a roar and the entire structure trembles. Then the train zooms by, again not slowing or stopping for anyone or anything. I watch until the trembling stops and the cars disappear around a bend in the distance.

Kiran was right. I don't like to admit it, but he was. The burned terminal lies below, forgotten or ignored by the train operators. No passengers, no commerce, no movement of resources. As if the sprawl has been cast off by TerraCo. And if Kiran is right about this, what else could he be right about?

"Hey." Sena appears next to me, her ashen skin now clear of any trace of tears. Iska sticks her nose over the ledge with a huff.

"I know how you feel," I tell the wolf, leaning back and scratching between her ears. There's nowhere for her to really run in this maze of levels and ladders.

Sena eyes me and I explain why I rushed up here. "Kiran told me the mag train wasn't stopping at all in the sprawl anymore. I noticed it passing earlier, but I wanted to confirm it."

She purses her lips. "There's a lot of moving parts here. The corpo city, the syndicate outpost, the sprawl. A train that doesn't stop." She pauses, considering. "What about the scavvers?"

I almost tell her I have no idea how anything works on this planet anymore, but I catch the longing in her eyes and realize she's asking because she wants to know more about how her äma might've fit in here.

"The scavvers live out in the wilderness, like they do on Tundar. But instead of one city, they have a number of bases and camps that dot the mountains beyond the mag zone. And the people of the sprawl don't hate the scavvers the way they do in the Ket. Groups of scavvers come to trade goods with the sprawl residents. They exchange plants or animal meats for building materials or other resources."

"Do the scavvers deal with the syndicates or the corpos?"

"The syndicates sometimes. Even though the Vega are supposed to act as security for the corpos, they turn a blind eye to the scavver dealings because they use the same goods, too."

Sena frowns. "Yeah, that's not surprising. When there's money or resources changing hands, profits usually win out over loyalties."

"The corpos never liked it regardless. Before, if they caught wind of any trading, they'd force a syndicate raiding party into the jungle to remind the scavvers to stay in their place. To remind them who won the war all those years ago and who holds the true power over Maraas, Edge World or not."

"Did the syndicates kill the scavvers?" she asks quietly.

I nod slowly. "Sometimes, a more zealous group would be sent on the raids. Other times, the ones chosen were more sympathetic to the scavvers they traded with. Alora's father, Rixus, tried to strike a balance between yielding to corpo demands and not pissing off the scavvers whose goods they often relied on when corpo shipments were delayed because of the hellstorm. But after he was murdered, I don't know what happened."

Sena considers this. "Based on all that we've heard and now with Lyria meeting one of the scavver leaders, probably nothing good."

I hum in agreement. Dekkard didn't care about the scavvers; he didn't really care about the actual running of the syndicate. Just the power that came with the position. But he was the one that the Nova execs chose when the corpos came to them, asking for a change of power. And now I'm realizing that's exactly why they chose him. To slowly chip away at the hold the Vega had over this world. To tilt the balance back in the favor of the corpos. They've been playing the long game while everyone else is struggling to survive.

And they don't care who gets caught in the crossfire.

I think about my promise to Alora, that night in the jungle. A promise to be better than what I was made for. To do something more with my life than serve corporate puppet masters. While I don't know how to feel about the changes on Maraas, I do know how she would feel about me refusing to get involved.

Guilt stabs me deep in my gut. The last two years, I've been so focused on finding her, on chasing Kiran. But maybe that was merely an excuse so I wouldn't look too closely at the problems I encountered jumping from world to world. At the suffering caused by the corpos. At circumstances that I was capable of changing but chose to ignore. At what Alora would want after I saved her. I was trying so hard to make up for my failure to my friend that I failed to see the truth.

That I was failing all over again.

And that I haven't kept the one promise I made.

A ringing fills my ears along with all of Kiran's accusations. Like knives, his earlier words scrape against my skin. Has he been right about me this entire time, or does he know how easily I can be manipulated through Alora?

Iska suddenly perks her ears forward just as I register a low hum. Not the mag train.

The sound of a ship engine.

Shit. I push my senses further. The rain has lessened to nothing more than a light mist, though gray clouds still dominate the sky, giving the perfect cover for a flyer. And a flyer only means one thing.

TerraCo.

I climb to my feet, concentrating on pinpointing the origin of the sound. It's not coming from the direction of the city, but rather the jungle. The same general area where I followed Lyria and the scavver out of the mag zone. Two things hit me at once.

The batimalu that landed on the tree limb next to me. It had a light on its collar that emitted a frequency. But more than that, there was a dark dot below it. A camera. I was so focused on getting rid of the thing, my brain didn't register the importance of the camera lens until now.

Taggert saw me hiding in the tree.

My feet are already moving, my body sprung for action as I leap down to a lower bridge. Sena pounds after me as Iska begins to bark.

"What is it?" Her shout follows me.

"We have to warn them!" I shout back. Because the second thing I should've realized earlier is that Taggert's probably been tracking me ever since the batimalu spotted me in that tree. Which means this ship isn't on some routine inspection or flyby. It's here to—

A sharp whistling pierces the air. Laser-guided missile.

"GET DOWN!"

I grab Sena and pull her behind a life pod as the world around us explodes into fire and smoke.

CHAPTER 18

We fly backward from the force of the blast, tumbling down a ramp into mud. I scramble up and force my eyes to focus through smoke and fire. Instant relief fills my gut; the tavern is still standing.

But the terminal building is in flames. Debris rains down from above. Shouts and screams fill the air. Most of the building is gone, pieces scattered outward from the explosion. Chunks of debris are lodged in the ground, on other levels, on top of the homes of unprepared sprawl residents. Next to me, Sena coughs while Iska shakes off dust and mud from her fur. They're all right, but what about so many others?

I glance back to the station being consumed by flames. Only the one wall affixed to the mag rail support beam remains. Metal screeches on my left. The platform lift far above us has come loose from its bearings, tilting at an impossible angle as the last few bolts attempt to hold the weight.

"It's going to fall!" Sena shouts. People underneath are already scattering. An older man trying to salvage what's left of his hawker cart remains in the lift's shadow.

I'm already moving.

I will not let more people die because of my mistakes.

Ten steps away and the caged platform shudders, one corner tearing loose from the beam. I force speed into my limbs and plow into the man. My arms wrap around his waist, and I drive him forward, out of the platform's path.

Three more steps and a ripping sound screams through the air as the last bolts tear free. I throw my momentum into a jump, clearing the area as the platform crashes into the ground.

The levels vibrate with the force of the impact. The man's cart is gone, smashed and buried underneath a mound of concrete and metal mere inches away from my feet. Then Sena is pulling me, helping me up. Together, we steady the man as he gets to his feet. He nods his thanks and then is gone, running away from the smoke. Others rush by, escaping the flames.

The roar of the burning fire and screams of the sprawl fill my ears. I push my hearing harder, beyond that, to the tavern not fifty feet away. Just underneath the chaos, I detect movement and heartbeats. Still alive. Kiran, Lyria, the others. Still alive.

Sena is already ahead, Iska beside her. Together, we clamber through the smoke, making our way to the tavern. A figure dashes through shadows and I recognize the shape and movement. Kiran. I squint as he disappears up a ramp, moving so fast I can barely track him.

Where the hell is he going? He's leaving us.

Leaving me.

Again.

For a split second, I consider following him, catching him. But a familiar sound has me grabbing Sena's arm.

The flyer is back, coming to a hover above the treetops, just beyond the tavern. A large chunk of debris has blocked the main entrance to the building. I can sense the people now trapped inside. The flyer dips lower, the side hatch of the ship swinging open. Taggert appears, leaning out of the opening, a smirk on his face. His eyes spot me, and the smirk turns into a grin. He disappears back inside, and I glimpse more commandos in the flyer's cargo bay, a whole unit ready for the attack. He must want to take some of them alive and I cannot allow that.

"Go and get them out of there!" I shout at Sena, pointing to the building. "There's a side door around the back."

She doesn't hesitate; she runs, the wolf by her side.

I'm already turning, my mind calculating distance and force, mapping out the best path to take. Kiran may have disappeared, but I won't. Not anymore. I refuse to let anyone else die at corpo hands. I already know what Taggert is planning. He still thinks I'm Revas. He wants me to watch as he captures the syndicates. He wants me to feel it.

But I'm not really their leader.

I'm something much more dangerous.

I don't have to think; my training takes over.

And.

I.

Move.

Up a ladder and across a bridge. Leap to the roof of a low-hanging life pod. Seconds tick away and I push myself faster. My senses and instincts do the rest. Wind speed, smoke cover, blast radius. I control this situation, not him.

Taggert reappears, this time with a loaded carry cannon, an RPG he's aiming directly at the tavern below. But I've already pulled a flash bomb from my pocket, already activated the trigger. With three leaping steps, I launch myself off the top of the roof, soaring through the air as the world slows, and hurl the bomb as hard as I can.

Then . . .

The flash explodes a foot away from the engine exhaust.

I land on a metal bridge, tucking and rolling as the fire roars over my head. The explosion rocks the flyer; the ship lurches backward. The pilot attempts to correct, but they're too near the tracks. When the ship jerks again to avoid the mag rail, the pilot miscalculates the spin and the wing glances off the tracks. Total loss of control. Just like I planned.

The flyer rushes toward the jungle floor, commandos jumping out of the hatch like rats. Then the ship crashes into the ground in a fiery explosion as the engines catch fire. Burning oil and melted plastic fill my nose. The heat from the flames singes my skin. The taste of ash mixed with blood and jungle rain fills my mouth.

Bloody brilliant.

I rush back down the levels, making my way to the tavern. Sena's managed to hack open the side door; syndicates and smoke push out of the opening. I calculate a head count as they rush out; there's barely thirteen of them. Corpo flyers usually hold up to thirty commandos. Even if only half the bastards survived the crash, we're going to be outnumbered and outgunned.

"We need to get out of here," Lyria shouts as she emerges from the smoke, the scavver leader behind her.

"And lead them into the jungle where they can find our paths and trails? Not a chance," Emeko barks as she kicks aside the remnants of the door to clear herself a path. "Stay and fight first, Revas. Prove that scavver interests are the same as syndicates'."

Lyria's hazel eyes narrow as she steps closer to Emeko. "Don't worry about our will to fight. You just hold up your end of the bargain."

The world is crashing down around us, commandos are filing out of the jungle, and these two are having a stare down. Unbelievable.

I step in between them. "Neither of you are going to get out of here alive if we don't get some more firepower!"

Shots ricochet off the doorframe and we scramble back behind some fallen debris for cover. I steal a glance without exposing myself. Sena ends up a few yards away behind the corner of a life pod. Emeko crouches next to me, her honey-brown eyes scanning the commandos as they emerge from the trees into the slums. She pulls a gun from somewhere and carefully aims, firing over the debris when a commando steps into range. Other shots echo hers as the syndicates start firing around us.

I spot Taggert at the jungle's edge farther down from our position. Of course he survived the crash. He's got a finger to his ear, and I know that he's checking the status of his comms. If he calls for more backup, we're all screwed. I reach into my pocket, one explosive left. He's too far for me to take him out from here, but at least the blast will knock him and other commandos back a few pegs.

"Heads up!" I shout, tossing the flash bomb into the air; it arches up, and as it descends back down to earth, the flash detonates, releasing a surge of fire and smoke near enough to the commandos, forcing them back.

"Sena, we need to take out Taggert!" I shout as fire engulfs the treetops. She nods, and trusting that the blast is keeping the corpos busy, I dart out of cover and run along the edge of the sprawl. The commandos' shots go wild, the smoke momentarily blinding them. I take a higher ramp while Sena and Iska follow my path on the ground level. I hear Lyria shout something and the syndicates return fire, giving us more cover to make our way closer. Fifty feet away and Taggert's back on his feet. We're out of time.

Without stopping, I scoop up a foot-long piece of metal debris and hurl it in his direction. It slices into the tree he's half hidden behind, embedding deep into the wood. His eyes jerk to me and he raises a handgun.

But instead of pointing at me, he lowers the barrel, aiming below the level I'm on.

"Sena!"

A shot echoes. I skid to a stop, peering over a ramp railing. The shot missed. But Sena is pinned down behind a barrier with no sign of Iska, and another commando is coming in to flank her from the jungle. Without a thought, I dive over the railing, flying straight at the commando below.

I crash into him, and we both go rolling onto the mud, knocking into Sena in the process. The commando scrambles to his knees, trying to get me off his back, but I wrap my arm around his neck and lock my legs on each of his thighs, sinking in a chokehold. Then Sena's leg connects with his exposed ribs and he falls face forward into the mud. I squeeze his throat tight and feel as he goes limp. I shove myself off the unconscious thug just in time to see a red blur dart across my vision. Another shot rings out and I grab for Sena, but she's not screaming in pain.

She's screaming for Iska.

Because the wolf's jaws are wrapped around Taggert's arm,

sending his shots wild as he stumbles into the muddy jungle. Iska's fangs sink in deep, and she jerks her head back and forth, ripping the flesh and meat of his arm even through his armor. Sena's rushing toward her as another commando from the tree line raises his gun, pointing it at Iska. I move but I can't get there fast enough.

All I see is another death that I can't stop.

Another friend I'm going to fail.

A shot fires.

But the commando drops.

I whip my head around—and find Lyria lowering a handgun as she sprints down a ramp. Behind her is Kiran, a group of armed syndicates along with dozens of sprawl residents following in his wake, people surging toward us on every level.

My breath catches in shock.

Kiran went and got backup.

That's why he was running so fast. To get us the firepower we needed. He didn't leave us. Or betray me. Maybe, for once, he's actually supporting the side he claims to be on.

The wave of syndicates and sprawl denizens push forward, firing relentlessly at the commandos, who start to fall back into the trees toward the plateau. On the run.

I take off toward Sena just as she leaps in front of Taggert and plants a foot in his chest, sending him flying away from her wolf. Shots zing past him as he struggles to his feet, his gun arm now useless and broken by his side. Another commando nearby grabs Taggert's other arm and drags him out of our range. Without slowing down, I pull both Sena and Iska behind a large tree right before bullets whiz by our heads. Around us, the sprawl is in chaos as the firefight continues.

Sena drops to her knees, checking Iska for injuries. I peer out from behind the tree trunk, watching Kiran help a fallen syndicate and Lyria shout orders while firing at the commandos. Flames consume the area, devouring parts of the sprawl and eating away at the treetops. The stench of blood and burning fills my nose. A handful of syndicates make their way toward Sena and me while the commandos regroup farther down. The residents of the sprawl have joined in, firing whatever they can at the corpo threat invading their territory.

The battle is spilling into the jungle, showing no sign of stopping.

A large drop of rain slaps against my shoulder and my instincts prickle. I glance up at the sky as more rain begins to fall. Another sound, beyond the growing storm, registers low in my ears.

More flyers are headed for us.

"We need to disappear deeper into the brush. TerraCo backup ships are already en route." Kiran's voice catches my attention. He's made his way to us, pausing behind another trunk for cover.

Emeko darts forward alongside him. "Then we don't have a lot of time. Hope you lot can keep up."

With a quick look at Sena and Iska, she slips past us into the jungle. Other syndicates follow her, running as the people of the sprawl buy them more time. Lyria sprints past next, still shouting directives at those who follow and those who stay behind. Kiran shifts his weight from one foot to the other, antsy to move. But his near-onyx eyes are looking at me.

"Well? Are you in?" he asks, his voice laced with impatience, but still, he's asking. Not demanding. Not controlling. I have my answer, my plan. I'll help them, not because of Kiran or Lyria. I'll do it to keep my promise to Alora. To be better than what I was made for.

"For her," I say, daring him to question otherwise. But then I quickly look to Sena. Because the decision is no longer entirely up to me.

She stares back at me, but no words are needed. I can see the want etched into every line of her face. She's aching to know more about the scavvers and her äma. Sena nods. I glance back at Kiran, catching something in his eyes before he smirks and moves after the syndicates.

Guess it's time to join this ragtag revolution and get shit done.

I offer a hand to Sena. She climbs to her feet, urging Iska forward, and together, the three of us follow the rebels into the jungle.

CHAPTER 19

We sprint deeper and deeper into the jungle, following a small river as it snakes away from the sprawl. The rain continues to fall around us, soaking through my layers into my skin. The sun has long since disappeared, either with the clouds or the coming dusk. Branches scratch my exposed arms and face as we sprint. Mud cakes my boots as I stomp through puddles, the thick muck threatening to pull me into the wet earth with each step. Next to me, Sena isn't faring much better as we follow the dozen or so syndicates trailing behind the scavver leader.

But still we run.

I keep my vision glued to Kiran's back as he plows ahead. Shouts and explosions still ring out even as we put distance between us and the sprawl. The corpo backup must've arrived. Soon, they'll be flying overhead, using infrared to spot us under the foliage. Following along this river will make us easy targets. One missile and our little rebellion ends in mud and flames. But venturing into the thicker brush is to invite another kind of death.

Still, Emeko doesn't slow. Leading us farther and farther away, she weaves through the jungle like she's part of every fern and vine. My internal compass generally knows the direction we're fleeing, but here on the ground, it's hard to piece together exactly where she's taking us. Time slips by too quickly and I feel the terrain beginning to rise as the remaining light fades away. We're heading out of the valley and into the mountains.

As soon as that thought hits me, the low hum of the mag field disappears entirely as we reach the edge of the mag zone and cross the invisible line where the true jungle begins.

Emeko veers away from the river just as another hum fills my ears. Flyers. I can't see them through the treetops or fully pinpoint them through the rain. Though the dusk partially masks their location, Taggert must be flying completely dark to try and sneak up on us.

But he can't hide from my senses.

Emeko weaves between two massive trees, and then suddenly, we're in a tiny clearing, just big enough for a small gang of scavvers atop six transpo ATVs, waiting for us in the downpour.

"Hop on!" Emeko waves her arm and leaps onto a vehicle without a driver.

Each transpo ATV has extended fencing along the back, allowing them to carry more passengers or supplies. The syndicates don't hesitate to jump on the ATVs, hanging on behind drivers and perching on the fenced frames. Kiran leaps onto the seat directly behind Emeko, followed by Lyria. Sena and I clamber onto the back, both of us gripping the frame as Emeko guns the acceleration.

Sena's eyes shoot to Iska, but the wolf is sprinting alongside us, happy to finally be able to run. Her tongue hangs out and her legs fly as she races the ATV.

"At least someone's having fun," Sena mumbles, just loud enough for me to pick up over the rain. The scavvers have modified the ATVs to run on batteries instead of fuel. Smart in a jungle where the predators come after loud noises rather than run from them. Also handy when escaping corpo flyers.

Ahead, Kiran has his hand cupped over his mouth as he whispers to Emeko. I could make out the words if I tried, but I don't need to. Based on Emeko's maneuvering of the ATV, Kiran is telling her where the flyers are and where they might be headed. His hearing is as sharp as mine, and I don't have to look behind us to know that he's steering us away from the searching ships. He did come back after all, even when I thought he'd abandoned us.

The speed of the ATVs, brisk even through the thick brush, keeps the corpos off our tail as the dusk around us turns to full night. Next to me, Sena's got a death grip on the caged frame with one hand, her knuckles white. I can hear her erratic heartbeat. She could survive anything on Tundar, but this is Maraas and nothing about the jungle is familiar. It's a world of new threats. Her other hand stays close to the arken blade at her side.

As true dark envelops us, the drivers flip on their headlights, illuminating the path in front of the transpos and casting the rest of the jungle in shadow. Iska keeps pace with us, her ears perking and an occasional whine escaping her throat. I know she can smell the creatures out there because my own nose is picking up scents, though we're traveling too fast for me to register anything specific. Which is fine. I don't want to know what lurks beyond the beam of light. I have to trust that Emeko knows where she's leading us, that she knows this jungle even in total blackout.

We may have decided to tag along with the rebels, but I can't help but feel very unprepared as the jungle stretches out around us. All I have is the serrated knife in my boot. No arken blade of my own. No more flash bombs. No firepower at all.

Rain continues to blanket us as we move. I'm soaked through to the bone and the cold wind nips at my skin. Without the sun beating down, the heat of the jungle is gone, replaced by a wet, humid cold. Not like the unforgiving ice of Tundar, but a deep chill nevertheless.

The darkness here is different than on other worlds. On Ceren or Ish, the lights of the corpo cities make it impossible for true night to be very dark. Even on Tundar, the white snow and ice reflect into the night, casting everything in an eerie gray. Only when we were deep in the splinter wood or tucked into a cave did the ice world dip into full darkness.

But here, the night is utterly complete. Beyond the beam of the headlight, it's impossible to make out anything. As the light bounces off the trees directly next to our trail, I catch glimpses of glowing red eyes and movement too fast for even me to track. With the rain and the shadows, not even the slightest glow of the fiery tahuayo flowers penetrate the night.

The darkness and calls of the nocturnal creatures send a shiver down my spine. I spent one night out here before. One of the most harrowing nights of my life.

And it wasn't when Kiran dumped me here. It was before that. The night Alora almost died. The night I realized that I couldn't let anything happen to her. The night I promised her I'd be better.

The memory trigger begins to crawl up the edges of my mind, an echo becoming real.

Alora had convinced me that we should borrow her father's flyer and go on a late-night cruise over the sprawl. She didn't want to be stuck in her room, cooped up like a caged animal. Those were her words, but I knew what it was to be locked in a cage. Missions and training were the only times I was let out of my room on Nova's fleet of ships. Even mealtimes were solitary if Nova thought our squads were fraternizing too much with each other. We were their property, not their children. They didn't raise us, their genopaths. They owned us.

So, when Alora said that to me, I agreed. We borrowed her father's flyer and took off toward the sprawl. We'd been flying only ten minutes when the right engine blew. A half-assed assassination attempt by someone working for Dekkard. But as I kept us afloat and made a wide circle to head back, the other engine exploded, too.

And the flyer plummeted into the jungle.

Unlike when Sena and I landed in the storm, Rixus's flyer didn't survive the explosion and crash. I woke up minutes later to burning flames and a ship scattered to pieces. I was still in the pilot's seat, having activated the parachute mechanism.

But Alora's seat next to me was empty.

Now, as we rush through the jungle on the ATVs, soaked to the bone, all I can see in the darkness and shadows is the wreckage around me and no sign of my friend. The replay finally triggers fully, but I don't fight it. A part of me feels like I deserve to watch it unfold again, to remind myself of what I lost, what I owe my friend. So, this time, I let the replay consume my vision, my thoughts. Let myself remember the panic, the fear, and the promise I eventually made when I thought the worst was happening.

In the memory replay, I unbuckle the safety belt. My wrist is badly bruised. Lacerations pepper my skin, my layers in shreds. Blood rushes down my face. But I don't let any of that stop me as I peel myself out of the wreckage. The only source of light comes from the fire still burning through parts of the broken ship along with the faint glow of tahuayo flowers scattered on the ground and in the trees. But it's enough. Not even true darkness would stop me from searching the remnants of the ship for my friend.

It feels like hours before I finally find her partially buried under a wing fragment, the metal having landed across her ribs. She's covered in cuts and blood and barely conscious. Her pulse beats too slowly in my ears.

"Alora!" In my head, her name is a shout on my lips, but really, my voice is nothing more than a terrified whisper among the towering trees. I shake her shoulders, pat her cheeks, but she doesn't stir. Doesn't move. She can't be dying. She can't be.

My emotions threaten to drown me. I've never felt like this before. Like someone's punched me so hard in the chest my insides feel hollowed out. Some part of me knows that rain is falling, that the jungle is creeping closer to the wreck. But the rest of me has never experienced this kind of all-consuming desperation, and I find myself slipping into a pit deep in my mind where the absolute worst has happened and I can't do a damn thing.

A roar reaches my ears and my instincts prickle. Not the rumble of the thunder above, but the call of a predator nearby. The sound wakes me up, pulls me from the despair. My training kicks in and I command adrenaline to flood my system.

I will not let her die out here.

I drag the wing off Alora and wrap her torso up tight using the ship's safety belts, but there's nothing I can do if she has internal bleeding. I have to keep us alive until rescue comes.

The weapons I had onboard are lost in flames. My armor is in pieces. But somehow I fend off the anacrocs that find their way to us. Giant reptiles that slink through the marsh with jaws capable of ripping through even reinforced exocarbon. The scent of our blood is a beacon, calling to the massive preds. I use pieces of debris as barriers and blunt weapons to protect us from the monsters. We barely survive the night.

Just as the darkness shifts with the coming dawn, Alora opens her eyes.

"Remy," she croaks. Her voice is no louder than a whisper, but I hear it as loud as any shout.

"I'm here," I call, rushing to kneel beside her after erecting a final barrier between us and the wild.

"Sorry I got us in this mess." She coughs, wincing in pain.

I shake my head. "It's fine. You're going to be fine. Don't try to talk."

"Promise . . ."

I lean closer. "What? Anything."

"To be . . . better. Better than . . . what we're made for."

Despite her injuries, despite her exhaustion, she holds my gaze as I stare into her blue eyes.

"Promise," she whispers. "You . . ." She trails off, too weak to speak.

"I promise," I say. The magnitude of my words isn't lost on me even though they are a whisper in the middle of the jungle, far from the world we came from. I've only ever belonged to Nova, only ever been owned. But with those two little words, everything changes.

We choose to belong to each other.

As the jungle continues to come at us from all sides, I realize this promise is more than just saving her from the immediate threat. It means I have to stop the coup. I have to stop Kiran and Dekkard. I don't know how I'll go against orders, but I'll find a way.

The hum of a flyer reaches my ears minutes before one zooms overhead, then lands in the clearing. Alora's father.

When he sees Alora, near broken, I watch as a piece of his heart fractures, the pain clear across his face. The hollow despair from earlier magnifies and stabs into my gut, sharper than any real stab wounds I've had before. Syndicates flood the area, taking out the final anacrocs, attending to my friend, putting her on a stretcher. As they load Alora into the ship, Rixus finds me trailing after her.

"Remy." His voice cracks when he says my name. "Thank you for saving my daughter."

I open my mouth to say what I've been trained to say. That it's my job. My duty. But instead, other words spill out. "I couldn't live with myself if anything happened to her."

Alora's father stares at me on the ramp to the flyer, his daughter—my friend—unconscious three feet away. He finally nods as I tear my eyes off her form and look back to the syndicate boss beside me.

"I believe you," he says. "You won't let anything like this happen again, will you?" His voice is no longer soft; it has a sharp edge to it. He's not fully blaming me for what happened but not letting me off the hook either. I think he knows everything about me in this moment. About what I am and why I am truly on his world.

Without hesitating, I shake my head. "Nothing will hurt her

while I'm alive." I meet his eyes, showing him some of my own sharp edges. I repeat the same words from earlier, a second commitment, just as important as the one I made to Alora.

"I promise," I tell him. And I mean it.

But three days later, I would lose everything. I didn't even get to see her again before she was taken from me.

At that thought, the replay in my head begins to dissipate, the claws letting go of my mind, bringing me out of the memory. The wreckage of the ship disappears, but the jungle remains, haunting me.

Because three days after that crash, Kiran drugged me, dumped me in this very same jungle, and went to finish the coup. Rixus was dead by the time I hacked my way back up to Verem. Kiran and Alora were both gone, and everything I finally belonged to, finally chose myself, was taken from me.

And I didn't keep either promise at all.

CHAPTER 20

The slowing of the ATVs draws me out of my haunted memories. The rain has lessened into a thin mist. Artificial lights peek through the brush and spider vines up ahead. Voices and heartbeats of a couple dozen people, the movement concentrated around a few structures. A scavver camp.

The transpo breaks through the trees into a clearing, smaller than a city block. Piles of wood and other materials litter the space, the broken-down remains of makeshift buildings. Some structures still stand, though they're mostly posts and cloth. Lights hang throughout the trees around spider vines, illuminating the clearing. Small magnetic generators sit along the border, emitting a low-frequency pulse to keep the major preds from coming too close. We're too far out in the jungle for the mag zone, so the scavvers have made their own. Though I don't think the puny generators would be enough to keep out a herd of batimalu. Especially the crazed ones controlled by Taggert.

Emeko pulls over beside the structures along with the other ATVs, where more servo trucks are parked, and kills the engine. The scavvers who were scurrying around before slow and stop in their tracks. Waiting.

The scavver leader grins as she faces them. She raises her voice loud, letting it carry across the clearing.

"The Vega stands with us."

A few cheers and whoops erupt from the scavvers, but not all seem thrilled to see syndicates standing in their jungle. My brain subconsciously marks their faces as Emeko raises her arm for silence.

"We move at dawn." More cheers at that, more genuinely pleased expressions. Emeko grins once more, then lets the authority slip away from her tone as she turns to the dozen or so syndicates around us. "But right now, I'm guessing you lot are hungry. Hope you like bush meat stew."

She points to a half-standing structure. "Over there's what's left of the kitchen. Barracks are behind. Find a cot and get some shut-eye. I'll send the doc over if anyone's got wounds that need tending."

The syndicates climb off the ATVs and head for the kitchen. Sena lingers, watching as they mingle with scavvers. I stretch my back, idly staying near her, then I turn and find Kiran behind me. His damp dark hair is pushed back from his face; his expression is oddly open as he looks at me, glancing down, scanning for injuries.

"What?" I snap, trying not to focus on the scar I gave him.

His near-onyx eyes jump up to mine. "Are you . . . okay?"

I stare at him. "Yeah. You saw me run through the jungle for miles. I'm clearly okay."

He nods to Sena on the opposite side of the ATV. "What about your . . . friend?"

My stare turns into a glower at the emphasis he puts on the word "friend." He didn't like it when Alora was my friend, and now he's got a problem with Sena? Or is he trying to remind me that I involved her because of my instincts?

"My friend is fine." I decide right then and there that Sena is here because we are friends, regardless of why I asked her to come. I wouldn't have made it this far without her, and that means more than my instincts and genetic impulses. "You don't have to worry about her because I've got her back. That's what friends do, not that you'd understand."

"Remy, I—" He runs a hand through his hair, but before he can attempt to say anything else, Emeko interrupts.

"You four, with us." She's standing beside Lyria, motioning us to follow. I realize she's counting Iska as one of our little troupe. At least someone understands friendship.

We trail behind her toward the structure opposite the makeshift kitchen, more of a tent than a building. I feel Kiran behind me as we walk. The memory of the jungle is still clinging to my skin, and it's hard not to be angry as I watch him out of the corner of my eye. Even if he suddenly acts like he cares, like he has changed, I shouldn't trust him, no matter what.

It's his fault I lost everything.

His sharp eyes reach mine, and I turn my attention away from the concern in his face. Another scheme, another lie. I ignore him and keep my focus on Emeko's back as she pushes aside the canvas flap of the tent. We slip inside, finally out of the wet rain. An older man with pale, sallow skin and white hair stands behind a collapsible, ancient-looking holoscreen, watching us file in. His brown eyes are so light, they're nearly colorless. His pulse catches my attention; it's erratic and slow. His breathing is labored, fluttering. He's not afraid or nervous; he's either sick or very frail.

Emeko tosses over some clean rags from a stack of discarded clothes. I catch one before it hits me square in the face.

"You all have more mud on you than the wolf," she says. I grumble silently to myself that it's probably her fault for driving so erratically, but I begin to wipe off the muddy water as Kiran and Sena do the same.

Emeko points to the man. "This is Mirko. He may be older than dirt, but he's been on Maraas longer than anyone and knows all the players and moving parts. He's in charge of our scouts and guerilla groups." She gestures in our direction, introducing us one by one. "The de facto boss of the Vega here, Lyria Revas, the one and only." Her eyes slide to me momentarily. "Though maybe that's up for debate."

Emeko points to Kiran next. "Kiran Lore, the catalyst for the shit that went down two years ago," she continues. "I know you recognize him, Mirko. Quit giving him that blank face. These two, Remy and Sena"—she points at us—"crashed from Tundar or some such nonsense. They might be with us, or they might be spies."

"We're not spies," I mutter, crossing my arms. Mirko gives me a nod, but his eyes linger on Sena.

"I'll vouch for them," Lyria says. "They're not spies and they're not working for TerraCo. They're here for their own reasons, but those reasons align with our cause."

Emeko rolls her eyes. "All right, they're probably not corpo spies at the very least." The scavver leader's gaze locks on me. "But you two are in this room now, so either you're with us to the end or you turn tail and get out. You stay and betray us, I slit your throat, simple as. Got it?"

I look to Sena, who, after a moment, nods once.

"We're in," I say. I made Alora a promise to be better, to be more. That means no more operating from the sidelines like I did on Tundar. It means getting my hands dirty again and this time for the very syndicates I helped destroy. This time, I'm going to get it right.

"Outstanding," Emeko drawls, her bored expression contrary to her word choice. "Don't make us regret it or that throat slitting will happen sooner rather than later." She turns to Mirko. "Now that we're all on board, give us the rundown, old man. What did you find out?"

Mirko takes his time tearing his eyes away from Sena, no matter the glare coming from Emeko as she waits. I note the look, immediately wondering if he recognizes Sena and knew her äma. One glance at Sena and her furrowed brow tells me she's thinking the same thing. Finally, Mirko waves a gnarled, slightly shaky hand over the holoscreen, and a map of the valley blinks to life over the table. He points at various markings dotting the flickering holo.

"Our intel gathered over the last few weeks concludes that there are a number of corpo substations that have popped up across the jungle. They appear to be fairly new, only a few months old according to our data. Generally, they're well-hidden and hard to find—"

"Except for that one within spitting distance of the sprawl," Lyria chimes in. The one she and Emeko were casing when I followed them. At least, they were casing it—until Taggert released his batimalu on the commando and spotted me through the camera.

"With the exception of that one substation," Mirko continues, "the rest of them are deeper in the jungle. We assume they're using the one near the sprawl to keep an eye on residents, as it's one of the more active and busy stations. Though we don't know why exactly."

He takes a breath. "We also don't know the purpose behind any of the substations yet. The security is too tight, and we haven't gotten an opening to get closer and determine what the equipment is for or what the smokestacks at each one are producing. We haven't even been able to capture a sample of the substance."

"I'll find out," Kiran volunteers. "It won't be hard for me to sneak in alone and figure out what they're up to."

"Put those fancy enhanced senses to good use, then," Emeko says with a smirk. Kiran moves as if to leave now, in the dead of night in the middle of the rain, but Lyria puts a hand on his arm.

"Stay awhile first. It won't do any of us any good if Weiland discovers you sniffing around those substations. We need her to think you're playing all sides."

Kiran grows still under her touch, and something about it makes my pulse speed up. His stone face tells me he's not happy about it. But then after a beat, he nods. "I'll go at first light."

"This one is closest to our current location." Mirko points to a spot on the holo, his finger trembling slightly. "According to the scouts, security was lightened in the last few days. It would be a good place to get intel without getting caught."

Kiran studies the map momentarily. I watch as his eyes jump from dot to dot, watch him scheme. I can almost see the calculations happening in his head. The outpost Mirko pointed out may be closer to us, but it might not be the one Kiran thinks is the most important. I know he's analyzing the data, piecing together possible scenarios, and coming up with odds complex enough for a computer to calculate. It's the part of his brain that is infinitely different from mine.

Strategizing based on intel and potential data is what he was built for. He's the planner whereas I'm the improviser, made to react based on observations—data made not of facts but rather people's facial expressions or elevated heartbeats. Mood shifts and tone changes. Hesitations and breathing patterns.

And I sense a shift in Kiran as he stares at the map. A tick of his eyebrow or the look in his eyes. He's realized something, something important that he's not letting on. Then he nods to Lyria and disappears out of the tent. My body instinctively wants to follow him, to keep an eye on his movements, but Lyria asks a question that cuts into my focus.

"Why would Weiland build a bunch of substations in the middle of the jungle? They're not settlements or future mag rail expansions. From the intel I gathered in Verem, Weiland is no longer focusing on the exocarbon or other resources from the mountains. The storms are getting worse, but she doesn't seem to be bothered by the changes. Why build these stations deep in the jungle at all? None of it makes sense."

Emeko shrugs. "Does it need to make sense? Corpos always act on profit. Whatever she's doing out there, it's definitely not for our benefit."

"Maybe they're planning to build something that will mess with the environment?" Sena's voice is quiet but firm. "That's what they did on Tundar. Set off an explosion at a factory out on the ice. All to increase the planet's temperature a fraction so they could mine more exocarbon. Maybe these bases have something to do with mining, but we just don't know how yet."

Lyria considers her. "That's not a bad guess. Maybe she intends to start mining in these areas despite the storm and lack of infrastructure."

Emeko waves her hand through the holomap. "You're focusing on the wrong thing. It doesn't matter what they're planning—it only matters that we stop them."

"You're right," Lyria says with a sigh. "We could sit here and argue about their motives all night, but ultimately, it won't change our plan. We have to stop them before things get worse."

"And we certainly can't change anything in one night," Mirko says, a hint of worry in his voice. "It's been a long journey and I think rest is in order for all of us."

Emeko rolls her eyes at him again but pats the man affectionately on the arm as she turns to go.

"Oh, I almost forgot. Sena is—" she starts, but Mirko holds up a hand.

"You think I wouldn't recognize the granddaughter of my oldest friends?" He turns to Sena. "You are Neran's child, are you not? You are her spitting image."

Sena swallows loud enough for me to hear. I move slightly closer to her on instinct, but she gives me a reassuring look.

She finally finds her voice. "I am." The old man smiles, his eyes full of light and tears.

"Welcome home, Sena. Though it may not feel like it after being on Tundar, your äma was born here. Her parents were among my closest friends."

Sena shifts uncomfortably, wrapping a protective arm around Iska's back. "I never knew my grandparents. They . . . died shortly after landing on Tundar. That's all Äma ever told me."

Mirko lowers his head briefly. "Their health, like mine, was

I pause, letting her know I heard her, but I don't turn back. I just nod over my shoulder as I walk away from the syndicate.

My feet lead me to an empty cot in the barracks, but then I spot Kiran dozing not far away. I try not to think of our conversation in the burned building back in the sprawl. Instead, I wonder what he saw on the holomap that piqued his interest; wonder how all of this fits in the bigger puzzle of TerraCo and Nova. I need to know the truth. For Alora and for myself. I know there's more, more Kiran hasn't told me.

He said he'd move out at first light. He could wake up at any minute, rested and ready to go, but I need fuel and rest myself. I grab a bowl from the remains of the kitchen area and slurp down the bland stew. Then I pick a cot near Kiran's and I wait, half asleep, half awake. My internal clock keeps track of the time as I doze.

A quick few hours later, the total darkness has slipped away, covering the clearing in a predawn gray. My body is somewhat rested. Enough so that when I sense Kiran moving, I'm ready to follow him. No matter where he's heading.

I hop up and stretch, taking quick stock of the barracks. The scavvers have switched shifts. Those working last night are sleeping while others are beginning to move about and finish the teardown of the base.

My senses gravitate toward Sena and Iska, dozing a few cots over. I hesitate for a second but decide against waking them. Sena could use the rest after everything that's happened. I wonder what sort of things Mirko told her about her äma. Hopefully good things. She deserves that a lot more than she deserves getting dragged out into the jungle to tag along with me. She could belong here with them.

My footsteps make no sound as I slip by them both. Iska's nose twitches, but the wolf doesn't wake.

Moving silently across the base, I follow my nose to Kiran, staying downwind so he won't pick up my scent. He's grabbing a few provisions from one of the servo trucks, a long arken blade strapped across his back. Prepping for the jungle. To my surprise, Lyria appears from the other side of the truck. I guess I'm not the only one keeping tabs on Kiran. They have a short discussion too quiet for even me to hear, and then they fade into the shadows of the trees.

I wait one minute. Then another as I calculate their direction and compare it to the holo Mirko showed us yesterday, the map's image perfectly clear in my head. As I suspected, they're not going to the substation closest to us. I follow in their wake, peeking into the servo truck and finding a few extra water canteens and some homemade jerky. I grab a canteen and shove some meat in my mouth, and as I chew it down, I spot a small box of flash bombs pushed halfway under the front seat. Perfect. I needed to restock. I take a few, their weight reassuring in my pockets.

With a smile, I follow Kiran and Lyria into the wild.

A light mist of rain blankets the jungle, and the night chill dissipates as the sun begins to rise ahead of me. On nearby spider vines, I catch sight of a few tahuayo blossoms closing their petals as the dawn arrives, their glow fading when the sunlight hits them. And with the sun comes the heat. My wet clothes begin to dry and then dampen again as sweat replaces goose bumps. After just fifteen minutes, the sun is peeking through the treetops and the warmth of the growing day presses against my skin.

Kiran leaves very few tracks, just as he was trained. Lyria's footsteps are careful, too, almost as undetectable as his. Not that it matters. I can easily catch their scent even with their five-minute lead. I stay as downwind as possible to keep Kiran from sniffing me out, but I know there's a chance he's predicted my move.

But their trail doesn't really matter since I've already deduced where they're going. They're heading back the way we came, toward the busiest substation. The one where Taggert released the batimalu on his own commando. I saw the smokestacks and the buildings when I was perched on that branch. Kiran doesn't want to gather intel from a quiet base. He needs to learn as much as possible, and the only way to do that is by going to the most active one. It's farther away and the risk of getting caught is higher. But the higher the risk, the bigger the reward.

While he's the strategist, intel is my forte, so as I follow them through the jungle, I piece together what I know about TerraCo and the substations.

TerraCo is an energy company at its core. Its main business is producing sub-cell energy modules that power ships and flyers. It also controls power sources across the Assembly worlds. Hydroplants, nuclear power, solar energy—if there's a power station on a world, it's most likely owned by TerraCo. The company established bases on Maraas years and years ago to mine the mountains, not only for exocarbon, which lines the tubes in the power supply chains, but for other potential mineral deposits to help with overall fuel production.

The substations are a mystery, though. The smokestacks were not the kind used in energy production. No, they looked more like they were pumping something into the air on purpose. Whatever the corpos are doing, it's tied to what happened two years ago. It's tied to Nova and the Vega.

And maybe even to Alora.

Because if Kiran is right, then all of this—the corpos, the syndicates, and Nova—is connected. And maybe that's why Kiran won't just tell me where Alora is. Maybe she's in as much danger as the scavvers or the people in the sprawl. If that's the case, I'll do anything in my power to make sure she's okay.

I made a promise to her father. I made a promise to her.

I won't break them again.

Harsh light illuminates the wild around me as the sun moves higher in the sky. The gray-dark shadows of the jungle turn into lush greens as I continue to trek up and down the hilly terrain, across streams and puddles alike. I check the direction of the substation against my internal compass. Still on course, we've probably hiked eight miles in the last few hours. Little signs of humanity catch my eye: a lost piece of plastic, cleared-out sections of trees. Must be getting closer to the sprawl now. I still don't hear the strong hum of the mag rail, but another sound, lower and nearly unnoticeable, pulls at my ears. A smaller mag field. I veer toward it; it has to be the substation.

Another ten minutes of trekking and not only can I hear the hum of a magnetized fence and smell the tang of metal and sweat, but also, down a small hill ahead, I can see a clearing peeking through the predatory spider vines and underbrush. I pick a tree and scramble up to the higher branches just like before; only this time, there are no commandos out past the perimeter even though the main gate is wide open.

From this vantage point on higher ground, I can make out the entire substation.

The fenced-in area has a flyer landing pad on one side and, on the other, a bunch of machinery I don't recognize, even after two years of posing as an engineer across multiple worlds. I can identify the various parts: pipes and tubes hooked up to generators and turbines. But from this distance, I can't tell what exactly the machinery's purpose is.

Four pipe-like towers as tall as the treetops jut out in a line between the generators. In a far corner, a surface-to-air missile carrier sits unguarded with three cannons pointing at the sky. Pretty serious security for a small station. Who the hell would the corpos need to fire at when they're the only ones with flyers on this world?

A short watchtower looms over one end of the square compound, and life pods are set up underneath it. A giant radar dish is perched on the top of one of them. Must be the operating room for whatever this place is. On the far side, across from the life pods, a small building pushed up to the fence stands on its own. My nose tells me it's the outhouse.

The perimeter fence encasing the whole place is magnetized just like the rail line; the slight magnetic force pulses in my ears and hums across my skin even up here in the tree. The range isn't as powerful as the mag rail, but it's strong enough to keep bigger preds away from the station.

I count three corpo commandos on guard duty. One's up in the watchtower; two others pace below just at the fence gate. Well, one is pacing. The other looks like he's taking a nap. More commandos are inside the life pods, but luckily there are no flyers on the landing pad, meaning Taggert probably isn't out here. I scan the trees and the brush surrounding the station, and I don't see any sign of Kiran or Lyria, though I can still detect their scents.

The generator whirs to life, and one of the large towers jutting out of the machine begins to flame at the top. They're burning something? As the smoke grows and the fire burns, a turbine fan next to the tower kicks on. The noise from the giant fan blades is a racket compared to the general quiet of the jungle. I need to get downwind of the smokestacks. Maybe then I can detect what they're pumping out. I climb silently down the trunk, keeping a lookout for commandos.

Movement to my left has my instincts prickling, but then a familiar voice calls out just loud enough for me to hear.

"Looking for us?"

CHAPTER 21

I step out from behind the tree at Kiran's voice. Like me, he drops down from a nearby branch. He's pulled his hair back and off his face, like he's done hiding behind the dark brown strands. Lyria follows him, her feet near silent even in the mud. Her own red hair is pulled back tightly. Gone is the black cap, and somehow, she looks more serious without it. Less like an undercover syndicate and more like someone leading a small-scale revolution. Kiran studies me with interest, but Lyria speaks first.

"What are you doing here, Remy?"

"Gathering intel." I cross my arms.

"And who exactly are you gathering intel on?" Kiran smirks. "The corpo substation down there or us up here?"

I glare at him, and to my surprise, so does Lyria. Guess she doesn't like conjecture and accusations either.

"Like you, I came to see the substation," I say to him. "I volunteered to help this ragtag rebellion. I'm good at intel, so this is me helping."

Lyria crosses her arms, mimicking my posture. She looks from me to Kiran and then her eyes lock on me again.

"We can trust you, right?"

Last night, she was glad I'm here. This morning, she's questioning my loyalty. But something about the intensity in her gaze compels me to answer with the truth.

Well, some of the truth.

"You can trust that I want the Vega back in control and Weiland gone. We"—I point at Kiran—"got played by Nova to put Weiland in power. I won't be their chump, not now, not ever again." There. That was mostly truthful. Lyria stares at me for a beat; some emotion that I can't quite pinpoint flickers in her hazel eyes. Then she nods.

"Good." Her jaw sets; any softness in her face from our conversation last night is gone, replaced by hard edges and sharp eyes. The shift happens in an instant as she points to the substation. "The answers we need are in that station. You and Kiran are going to sneak into the base together, since he tells me your strengths are getting into places and making people think you belong."

Her words dig into my skin. I don't know if she chose them on purpose, but they're like salt rubbing in an old, festering wound. Because that is all I'm good for. Making people think I belong. Not actually belonging.

"Remy." Kiran steps toward me, softening his voice, like he can see the hurt under my skin. "You don't have to go." Then he quirks an eyebrow. "I know you're a bit . . . rusty. Maybe even a little slow. I'll go alone. I'll be fine."

I gawk at his shift in tone. "Excuse me?"

"You were at your peak two years ago, but you've been pretty lax since then. No training, no practice. The chances of you getting caught are much higher than if I go down there."

Is he . . . baiting me? Or genuinely judging me? Is this him falling into our old dynamic or him using the taunt to redirect my focus from the sting of Lyria's words? Friend or foe. Partner or enemy. I never know with him. And maybe yes, a part of me is thankful for his distraction, but the rest of me is pissed he still knows exactly what sets me off and is using that to get a rise out of me, even if it is for my benefit.

"I'm not out of practice nor am I slow." I grind out each word. "Instincts and skills don't fade when they're hard-coded into your genes, you chump. I can easily get in and out, probably faster without you to slow me down."

"Are you sure you can do it alone?" Lyria's looking at me like she can't tell if I'm going to break under the pressure. She doesn't know me, though. I don't break. And she obviously doesn't know how well I can play this game.

"Of course I can. But what are you going to give me in return?" I ask them both, then repeat Kiran's words from the outpost: "Nothing taken, nothing given."

Lyria's lips suddenly curl into a half smile, an expression that's oddly triggering. Alora would smile in a similar way when she was scheming up some new plan that would inevitably put the two of us in danger. And now, for whatever reason, I see an echo of that. An old ghost haunting me in a strange girl's smile. I shake off the unnerving feeling quickly. I don't need any triggers setting off replays right now.

"If you find out what they're doing without getting caught,"

Lyria replies, her smirk growing, "I'll make Kiran tell you the an-swers to those questions you've got about your friend."

Kiran's head jerks to Lyria in surprise, anger flashing across his face. He didn't expect that. I didn't either. It's too obvious, too easy. Here I am, having a thought about Alora, and then Lyria comes in, offering the information of her whereabouts to me. She clearly knew what I wanted the whole time and only now offers the info? It's suspicious as hell and makes it clear to me that Lyria is playing her own games, especially if Kiran is pissed by her offer.

Maybe he and Lyria aren't as close as he thought. Maybe she's using him as much as he is her. Regardless of her motivations, the fact that Lyria is pissing Kiran off makes me smile despite the mess I'm standing in.

"Deal," I say. Might as well take her bait. I'm going to check out the substation anyway.

"You can't make me do anything—" Kiran starts. Lyria silences him with a look. Interesting. He presses his lips together, swallow-ing whatever else he wanted to say. For now. Instead of arguing further, he gestures to the base down the hill.

"Better hurry up, Remy," he says.

I smile with fake sweetness at him. "Don't go anywhere, partner."

He glares murder at Lyria and me both, and that fuels me even further. With a chuckle and a real grin, I slip silently down the hill.

※

After I circle the base a few times, carefully watching the com-mandos' movements, an idea wiggles its way into my head. The light mist still falling makes for good cover, but it will only get me so far. I need something stronger to make the idea work. As I start moving closer, a flyer appears over the treetops. Inside the fence, commandos scramble to prep for landing, and an even better opening presents itself.

While the commandos' attention is on the flyer, I rush to the perimeter fence and press myself as close as possible to the metal, then make my way to the open gate. None of them even look in my direction as I slip inside; the commandos' focus is wholly on the ship and its descent. I duck into a corner behind the support posts under the watchtower. No one notices me as I take in the layout of the substation.

To my left is the control room and the second life pod; a stack of large crates lies just outside the life pod entrance—a good place for cover. Beyond that, there are plenty of other hiding spots among the mess of equipment and machinery that lead to the four towers in the middle of the substation. The towers themselves make a nice barrier between me and the flyer. It'll be near impossible for anyone in the air to spot me through the smokestacks. I peek around to my right. The surface-to-air missile carrier, still unguarded, sits just beside the landing pad. A loud option, but one that could work in my favor if worse comes to worse.

As the ship touches down, the commandos line up in front of it, and warning bells sound in my head. Whoever or whatever is inside must be high priority. Which means the risk of getting caught just tripled. I push adrenaline into my veins as the flyer's side hatch opens and more commandos file out.

Using the noise and movement to my advantage, I steal forward, sprinting the ten feet to the control room and ducking behind the large shipping crates. My position is still too close to the watchtower for the guard stationed up there to take notice. He'd have to lean far over the railing to spy me hiding between the crates, and I know his attention is currently occupied.

Another quick glance over the crates and all eyes are still on the flyer. I take the moment to pry open a corner of the crate closest to me, and a whiff of acidic chemicals hits my nose. Inside are what look like missiles, but the sleek metal tubes are not filled with explosives—that much I'm instantly sure of. My mind catalogues the scents, quickly identifying what chemicals lie within. Puzzle pieces click together as I realize what the chems are for. I am taking a deep breath to confirm my suspicions when shouts draw my attention.

I duck back down but don't see anyone close enough to be a threat. I peer around the side of the crate; the commandos are waiting as a tall figure steps out of the ship's bay.

Taggert. Of course. Just my luck. He's got his arm in a sling, and I smile thinking of Iska's teeth in his skin. Chump.

He shouts at a few commandos, and they peel off, heading straight for the crates I'm behind. I move slowly so as not to draw attention, keeping low and slipping into the open door next to the control room. It's a converted life pod that I guessed correctly were the barracks. Cots and lockers fill the small space. Not a soul in sight either. All hands on deck for Taggert's arrival.

This will be almost too easy.

I open a few lockers and find a vest and helmet that I quickly slip on. I tuck all my hair inside the helmet and make sure that it's tilted forward, casting a shadow across most of my face. Adjusting my posture, stiffening my spine and raising my chin, I head back outside.

I keep my pace unhurried, just an average soldier on patrol passing the barracks, then a locked equipment closet, and then making my way to the perimeter fence. I walk until I'm nearly next to the flyer's tail, keeping an eye on Taggert in my periphery the entire time, watching as he points at the crates and calls out orders. Everyone is too busy buzzing around him to notice a lone commando at the fence. Then, just when I reach the corner closest to the flyer, he walks away from the ship and toward the crates.

Another opening I won't waste.

While Taggert's got his attention on the crates, shouting about some being loaded and others left behind, I move closer to the opened ship hatch. The commandos seem to have left the cargo bay mostly unattended. How nice for me.

I walk right up the ship's loading ramp and grab the manifest datapad by the door release. All ships have them, especially corpo ships. Heaven forbid TerraCo loses even a chit of profit from a lack of organizational oversight.

Quickly scrolling through the supplies listed for the last couple of runs, I glimpse enough to confirm my suspicions about the crates. My mind begins to put the pieces together, my stomach sinking at the implications. I keep one eye on the data and the other on the pilot as he busies himself in the cockpit, tapping out coordinates for their next flight.

Voices and footsteps approach, so I keep my head dipped as I continue flipping through the manifest like it's my job, like I belong here. The pilot calls out at someone from the forward entrance.

"Sir, can you confirm the coordinates for the next drop? They're not located at any of the other substations."

"Stop asking questions, trooper," Taggert's voice responds, dripping with disdain. "You may have moved up in the ranks since Graves got himself killed, but that doesn't give you the clearance he had. You earn that, like everything else."

My heart speeds up at the mention of Graves and the long-reaching consequences of a simple bar fight, but I don't let it show. I can't change what happened; I can only make sure it doesn't happen again. The pilot snaps his mouth shut and nods.

"Now, finish helping them load up the crates. I'll fly myself to the next drop zone. You find your own way back to HQ, got it?"

I keep the datapad mostly in front of my face as the pilot rushes out, and Taggert doesn't seem to notice that someone else is in the ship.

Whatever those coordinates lead to, I need to know. I slide the datapad back into its holder and turn away from Taggert, peeking out the bay doors, looking for a way to distract him. Just beyond the cargo bay, four commandos lift up one of the crates and head straight for me.

Without a second thought, I pull a flash bomb out of my pocket and roll it down the ramp, right toward the men, before I move back into the shadow of the loading bay.

"Flash bomb!" a voice calls.

"Watch out!"

"Get down!" someone else shouts. There's a crash as the commandos drop the crate, followed by instant commotion. I chuckle silently. Of course, I didn't activate the trigger mechanism, but they're too panicked to notice. The distraction works because Taggert's out of the cockpit and outside in a flash.

"What the hell is going on?"

I steal forward to the pilot's seat and quickly bring up the coordinates on the holoscreen. The spot isn't too far from here, right along the base of the mountains. But the pilot was right—the location doesn't correspond to any of the substation coordinates I memorized from Mirko's map.

"Who the hell dropped a flash bomb?" Taggert's voice has reached new decibels.

Better work on my exit strategy.

I squat down and unlatch a panel underneath the flyer's dashboard. My fingers feel their way across wires and chips and finally find the section I'm looking for. With a solid yank, I pull out a nest of wires that connect the stabilizers to the thrusters, effectively making it impossible for the ship to take off safely. I shove the wires in my pocket and reattach the panel. The holoscreen will alert Taggert, but getting a fix will take time.

Time enough for me to get out of here and figure out what's so secretive about those coordinates.

Keeping my eyes forward, I walk right back out of the cargo bay just as the commandos are lifting the crate again. Taggert's storming toward the cockpit, and someone has removed the deactivated flash bomb. Without stopping, I scoop up some broken wood from the dropped crate as if I got stuck with cleanup duty. I walk past the towers, slowing my pace to get a better look at them now that I'm beginning to understand their purpose.

The turbine fans kick on and the generators whir to life as I pass.

The heat from the flames within the thin towers makes the humid air even heavier, hotter, and sweat pools underneath my layers and the commando vest. Even my hair is sweating at this point. My gaze lands on the mechanisms and control panels, but tinkering with them would bring too much attention, and I wouldn't be able to slip back out the way I came. The towers need to be stopped — I'm sure of that now. But first, I need to get out of here, and fast, before Taggert attempts to take off and realizes someone's been tampering with his ship.

I round the final tower and find myself facing the barracks.

The lock on the equipment room door gives me no trouble as I punch in a universal override code that Nova taught us years ago. Once inside, it takes me only a second to find some comms being charged. I switch one on and lower my voice an octave.

"Base, this is watchtower," I say urgently. "We've got movement in the trees up here! Scavvers, I repeat, scavvers on the horizon, heavily armed with ATV transpos, heading this way. Full lockdown, go into full lockdown!"

I shut off the comms just as multiple voices crackle in response. An alarm goes off and I slip back outside, the sirens piercing through the noise of the base. The commandos are springing into action, rushing to posts along the perimeter fence. Using their movement as cover, I race toward the now-closing gate. Shouts ring out.

"What's their location?"

Forty feet away and the gate is closing fast.

I break into a sprint.

"Watchtower, do you copy?"

Twenty feet.

The main gate is nearly closed, but I will speed into my legs.

"I've got no eyes on enemy movement. Nothing on visuals!"

Ten feet.

"Who gave that order?"

I slide across the ground, squeezing through the opening just before the gate snaps shut behind me. I hug the perimeter fence, quickly darting away from the watchtower corner before I can be spotted. Once I'm on the opposite side of the substation, I hold my position in the shadow of the fence, waiting until the commando in the watchtower is looking at another part of the jungle. Then I slip into the trees unnoticed.

I keep my movements slow and careful back to where I left

Kiran and Lyria. Hopefully, they're waiting behind cover and not moving around like targets while the base alarm echoes through the jungle. I quickly dump the commando vest and helmet, glad to lose the extra layers.

Cooler, heavier rain begins to pitter-patter, falling lightly across the jungle, each drop sinking into my sweaty layers and exposed skin. On Tundar, I was constantly cold. Here, I'm constantly wet. At least the rain provides extra cover as I make my way up the hill. But I know the truth about the storm cycle now.

The rain is a symptom; the corpos are the disease.

And this drizzle is just the beginning of the true storm coming our way.

CHAPTER 22

"You weren't supposed to alert the entire jungle to your presence." Kiran's near-onyx eyes follow me as I slink around a tree, finding him and Lyria exactly where I left them.

"Please," I drawl, brushing raindrops off my face. "We both know that alarm isn't because I got caught."

"What did you find out?" Lyria says briskly, but her gaze looks me up and down. If I didn't know any better, I'd say she was looking for injuries. I pull the wires out of my pocket and toss them at her. She catches them without a blink, but her brow furrows as she studies them.

"Ship stabilizer wires?"

"Borrowed them from Taggert's flyer. He'll be grounded for a while, which is good for us, considering his ship was loaded with cloud seeder missiles."

Lyria and Kiran exchange a glance that I can read even through the drizzle.

"Are you sure?" she asks me.

I nod once. "I saw the shipping manifest, smelled the proof myself. They're using a dozen different chems to seed the storms and make more rain. That's what the towers do, too. The turbines disperse the chems high up past the canopy. Towers and missiles mean they must be constantly putting out seeders, and that's why the storm cycle has been so erratic. But let me guess, you suspected that already." I knew as soon as they glanced at each other that my words weren't a surprise. "It would've been nice to know what I was looking for before going down there."

Kiran opens his mouth, but Lyria speaks first.

"All the evidence we had was flimsy and circumstantial. I needed real proof to be certain."

"Certain that TerraCo is making the storms worse?" I think about how ridiculous the words sound now that I've said them again. "It makes absolutely no sense. Why would they increase the rainfall on a planet already consumed by a giant hellstorm? Shouldn't they want to stop the storm?"

Kiran glances down the hill. "We should move. They might get antsy and send out a search party." Without waiting to see if either Lyria or I will follow, he starts walking into the brush. "TerraCo is using the hellstorm to drive people away," he says. "To weaken their resolve to stay here. To give them little to no chance to recover in between the storm cycles."

"Yeah, I get that," I say, slightly annoyed he's explaining it to me like I'm a child. I fall in step beside him. "It's the why I don't understand. Why would TerraCo want an empty planet stuck in a permanent storm?" I gesture to the jungle and rain around us. "It's hard to lord your power and money over people if there aren't any around. And how will they make a profit off unending rain? Because whatever this scheme of theirs is, we both know it has to do with chits."

Lyria's voice cuts in behind us. "It doesn't matter why or what their endgame is." Kiran pauses and the syndicate steps next to us. "At this point, I have to agree with Emeko. We don't have time to figure out their true goal; the weather is getting worse by the day. It only matters now that we stop them. With the scavvers on board, we can cover more ground and take out the bases all at once and stop Weiland from creating this never-ending storm."

"What about Taggert's flyer?" I argue. "It was loaded with missiles. Even if you take out the bases, what about the fleet of ships TerraCo has up on the plateau? I saw at least a dozen when we were taken to the hangar."

"One thing at a time," she says, her voice low enough it almost sounds like she's talking to herself. "We need to deal with what we know first. No point wasting resources. The unknowns can come afterward." Lyria pauses, her eyes drifting past me as she thinks. After a second, she hands the nest of stabilizer wires to Kiran.

"We need to get back to the base and plan out a coordinated attack. If every single one of those substations is currently spitting out cloud-seeding chems, it's a wonder the hellstorm hasn't enveloped the whole planet. We can't let them operate another day." She sets off in the direction of the scavver base.

I jog to catch up. "Hey, what about your end of the bargain? Kiran still owes me answers."

"You can ask him when we get back, after we plan everything," she says without turning around or stopping. Nerves pool in my stomach at the thought of finally getting answers. What if Kiran tells me something terrible?

But Kiran isn't following her. He's studying the nest of wires like they hold the secrets to TerraCo's nefarious plan. I can practically see the gears turning in his head, and I know what he's about to ask even before he asks it.

"Why are you two not walking?" Lyria stops, staring at us expectantly.

But Kiran looks at me. "Why did you pull this out of Taggert's flyer?"

"To stop him from firing off more missiles," I answer without hesitation.

"And?"

I can't help but smile. This asshole is impossible to keep secrets from sometimes.

"And because he was taking off to some secret coordinates deeper in the mountains where there are no substations, and I figured he probably wasn't going for any good reason." I shrug. "So, it seemed useful to keep his ship grounded."

"Where in the mountains?" His voice is distant despite how close we stand. I know that he's piecing together a thousand different snippets of information, looking for the ones that make sense. The ones that fit.

I point into the bush. "Probably ten or so miles northwest of here."

He blinks and I can almost see some spark in his dark eyes, some recognition of that one puzzle piece that just fell into place.

"What else do you suspect that you're not telling me?" I know that whatever's in his brain has to do with all the other things he's been hinting at but won't explain.

"Can you find your way back on your own?" Kiran looks past me to ask Lyria.

She stares at him, appearing to read him in a way that surprises me. Just how well does she know him?

"No," she finally says. Her eyes jump to me and then back to Kiran. "I'm not going to plan a huge attack while you gallivant off in the jungle."

"Lyria," he starts, a growl growing in his voice. He never did like being told what to do.

"What if you get caught? Then you're gone, and we're left planning this rebellion on our own. It's too risky."

"I can't just leave this," he argues. "Not following up is a different risk in and of itself."

"A smaller risk."

I watch them go back and forth, wondering what it is they're not saying. Though the way Kiran's jaw is clenched, I can guess that whatever's at those coordinates is not good. I can think of only one thing that would set him on edge like this.

Nova.

"I'll go instead," I say.

"Absolutely not," Kiran says at the same time that Lyria says, "Not happening."

I raise my eyebrows. "Last time I checked, you"—I point to Kiran—"have a revolution to plan. And you"—I point at Lyria—"are supposed to be leading said revolution. That leaves me free. And since I'm the one who excels at gathering intel, I'm going to be the one to check out the coordinates."

There's a moment of quiet as they stare at each other.

Lyria steps forward. "I'll go with Remy."

Kiran opens his mouth to argue, but the syndicate doesn't give him a chance.

"You have to be the one to plan the attack. There are too many moving parts to leave anything up to chance. And that means we need you on it. I'll make sure that we get back to the scavver base safely before dark."

Kiran glares at her with such intensity that I feel it in my own bones. Whatever their relationship is, it's a mess. I've only ever seen him look at our Nova handlers with that calculated malice. And only a handful of times. A memory sparks, momentarily taking me out of the jungle and putting me right back in Nova's labs.

He had that same look on his face when I got dragged away for reconditioning after our first mission together. I'd never seen him so angry, so full of hatred toward our handlers. I shake the memory loose quickly, focusing on Lyria next to me. Her familiar scent of light sweat and clean soap brings the jungle back as fast as the lab took me.

Kiran's expression has reverted back to his mask of boredom. "I'm coming. No more arguments. I'll use the comms to start the planning. Mirko and Emeko can get everything prepared. I'm not letting you two go alone." Even though his expression has calmed, his words are clearly more like a threat than a compromise. Guess he's back to his typical controlling self. And I almost wanted to believe he was different like he claimed, that he'd treat me differently.

Before I can argue, Lyria glares at him, steel in her eyes. "Fine. Do what you need to do, Kiran. We both know that you acting on your selfish impulses is what led you here in the first place. I'm fighting for something bigger than my own self-interests, and I'm not going to let your stubbornness screw that up."

Something in her tone gives me goose bumps despite the jungle heat. I've seen a number of Lyria Revas's faces since getting on that elevator, but this one is new. This side of her has true bite. Enough that I can finally see her as the revolutionary syndicate boss she claims to be. I see it clearly in her posture and the set of her jaw, her fiery hair, and the flash of defiance in her eyes.

I might not know how Alora would feel about the state of the Vega, but something tells me she'd probably like Lyria.

After a moment, Kiran tucks the wires into one of his pockets and pulls the long arken blade from his back. "Let's not waste any more time. And you'd better keep up," he says flatly to her, then disappears into the bush, cutting a path with his blade in the direction I pointed. I catch a momentary flash in his eyes and I suddenly realize that, just this once, his controlling nature might not be targeted at me.

"So stubborn," Lyria whispers after he's a few feet ahead. She lets out a small sigh before turning to me. "You're sure about the direction of the coordinates, right?"

I blink at her sudden change in tone. All the bite in her words is gone; now her voice sounds slightly worried.

"Obviously," I say.

"Just checking," she replies with a smirk, but it doesn't fully hide the unease. Did she really just tell Kiran off and then panic about whether she'd done the right thing? So much for the regal syndicate leader. I shake my head and point at Kiran's path leading us toward the mountains to the north. Lyria nods and sets off into the jungle after him. I trail behind the girl, wondering where the other version of her went and what the hell is going on between her and Kiran. Whatever it is, I'm not sure I like it.

For the first hour or so of our hike, the three of us trek in near silence. I'm not sure if there's still tension between the two of them or if they're not talking because the terrain gets harder and harder the deeper in we go.

Kiran eventually lets me lead, falling back a ways to talk to the scavvers and syndicates over his comms. The murmur of his voice is the only human sound as the undergrowth around us thickens. Everything else that my senses pick up is wild, from the birds singing to the insects buzzing around my head, nipping at my skin. Not one sign of humanity as we navigate the ever-changing terrain of the jungle.

Creeks and rivers of muddy brown water appear seemingly out of nowhere, the drizzling rain adding to their currents. We have to double back more than once to avoid herds of wild batimalu hanging from tree limbs, the ape-bats thankfully asleep during the heat of the day.

Leaves and spider vines slap against my exposed skin and tangle in my hair as we hack our way through the weeds with the long arken blade. I may be engineered to be faster, stronger, and smarter than most humans, but the Maraas jungle is unforgiving and unending; I've long given up on ever being dry or clean again.

After another hour, the rain lessens the slightest bit, morphing into a dreary sort of sprinkle. The terrain has grown hilly around us. At the top of a steep incline, I pause to give Lyria a minute to rest. My thighs are only slightly burning, and I know Kiran and I can keep pushing, but I don't know what her limits are. Kiran's a few yards back, still on his comms.

Lyria opens her canteen and takes a swig before passing it to me.

"Late breakfast? Or is it lunch already?" she asks, pulling something out of her pocket. "I've got two options. Dried jerky or dried jerky."

I raise an eyebrow at her outstretched hands, each holding a piece of dried meat from the scavver camp. I really can't get a beat on this girl. She's fiercely squaring off with Kiran one minute and making lousy jokes the next. But I take the food from her and quickly munch it down.

"Let's go," Kiran practically growls as he catches up. "I told you to keep up."

"I'm ready," she says with a smirk. "I may not be a genopath, but I'm good. Don't feel like you need to slow down on my account."

"Don't worry. I won't." He looks at me expectantly. I know what he wants even without asking. He may be infinitely analytical, but patience was never his thing.

I point down the hill at the mountain rising up beyond it. "About another mile or so that way."

He nods. "Good. Let's just get there and get this over with." I realize he's on edge, not just because of Lyria, but because of what could be waiting at the coordinates.

Nova.

My annoyance with him slips at the thought. "You lead," I say. "We'll follow. I'll let you know if we veer off course." His eyes lock on mine and the furrow between his brows lessens the slightest bit. Then he's back on his comms, moving again down the incline. I wait a few beats before following to allow him some space. Why I'm giving him any measure of control, I'm not sure. He's been nothing but a huge pain in my ass since I landed on this planet.

Lyria's watching me out of the corner of her eye, a look on her face I can't read. But this time as we trail a few yards behind him, the silence from her feels heavier. I don't know if it's my training, but I feel compelled to fill the empty space, to put Lyria a little more at ease. Not because I'm trying to be friends or anything. The time will pass quicker if we talk.

So, I clear my throat and ask: "What's the deal with you and Kiran?"

Okay, and maybe I want to pry for information.

Lyria pauses midstep to look at me, uncertainty playing across her features. She checks the distance between us and him before she continues down the steep hill. He's just far enough away that if we talk low, he probably won't hear. Especially while he's busy on the comms. Lyria must realize that because she answers my question.

"Kiran and I met over a year ago," she says softly over her shoulder. Her pulse beats a little faster. Is she lying or just nervous? "Though maybe it was longer than that; it's hard to remember exactly. Sometimes I feel like he's been around forever, annoying me."

A reluctant smile tugs at my lips. That part isn't a lie.

"We were on Abydos. I knew what he was." She looks at me, red hair falling in her face momentarily. "You're not the only one good at gathering intel. That was my earliest role for the Vega. I was just getting my feet wet with the syndicates, learning the ropes, when we crossed paths."

I try to imagine what a younger Lyria was like, but I've seen too many faces to be sure of anything with this girl. Even now, I'm the genopath, but she's the one pointing out twisted roots in our way and snaking a path through the jungle like it's second nature.

"We didn't exactly hit it off, you might say." She leaps over a deep puddle, and I follow with ease, landing beside her. The ground has turned into a swamp now that we've reached the bottom of the hill.

"The short version of the story is that I caught Kiran doing something that his Nova handlers would not approve of. So, I used it to force him to help me."

This time I stop midstep, my gaze jumping from her to Kiran up ahead and back again. "You blackmailed Kiran?"

Lyria nods. "I was born here actually." She sweeps her hand through the air, claiming the jungle marsh, lush and green and humid around us. Then she chuckles.

"Well, not here in this swamp. My father was stationed at the outpost, and I grew up on this world before we moved to Abydos. It was one of the few places we were happy before he died."

She takes a tentative step into the small river in front of us, water rising up to her knees. I follow, my boots sinking deep into the soft mud under the flowing water. Ahead, Kiran's already climbing out onto the muddy bank of the other side.

"I was rising in the ranks, and I knew that Dekkard had given up on Maraas," she continues as we slowly work our way across the river. "I'd been looking for a way to come back here and rebuild our power base. And suddenly, this genopath with extremely useful abilities lands in my lap. So, I made an opportunity for myself."

"And Kiran went along with this?"

She smirks again. "You think I gave him a choice?"

Now I'm dying to know what she caught him doing.

"That's why Kiran doesn't like it when I order him around or remind him about his past. Especially now, when he's already on edge because he suspects Nova might be at the coordinates," Lyria finishes.

I'm surprised by how well she knows him, all the way down to his current suspicions. Surprised he let someone see him so clearly. Though, now his anger and hatred earlier make sense. This deal between the two of them probably makes him feel the same way Nova does—like he has no control. I sigh internally as I realize something else. He's not helping Lyria because of some misguided attempt to fix the mess we made with the Vega. He's being forced to help.

I should've known.

"What is it you have on him that's more powerful than Nova?" I ask her the new question burning up my brain. Lyria stops walking and studies me. I can see her debating within herself, trying to decide if she should tell me or not. Her pulse skips faster than before. Whatever she knows, it's big.

Lyria's eyes suddenly go wide as her gaze drifts past mine.

"Climb!" Kiran shouts, his voice laced with urgent panic. Lyria pushes me toward the nearest tree.

Only then do I see the swirling movement in the water behind us; only then do I feel more heartbeats. And not human ones.

As I scramble up the tree's giant roots behind Lyria, a breeze changes direction, pushing the unmistakable stench of carrion and death up my nose. Scales slice through the shallow water's surface.

Anacrocs.

Not just one or two, but a swarm of them.

I was so focused on Lyria, on reading her lies and truths, that I didn't notice them surrounding us. Kiran scrambles up a nearby tree while Lyria pulls herself onto a branch above us. I quickly jump, catching a low-hanging limb and wrapping my legs around it. I swing myself up and perch precariously on the branch. Back down in the mud, a half dozen anacrocs surround the base of our tree.

Must climb higher.

They may be mostly amphibious creatures, but I've heard of them stretching up, leaning on trees as tall as their body length so they can chomp down foxbats or even batimalu on lower branches. I reach for a higher limb to get more distance on the creatures and Lyria follows suit, keeping up with my pace.

"I don't think we can stay here," she says, pulling herself on a branch near me.

"Definitely not," I reply as the wood cracks under my weight. My eyes dart around, looking for some means of escape. Other than our arken blades, Lyria's handgun, and the flash bombs in my pockets, the three of us are gloriously unarmed to take on a whole pack of fifteen-foot crocs. The small caliber bullets won't pierce their hides and dropping a flash bomb would certainly give me the satisfaction of wiping out the whole colony, but at this distance, we would be blown up in flames along with everything else.

"This must be a nesting area for them," I mumble as I balance on the slowly bending branch.

"Any bright ideas?" Lyria calls to Kiran as she tugs on a limb from his tree that's close enough to touch. It holds even as she pulls it lower.

"Working on it," he says. Then he yanks at a hanging spider vine, testing its durability. It doesn't snap.

"That's probably not going to work," I say as I realize his plan. Kiran tosses the vine toward Lyria, and she catches it with her other hand.

A stupid smile crosses her face. She's . . . enjoying this?

"It's totally going to work." She takes a breath, then swings herself across the open space using the vine and lands on the branch just below Kiran's. I glance down as a few errant leaves and twigs flutter to the ground. The anacrocs are hovering in the puddles near the trees, as if they're waiting for one of us to fall and become lunch. Lyria swings the vine back to me.

I wrap my fingers around the plant and shake my head. "This is insane."

"We can't go down and we've got to get across," Kiran says, scanning the small valley we've found ourselves in. "This is the only way."

Lyria stretches out a hand toward me. "I'll catch you if it breaks. I promise I won't let them eat you."

I stare at her outstretched hand, transfixed for a moment. I barely know this girl. She's got a dozen different faces hidden up her sleeve, not to mention motivations and ambitions that I have only scratched the surface of. I'm not one of her syndicate lackeys. My eyes jump to Kiran. He's watching us silently, his face pinched as if he wants to say something, but he doesn't. And even though I can see the muscles clenching in his jaw, he gives me the slightest nod.

Kiran's reluctant encouragement aside, somehow, on an instinctual level, I know that Lyria won't let me fall and get eaten by hungry reptiles in the middle of the jungle.

With another shake of my head, I take a breath and launch myself across the space. Lyria catches my hand in hers and pulls me forward. I land on the tree limb next to her with ease despite the misty rain and slick branches. Nothing like the threat of death to send my instincts and reactions into overdrive.

Lyria looks at me with a grin.

"You're smiling," I say. "We're gonna get eaten by crocs and you're smiling."

She shrugs. "You have to admit. This is kind of fun."

I choke out a laugh. "Fun if you like sharp teeth and the stench of death."

She wiggles her eyebrows. "Guess I have weird tastes."

"If you two are done chitchatting, can we get a move on?" Kiran's voice is an annoyed growl as he moves toward the next tree, testing more spider vines as he goes. Lyria and I exchange a glance, and she rolls her eyes, and I find myself smiling despite the mess we're in. I reach for another neighboring branch that Kiran points out and give it a tug. Then I'm jumping across to the next tree with Lyria in my wake.

The three of us work our way around the anacroc nest, climbing up branches and jumping across trees, using the spider vines to help. I test each vine carefully to make sure it's firmly attached to something and that my grip won't slip. The last thing I need is one of these to snap and send us careening to the mud and teeth below. I'm shifting onto a fourth tree when a truly awful stench stabs up my nose. I gag at the sour, putrid smell. Not even the sweet scent of the closed tahuayo buds on the spider vines helps mask the awful odor.

Kiran extends a hand while balancing on a branch next to me, his face wrinkled with distaste. "Guess we found where they mark their territory."

"I didn't know shit could smell this bad. It's like something crawled into my nose and died horribly." I let him pull me closer, covering my mouth with my other hand as more of the stink slips in on my tongue. Kiran's mouth is pressed into a hard line, his own effort to keep the stench out. He jerks his head to the next tree, letting me take the lead.

"Got to love our enhanced senses," I say, then push off the

branch hard and leap down to a lower one on the next tree, where the smell is worse. I promptly scramble higher.

Kiran follows me without missing a beat. "Next time I see anyone from Nova, I'm going to thank them personally for our heightened sense of smell."

"I'll give you a flash bomb to toss at them for it," I mutter, trying to climb and cover my nose at the same time.

Farther down on the branches, Lyria points to the mountain rising in front of us.

"We're almost out of the valley."

There's a rocky outcrop at the base of the mountain. The boulders are too high and too smooth for the crocs to climb up, especially with the falling rain, so it's as good a place as any for us to aim for. I grab another vine and swing myself closer to the rock; Lyria follows while Kiran's just ahead of me. Two more trees and then we're nearly close enough to jump to the outcrop. But there's a gap between us and the rocks, and I'm not sure the vines will make it all the way. Kiran holds up a hand for us to wait as he judges the distance.

"I'll go first," I say to Kiran while Lyria struggles to balance on the branch next to me. "I'm the lightest and I can jump farther than Lyria. Once I land, I can make sure whoever's next gets safely on the rock."

Kiran nods. "I'll go last."

But Lyria grabs my arm, glancing between the ground and our tree.

"You sure? We can both swing—"

"No," I interrupt. "The spider vines won't reach all the way. One of us has to jump first and that's me. Don't worry, it's an easy jump."

Without waiting for an argument, I head higher up the tree. Up and up I climb, then I scoot out on a far limb to assess the distance, to find the optimum angle for jumping. The ground stretches far below me.

Almost there. Just a bit higher and I'll easily make the jump to the rock. Above me, one branch juts out a little farther than the rest. The perfect angle. I can swing from it right to the center of the rock. I reach for the limb, nearly at the tip of the treetop, stretching onto my tiptoes to grasp it.

Just as my hand wraps around the wood, the branch under my foot snaps.

My balance teeters. Fingers lose purchase. And I slip toward the jungle floor.

For a second, it's free fall as gravity pulls me toward the swamp below.

Then a body crashes into mine, a steel-like arm wrapping around my torso.

Kiran has swung off the tree and caught me in midair. As our momentum drives us forward toward the rock, his grip on the vine slips a fraction. Using my legs, I kick our weight farther. As we reach the pinnacle of the swing, I strain toward the rock, willing us closer to the outcrop.

I feel the moment his grip loosens entirely, the moment gravity grabs us again. But this time, I'm the one who catches us from falling.

I slam into the side of the outcrop, my ribs cracking in more than one place. The breath rushes out of me as pain explodes up my side. No time to deal with it, though—we're already sliding down the wet stone. But my fingers dig into the rock, looking for purchase even as my nails crack and rip. At the last second, I find a handhold and clutch at it with all the force in my muscles. I dump adrenaline into my system, increasing the strength in my grip.

We stop sliding.

Kiran's still got an arm tight around my waist.

"Don't let go!" Lyria shouts from somewhere behind us. I can smell decaying meat and animal feces. The anacrocs must be below us.

"Not planning to," I answer, readying myself for the pull that comes next. "Why do you have to be so damn tall?" I grumble at Kiran.

Before he can answer, I flex with everything I've got, straining my muscles to pull us up. But then the weight lessens. I steal a glance and see Kiran using his free arm to help me as I climb the rock.

Together, we inch up and up. Then my torso is over the ledge and Kiran is scrambling past me. My boots find the side of the rock just as his hands wrap around my arms. I push at the same time he pulls, and with a final lunge, we both collapse onto the solid surface.

I lie there, my body facing the clouds. Small drops of water dance across my skin. As my lungs remember how to work, a sharp pain cuts into every breath. My ribs might not be fully fractured, but they're most definitely cracked. At least I'm not croc meat.

Kiran peers down over me, loose strands of his dark hair tickling my cheeks.

"Are you all right?" His voice is barely a whisper.

"Everything hurts, but I'm alive," I droll.

He lets out a breath and sits on the rock beside me.

"Thank you for catching me," I mumble, now taking slower breaths to counter the pain. The sweet smell of rain and rock fills my nose, blessedly washing away the putrid scent of the anacroc nest below.

"Thanks for pulling us up and not dropping me," Kiran says softly. "The anacrocs are disappointed, but I'm sure not."

"And why didn't you notice them sooner?"

"I was talking over tonight's plan with Mirko on the comms."

I raise an eyebrow. "And?"

He blinks at me and then smirks. "And trying to eavesdrop on you and Lyria at the same time."

"There it is." I laugh and pain smarts up my ribs again. "Predictable to the end."

"But you knew I wasn't going to let you fall, right?" He stands next to me, offering a hand to help me up.

I eye his outstretched fingers.

"Hello!" Lyria's voice cuts into my focus. "A little help here?"

Kiran's fingers fold inward and then he's moving away from me, toward the edge of the rock, ready to help Lyria, who's found a spider vine to carry her some of the way over.

She points at Kiran menacingly. "Don't drop me."

He wiggles his fingers at her impatiently. "Don't worry your little syndicate head."

I smile softly to myself because I know he won't. He may be a traitor and a liar. He may be keeping secrets and pissing me off every other minute. But he won't let us fall prey to the anacrocs. I think back to our missions together; he never did let me get hurt if he could stop it.

Slowly sitting up, I watch as Lyria swings herself into the air and lets go of the vine at the last possible second. Her momentum carries her up, and for a moment, it looks like she's going to fly right into the pit below. But then Kiran dives down and catches her outstretched arms. She collides with the rock, but neither of them loses their grip, and seconds later, she's clambering up on the ledge.

She rushes over and crouches next to me.

"Are you okay?" She's looking at me like I'm something fragile, like I might break. Her worry is unwarranted. I won't.

I shrug and give her a half smile. "Never better. Who needs ribs anyway? You were right, this was fun." It will take a lot more than some anacrocs and injured ribs to break me.

Her eyes find mine and she grins.

As I push myself to my feet, Lyria starts to protest.

"You should rest for a minute at least. We need to figure out where we are anyway."

I wave her off. "I'll be fine. We don't have a ton of time out here, remember? We've got a revolution to plan."

"And questions to answer," Kiran adds. I catch his gaze, noting how it's shifted since Lyria grinned at me. Is he finally going to give me answers, after all this? I don't know what's made him decide to change his tune, but before I can ask him, something else catches my attention.

"I really think you should take a minute to recover," Lyria continues. "We still have to find the exact coordinates—"

I point behind her. Her gaze follows my finger. There, tucked into the side of the mountain, half hidden under vines and mud, is a heavy metal door.

"Found them."

CHAPTER 23

All three of us stare at the door. Then I tentatively cross the outcrop, looking elsewhere for signs of another entrance. But there's nothing but more rock and jungle. And the anacrocs still swirling below.

"Are you sure these are the coordinates?" Lyria asks, moving aside vines and inspecting the handle.

I do some mental math. "We're close but not exactly on top of them."

She glances around the outcrop. "Taggert's certainly not landing a flyer here."

I nod, pointing to the side of the mountain. "The coordinates are farther that way. Maybe there's a hidden landing pad somewhere higher up."

With a quick move, Kiran smashes the handle and pulls the door open, letting some light into the shaft. "I don't really feel like climbing anymore, so I guess we use this door then. It's probably an old mine entrance."

"These old mines have dozens of tunnels for miles under the mountains," I say, peeking around him to look into the shaft. "We could stroll into this one and never see a soul. Or we could stumble right into whatever nefarious thing Taggert is coming to inspect."

"There's a huge gulf between those two outcomes," Lyria replies dryly.

We peer into the dark.

"Only one way to find out," I say.

Kiran puts out an arm to stop me from stepping into the tunnel. "One of us should stay here. In case something happens."

Behind me, Lyria sighs. "Damn, you're probably right."

I open my mouth. "I'm going in."

Kiran rolls his eyes, but I see a smile playing on his lips. "Yes, yes. We know." He glances at Lyria. "You stay. You're the one the syndicates are following. If something happens to either of us, you can still carry out your mission."

She crosses her arms. "If something happens to either of you, the mission can wait."

"Do what you need to do, Lyria." His words echo hers from earlier. "If we're not out in an hour, go back without us. Do not come in after us."

The syndicate grinds her teeth, the muscles in her jaw working overtime. But finally she nods, looking at me. "If it is Nova in there, don't let them take you off this planet."

I answer her this time. "We won't."

With a grim face, Kiran steps into the tunnel and I follow on his heels.

Nothing but darkness greets us. No sounds, no movement. Just still air and dark shadows. The dull ambient light of the misty sun outside illuminates nearly nothing beyond the door's threshold. The shaft is in disarray; fallen boards and rusted support beams dot the tunnel as it sinks downward into the mountain. The air is stale, smelling of damp dirt and stagnant moisture. Clearly, no one's used this entrance in a while, so at least we'll be able to get in without being noticed.

"Do you smell that?" Kiran asks as we venture deeper in.

Underneath the musk of earth and damp mud is another scent. A sterile and acidic scent. One that I hate with my entire being. I want to be imagining it; I don't want it to be real.

"It smells like a lab," I reply. The smell is practically etched into my DNA from spending most of my life in and out of labs at Nova. Labs for reconditioning. For testing. For dissecting.

And now that scent is here. Something is happening here that Weiland and Taggert clearly don't want others to know about. Something that Nova is definitely involved in. Which means it can't be anything good.

I swallow past the memories that are trying to force more replays up my throat. The smell is enough to send me back to that place if I let it control me.

So, I don't. I push the memories and emotions and triggers down.

"Did you know Nova had a lab on this world?" I ask to break the silence of the tunnel. It feels too much like a tomb, more so the farther we get from the entrance and sunlight. My eyes adjust to the dimness automatically, but the feeling doesn't dissipate.

"I had my suspicions," Kiran answers.

"You couldn't have shared them?"

Despite the near dark, I can see the shrug of his shoulders. "I needed to be sure."

We fall back into silence. Not a comfortable silence but rather one that itches at my skin. One that has me wondering what else Kiran knows but isn't sharing. What he's hiding. What Lyria black-mailed him with. All of it. I try to ignore it as we follow the tunnel deeper into the mountain, try to tell myself it doesn't matter. That he's always concealing things and that knowing more of his secrets won't change my plans. The warm, damp air of the tunnel sinks into my layers, plasters my hair down so it clings to my neck, to my cheeks, strangling me just like the thoughts in my head.

"Are you going to ask or just stew back there?" Kiran inter-rupts the growing quiet.

I force a few errant strands of hair out of my eyes. "Are you going to actually answer me this time?"

"That was the deal."

"A deal I made with Lyria, not with you."

"Does it matter? You'll get what you want."

Annoyance sparks in my throat at the tone of his voice. The disdain. I forget about the blackmail and the rest and snap at him. "What is it you think I want, Kiran, since you're so sure about everything?"

"I'm very sure you don't even know what you want." He pauses in the middle of the tunnel, not turning around, just standing there. In the near darkness, I watch his shoulders move with his breathing. I can tell by his posture that he didn't mean to say those words. That he'd take them back if he could. He constantly treats me like I'm a child, like my impulses need to be controlled. Finally, here he is admitting it. A bit of truth slipping out in the dark.

Instinctually, I want to fall back into our old pattern. To shout at him, to yell and fight. But the fire isn't there like it was when I first saw him at Arun's den. I'm tired of the constant arguing and his deliberate misunderstanding of my actions. Even though he brought backup in the sprawl, even though he led me to the syndicates to save Alora's world, even though he caught me before I could fall into the anacroc pit, his words and secrets are a constant reminder that he can't be trusted.

"What I want is to help my friend. I want to find her," I say at last, the fight gone from my voice.

He turns slightly so that he's looking over his shoulder at me. "And then what?"

I shrug. "What does it matter?"

"If you can tell me what it is you're going to do once you find Alora, then I'll tell you where she is right now. Your honest answer for my truth."

I open my mouth.

But nothing wants to come out.

"I'm going to be with my friend," I say quickly to cover the hesitation.

"Be with her? How? Where? You're so wrapped up in her memory you won't look at the bigger picture. You won't even consider whether she feels the same way about you."

"What same way? We're friends. We made a promise."

He rolls his eyes. "Keep telling yourself that's all it is. That you don't want anything more."

I stare at him, heat and confusion crawling up my stomach. At the look on my face, Kiran sighs, almost inaudibly. "Forget it. This is the problem you have, Remy. You never think anything through or consider the consequences. You don't want to. You just do whatever it is your impulses tell you. Whatever feels right in the moment."

At his subject change, I swallow past the lump in my throat and cross my arms. He doesn't know what he's talking about. Not with Alora and not with me.

"I follow my impulses because that's how Nova wired me." I stride past him, but his voice follows me in the dark.

"Maybe that's it, and you're just like me, so caught up in the mission you don't dare to think about what comes after. I know the after is terrifying." I glance back at him, and even with the lack of light, I can see the ghosts in his eyes. His own replays of what often awaited him after the missions were through: reconditioning. I watch him push his triggers away, but part of me is wondering what about the "after" could terrify even him.

"Alora isn't a mission," he continues, pulling me back from my thoughts. "She's a person. She's got her own life. And before you go running off to her, you should decide what you want. For yourself. Not for her. Not for some mission. Not for Nova. For you, Remy." He steps forward as if that's the end of the conversation. But I reach out and grab his sleeve before he can shuffle past me.

He freezes under my touch.

"Why do you even care so much about what I do afterward, Kiran?"

He keeps his eyes forward, away from mine. "I'll always care what happens to you. Someone has to since you don't."

I let go of his arm like it's burned my fingertips.

"Did you care when you dumped me alone in the jungle?"

He sighs. "I did that to protect you"—I start to interrupt, but he keeps talking—"from Nova. If they knew that you'd decided to go off-mission to help her, you would've been dragged to reconditioning indefinitely. They would've done everything in their power to erase the person that you are. We're not talking days or weeks in those rooms, Remy. More like months or years." He pauses, swallowing. "And I figured at least if you were out there, I could claim you were dead. Keep you away from Nova and their reconditioning. And save you that way."

I hesitate. Sena told me that he probably had a reason, and even though I've been ignoring Kiran's excuses about protecting me this whole time, she was right. He was trying to protect me the only way he knew how. But that doesn't erase how powerless it made me.

"You might've saved me from them, but you took away all my choices," I say, not expecting an answer.

"There were a dozen other variables I had to consider. . . ." His voice trails off, then he sighs. "I know I did. And for that I'm sorry." He coughs to cover his near-whispered apology. "We're wasting time. Let's go."

I stare at his back, trying to work out what's going on in his head. His words about Alora, his sudden apology, they were all too personal, too raw to be a manipulation. Weren't they? Or maybe I don't know what to think. Things keep getting more complex, more complicated. Usually I see that as a challenge. But right now, in this stupid tunnel, I wish like hell things were simpler.

I trudge after Kiran, trying to decide if I should press him to explain or if I should just forget the entire conversation ever happened. I don't want to forgive him for leaving me in the jungle. But if our roles had been reversed and I needed to protect him from Nova, I might've done the same thing. And just because I understand his motivations doesn't mean I have to excuse his actions, does it? Because it definitely doesn't excuse him for all the other things he said. About my impulsiveness. About what I'll do after I find Alora.

Fortunately, I'm saved from having to decide anything when our descending path suddenly branches into three tunnels.

I put our conversation aside to deal with later, and focus on my physical senses. Different scents hit my nose from each tunnel. The dampness of mud and water in the first. Something sour and spoiled, like death, lingers just behind the threshold of the second. Blood and something astringent floats in on a draft from the third.

Kiran glances at me and nods at the third path. Guess he also thinks our discussion is over and we're back to pretending like this is any other mission. Fine, it's better that way. I don't have the energy to deal with his mood swings, so I nod back and follow him through the archway.

The new path cuts deeper into the mountain as it winds through rock and stone. Slowly the ceiling opens up, and more scents and sounds drift down the tunnel. We both stay silent as we get closer to the source, knowing that stealth is what matters most now.

The tunnel abruptly ends at a haphazard pile of boulders and rocks, but light is shining through the larger cracks. Shouts and the sounds of machinery filter through, too. There must be a big space on the other side.

Without saying a word, Kiran and I start moving the smaller rocks, slowly and carefully, to create enough space to crawl through. Sweat trickles down my spine as we move stone after stone until the hole is large enough. Peeking through, I can just make out a small ledge before the cave widens into a cavern. I squeeze through the opening first, crawling onto the ledge and staying hidden behind the rocks around us. Kiran follows and we crouch, the ledge providing a bit of cover as we take in the space.

The cavern floor is about ten feet under us, but the ceiling rises impossibly high. My gaze follows it up and up despite the noise and movement demanding my attention below. At the apex of the ceiling is a giant shaft with a large hole at the top. Cloudy light filters down from the sky far above. The shaft is big enough for a ship; there's even a landing pad marked out on the cavern floor. Guess we know how Taggert gets in here. Kiran nudges me and my attention jumps, following his line of sight.

What was once an exocarbon mine is now a full-on testing lab. People in white coats and drab uniforms dart about here and there, all seemingly in the middle of something important. Stacks of crates and various equipment line the space around the landing pad. Small life pods have been set up, most likely acting as barracks or rooms for experiments. I don't know what is worse: the fact that there are scientist hacks staying here full time or that even within a secret lab hidden in a mountain, they still need rooms for privacy.

Directly underneath our ledge, stacks of cages hold a variety of animals. Some are pacing in the tiny spaces; others are sleeping. The few birds and monkeys make enough noise to fill the massive cavern.

Kiran inclines his head toward the machines stacked by the landing pad.

"I recognize some of those," he says, his voice barely a whisper. "They're for studying weather effects. Wind, air pressure, that sort of thing. They must be studying the storm from here."

"Among other things." I catch sight of batimalu in some of the cages below us. They're agitated, and most are wearing the same collar, with the camera and transmitter, that I saw before. One has its claws locked in the cage fence, shaking it so violently that the other animals are beginning to squeal in annoyance.

"This is how they're controlling and training the batimalu to attack people," I point out. Kiran nods, his lips pressed into a tight line. As if in answer to my statement, one of the lab hacks approaches the cages and activates something on a datapad. The agitated batimalu screams, releasing the fence and falling onto the cage floor.

"Electric shocks." The whisper escapes my lips without thinking, horror clinging to each word. We've both been subjected to electric shocks. During reconditioning. During testing. Even though the ape is a flying demon, I still wouldn't wish that pain on the predator.

"One of Nova's ships just outside of Abydos's orbit was caught and grounded," Kiran hisses through clenched teeth. "My guess is they're using this as a makeshift stronghold until the Corporate Assembly releases the ship back to them."

"We have to destroy this place," I breathe.

Kiran squeezes his eyes shut, frustration spelled out in the tightness of his jaw and the furrow of his brow.

"We can't, Remy," he whispers. "If we try anything here, we'll expose ourselves and compromise the attacks that Lyria and Emeko are planning. It's more important for us to stop the substations first. And for that, we'll need the element of surprise."

I know he's right, even though he looks as pissed about it as I feel. We may bicker and fight, but on the subject of Nova operating here, our feelings align. This place is straight out of our nightmares. And I can't let it exist, not on a planet I'm trying to save for Alora. I made a promise to be better. A promise that I failed on over and over.

Not anymore.

"Kiran, I can't just leave," I argue, still keeping my voice a whisper. "This place is the same as the hell we were raised in. TerraCo is clearly allowing Nova's operations here if Taggert had these coordinates in his flyer. Which means Weiland knows about it, permitted it. We can't stop her and not stop this."

Kiran glances at me, a careful mask covering his emotions. "Nova is all the more reason to get the hell out of here without anyone seeing us. They thought you were dead for two years. You think they'll let you slip away again if they find out you're here, on this world?"

Fear sends more adrenaline rushing through my veins. I will not go back to that lab. But I can't leave this one operational either. I won't.

I rack my brain as I scan the space, looking for any sort of option. Any way to engineer a mess that won't point back to us. Noise from the cages draws my attention again, and then I know exactly what to do.

"All right," I whisper. "I won't totally blow up everything and I won't get caught. But I'm going to need you to pull me back up, so stay here."

"Pull you back — Remy, wait!" he hisses.

But it's too late. The lab hack by the cages turns his back to us, giving me the opening I need. Without making a sound, I slip my legs over the edge of the rock and lower myself down far enough to drop the last few feet. I land soundlessly behind the stacks of cages and quickly duck low as the scientist drifts back over.

After a minute of the lab hack taking notes on the batimalu, he moves farther down the line of cages. Monkeys, birds, small mammals I don't know the name of; even a paka tiger slumbers toward the end. What Nova is doing with the animals I can only guess. Based on the way the batimalu tore after the commando in the jungle, the scientists must be programming them. Like they did to us when we went off-mission in any way.

The triggers bubble under my skin, dredging up recalls of small, dark rooms and bright lights. Gene hacks and other quacks poking and prodding while asking us a million questions. Questions about our loyalties. About our performance. About our most intimate thoughts. If the answers weren't satisfying, then the more extreme and invasive procedures began. Simulated drowning in the water tanks was just one method in their arsenal.

Time and time again, they used physical and mental torture to condition us to believe that our actions were not our own. They were Nova's. Any hint of independence was shocked out of us, programmed to be suppressed and forgotten. To the point that even our thoughts belonged to Nova. Only Alora pulled me out of that pattern.

But the hacks at Nova didn't see anything wrong with what they were doing. How could they be committing atrocities when we were just their property? We weren't people. We were profits or losses, viable assets or wasted investments. They gave us all abilities that no human should have, and then they forced us to use them to their own advantage.

Maybe Kiran's right, and I do things impulsively. I just jumped down into this hell without a second thought. But the only thing I'm thinking about now are the consequences of leaving this place intact. And I can't live with them. Maybe it's time I use my impulses against those who made us and broke us. Use them to show the Nova chumps that I don't belong to them; I never did.

That none of us do.

By now, the scientist is at the end of the cages, prodding at the slumbering paka tiger. I hope it bites his arm off.

I slowly pull the serrated knife from my boot and sneak over to the batimalu's cage. The demon ape-bat snarls at me from the corner but makes no move to come closer.

Keeping an eye on the lab coat at the opposite end of the row, I start sawing through the fencing, starting at the top of the ape's cage and working my way straight down to the next cage below. I keep the cuts jagged instead of straight, pulling and pushing bits of the fence in or out as I go to make it look like the ape forced its way through. I make quick work of it, pushing more oxygen into my veins, willing strength into my arms.

When I get to the bottom of the cage, I slice over and then up again. The batimalu in the cage underneath watches me, too, now, its beady eyes following the path of the knife. When my cuts approach the cage's top, the ape is bouncing up and down as if it knows what's coming next. Monsters they may be, but the flying apes are smart. Far too smart to be kept in cages.

Before I can finish, the ape begins to peel back the ruined fencing with its claws. I slice through a few more inches and the batimalu forces itself through the opening. Just as it squeezes through, I slip back behind the cages, away from the pred. The ape tumbles to the floor with a screech.

The lab hack turns around, his eyes going wide. But the batimalu is already up, locked on the nearest prey. With a snap of its now freed wings, it launches itself directly at the scientist's head before he can activate any shocks on the datapad.

The beginnings of his scream are swallowed by the howls of the batimalu.

Then another ape in the lower cage slips free, staring at me through the fencing as it, too, spreads its wings. I hold my breath, waiting to see if it will come at me. A moment passes. The batimalu leans forward and screeches loud enough to split eardrums.

Then it flies.

But not at me. Toward the other batimalu and the gene hack in its jaws. The two of them tear at the scientist. I rush forward, grab the datapad, and activate the locks on the rest of the cages as quickly as I can. The noises of the freed animals echo through the cavern. I have seconds before someone realizes that they're not normal.

One more cage to go.

The paka tiger's eyes are now open, surveying the chaos of fluttering birds and squealing mammals. I catch more movement in my periphery, white coats coming closer, shouts closing in.

Without skipping a beat, I clamber onto the top of the cages, then tap the screen; the lock clicks free. A blur of spotted black and green fur flies past and I scramble backward, hurling the datapad toward the ground hard enough so the screen and case shatter, erasing all traces of my presence.

I scramble across the cages, back to the ledge where Kiran is waiting, his arm already stretched down toward me. I leap up and catch his hand, then he's pulling me up over the rock as the scientists below finally realize the extent of the damage, the animals now swarming all over their lab. Sena would be proud.

Kiran's looking at me like I'm in trouble, but something sparks in his eyes, undermining his stern expression.

"Nicely done. Can we go now?" he says. "We've got the other bases to destroy."

I nod and follow him as he crawls back into the mine shaft tunnel. With a quick and final glance over my shoulder, I make a silent promise that I will come back to finish burning this place to the ground.

As we sprint through the tunnels, the beautiful sounds of chaos follow me out of the caves.

CHAPTER 24

As we rush back through the empty mine, the elated buzz from causing mayhem at the lab energizes me while adrenaline and the need to escape keep the fatigue out of my limbs despite my ribs still smarting from slamming into the rock.

Once outside, Kiran gives Lyria a quick rundown of what happened, and she then directs us to a new scavver base, one she visited with Emeko before. We're forced to go the long way around the mountain to avoid the anacroc nest, but at least the syndicate knows her way around the jungle. We hike in near silence, interrupted only by Kiran or Lyria responding to their comms. I can tell something about our involvement in the mine bothers her, but whatever her thoughts are, she keeps them to herself.

Trailing behind me, Kiran doesn't press me about our actions, doesn't interact with me at all. And for once, I'm not sure if I'm glad he's not annoying me or if I want him to. Something changed or broke between us after the conversation in the tunnel. I keep replaying his words but can't seem to pinpoint what exactly made him clam up. The silence between us seems to grow the farther we hike.

As the sun sinks toward the horizon, the awkwardness between us leaves me feeling hollow. I can't stop focusing on Kiran's accusations. Now that we're out of the mine, the consequences he claims I always ignore are all I can think about. Did I do the right thing, releasing the animals? What if Nova decides they're all failures and puts them down?

I wasn't programmed to care about the aftermath of my missions or the lives I destroyed for Nova's gain. No matter how hard I try to do better and be better, I can't ever get past my genes and training. Kiran's right. I don't think, I just react.

The last two years have been nothing but me reacting to Alora's disappearance and Kiran's involvement. I've chased him across worlds, leaving messes in my wake. Just like on Tundar. I helped Sena save Iska from Kalba, but she was forced to kill him and now has a bounty on her head. A long-reaching consequence of my actions. Now Sena's stuck here in this mess with me. Another "afterward" I didn't think through because I was too focused on my own search for Alora. Another life I helped destroy.

I can blame Kiran and I can blame Nova, but the fault is mine to bear. It's partly what's been driving me to find her, the shame and guilt. I don't know what Kiran meant when he brought up how Alora might feel about me. She wants me to find her—why wouldn't she? He doesn't know what he's talking about. I want to keep my promise to her; there's nothing more to it than that. But as soon as I have that thought, Kiran's other words echo in my head.

And then what?

As much as it pains me to admit, I haven't been thinking be-yond finding her. The truth is, I don't know what comes next. I don't think I have any idea what an afterward even looks like. Maybe my afterward will always be like this planet. Like Maraas, a tangled jungle drowning in storms. A once beloved home to the friend I swore to protect, now nothing more than tatters and mud.

Maybe I don't deserve an afterward.

"Almost there." Lyria's voice registers somewhere in my head, but even approaching our destination doesn't pull me out of my thoughts. Some part of me knows this mood dip is also a conse-quence of all the adrenaline dumping and the energy I've been expending for the last eight hours. Hell, the last three days. Nova would see this as my own fault for not regulating my hormones more closely and probably send me to reconditioning.

And that causes my mood to sink further as I fight replays and triggers in one corner of my mind and the spiraling guilt and shame in the other.

The heavy mist continues to fall. It hasn't stopped since Sena and I left the sprawl yesterday, and a small part of me fears the worst. That this is permanent. That the corpos have already won. The clouds and coming dusk push away the sun by late afternoon, taking away the sting of the heat with it. But the warmth in the jungle is more than just sunlight. The humidity and drizzle have sunk into my very bones. Heat still presses down on my skin, a blanket of warmth smothering me as we slog through the mud and rivers. Even the mosquitoes surround me like a cloak.

I slap one on the bridge of my nose as Lyria pushes a final fern out of our way, revealing a partially cleared glade tucked away in the shadow of a steep hill filled with human activity.

Buildings and tents are spread out across the clearing—some built among trees, others directly next to the rocky cliffs behind, making this location difficult to spot from the air. Everyone is hustling, rushing off to fulfill some task in preparation for the attacks later tonight.

This base is bigger, more permanent than the one we spent the night in, with clearly marked bunkhouses, supply sheds, and other structures.

And while everything is busy, there's a method to the madness, an order to things. This is not a settlement or a community like the scavver city under Lake Jökull on Tundar. This is a structured base. No sign of kids, no animals running around. It comes as a surprise. I didn't realize just how organized the scavvers are on Maraas, how militant they've become.

We pass a bunkhouse, and the moist smell of clean water and soap hits my nose. Suddenly, I want nothing more than to be alone. To not have to face any more of my failures or hear Kiran's continued accusations. To not manage the schemes of the scavvers and syndicates. To not deal with any of it.

"Why don't you two go ahead and find the others?" I say, stopping between them. "I'd really like to shower."

Lyria's brow furrows as she studies my face. She glances at Kiran and then back at me. "You should be there when we're discussing the plan. Mirko and Kiran will have everything laid out, but I'd like your opinion, too."

I shake my head. "You don't need me for that. That's his thing. I'll catch up when I'm clean."

"Remy . . ."

I wave her away. "The anacroc stench is killing me and I could use a catnap to reenergize."

She looks like she wants to say more, but I point to the bunk-house, avoiding Kiran's all-too-knowing eyes. "Come on, I can smell the shower. Just find me when you're done and tell me what the plan is."

She presses her lips into a line. "The plan will be better if you're involved in making it. And you still can ask Kiran your questions about your friend. He'll answer them."

I'm not sure I want to hear those answers anymore.

Kiran gives a single nod. "If that's what you want, I will." Then he falls back into silence beside us, but I can still feel unease radiating off him. I don't know if his agitation is because he's worried about my state of mind or because he said too much earlier and regrets it. Either way, I don't really have the energy to figure out his machinations.

"Just go, Lyria," I say, steel in my voice. Without waiting to see if they'll leave, I start toward the bunkhouse. I don't look back over my shoulder or listen for their voices. I don't even care if they talk about me.

I step inside the bunkhouse, blissfully devoid of people. Every-one must be gearing up for the attacks later tonight. Mirko sure did mobilize everyone quickly. Or maybe the scavvers have been prep-ping for a while, itching to do something about TerraCo. There are so many angles and elements, but they make me more tired. This sort of thing is supposed to excite me — Nova basically engineered us to react to threats and danger as if they were stimulants. But all the manipulations of today feel too heavy for my brain to handle; I want to push them all aside.

I didn't want this, this mess. I only wanted to find my friend. To make sure she was all right.

But with every move I make, everything ends up more tangled

than before, and I still feel no closer to finding Alora than I was when we landed on this planet.

Feeling my energy level sink further, I open a few lockers to find some clean layers. I'm sure they won't mind if I borrow some clothes. Mine are beyond saving. I empty my pockets of explosives, take the serrated blade out of my boot, and peel off my mud-caked clothes, tossing them aside in the communal bathroom. Turning on one of the showers full blast, I stand under the icy stream for a long time, letting the water clean off the sweat and smell and sticky heat of Maraas. Must be spring water from somewhere to be this cold. Though it's not enough to wash away all my thoughts, I do feel better once the stench of anacroc shit isn't lingering in my nose. The clean layers help, too.

I'm shaking water from my hair when footsteps sound outside the bunkhouse, accompanied by softer padding. I turn and find Sena in the doorway. Iska bounds over and buries her nose in the pile of dirty clothes before sneezing.

"You found me," I say, managing to conjure a smile but faltering at the expression on Sena's face. Her dark eyebrows are drawn forward, lips in a slight frown. Her eyes hold a storm of emotions, but I can't pinpoint why. Is it the scavvers? Or did Emeko tell her something about her äma?

"Iska took off when Lyria and Kiran showed up without you," she says, watching me from the entryway. "It didn't take her long to track you down."

I sit slowly on a cot, unsure what to say. I'm supposed to always have the right words that people need to hear. But after the draining day, and now, looking at Sena, I've got nothing but Kiran echoing in my head. That I never think of what comes next.

Iska sticks her nose in my lap, pulling my focus. Dutifully, I scratch her ears as Sena comes in and sits on a cot opposite me.

"What is it?" I ask, my voice suddenly hoarse, knowing it's none of the other things that have upset her. Knowing only one thing could be the cause. Me.

"You left us. Without saying anything." Sena pauses and looks down at the floor as she fiddles with a few dark curls that have come loose from her braid. "We didn't know where you went or if you were okay. Nothing, Remy."

I blink, not surprised. Another consequence I didn't bother to think through.

"I'm sorry," I say, managing to keep some of the emotion out of my voice. "I didn't think. I just followed my instincts and that meant chasing after Kiran and Lyria. I had to know what was going on."

"I know why you did it, Remy. That's not what bothers me."

"Then . . . what is it?" I stumble over my words as the hollow feeling in my chest grows. As I worry that I've pushed her too much. That she's realized I've caused all her problems since I told her she had to race with me. That she knows I must be using her.

But to my surprise, Sena laughs. "You know, I'm not great with people. But for someone supposedly engineered to read others, you're not doing a very good job at it either."

I flinch at the unintended sting of her words.

Her face softens along the edges. "You left me and Iska behind. You didn't tell us you were going or ask if we wanted to come."

"You were sound asleep after talking with Mirko," I say quietly. "You obviously needed rest. You'd just found your äma's people; I didn't think you wanted to go traipsing through the jungle with me, chasing after Kiran and Lyria. I figured you wanted to stay with the scavvers."

She shakes her head, her gray eyes flashing. "You don't get to decide what I want without even discussing it with me. I might not have a lot of experience with friends, but I'm pretty sure that's not how you treat them."

"But . . ." I say, pushing aside that I practically said the same thing to Kiran back in the outpost; that he treats me like a child who doesn't know what I want. I'm not like him. I'm not.

"Sena, don't you want to be with the scavvers? Don't you want to find out more about your äma's family? Because I know you want that without you having to say a word."

Suddenly, her anger turns into a sigh.

"Of course I want to learn more about my äma's family. But I'm not just going to drop you for a bunch of strangers I don't know, even if they were friends with my grandparents. You are the only one on this planet that I trust. The only one who knows what . . . I've gone through. And the only one who's gone through it with me. No amount of surprise family secrets is going to change that."

I stare at her, confused. Trying to understand. "How can I be more important than the family you lost?"

She laughs again, but there's no humor in it. Iska pads over to her and licks the hand that automatically reaches for the wolf.

"I never truly lost them," she says. "My mothers have always been with me, even when they were gone. It took me a long time to understand that. And it took me even longer to understand that family is who you make it, not who you were born to. You and Iska are my family, Remy. Even when you mess up. We still choose you."

I stare at the girl on the cot and the wolf on the floor. I've done the same thing to Sena that Kiran did to me. Taken away her choices. A lump forms in my throat. I don't want to be that type of friend. Is that what Kiran thinks he's doing? Being a friend? Maybe he's struggling to understand my emotions, just like I am with Sena right now. Something loosens in my chest at the thought. He doesn't know how friendships work.

But I do.

I've dragged Sena and Iska across planets. I got them into a mess with a bounty on their heads. I never once really thought about the afterward. But . . . Sena is still here, even after all that. She doesn't care why I brought her along with me. Doesn't care if it was my instincts inviting her to the stars. She still chooses me. Like Alora once did before.

It's time I choose her back.

"I'm sorry, Sena. You're right. I—" Words won't form past the lump in my throat.

"You don't have to make me any grand promises, Remy," she says softly, reading my intentions. "Just don't disappear on me or push me to the side." The corners of her mouth tug into a small smile. "Don't stop dragging me around with you."

"I won't," I say, meaning it. "You're stuck with me," I add with a chuckle, using the motion to swipe at the tears in an effort to rein my emotions back in. Somehow, Sena doesn't care that I failed her. I don't deserve her, but still, she gets up and sits next to me. Neither of us moves despite the cot sinking a bit under our weight.

Sena nudges me with her elbow. "Or at least tell me where you're going. That way I can decide whether I want to tag along on whatever harebrained scheme you're planning. Seriously, I was worried sick. I almost convinced Emeko to send out a crew of ATVs to look for you."

I sniff and suck in a breath. "Emeko? Look for me? Highly doubtful. I don't think she likes me very much."

Sena smirks. "I could've convinced her."

"At least someone likes one of us," I laugh.

Sena chuckles in return. "It's surprising it's me, though, right? I figured only you and Iska would ever put up with me."

I scratch the wolf's head where she lies on the floor. She huffs like she understands our words perfectly. Funny wolf.

"What about Kiran and Lyria? You were with them, weren't you?" Sena asks.

I nod. "We found out what TerraCo is doing with the substations."

"Kiran told us." Her eyes search mine. "What else?"

She really does know me. I guess surviving an insane ice planet and nearly dying for each other will do that to people.

"After fleeing a half dozen anacrocs, we found a lab," I say.

She considers this, glancing to Iska and then back to me. "Nova? Like the one you came from?"

My silence answers her question.

"What did you do?"

This time I look up, a smile tugging at my lips at her intuition. Unlike Kiran, who sees what he wants, Sena sees all of me.

"My friend inspired me to free all the animals and cause a ruckus."

She grins. "Bloody brilliant."

And I smile back, the most genuine smile since we landed on this planet.

"Oh," she says, reaching into her pocket. "I grabbed you more protein bars. Figured you hadn't eaten. The canteen's got pretty decent stew that you can grab instead. They said it was some sort of croc meat."

I make a face, thinking back to the awful anacroc stench, and take the protein bars. "I'll stick with these, thanks."

She laughs and Iska barks along with her.

"How was your conversation with Mirko?" I ask tentatively.

She chews on her lip.

"He's . . . a nice man. He told me a lot of things even though I could tell he was tired and needed rest. Said he was used to feeling sick, and telling me about my äma was more important than sleeping. Apparently both Mirko and my grandparents used to work for TerraCo. They were scientists. Like Pana going to Tundar, they traveled to Maraas to study plants and animals. And when an expedition in the jungle went bad, the scavvers saved them when TerraCo left them to die. So, they sort of switched sides. Just like Pana."

"Wow." I try to think of the right thing to say and end up with nothing but the truth. "That's surprising."

She nods, looking off into the distance. "I'm not sure how to feel about it. My mothers were both so anti-corpo. I guess it was based on personal experiences for them. But just the fact that my grandparents used to belong to that world . . ."

"Hey." This time I nudge her slightly with my elbow. Her eyes focus on me again and I smile. "I used to belong to that world, so it looks like we both have corpo origins."

She considers that and then smiles back. "Iska, too. Aren't we a trio?"

"Seems even more fitting that we all found each other."

"And that we're fighting against them now. Just like you said we would," she finishes with more confidence. "Guess my mom's saying is true. It doesn't matter where or how you start. It only matters what you do to change things and where you end up."

Her words echo in my head as we spend the next half hour together. Some part of my mind is still thinking about Kiran and the answers he promised he'd give, but I'd rather stay here with Sena than seek him out. I munch on the protein bars while Sena tells me what she learned about her äma, about the base around us, and about the scavvers. About Emeko, too; apparently they spent most of the day together. My emotional mess fades from my mind, and though sweat still soaks through my layers, the heat is somehow less intense.

Footsteps sound on the stairs again; this time the scavver leader herself peeks her head in the door. She's added more braids to her hair and pulled them up high, showing off the tattoos inked on the sides of her head, their designs swirling against her deep brown skin. Sena sits up a little straighter as Emeko strides into the bunkhouse and plops down on the cot across from us.

Her sharp eyes slide from Sena to me and back again. "Everyone's waiting, but you two seem cozy enough in here, so, you know, why not kick back? Relax. We can totally manage the raids without you."

To my utter surprise, Sena laughs. "I don't think it's even possible to be cozy on this planet. It's too damn hot." From the floor, Iska huffs like she agrees. Her yellow eyes track Emeko, but the wolf doesn't move from her spot. Interestingly, Iska doesn't seem to think the scavver is much of a threat anymore.

I open my mouth to say something about the raids, but Sena beats me to it.

"If everyone's so impatient, they could've come and gotten

us earlier." She stands and crosses her arms, staring down at the scavver. Not with malice but with a slight smile. Emeko stands, too, not as tall as Sena, but the scavver doesn't seem bothered by the height difference.

"Well, we didn't want to interrupt." Emeko looks at me. I roll my eyes.

"We were just talking," I drawl.

"And now you're the one wasting our time, Emeko," Sena says, still smiling. "Come on. Show us the way, oh benevolent scavver leader."

Emeko chuckles as if it's some sort of joke between them and then waves a hand beckoningly as she heads toward the door.

"All right, chumps. And you too, spy." I realize she's referring to me. "Let's go set some shit on fire."

"About time." Sena smiles at me and follows Emeko, Iska on her heels.

What exactly did the three of them get up to when I was out in the jungle? I'll have to ask Sena more about it, and why she didn't mention . . . whatever this is between them. But later. First comes the substations. I grab my serrated knife, shoving it back into my boot, and then pocket the flash bombs again before pulling my damp hair off my face into a tight ponytail.

Time to get my head back in the game.

CHAPTER 25

The lights of the substation peek through the darkness as we approach from below. There's no sign of flyers or activity; everything is quiet in the late hours of the night. The rain has slowed for now, but the mist remains, bringing with it a humid chill that sinks into my very bones.

The artificial light filters down through the trees, illuminating the faces of the raiding party with harsh shadows: Sena and Iska beside me, Kiran just ahead, Lyria and a handful of her Vega syndicates on our tail. We're at the base of a mountain far west of the scavver camp. We were assigned this substation since it's one of the most difficult to reach.

Because that's where Kiran and I come in.

The substation is above us, situated on a plateau jutting out of the side of the mountain, similar to the outcrop by the anacroc nest but much, much larger. Behind it, the mountain rises in a steep ascent, too steep for us to launch an attack from. There's no tree cover, no way to circle around, no easy route up this hill — unless you're a pair of genopaths engineered for subterfuge, infiltration, and situations exactly like this.

Lyria puts a hand on my shoulder. She's in full Vega boss mode tonight, but there's a hint of real concern in her eyes as she says to me, "Get in, plant the explosives, and get out. Don't try anything else."

"Yeah, we know," I say, giving Kiran a sideways glance. We haven't talked since the mine, and his words still hang heavy between us. Ever since my conversation with Sena earlier, I've been wondering if all his controlling actions are some misguided attempt at friendship. At something he doesn't really understand.

"We're not going to mess it up and let them alert the other stations," I finish, pushing the thoughts about him out of my mind. I need to focus on the mission, not our weird, convoluted history.

A small exasperated sigh escapes Lyria's lips while her fingers squeeze my shoulder harder. The glow from a tahuayo blossom hanging near her head paints her freckled face in a red-orange tint that does nothing to disguise her apprehension.

"I'm not worried about the other stations. I don't want anything to happen to you. To either of you."

"We'll be fine," I say. Her concern unsettles me. Even after our escapade in the jungle, I'm not one of her syndicates. "We've broken into worse places dozens of times."

She eyes me like she wants to say more but presses her lips together and nods.

"If you're not back in twenty minutes and we don't hear anything on the comms, we're coming in to get you."

Kiran cracks his neck twice and steps toward the trees as he reties his hair at the base of his neck. "You won't have to."

Sena whispers as I move to follow him. "Just whistle if you need us. Iska and I will come running."

"Stay ready," I say back. She nods, and then Kiran and I are slinking through the trees, closing in on the rocks above us.

I don't know why they're so worried. When I said we've infiltrated places worse than this, I wasn't kidding. We ran dozens of missions breaking into syndicate strongholds on desolate worlds like Abydos or rival corpo offices on busy Assembly worlds. Besides, despite all the trouble we've caused Weiland, I suspect she wants to capture us alive. The commandos may be dumb and trigger-happy, but they're more scared of her than anything else.

We hit the base of the plateau, and without a word, Kiran and I begin to climb, working in tandem up the rock. He slowly begins to take the lead, pointing out handholds, offering an arm up. I ignore his suggestions. Even if he's trying to be friends in some messed-up way, I'm still mad about all the shit he dumped on me earlier and his constant misunderstanding of my relationship with Alora. I can see him making a face at me at one point, but I ignore that, too. Despite the tension between us, we make good time, reaching the top in less than five minutes.

We scramble up the final edge and crouch low beside the substation fence. Like at the other station, the fence is tall, topped with barbed wire, and emitting a low hum. But the wire and the mag field are meant to keep out animals, not genopaths with arken blades. Kiran makes a move toward me, his expression suddenly soft.

"Remy—" he whispers.

"I'll go first," I say quickly, cutting him off before he can say whatever is on his mind. I didn't seek him out at the scavver base earlier because I didn't want to ask for the answers that Lyria promised. He might be right about my impulsiveness, but I don't want to know if he's right about Alora not wanting me to find her. Besides, now's not really the time to get into any of it.

A muscle in his jaw ticks, but he nods before hoisting me up. I glance over the top of the fence, checking the area below for commandos looking our way. Seeing none, I make quick work of a section of the wire; the flash of my arken blade is on and gone before anyone registers its glow.

With a leap off Kiran's shoulders, I pull myself to the top. It's just wide enough for me to balance in a crouch to offer him a hand up. But he's already climbing the fence, so I slip down the other side and land silently on my feet, right beside a stack of crates and a supply shed. As quiet as a shadow, Kiran follows.

And just like that, we're in the substation.

Like the other one, there are a few life pods—barracks and the control room—and the same maze of pipes and machinery leading to the towers in the center. Two, not four; thankfully this station is smaller than the one near the sprawl. No room for a flyer landing pad, but a similar surface-to-air missile launcher sits in a far corner. A strange, low pulse vibrates from the life pods. Some sort of comms signal? Or maybe an extension of the mag fence.

Beside me, Kiran nods and then, staying low, sneaks forward through the pipes toward the towers. Though there are only two, they're bigger than the ones at the other stations, so we need to plant mines under each. I move to follow, but before I do, I mark the distance from the shed's roof to the fence, as it could make an easy exit. Always have an escape route ready. Despite two years on my own, Nova's training resurfaces like I never left. At least right now, that's a good thing.

Exit established, I use machinery and crates as cover as I make my way to the towers, casing the place as I go, knowing Kiran is doing the same.

Fortunately, there are relatively few commandos on night duty. Two I spot in the watchtower. I can read at least two other heart-beats coming from the control room along with that deep pulsing sound. Not sure what machine makes that noise, but it doesn't matter. Turning my focus away from it, I catch a few other pulses from commandos patrolling the grounds. All in all, maybe ten or so.

But my guess is that those on duty aren't paying close attention. That they've more than likely gotten lazy over nights and nights of no activity. As we cut a path to the generators beside the two towers, no guards shout in our direction. No alarms sound. Nothing.

At the towers, Kiran and I split up, each of us taking one. Heat radiates from the pipes, pushing away any lingering chill from the jungle mist. I duck behind a generator, pull a compact sleeper mine out of my pocket, and activate the timing function. The scav-vers have been stockpiling explosives ever since Weiland came to power, stealing them from TerraCo's own shipments. Now we're giving them back to Weiland in a way she deserves.

A big drop of rain lands on my neck and slips down my spine. I glance up to the dark clouds blacking out the sky. The mist still lingers as another drop hits me in the shoulder. Then another. A bigger storm is coming. At least we'll have more cover.

Shimmying underneath the pipes and machinery, I crawl as close to the fuel tanks as I can, then attach the mine to the under-side of a tank's metal casing. I'm about to scoot back out when I spot the pipe that carries the fuel from the tanks to the turbine fan. It's always good to have a backup when you need things to explode. That's not really Nova's training; that's just me and my instincts wanting the biggest bang possible. Kiran would call it my impulsiveness, but it worked on Tundar when Sena needed to escape Kalba's den. It'll work here, too.

And I just happen to still have a few extra flash bombs in my pocket.

I crawl deeper into the maze, sweat drenching my back as the heat grows sharper, more oppressive. A hiss from the pipes screams, nearly splitting my eardrums. My eyes water as the heat intensifies, radiating off the metal in waves. But I keep crawling.

At the junction where the pipes meet the tower, I press down on the activation switch and carefully place the flash bomb switch-side-down on the pipe. It won't go off as long as it sits untouched with the activation switch pressed against the surface of the pipe. But as soon as the sleeper mine explodes, the flash bomb will get knocked off, activate fully, and explode into flames.

Overkill, maybe. Impulsive, probably. But sometimes I guess I can't help myself.

I scoot carefully away, making sure not to bump anything as I make my way back through the maze of machinery. Fresh air teases me as I crawl, the chilly mist finally hitting my face as I pull myself out from the last tangle of the machine-confined space.

Floodlights snap on, blinding me momentarily. I dash toward cover as my eyes quickly adjust; running boots and angry shouts fill my senses. Movement to my left has me sliding down in a dodge, but the butt of a gun still glances off my head. I stumble and lose my balance, then someone grabs my arms, yanking me to my feet and stripping me of my arken blade and the comms in my ear.

I let myself be loose, pliable. Let them think I'm down for the count as adrenaline rushes to my limbs and clears the blood pounding in my head. The blanket of mist has turned to a soft rainfall. Thunder rolls, closer than expected.

A light shines bright in my eyes, but they've already adjusted, already counting the guards around me. Already spying Taggert moving forward through the crowd as Kiran is dragged into the circle of commandos. My stomach plummets. Kiran is in worse shape than me. They must've caught him while I was still buried in the pipes and couldn't hear anything.

Anger begins to crawl up my skin as I take in the bruises already forming on his face. Kiran may piss me off most of the time, but that doesn't mean Taggert should get a piece of him. I jerk against the hands holding my arms, testing the commandos' grip as they drag me closer to them both.

"Well, well, well. It seems to be my lucky night," Taggert drawls as he crouches in front of us. "Where are the others?"

I smirk at the commando, letting him see nothing but confidence and cockiness. The same mask I used on Weiland at the syndicate outpost.

"What others? Can't I blow up your station all on my own? I have a reputation to uphold."

"You're clearly not alone." Taggert kicks Kiran's leg with the toe of his boot. "Whose side are you on anyway?" Kiran smiles through his now-messy hair, revealing bloody teeth. My pulse speeds up at the stark red color.

"The one with the most to gain."

Taggert barks out a laugh. "I always thought you were full of shit." He leans closer to Kiran, lowering his voice. "I'm sure your Nova handlers will be happy to see you once we turn you over to them. We both know that they get off on poking things in cages. I'm sure they'll love putting you back in one."

Kiran lunges toward him, but multiple commandos grab his arms, yanking him back as Taggert kicks him square in the chest. My fingers clinch into fists. He's going to pay for that.

"Just take us to Weiland before I beat your ass." I raise my voice over their jeers. He still thinks I'm Revas. I can still get us out of the mess before the explosives go off. A low hum under the growing storm buzzes in the back of my mind. Flyers. Not far off now. But the timing can still work.

Except then, to my annoyance, another commando tosses the two sleeper mines in our direction. They clatter on the ground, useless and deactivated. Bloody chumps.

No sign of the flash bomb, though. The flash bomb was my own, last-minute addition. Either they didn't find it or . . . they had intel on our strategy and only knew to look for the mines.

My stomach sinks at the realization. They knew about the mines, which base I would be at, and the time of the attack. The only explanation is that someone leaked the information to them.

"I think the time for negotiation has passed." Taggert snaps me from my thoughts. "Especially since we know you're not really Revas." He raises his voice. "Come out, come out, Revas. We know you're there."

The number of people who could've betrayed us gets smaller. Only a select few know about Lyria's identity. And most of them are right outside this substation.

Or inside it.

My attention jumps to Kiran, grunting as he pushes himself to his knees. Familiar doubts begin to creep back in.

Did he double-cross us all?

But he wouldn't, would he? Sure, Kiran's always playing every angle, but is this his endgame? Have Taggert round us all up just as we're about to strike against TerraCo? No, that can't be right. He wouldn't.

"Remy," he whispers, too low for anyone other than me to hear. "Get ready to run."

Then I catch the sounds of hushed boots on the rocks beyond the fence. Lyria, Sena, the others. Do they know it's a trap?

A shot zings through the night, and one of the floodlights shatters.

Kiran's already moving, plowing into the commando in front of him. I follow on instinct, dropping my weight down and yanking the two men holding my arms. As they stumble, I elbow one in the jaw and knee the second in the groin. They both go down as the other floodlight winks out. Half the commandos rush toward the fence and the watchtower. There are definitely more here than I counted earlier. That pulse sound. It must've hidden their heartbeats from us. Someone knows exactly what Kiran and I are and what we're capable of.

Nova.

Nova knows we're here.

My blood boils at the thought.

A commando stupidly rushes straight at me, but I plant my boot right in her chest. She goes flying as I kick her away, and then I'm ducking under another arm, slamming my fist into a chin with an uppercut as I rise. The rain falls faster, harder.

Movement in my periphery grabs my attention.

Taggert. He's raising his gun at me, but then Kiran rushes into him, tackling him to the ground. The two go rolling away. I use the opening and snatch up the forgotten sleeper mines, slinging them across the ground, watching as they slide underneath the maze of pipes. I grab a gun dropped by a downed commando, and rush toward Kiran and Taggert.

I've barely taken two steps when spotlights flare brightly. My eyes leap up; three flyers hover just above us. I was waiting for them to show up. Still, I don't stop running as I close the distance to Taggert and Kiran. Thunder crashes and a true downpour erupts across the station, stinging my exposed arms. I ignore it, fully focused on the fight in front of me.

No matter what Kiran's done to me, I won't let them take him back to Nova.

Taggert's managed to pin Kiran underneath him and is pummeling him with his fists. Kiran takes a blow but then snaps his hips up, not to throw Taggert off but to make him an easier target for me.

As Taggert flails back, I raise the gun and fire two quick shots into his chest. The impact forces him backward, flying away from Kiran. I know the bullets won't pierce his armor, but it doesn't matter. I grab Kiran's arm, pulling him up as I run through the rain toward the supply shed. Kiran takes the gun from me without breaking stride, then twists and fires up through the rain at the closest flyer as I lead us both.

But the spotlight isn't on us.

None of the flyers are following our movements anymore. They're searching the rocks surrounding the station. They're hovering just over the trees, illuminating the jungle below as the storm gathers strength around us. They're going after the syndicates.

They're trying to catch Lyria, the real Revas. That's why they were waiting at this substation.

We skid to a stop on the now-slick ground next to the crates stacked up against the supply shed. Time to ruin Taggert's day.

I hold out my hand and Kiran tosses me the gun without question. Pointing the barrel at the towers, I recall the exact spot of the flash bomb hidden on the pipe. I don't have to hit the bomb itself, just near it. Easy shot. Water runs down my face, rain dripping into my eyes, but I was engineered for this.

And I don't ever miss.

Letting out a breath, I squeeze the trigger.

And then, despite the torrential rain, the towers erupt into flames.

CHAPTER 26

A split second after the flames engulf them, the towers explode outward as the sleeper mines ignite. Kiran and I are thrown into the perimeter fence from the force of the blast. The flyer closest to the towers slams right into the mountainside, flames crawling up its wings. The fuel cells catch, blowing up the ship, and fire spreads farther across the sky.

Strong arms pull me up, and then I'm clambering onto the crates with Kiran, trying not to slip on the wet surface. Then we're over the fence and leaping off the rock ledge into the trees.

For a heartbeat, I'm frozen in the air, nothing but treetops below and fire and heat on my back.

Then gravity kicks in and I plummet toward branches through the downpour of rain. My bruised ribs slam into a limb, but my hands find purchase and I manage to stop myself from total free fall. Using branches and spider vines, I slip and bump my way down the tree and drop the last few feet into the mud below. Kiran's already there, already helping me up.

"We can't let the flyers find them," I shout over the storm, trying to catch my breath as I clutch my ribs.

"I heard shouts leading deeper into the jungle. But I think Lyria's still on the rocks above. She's one of the few with the skill to shoot out the lights."

"Shit."

Sena could be with her. What if that flyer exploded right on top of them?

I take off toward the mountain, trying to find a way back up the boulders. I can see a spotlight from one of the ships through the trees; it's holding steady. Heat from engines hits my face as the other flyer zooms overhead. Shit, shit, shit. They're boxing them in. I think about the ATVs we parked farther downhill, but they won't help us get up the rocks. I push power into my limbs, running flat out.

Then Kiran and I burst through the trees, and I can see them, up on a rock ledge above, silhouetted by spotlights in the storm. Sena and Lyria. Surrounded by flyers. Where are the other syndicates?

I'm about to leap onto the rock to start climbing when Lyria pulls out a gun and fires a few shots at one of the flyers. She's waving at Sena, trying to tell her to run. The other ship returns fire, bullets ricocheting off the rock around their feet. I can just make out Taggert's figure at the gun. The asshole must've gotten out of the station and onto the ship. But he missed the shot on purpose, confirming that Weiland wants at least Lyria alive.

Sena stands her ground; she won't leave Lyria alone. And I know that Lyria sent her troops into the jungle to escape while she distracted the commandos, letting herself get captured rather than allowing any of them to get hurt.

A red blur bursts from the jungle, barking desperately as the flyers sink lower and trap Sena and Lyria completely. I latch onto Iska's fur, holding her back as the rain pelts my face. There's no way she can make it up there on the slick rocks, and the commandos won't hesitate to shoot her after she attacked Taggert. She struggles underneath me, her barks turning to whines as commandos jump from the flyers, their guns pointed at our friends. Lyria tosses down her gun when they point their barrels at Sena.

Then they herd the two of them into the flyer opposite Taggert's as he watches from his ship.

"The ATVs," I shout. "We can follow them."

But Kiran's already running into the trees, a step ahead of me.

"Come on, Iska. We'll get her back." I tug on the fur on her neck, but her eyes don't leave the flyer as it rises up off the mountain. The ship turns eastward, no doubt heading back to Verem on the plateau. Iska breaks from my hold, racing in the flyer's path. I rush after her, catching the sound of crashing branches as Kiran plows through the brush behind us on the ATV.

I track the noise until the ATV appears alongside me, Kiran deftly weaving between the trees. He guns the engine, pulling ahead, and without hesitating, I grab his outstretched hand and leap onto the back as he slows a fraction.

We tear after Iska as the flyer skirts the mountain.

Mud flies in my face from the wheels, my layers are soaked from the rain, and the rocks rush by in a blur, but my focus is on the disappearing ship. Nothing else matters.

"We won't be able to catch up!" Kiran shouts over the storm

as he forges a path through the undergrowth, keeping close to the mountainside. But the jungle is getting denser as we move away from the rocks and boulders.

"We have to! We can't let them get away!"

Light floods the trees. The second flyer, Taggert's ship. Bullets zing past us as he opens fire. Kiran steers us closer to the rocks, looking for some sort of cover. I reach into my pocket and pull out my last flash bomb. Shifting on the platform so I'm sitting backward, I activate the release and hurl the bomb as hard as I can at the ship.

But even my strength and fury aren't enough.

The bomb explodes below the flyer's belly, barely causing it to rock. I gasp as the ship's missiles lower from one of the wings, pointing straight in our path. I don't have to guess that these missiles aren't full of cloud seeders.

"Faster, Kiran, faster! He's arming missiles!"

Kiran revs the engine, pushing it hard as he somehow maneuvers through the rocks and trees. I glance back at the ship, fully expecting a missile to be heading straight toward us.

But it isn't. Taggert's now pointing the missiles at the mountainside. Before I can comprehend why, he fires every single one of them into the rocks near the peak in front of us.

For a moment, nothing happens.

Then I hear it. The entire mountain rumbles. And suddenly I understand.

"Kiran!" My shout is swallowed not by thunder but by the roar of cliffs collapsing into mud and rock and debris.

Taggert's started a mudslide, and nothing will stop the mountain from burying us.

Kiran slams on the brakes, twisting the ATV in a sharp turn

away from the oncoming destruction. We can't possibly outrun it, but he revs the engine and we take off back the way we came.

"Where are you going?" I squint over my shoulder as the rumbling grows closer. Even in the dark and rain, I can see the shadow of the trees as they disappear, swallowed by the flowing onslaught of mud and earth.

"I saw a cave not too far back," he shouts. "It's our only shot!"

Gripping the platform tight with one hand, I raise my other fingers to my lips and whistle, loud and shrill.

"Iska!" I shout before whistling again.

But I see no sign of the wolf as we race the mudslide. I have no idea where she is or if she's in the path of destruction. Then the ATV is jerking to a stop and Kiran is yanking me off the back. Part of me registers the cave tucked into a sharp outcrop of rocks—the rest of me is screaming for Iska.

But the storm swallows my voice, and the wall of debris is barreling down on us. With a final desperate cry for the wolf, I let Kiran pull me into the cave.

All I see are the ships disappearing into the storm.

I didn't save them. I failed.

Again.

Then mud and moving earth swallow the entrance, burying us in darkness.

CHAPTER 27

Above our heads, the earth rumbles as debris plummets into the valley beyond. My mind flashes to all the things that will be destroyed in the landslide's path. The scavver base camp. Miles of untamed jungle. It could even reach all the way to the sprawl. With the torrential rain, massive destruction is possible.

And I couldn't stop it.

I turn and stare at Kiran. He's pulled a chem-light out of his pocket, illuminating the small cave around us. Not that we need the light. Our eyes adjust fine even in true darkness. The area is about as big as a room, but a tunnel behind him winds farther into the mountain. A potential escape route.

Except escape is the last thing on my mind. I stare at Kiran as he studies the cave walls. Somewhere along the line, I began to trust him again. Maybe I shouldn't have.

I stomp toward him and shove him backward with all my strength.

He stumbles and catches himself on the cave wall. "What was that for?"

"Did you do it, Kiran?"

Now his eyes narrow. "Do what, Remy?"

"Give us up to the corpos." My voice is a whisper.

He stares at me while I search his eyes for some shred of truth. Part of me doesn't want to believe it, but I don't know who else it could be. Who else knew everything and knew exactly how to play everyone? Only Kiran.

"What are you talking about?" His voice is ragged. "After everything that's happened, you think that I betrayed you —"

I shove him again. "Like you did before? It's not a very far-fetched assumption when the corpos knew everything, Kiran. They knew that Lyria is Revas and which base she would be attacking. They knew about the sleeper mines. They knew it was going to be you and me planting them. They even know what we are. How would they know that, Kiran? How would they know every detail of your plan if you didn't tell them?"

He shakes his head, anger now in his eyes. "A handful of people knew the plan, Remy."

"Oh, right. So that's who? Emeko. Mirko. Lyria. Sena. A few others. But do any of those people have a history of betrayal? No. Just you."

I jab my finger into his chest hard. He doesn't stop me; he just stares at my finger.

"You have been lying to me this entire time. You purposely tried to rope me into this mess and keep me on this world. Why? To turn me back over to Nova? Because the only thing that makes sense is that you're either working for TerraCo or working for Nova."

Kiran squeezes his eyes shut, frustration spelled out across his bruised features. "Remy, you're not being fair. You have to know I would never let Nova get to you. Everything I do is to protect you from them. Everything I have done on this planet has been to keep you safe."

"I don't need you to keep me safe! I need you to be honest with me, to tell me the truth."

"Fine, you want me to be honest?" He pushes off the cave wall, pacing past me in a flurry of movement. "It's shitty of you to assume I am a traitor at every single turn. Why would I be here with you in this cave if I was working with the corpos or Nova? We just escaped from them together. The two of us, Remy. Working like a team. Like real partners. Are you just going to ignore that? Why is it, as soon as things go wrong, you automatically assume it has to be me? Why do you do that?"

"Because every single time something has gone wrong, it has been your fault. You left me in the jungle—"

"I explained the reason for my actions and apologized, but now you're ignoring that, too," he interrupts.

"It goes beyond that," I shout over him. "All the missions we ever ran, you pushed me off to the sidelines or sent me away from the action." I think about the weird relationship between him and Lyria. "You make deals that no one else knows about. You don't let me in on any of it. You never trusted me to be an actual partner, ever."

He stops pacing in front of me. "Remy—"

"I'm not done! You turn me in to Weiland and then save us from her five minutes later. You catch me from falling into the anacroc nest, but then in the mine, you tell me I don't know what

I want and I never think things through. I assume you're the problem because you always treat me like this. Like I need controlling. And you're still doing it. Not telling me where Alora is—that's just another way for you to manipulate me into doing what you want."

"I haven't told you where she is because it isn't my secret to tell!" He raises his voice to match mine, but I can still hear his heart skip a beat, confirming that I finally caught him in his lies. The mountain begins to shake again, a thunder growing to match the roar in my head, as a second landslide, aftershocks of the first, crashes around us.

"For once, I'm not manipulating you," he argues after the shaking has stopped. "I was waiting at the scavver camp for you to come and ask me about Alora, to follow through on the deal you made with Lyria. But you stayed away. So, I gave you space."

I scoff. "Oh, right, like I'm supposed to believe that. I barely had time to shower, let alone come and talk with you."

He points a finger back at me. "Now you're lying to yourself. You know what? Don't blame me because you don't want to hear the truth. That Alora might not want you to find her."

My fist lashes out without a thought, punching him clear across the jaw.

Then, like a dam unlocked, I rush forward, driving him to the cave wall. My knee finds his gut and he drags me to the ground with him as he collapses. We struggle in the damp earth, me attacking, him deflecting. He dodges my fists, but I catch him with my nails. It's easy to fight someone who won't fight back. I scrape three red lines down his cheek, right next to the scar I gave him. He howls, and as I lunge at his face again, he flips me, pinning me underneath him. He locks one of my arms with his and catches my other wrist in his hand.

"Remy, stop! I don't want to fight. I don't want to hurt you."

"Then stop lying to me! This is all your fault!" I scream.

It's all his fault. It has to be.

A sob escapes my throat as his words from earlier echo in my head. That I'm impulsive. That I never think about the consequences. The things he told me in the burned-out terminal building in the sprawl.

I see you. . . . You go to extremes. . . . Consequences be damned.

Tears stream down my face, the words burning in my mind like a brand. Kiran blinks down at me like he's finally seeing my true self for the first time. I don't care if he sees me unhinged or wildly desperate. I don't care that I'm blaming him for everything. It's his fault Alora is gone. It's his fault that Taggert took my friends. It's his fault that Iska was left in the storm alone.

Kiran's face suddenly softens and his grip loosens. I take the opening and flip him over with my hips in one move. My fingers curl into a fist, ready to lash out at him again because I can't stand the emotion swimming in his eyes. Because I need him to be responsible.

Because if I can't blame him, then the only one left to blame is me.

Kiran watches me but makes no move to protect himself or stop me. I can see myself reflected in his dark eyes. I suddenly see what he must see.

That everything is my fault.

That I'm the one who did this. That I fail the only people who matter to me over and over again.

I scramble off him, stumbling away as I realize the awful truth. I can't be better. I can't keep my promises or stop my impulses that lead to awful consequences. I'm just a mess of broken programming and tangled instincts. No matter how hard I try, I always end up losing the people I love the most.

The truth is that I don't deserve Alora. Or Sena or Iska. I don't deserve any friends. I deserve cold walls and probing instruments. Lab coats and no warmth. Alone, where everything hurts but I can't hurt anyone. We weren't designed to have feelings, to have friends, and clearly this is what happens when we deviate from what we were engineered to be. I should've just stayed with Nova, should've accepted my life as a corpo tool.

I lean against the cave, ignoring the tears on my cheeks and the hair in my face. "You're right," I whisper. "I know it's not your fault. I know you wouldn't betray us. I do know that now. In the end, it doesn't matter who leaked the intel; it's my fault that they got taken away. I brought this down on everyone the second I pretended to be Revas. Maybe even the second I crashed on this stupid planet."

Kiran sits up slowly, keeping his voice soft. "It isn't your fault they got taken, Remy. Weiland outplayed us both."

I shake my head. "No, I let her win. I was too focused on getting what I wanted and not on the afterward. Just like you said."

Kiran sighs as he leans on the opposite wall. I watch a drop of blood run down his bruised cheek, following the ridge of his older wound, the scar I gave him. Guilt tugs at my gut. More proof that my impulses lead to nothing but blood and pain for everyone.

"Then it's my fault, too." Kiran's voice draws my attention from the scratches on his face. His eyes are down but his voice is clear.

"When I first saw you at Arun's, I wanted to show you that I wasn't the same as before. That I wasn't Nova's toy anymore either. But I couldn't tell you where Alora was yet, so I goaded you. Baited you. Because I needed you." He clears his throat. "Needed you in this fight. But also because it's easy for me to fall back into old habits. That stops now."

He pauses, his eyes coming back to mine.

"Alora is here. On Maraas."

I stop moving. I think I stop breathing. Is he lying? His pulse is steady, his expression unguarded. I open my mouth and shut it again.

"What?" I finally find my voice. "What do you mean she's here?"

He sighs, his breathing heavy. "She's been here on Maraas since before you landed."

I stare at him, stunned. He avoids eye contact, brushing dirt from his shirt. I lean closer to him, willing him to look at me.

"Why didn't you tell me before?"

"It wasn't entirely up to me. We thought . . ." He hesitates, his shoulders tensing, his breath catching. Then he sighs again, deeper this time, and shrugs. "I," he corrects. "I was worried that you knowing where she was would mess up our plans."

I glare at him, unsure what he means by 'our plans.' Him and Alora . . . working together? But if he and Alora did have plans, then she was talking to him; she was with him at some point. Which means she knows I'm here. Shouldn't I have seen her or known somehow? Why didn't she come find me? Unless . . .

"Is she hurt?"

"Not yet."

"Where is she, Kiran. Where is she right now."

He takes a breath. Then stares directly at me.

"On that flyer. Headed for Weiland."

My heart sinks down, down, down into my knotted stomach. The realization hits me full force as errant puzzle pieces fall into place, and I want to disappear into the cave floor. Alora has been with him, with me. She saved me in the restaurant. She led me through the sprawl. She rallied an army of syndicates and scavvers. All of that and I didn't see the truth.

"Alora . . . is Lyria?" I squeeze my eyes shut. My emotions whirl, not wanting to accept what my brain has already figured out. "But she doesn't look like . . ."

Kiran huffs. "You know how easy it is to modify facial features. Some plastic surgery, gene alts. Change her hair, her eyes, her bone structure. She became a different person."

I was with Alora the entire time. Since the elevator from Verem. Since she led us through the tunnels. Meeting with scavvers, fighting against TerraCo.

Alora has been here with me every step of the way.

For a moment, I forget how to breathe entirely. My friend changed her face, altered her genes even more. She hated gene mods, but she went through all that. Why? That answer I can guess. To take her father's legacy back. To reclaim Maraas as her world.

She must've decided to embrace her fate after all. Her entire outlook must've shifted the night her father was murdered. I was fighting through the jungle to save her, but . . . the Alora I knew, the one who wanted to be free and choose her own path, was already gone. Died along with her father. This girl—Lyria—this is the girl she decided to become. The girl who survived.

And Kiran has been helping her.

"Tell me what happened. From the beginning," I say, giving him a chance to break his habit of keeping secrets.

Kiran makes a face, a real face and not a mask. It's an annoyed but playful look. It reminds me of the boy he was ages ago, before Nova conditioned the playfulness out of us.

"Please, Kiran," I add.

His eyes meet mine. "Alora and I came to an arrangement."

"Before that. Start with you dropping me in the jungle."

He chuckles but there's no humor in it. "I had confirmation Nova was going to send you to reconditioning as soon as the coup was done. I couldn't let them do that, so I took it upon myself to ensure that you avoided that fate."

"By drugging and kidnapping me."

He sighs again. "Yes, I did. Was it the best method? Probably not. If I had to choose all over again, I wouldn't do it. But you're still here, aren't you? All memories and feelings intact. No Nova programming. You could be a little thankful."

"I'm not going to thank you for taking my choices away. What happened next?"

He closes his eyes momentarily, his voice growing serious once again as he looks back at me. "You're right. Again, Remy, I'm sorry I did that to you."

I glance away from his gaze, swallowing past the lump in my throat. "What happened when you got back to Verem?"

"Dekkard killed Rixus. I went to find Alora." He pauses and I see something in his eyes as he looks away for a second. And then I understand what he's not saying.

"You went to finish the job."

He runs a hand through his hair, pushing it out of his face. "Nova gave me orders. Capture her for them or kill her if I couldn't. But I couldn't follow through with either, knowing that you would never forgive me. So, she and I made a deal. I helped her escape and plan her revenge. And here we are."

As if that explains anything at all.

"Why did you agree to help her, though? You could've just

left her anonymous on another world somewhere," I say, remembering what he said earlier, that he made a deal to pull off the coup. And Lyria, she said she had something over him, something Nova wouldn't approve of. Something big enough to blackmail even him.

Kiran watches me piece it together. "I helped her because she's very convincing. I helped her because I had to. And because some secrets are my own to keep." His posture makes it clear that he won't say another word about the whys.

But I know Kiran doesn't make deals unless there's something in it for him. Something for him to gain. What could he possibly gain from Alora? He always disliked her. Hated our friendship. Why would he make a deal with her? My brain whirs through a few scenarios, but I catch the pained expression on his face and decide to let it go. To not push him on this.

Though I get it now, why he was so mad when Lyria volunteered to go look for the coordinates with me and wanted to give him orders. He didn't like being reminded that she had all the power in their relationship. The Alora I knew wouldn't want to use someone's feelings against them, wouldn't want to control someone the way she felt controlled by her father's will. I guess she really isn't the same girl at all.

I don't know how to feel about that.

"Are you okay?" Kiran's soft voice interrupts my thoughts.

I shrug. "You asked me why I never thought of what I'd do after I found her. I told you it didn't matter, that we belonged together and the afterward wasn't important. But now . . . I don't know who this Alora is—who Lyria is. I don't know if we belong together anymore."

"Is that why you wanted to find her so badly?" he asks slowly, his expression suddenly inquisitive, like he's actually trying to understand. "Because you belong to her?"

"She's my friend," I reply. "I don't belong to her. I promised to be a better person for her."

He's quiet for a minute. Then he barely whispers, "You . . . love her."

"Love?" I cough, my ears burning slightly as I realize what Kiran must've thought of our relationship this whole time. "I never really thought about it like that." I look at him in the near dark of the cave, the chem-light casting long shadows on his face. His posture is tense, like he's waiting for something. For what, I don't know.

I look past him then, considering his words. "Are we even capable of such a thing, or are we too broken, too tainted by Nova?" I shake my head, squeezing my eyes shut. "It's not romantic between us but I don't know if it's love. Look at where we are now. She's in Weiland's hands and I'm trapped in this cave. Failed her again because of my genetics and engineering." A tear slips down my cheek. "I don't even know who I am without her. Just a washed-up genopath with nothing."

"That's not who you are," he says, louder than before. "I see who you are."

I look up at him. "And who is that?"

"You're Remy. My impulsive partner—ex-partner," he corrects with a small smile. "You push boundaries, push everything a bit farther than we were ever supposed to. You don't let anyone put you down. Even the hacks at Nova could barely ever rein you in."

I raise my eyebrows. "What are you talking about?"

He looks at me, a confused laugh on his lips. "You know what

I'm talking about. You always had to have more fire, more explosions, more anything than was ever necessary on every single mission. You were supposed to just gather intel that directly impacted our decisions, but you'd try to affect things that were not related at all."

"That's how I was programmed," I argue.

"No, Remy. That's who you are. You were that way before we ever came to this planet. You push limits and rules to the extreme. Hell, you decided to become friends with Alora even though you knew Nova would never allow it. That's just what you do. It's one of the things about you that always amazed me. How you could decide to act without overthinking every move. How you do things because you want to, and you don't let consequences hold you back."

His earlier words about my impulsiveness didn't sound like this. Like a compliment. It's strange, something nice coming from him. I squirm a little, unsure how to take the awe I hear in his voice.

"I . . . admire you for that," he finishes.

"Even though I don't think of the afterward?" I say in disbelief. "Look how well that's turned out. I failed everyone."

His eyes pierce mine in the dim light. "But you never let that stop you. I'd move you away from the action on our missions, but you'd always end up in the middle of the battle, turning things in our favor. I gave you the slip on Tundar, but you still raced across the ice just to help a girl you hardly knew. Even when Weiland had you cornered in the outpost, surrounded on all sides, you found a way out and still managed to throw a flash bomb in her face at the same time."

I blink at him but he just shrugs. "I told you. I know who you are."

I stare and stare at him while all my actions over the past few days reassemble in my head as I try to see myself the way he sees me. I thought he only saw what he wanted to, thought he didn't know me at all. But I was wrong.

Kiran sees me more than I ever realized. As much as Alora did, as much as Sena does. He isn't the enemy or traitor I thought he was. I don't know what exactly this new relationship is between us, but I don't think it's a bad thing. To have someone else who understands me.

He glances away, as if my gaze has gotten too heavy to hold. "And I know that Lyria knows who you are, too. And Sena. They know you won't give up on them, no matter the consequences or afterward."

I think about my friends, now in Weiland's hands. Every move I've made since we came here is proof that I do ignore those consequences, that I go above and beyond when I'm in the thick of it and never think things through. And now Sena and Lyria are suffering because of it. I've failed my friends many times over. I've made a giant mess of things.

Kiran shifts against the wall, his gaze back on me. I think about his words, all of them. Maybe I am broken, a little too messed up from Nova's programming. But maybe he's right, and my impulsiveness doesn't have to always be a bad thing. Maybe my pushing limits is the only way I know how to help the people around me. The only way I can show my friends that I care. It might not be conventional love; it might not always work, but it's my way of doing things. One thing that is truly mine and not an instinct programmed into me.

Right now, it's the only thing I've got.

And the only chance my friends have.

"I helped make this mess," I begin slowly. I won't just sit here wallowing anymore. I'm going to do something, even if it ends in more disaster. "And the consequences are the only thing I'm thinking about now."

Kiran interrupts me. "Remy, I told you. You think it's your fault —"

"That's enough," I stop him, my voice soft but firm as I push off the wall and stand. "Whether it's my fault or yours or Weiland's, it doesn't matter. But you telling me how I think, that ends now." I point at him as he stands in front of me. "No more deciding what's best for me. No more protecting me from myself. That isn't your job."

Kiran opens his mouth to argue but then lowers his eyes. And nods.

"Your job is to figure out how we get them back. Someone tipped Taggert off and told him our plan. Someone who's still out there. We're going to find that person and we're going to stop Weiland. That's the only consequence I care about right now. I won't be stuck out in this jungle while my friends get hurt again."

I peer into his face, looking past the shadows and scars.

"I'd like to get out of this cave now and go save our friends. I made Sena a promise. And Lyria. We can't let Weiland take this planet." I extend a hand to Kiran.

"Are you with me?" I ask.

His near-onyx eyes lock on mine. "Of course I'm with you. I'm always with you."

I scoff. But he steps closer.

"I mean it. If I'm going to stop telling you what to do, you have to stop assuming that I'm not on your side. I'm not going to betray you, Rem. Not again. Not ever." There's a fierceness in his gaze that unsettles me even more than his awe a few moments ago. A lump forms in my throat, but for once, I don't have to read him to see whether he's telling the truth; I trust that he is.

"Deal," I say, then cough, trying to clear the sudden emotion in my voice.

Kiran eyes me and then my outstretched fingers. Finally, he squeezes my hand, the warmth from his skin a comfort in the dark, the heat not bothering me even in the humidity of the cave.

"Let's go cause a ruckus, partner," he says, raising an eyebrow.

I don't scold him or correct him this time; instead, I smirk back at him.

"Let's get out of the cave first."

After another second, I untangle his hand from mine because we need to move. I grab the chem-light and head for the tunnel at the back. "This way seems the most promising. Unless you want to dig by hand through the muck and debris."

"Tunnel it is," he replies. "I've had enough muck to last me a lifetime."

The tunnel twists and turns, but neither of us are afraid of getting lost. Even after our chem-light dies, we wander through near darkness for over an hour. And then soft light appears at the end of one of the turns. The tunnel has led us out of the mountain. I brush aside branches and we climb over a fallen tree.

Then we're out of the cave and standing at the precipice of mass destruction.

Rain still falls around, steady and heavy. But even the sheet of rain cannot hide the sheer size of the landslide's path. As the dawn's light grows around us, the true devastation sinks in.

A line has been cut across the jungle.

An area of no trees, no animals, no signs of life. Only thick mud and endless debris cover the landscape like a blanket made of chaos. Roots and branches stick up out of the still-wet mud. As we walk closer, I realize the landslide's debris rises taller than my head, taller than Kiran. At least twelve feet deep at the sides of its path and even thicker in the middle.

"The scavver base camp?" I breathe my question loud enough for him to hear over the rain, fearing the answer.

"Directly in its path," Kiran says softly.

"Let's hope they managed to get out in time."

We start to pick our way down the rocks, following the path of mud and jungle flotsam, staying slow and careful as the raindrops pelt us. With the constant rainfall, the muck still moves, like a lazy river winding downhill. The corpos have done awful things to worlds in the past in the name of profit. Look at Tundar. With one explosion, they raised the core temperature a few degrees, all so they could mine a little more exocarbon.

But this . . . this is something else. This is the calculated, intentional destruction of human lives and livelihoods. For a reason I can't even fathom. How does TerraCo profit off destroying settlements and murdering people? The same people who prop up the economy. Who will the corpos exploit if there's no one left alive?

After another hour or so of hiking, I'm drenched and sweaty and covered in cakey mud all at once. It's hardening in the cracks of my skin where the rain can't reach. Between my toes, in the crooks of my elbows, under my chin. My layers are completely soaked through. The clouds keep the sun from warming us, and a slight chill has worked its way to my bones. I hate the bloody jungle.

Finally, Kiran steers us away from the mudslide's path. Toward another scavver settlement, he says; a place they would retreat to. I follow, still trying to comprehend the reason behind the destruction.

A familiar bark pulls me from my thoughts.

"Iska!" I shout without a second thought.

And then red fur and amber-yellow eyes are rushing at me full speed through the trees. The wolf leaps up on me and licks my face, sniffs my layers, whining for the girl she's missing. I wrap my arms around her neck, inhaling the scent of her fur. Beyond the mud and dampness, I can still smell the cold ice and splinter wood. The familiarity grounds me. I will not let Sena be hurt. I will not let Weiland win. I will use every tool in my engineered arsenal to make sure of it.

An ATV pulls up a few seconds later. Emeko and another scavver.

"That wolf's practically a bloodhound," she says in lieu of a greeting. "Led us straight to you." She glances from Kiran to me.

"Is there no one else with you?" Her voice grows hard as her eyes narrow.

Kiran shakes his head, water dripping from the mess of dark brown strands. "Taggert took them. Someone leaked our plans to the corpos. We took out the base but lost Lyria and Sena."

Emeko's lips press into a line, and her honey-brown eyes practically flash with rage.

"Then what the hell are we standing around here for?"

CHAPTER 28

The scavver settlement Emeko takes us to is hidden deep in the mountains, and it's nothing like the base where we planned our attack. Built around rocks and in caves that dot the mountain face, it doesn't feel like a military camp.

It feels like a home.

In the morning light, I watch from the back of the ATV as people come in and out of rows of stilted life pods. Others are tending small patches of crops spread across terraces. I catch sight of livestock pens made from old flyer parts and even shops and stalls built into the mountainside, like the syndicate outpost in the cave. Kids hide under the homes and dart around servo bikes to wave at Emeko and smile at Iska running alongside us. It feels familiar. Like the sprawl far behind us but much less desperate. Like the settlement on Tundar but less rigid. Less cold.

Emeko drives us straight to a cave tucked off to the side. There, a group of people are just finishing breakfast. The scavver council,

Emeko tells us. They insist we sit and eat, despite the panic and urgency pushing at me to do something about my missing friends. But I scarf down the barbecued meat and eat my fill of rice and potatoes. I need the energy; fumes and fury will only carry me so far.

Once the food has been cleared, Emeko finally begins to break down the events from the night before. TerraCo and the commandos were prepared for our attacks at every station. Someone definitely leaked information. Despite the mole, four of the corpo substations were totally destroyed. Three others, partially. Dozens of scavvers and syndicates were killed or taken. When the landslide triggered, some of the base camps were evacuated in time.

Two others in the direct path of the landslide had no chance.

My heart nearly stops at the number of scavver and syndicate lives that have been lost. The base camp where we organized everything was completely wiped out, buried underneath debris.

The entire time Emeko is talking, the guilt and rage and fire in my stomach take hold, growing with each of her words. I didn't think about the syndicates who died two years ago in Dekkard's coup, but now my heart aches for the lives lost in the last few days. I might've helped the TerraCo corpos become the monsters on this world, but I won't let them swallow it completely.

"TerraCo has to be stopped." Emeko's final words echo the thoughts in my head.

One of the younger council members speaks. "We have already lost so many lives." Her expression is sad, thoughtful. "TerraCo may rule over a portion of Maraas, but we are free from their influence out here. Why should we continue to devote our resources and people to a fight we cannot possibly win?"

"Oh, so we'll just let them murder and kidnap us instead? Blow up mountains until there's nothing left in this jungle but mud and bones? How can you not see that the landslide was a direct attack?" Emeko's eyes flash with her words, but the council doesn't look convinced.

"If you do nothing, the storms will continue to grow," Kiran says. "They'll never stop. And life, even out here, will become impossible."

Another, older member waves a hand. "We are used to the rain, child. We were born to this world and know the dangers it poses."

"You don't understand." I pick up Kiran's argument. "It won't be just a little more rainfall. The hellstorm will become permanent and unending. That's TerraCo's endgame. To destroy all the human life on this planet. To create a storm that never stops. I know you'll be risking more of your people, but it's a risk we have to take to put an end to this."

Kiran nods. "You're not the only ones at stake. The syndicates and the hundreds of people living in the sprawl will be wiped out as well. This isn't just a fight for you. It's a fight for everyone on this planet."

The council members are silent as they regard us. Finally, Emeko sighs.

"It doesn't matter what you decide," she says, her voice soft but not weak. "We aren't asking for permission. Either you help us with supplies and more troops, or you don't. We're going after them no matter what. I won't let this planet get destroyed by bloody corpos. You chose me to help lead this movement. This is what I'm choosing."

The younger council member slowly smiles.

"A strong choice, Emeko Hasan. What is your plan?"

"Oh . . ." Emeko draws out the word. "Did you want more than just anger and conviction? Is that not plan enough?"

Eyebrows rise and heads shake, but the small whisper of an idea has formed in my head.

"Do we have any idea where they might've taken Sena and Lyria and the others?" I ask Kiran, but Emeko answers.

"Mirko said before that Weiland has holding cells under her tower on Verem."

"Where is Mirko?" Kiran asks suddenly, his brow furrowed.

Emeko shakes her head. "He was moved to another camp before the attack on the substations but he's unaccounted for now. He's either gone or taken."

"No." I sigh as the puzzle clicks into place, frustrated I didn't see it sooner. "No, he wasn't taken. He's the mole."

"What?" Emeko goes back to looking like she wants to pummel me.

"He used to work for TerraCo. He told Sena that he and her grandparents defected years ago."

The older council member practically growls. "Mirko has been an integral part of this community for half a lifetime. He wouldn't betray us for his old loyalties like that."

"He would if he had something to gain from Weiland. He was sick." I look to Kiran, his eyes telling me he's come to the same conclusion. "His pulse was erratic. His breathing was slightly labored. He told Sena he was ill. What if it wasn't about betrayal for him but rather offering information in exchange for some sort of medical treatment that he can't get out here? Something he needed to save himself."

The council members are silent again as they consider the implications.

"He lied about the holding cells," I continue, looking to Emeko.

"I was in Weiland's tower. The only things underneath it are the train station and the ship hangar."

She crosses her arms. "How can you be sure?"

My mind rushes through the last few days, going back to that first meeting, getting a feel for the building and the people. Listening to what Weiland said and what she didn't have to say. Sena and I trekking across the rest of the run-down city. All the intel weaving together in my head.

"She made sure that the tower was tall enough to be seen anywhere in Verem," I think out loud. "So everyone could see her triumphs and wealth and grandeur. She wouldn't spoil that by keeping prisoners in it."

Then I remember the door in the Vega compound. The door leading to the interrogation rooms in the basement; the door that I didn't want to go through no matter that it was sealed shut. And the antiseptic smell seeping through the building. The scent of sterilization. Of labs and white coats. Of Nova.

"She's keeping them in the old Vega headquarters," I say. Kiran's eyebrows shoot up. "Down below. The syndicate tunnels underneath the city are still there, too; TerraCo didn't get rid of them or block them off. One of the tunnels in the ship hangar leads straight to that level in the Vega compound."

"I bet she converted all those rooms into cells," Kiran says.

"To prove her dominance over the syndicates who used to live there," I finish, locking eyes with him.

"So, if they're there, what's our plan?" Emeko is looking expectantly at Kiran and me.

I keep staring at Kiran, his own eyes searching mine. He's the strategist, I'm the infiltrator, but suddenly my whisper of an idea falls into place. He is right about me. That I go above and beyond what Nova programmed in my genes. That it can be a good thing. My idea is a long shot, but if anyone can make it work, the two of us can. I still may not understand all his secrets, but I trust that he'll see this through. That he's got my back. Kiran's lips tug into a smile, and I know he's come to the same conclusion I have.

"The train," we say in unison.

⤞⤝

Unlike the other abandoned mines, deep under rocks and caves, the exocarbon one at the end of the sprawl is exposed, cutting into the cliffside like an angry scar, marring the earth.

Half the mountain has been carved out, the lush green stripped away to nothing but earth and mud, the orange-brown terraces a stark contrast to the untamed jungle beyond. Despite the heavy rainfall, a handful of sprawl workers still toil in the mines, some using machines, others handheld tools. There aren't many of them and they're mostly on the lowest levels. I spot only a few TerraCo employees around, safe from the rain in tiny container pods. The lack of proper tools and oversight is proof that TerraCo doesn't care about the profitability of this mine. Even the security is lax with commandos only around the rail depot.

The mag rail depot itself is next to a small plateau that over-looks the layers of dug-out earth. The farthest reaches of the sprawl sit underneath the tracks, mostly abandoned by the look of things and total lack of movement. I don't want to think about where all the people went. If they moved closer to Verem and the syndicate outpost. Or if they were edged out by either the corpos or the ever-increasing storm cycles.

Our raiding party is hidden in the jungle beyond the tracks, a small group of scavver troops along with Emeko, Kiran, Iska, and me, tucked in tight among the trees as the afternoon sun begins to sink in the sky. Iska shakes raindrops off her fur, flinging more mud onto me, but I don't mind. Despite showering at the scavver settlement, I'm completely drenched and muddy already. The corpo-created rainfall hasn't stopped since last night, and it isn't going to stop anytime soon, so I've just accepted the downpour and the mud caking me like a second skin. Helps keep us camouflaged in the jungle anyway.

The crew around me may be modest, but what we lack in numbers we make up for in sleeper mines and flash bombs. The scavver council members may have had their doubts about our plan, but they certainly didn't send us empty-handed. I've even got a nice-sized arken blade strapped to my thigh.

"I don't see the train anywhere." Emeko taps her boot impatiently in a puddle.

"The train hasn't been on a regular schedule for a while," I say. "We're probably going to have to call it and convince them to send it here."

"In this weather? The storm's getting worse by the hour. Pretty soon these raindrops are going to feel like bullets. You really think they'll send the mag train out in this for a few scraps of exocarbon?"

"Don't worry," Kiran replies. "Remy will convince them."

Even after our agreement in the cave, I'm still surprised by his blatant show of confidence in me without a directive to go along with it. I keep waiting for him to give me orders, but he hasn't. At least in this case, his confidence is merited. This is what I was made to do, what I trained for most of my life. I will get the mag train here. Because there's no other option.

Ignoring the skeptical look on Emeko's face, I tell her: "Just get us in there undetected and I'll take care of the rest."

"Oh, don't you worry about me and my part. I've been sneaking into this place since I was a kid. I know a way straight to the comms tower that won't get us noticed."

I raise an eyebrow. "You snuck into a mine as a child?" Not that I should throw stones. I was trained to do a lot worse things when I was young.

Emeko shrugs. "I liked to break into places I wasn't allowed to go. Rules are for chumps. Plus, the Vegas who used to work security had really good lunches delivered from the outpost."

I glance at Kiran, whose eyes slide over to me as we walk. "Risking life and limb for a bit of food. Such a great choice for a leader," I mumble.

"I heard that," Emeko snaps from ahead on the trail, just loud enough for us to hear over the storm. "Trust me. You'd do the same if you'd tasted the lamb jerky from Ish. Bloody delicious."

Kiran raises his eyebrows pointedly at me. We've been on Ish many times, in worse scrapes than this. Blew up an entire block of abandoned corpo buildings there once. Memories of our missions run through my head, and I smile at his knowing look. Like Emeko, I guess I also excel at breaking rules.

"You ready or what?" The scavver leader is staring at me, waiting impatiently at yet another tunnel entrance. I shake off the thoughts and wave at her to lead the way. She might not be my biggest fan, but at least we're both in good company. And she's not wrong. The lamb jerky that Ish exports is worth stealing.

Without another word, we head into the tunnel. The group sticks close and moves fast as Emeko leads us into the belly of what's left of the mountain.

While I trust she knows the way, my hearing is on high alert, searching for heartbeats and footsteps beyond the thundering rainfall outside. I rely on my other senses, too, sniffing for the stench of body odor or the tang of blood underneath the heavy earthen smell of the mine. Iska stays ahead of me, trailing just behind the scavver leader. Between the two of us and Kiran, no one should be able to get the drop on our little raiding party. Emeko's path leads us true, and we make it up to the level where the comms tower is without running into a soul.

The platform is partially covered to keep the communication equipment out of the storm. Crates and empty mineral canisters litter the area, like the corpos packed in a hurry and left behind the less expensive gear.

Thankfully, their carelessness is our gain; there are only a few commandos working this level. Two patrolling the terrace beyond the overhang. Three scattered near the short tower where the comms are. One inside working the control panel.

Kiran nods to Emeko, points to a few of the scavvers, and indicates where to flank the commandos. The group of them fans out, keeping low behind the crates. As they take out the commandos, I follow Kiran, heading straight for the tower where the comms operator is.

As Kiran and I slink in through the open door, the woman at the controls looks up, her eyes wide. I've got my arken blade pointed directly at her head.

"We'll take it from here," I say with a smirk. Before she can protest, Kiran removes her ear comms and hauls her outside to be tied up with the others. Emeko points to a life pod that's been converted to a holding cell tucked against the far side of the platform. The fact that there's a holding cell in the mine speaks volumes about

TerraCo's true intentions. While the scavvers disarm the comman-dos and drag them away, I start activating the comms, running through the various corpo protocols that Nova drilled into us.

"Mountain base to tower, mountain base to tower." I keep my voice low, bland, unrecognizable. "Do you copy?"

Static sounds momentarily before an answer comes over. "Copy, mountain base. What do you need?"

Kiran and Emeko both stand in the doorway, watching me. I ignore them and focus on the voice on the other end of the radio.

"We need the train out here, stat. We just hit a big exo deposit and want to get it back to HQ before the storm opens up."

"Negative, mountain base. The train is grounded per exec or-ders due to weather. It's too late to send it out now. You'll have to wait for the next retrieval run after the storm."

"We can't wait," I say, letting cocky impatience seep into my voice just as the meaning of his words sink into my head. I was wondering before what Weiland was transporting on the train. Here's my answer. And it's not people or supplies; she's salvaging what equipment she can from this place before the storm becomes permanent. "This cycle's going to be a lot longer than the last and I can't guarantee that the residents of the sprawl won't take a chisel to this hunk of exo. So, unground that train, soldier. Unless you want to be the one to report to the execs a total loss of millions of chits worth of exo because you were too afraid to send the train out in a little rain."

There's silence and static for a full minute. Emeko's already looking pissed, but then the voice comes back.

"Are you sure about the exo?"

I hit the button so hard my thumb goes numb. "We've got an extractor freeing a chunk of it as big as a servo truck. This haul alone would make us all chit-rich enough to buy a moon some-where."

Another beat passes. And then:

"All right, base. I'm sending the train, but you better not be exaggerating."

"Copy, tower. We'll pack it and be ready when you get here."

The transmission cuts off. I grin at Kiran and Emeko.

"See?" he drawls to her. "Told you she'd get it."

Emeko's shaking her head at me, but a smile is growing on her face.

"Weiland's not going to know what hit her."

CHAPTER 29

Train to mountain base, we're on our approach, but we haven't gotten your clearance code yet. Are we clear to dock?" The voice sounds over the comms about thirty minutes later.

I hit the button as I scan the holoscreen in front of me, looking for the code. Iska whines beside me in the control room, pawing at the ground. Her impatience is certainly palpable. Me too, girl. Me too.

"Copy, train," I say, nudging her gently away from the controls. "We're ready for you. The clearance code is . . ." My fingers fly through the data, looking for the daily codes I know they're supposed to put in here. Finally, I spot it.

"Clearance code is X5–452."

"Copy that, mountain base. See you in five."

I signal to the others outside, the scavvers now wearing corpo armor and helmets as they move into position on the platform. We pushed all the crates near the tracks so it looks like we're going to load the train. The rumble of the tracks grows as the train approaches us. Next to me, Emeko crouches down below the control panel. She refused to put on any of the corpo gear. Something about the principle, she claimed.

"Where'd you learn corpo comm-speak?" she asks as I pull one of the full-face helmets down over my chin. Iska growls for a split second, but I extend my fingers toward her slowly. She huffs and sneezes on my hand. She knew it was me. Just wanted to voice her dislike.

"We were trained to talk like corpos." I answer Emeko's question automatically as I switch on the speaker inside the helmet.

She eyes me. "Now you look just like them, too."

I mimic Iska's huff loud enough for Emeko to hear without the mic. "We were also trained in syndicate protocol and even scavver slang. We look like whatever we need to for whatever the mission."

"Ha. There's no way you could ever look like me, spy."

I roll my eyes in the helmet. "No, you're definitely one of a kind."

Luckily, the train pulling up to the platform cuts off her retort. Iska resumes growling as the doors to the five cars all slide open and a commando steps out of each. The scavvers don't wait. They quickly overwhelm the commandos, taking them by surprise. Who expects to get attacked by their own people? Five minutes later, the commandos are down and thrown into the holding cell along with their compatriots. And our little group files onto the train.

Kiran, Emeko, and I head straight for the control car, the wolf hot on our heels. She hasn't let me out of her sight since we lost Sena.

We'll find her, girl. I promise.

"Did they train you two how to drive these things?" Emeko says as I tear off the stupid helmet, Kiran following suit.

"Not this train specifically." I shrug. "But we'll figure it out."

The scavvers spread out across the train cars as we activate the door for the control room. It's a tiny space, only slightly bigger than most flyer cockpits. The entire dashboard is a mess of holoscreens and switches, but luckily the controls aren't that much different than my flyer, so it doesn't take Kiran and me long to figure them out. I finally jam the acceleration, and with a lurch, the train pulls forward, away from the platform. A few shouts sound from the cars behind, and Iska barks her displeasure with the sudden motion.

"Sorry," I call out.

Beside me, Kiran chuckles as Emeko and the wolf storm away from us. I took only one step backward, even though I expected the jerk. Kiran's hand shot out behind my back, but I glare at him, and he quickly pulls it away. He might've promised to not be so controlling, but old habits are hard to break. I keep my attention on the tracks in front of me instead of him.

Based on how long we waited at the mine, the trip back over the sprawl should take about a half hour. It's not a ton of time to prepare, and I need my head in the game as much as possible. Weiland and Taggert won't just be sitting idly by, even if they assume we were all buried in their landslide.

The jungle zooms by around us and my mind jumps back to Alora. Lyria. She planned this entire thing. Did she take into account that Weiland might get to her? I glance over at Kiran.

"So," I start, trying to figure out my words. "You helped Lyria with this . . ." I trail off, hoping he'll fill in the blanks without me specifically asking.

"This revolution?" He eyes flick to me, then away.

I nod and wait for him to say more. He looks back at the controls and makes adjustments while avoiding my gaze.

"This plan was the only way for her to get the Vega back from Dekkard. It required years of prep work. Years of splitting my focus between Nova and helping her gather resources. Training her."

"I thought you hated her," I say softly.

He's quiet for a moment and then shrugs.

"I only hated that she warped your thinking about our mission and put you in danger."

"And by helping her, you were able to keep us apart," I say, some understanding dawning on me. I still don't know what Lyria held over him to even get him to agree in the first place. But I know I'm right about this. Otherwise, why not bring me in earlier? Why else would he lead me on a wild goose chase across worlds?

"Yes, I suppose. But I was able to keep you safe," he replies shortly.

I don't know whether I want to shout at him or not. My anger at his controlling nature is still there under my skin, even though he promised to be different. But it doesn't change the past, doesn't change that he screwed things up because of his inability to let me make my own decisions and live with the consequences.

"You might've kept me from Nova," I say. "But you messed up everything else in my entire life."

He presses his lips into a line, not meeting my eyes again, and stares out ahead of the train.

"They were going to reprogram you, like I told you before. But it was more than that. They were going to send both of us and maybe even Alora to reconditioning. They knew you two had gotten close. And with her gene mods, if they'd captured her alive, they would've happily made her one of their other agents. I tried to warn you about their eyes everywhere, but you didn't listen. At the time, I thought the only way to keep them from erasing your entire personality was to separate you two."

He looks out into the jungle, then adds quietly, "I don't know what I would've done if they'd erased who you are."

I open and then shut my mouth, my mind trying to wrap itself around his words. Around these feelings of his that I didn't realize ran so deep, so intense. Why would he need to protect me so badly? Something flutters in my stomach, a nervousness edged with uncertainty and panic. So, I quickly remind him, and myself, of our conversation in the cave.

"You still don't get to make those kinds of decisions for me, Kiran."

He nods. "I know. I realize how much that hurt you."

Something else occurs to me. "And what about you? Did Nova send you to reconditioning after all was said and done?"

He doesn't answer. Which is answer enough.

"So, you left me in the jungle, then told them I was dead. You got Lyria off-world and then you had to deal with the fallout alone. Why? Why would you let them torture you?"

He shrugs, his bored mask a stark contrast to the pulse I hear beating rapidly under his skin. "I knew the risks. It didn't matter anyway. I've survived the reconditioning more times than you know. More than any of our squad. They can poke and prod me all they want; it won't change anything."

I let that sink in, but now I'm left with only one question.

"Why?"

The sprawl flies by underneath as the jungle spreads out around us.

"Why did Nova recondition you more than the others?" I ask,

the nerves building again in the pit of my stomach. "Why won't their torture change anything? What aren't you telling me?"

He keeps his mouth closed, a muscle flexing in his jaw. The rain outside continues to fall unabated. I think back to the memory replay of us in Nova's canteen, after his five days of reconditioning. I asked him if he was okay, and he looked at me before answering. Looked at me as if seeing me was the oxygen he needed to breathe. The same way he's looking at me now.

I'll always be okay.

I don't know what I would've done if they'd erased who you are.

Before I can say another word, Kiran starts to speak. "Remy, the thing is, I—"

"Are we there yet?"

I jump as Emeko's demanding voice interrupts us, my cheeks suddenly burning with heat. I quickly check the readouts on the holoscreen while Kiran clears his throat.

"We're almost there, impatient one," I grumble at Emeko, then point out the window while the back of my mind wonders what Kiran was about to say. "Look."

The train comes around the end of a curve in the tracks, revealing the rise of the plateau and the tower standing tall at its apex, a beacon even in the gray rain.

"Great, we'll prep the sleeper mines."

She says something else before disappearing into the cars, but my mind isn't fixated on her or even what Kiran started to say. No, I'm staring at the path ahead. Looking for something I can't pinpoint but I know is off, is wrong. We're coming in for the final approach to the tower station. I check the controls again. Nothing jumps out at me as incorrect or misplaced. I flip the switch to send a comms to the tower when it hits me.

When the train was approaching back at the mine, it required a clearance code from the base. We're nearing the tower, and yet no one has given us a code. Which can only mean one thing.

They know we're coming.

I slam the controls into a lower gear, trying to slow our approach. The train shudders and sends us all flying, even Kiran and me.

"What the hell?" Emeko shouts at us from behind as Iska begins to bark frantically.

"They know we're coming! Everyone hang on!"

I scramble back to my feet, reaching for the brake, but Kiran is already there.

"I got it!" He pulls hard on the lever and punches in the control sequence for the brakes. The entire train lurches as the mag fields change polarity in an attempt to stop our motion. I'm thrown backward out of the control room by the force and slam into a crate in the first car behind. The air rushes out of my lungs, and I gasp for breath as pain radiates through my already injured chest and ribs. Even from here, I can see the entrance to the plateau just ahead of us through the front window, the tower looming ever closer.

But we still haven't stopped, and suddenly I have a very bad feeling about what's waiting for us.

"Kiran!" I scream.

At the same moment, the tracks in front of the train detonate.

There's a split second following the explosion where the world is silent, frozen as the rail lines explode apart and a wall of flames rushes at us. Then everything jumps back into motion, physics catching up, and the cars are flung backward by the sheer force of the blast.

The train flies up and off the tracks, suspended in the air for seconds that feel like eternity. The crates, the scavvers, everything is flying. Then the magnetic hum disappears with a pop as we crash back onto the tracks and everything is thrown sideways.

I grab a bar on the side of the car's interior and pull myself halfway up, trying to recalibrate my bearings. Kiran's not far from me, still in the control room, getting his feet underneath him, too. I glance around; Emeko and others are still moving, still alive. Iska whines a few feet away from me, crouching close to the ground but unharmed.

Another crash echoes, rocking the car again, and more of the railing around the train disintegrates into pieces. The entire track shudders. The support beams below must be damaged.

"Everybody hold on to something," I shout, gripping the bar tighter as I reach for Iska.

But then more tracks in front of us collapse into the sprawl and jungle below. And with a sudden lurch, the train begins to slide down into the gaping hole ahead.

The world teeters on nothing but air as we balance on the very edge of what's left of the tracks.

Something snaps.

The train groans.

And the angle steepens with a jerk.

Beside me, Iska slides straight toward the front of the train, now dipping precariously over the edge. My fingers reach, grabbing on to the fur on her neck. She yelps but stops sliding. The window in the control room now looks at nothing but the debris and jungle and hard ground far below.

The train inches farther down and my stomach begins to drop. My fingers spasm as I struggle to hold the wolf's weight.

Kiran is climbing out of what is now an almost completely vertical control room.

I scream his name again as he attempts to move closer to me, but I have no free hand to reach for him.

Then my stomach jerks clean through my throat as the train plummets straight for the ground.

CHAPTER 30

My body is thrown upward as we crash through the wreckage of the rail line and the levels of the sprawl.

Then, with a jarring thud, the train smashes into the mud, and I fling myself through a window on instinct alone. Sparks and metal and glass explode every which way, slicing my skin before I hit the ground. The wind whooshes out of my lungs and I tuck and roll, everything a blur of pain and noise as shrapnel and rain pour down around me. My body keeps rolling and flipping through mud and debris alike until finally I tumble to a stop.

I open my eyes and find myself blinking up at mangled tree limbs and falling rain. I cough up dust and mud. My chest smarts with every breath, pain cleaving my ribs. Probably a few that were cracked are now fully broken. But I don't have time to lie here; my limbs appear to be working, no major injuries aside from dozens of bleeding cuts and gashes.

Slowly, slowly, I push to my feet, but I nearly collapse onto a tree trunk when my legs shake underneath me. Blood drips into my left eye. Mud runs down my face, in my nose. My right ankle and knee protest, but after a few slow movements, I put weight on them and stand again, walking carefully through the mud toward the wreckage.

The front train cars are a tangle of metal. The control car went sideways when it fell; half is smashed into the jungle around me while another section has collapsed onto the sprawl. Buildings have been dislodged, life pods destroyed. Screams pierce the downfall of the rain, dozens of heartbeats out of sync, racing or slowing. Pain and despair fill the air as fires burn around the debris. So much destruction. So much loss of life. Anger bubbles in my veins as I absorb the scene. Weiland isn't hiding her intentions anymore. She's coming for us and doesn't care who or what gets in her way. Doesn't care who she murders.

She's going to pay for this.

A creaking groan pulls my attention upward. The last train car is still vertical, hanging precariously from the tracks above. Which don't look like they'll hold for long.

My eyes scan the wreckage for movement, squinting through the storm for any sign of life. Iska, Emeko, the others. Where are they? Where is Kiran?

Panic rises in my throat, but a small whine cuts through the discord, barely audible in the rain—my ears just catch it. I focus all my senses on the sound.

The whine calls again.

Iska.

Without a second thought, I limp past a large piece of the train that tore apart and landed on a platform at the edge of the sprawl.

Bridges and ramps that were in its path are mangled beyond repair. Ropes and spider vines tangle around every part of the debris. I clamber through the mess, watching my step on the slick
surfaces, following Iska's call. Some of the rain is blocked by the
levels above my head, but water still soaks through my skin as I
make my way to the sound.

I squat down next to a large piece of metal, hissing as my knees
protest. Gripping the edges of the panel and bracing myself for the
worst, I gather my strength and lift. A roar tears from my throat
as I fight the weight of the panel and the injuries of my body. But
then it's cleared.

And Iska comes hobbling out from under it.

I drop the panel and fall to my knees next to her. I try to breathe,
but fear and dark spots pull at the edges of my vision.

Warm breath on my cheek. A soft nose on my skin. She's all
right. I bury myself in her damp fur. She's all right. I pull back and
check her body for injuries. A few gashes have opened across her
torso and legs, dark blood and mud matting her red fur. She's holding up one paw like it hurts—she must've landed on it wrong when
the train crashed, just like I landed wrong—but thankfully her old
wound didn't reopen. She tentatively takes a few steps, working
out the kinks.

"That bitch!" A voice and a crash sound as someone else moves
in the wreckage. A moment later, a face appears from behind a former bridge hanging from an upper level. Emeko. Blood runs down
her face and arms, stark red against her dark skin. Her braids are
a mess, and her pants are torn. She's cradling one arm but is otherwise okay.

"The others?" I call over the storm, pushing to my feet again
despite the ache deep in my bones.

She winces, her face etched with pain and fury. "I haven't seen anyone else yet."

Shit.

"Kiran!" I shout. He better answer. If I survived, surely he did. I scan the wreckage, looking for whatever's left of the control car. I spot half of the switch panel further down and start moving. The rest of the car is nothing but mangled metal.

I call Kiran's name again, moving aside part of a crate and kicking my way toward the panel, ignoring the pain in my ankle, in my knee, in my ribs. The injuries will heal; the pain will subside. But that stubborn jerk better not be dead. There's too much unfinished between us for him to go and die on me. Too many secrets left unsaid.

As I scramble deeper into the wreckage, Iska hobbles past me, despite her injured leg, sniffing at everything. I frantically search the debris, glancing under ruined panels and broken crates, pushing my senses to find one single heartbeat, one specific scent. I brush off everything else. The shouts of pain around us. More heartbeats marching toward us. The smell of gunpowder and plastic. I push it all away. Ahead of me and directly underneath the last train car hanging vertically from the tracks above, I catch a faint heartbeat just as Iska stops.

And howls.

I rush forward, my body protesting the entire way. I trip over some wires, but Emeko grabs my arm, pulls me forward. There's a large side panel, bigger than the one I lifted earlier. But just under it, I can make out a faint pulse.

"Grab that side!" I shout. My fingers struggle to find purchase on the slick surface. Despite her hurt arm, Emeko grips the panel with both hands. Together, we lift and move it, inch by inch. I can see Kiran's mess of dark hair. Then the rest of him, still breathing, heart still beating, face down against the ground. Iska moves in to lick his exposed cheek while we finally clear the panel and drop it off to the side.

I rush to him, scanning his back. There's blood soaking through his layers, soaking through even the commando armor. Gently, gently, I roll him over.

A jagged piece of metal juts out of his left shoulder. My hands shake as I slowly examine the wound. It doesn't look like any vital organs were hit. He's breathing with no wheezing sound coming from his lungs. But there's so much blood, and that is just as dangerous. We're engineered to heal fast, but we're not invincible. I smack his cheek and his near-onyx eyes flutter open, focusing on me before glancing down at his wound.

"I accidentally got some of the train in my shoulder," he says weakly.

"I see that." I snake an arm behind his neck. "Can you sit up? We need to move."

Emeko kneels at his other side. "Move where? He needs a doctor."

"I know," I snap. "But we've got to get out of here first. People are coming and I don't think they're going to be doctors, nor do I think they'll be sympathetic to our plight."

"Commandos," she breathes. I nod. With a grunt, Emeko takes his other arm, and we sit him up. His eyes squeeze shut, and his breathing is shallow. But he's still alive.

"We have to leave the shrapnel in for now, so the bleeding doesn't get worse and —"

A low creaking noise interrupts me.

"What is it?" Emeko asks. She didn't hear it. I hold up a finger, closing my eyes to better pinpoint the sound. Raindrops pebble my exposed face as I push my focus harder, farther than the rain cascading down. I catch another almost undetectable groan. Coming straight from above us. Iska starts barking.

"Grab his shoulder!" I shout, wrapping my arm around Kiran's waist and pulling him backward as hard and as fast as I can. Emeko doesn't question; she latches onto him with her good arm and together we drag him back. Iska's running alongside us and Kiran's shouting in pain, but I block it out, concentrating only on getting us clear.

"Down that ramp!" Emeko nods and we yank him to the left, getting him down the ramp just as whatever is holding the suspended train car finally snaps.

The car plummets down and I throw my body backward, not letting go of Kiran. The crash shakes the very foundation of the tracks, sending metal and glass debris flying. More life pods collapse, falling down multiple levels to the mud below. Sparks fly as wires rip. Screams erupt and are silenced.

I tuck my body around Kiran as much as I can, and pain slashes across my back in tiny cuts. Several more large pieces fall as we lie there, not ten feet away from total disaster. Finally, the crashing stops, and I open my eyes.

Next to me, Emeko peels herself out of a fetal position. She looks from the wreckage to Kiran and me, prone on the ground.

She locks eyes with me. "Holy shit, you saved us."

I let out a long, shaky exhale, trying to get my breathing under control, and check to make sure Kiran's okay.

As I rise, I help him into a sitting position. His normally bronze skin is sallow and ashen, but he's conscious and still breathing. Well, mostly conscious. He won't last long without some help. But

I can hear the marching footsteps getting closer even through the twisted wreckage.

"I haven't saved us yet."

Commandos appear in the rain and trees just beyond the sprawl.

"We need to go. Now," I say.

"What about the rest of my crew?" Emeko's eyes are wide. "We can't just leave them here."

"We have minutes before the commandos are on us and then we won't be able to help anyone at all. You have to make a decision," I tell her. "Stay and risk capture or run and complete the mission."

"I hate you," she growls. "I hope you know that."

"I would hate me too." I quickly take stock of where we are and spot the barricade that Lyria led Sena and me through only a few days ago. It feels like weeks have passed since that moment. Now both of them are in Weiland's clutches and we're down here bleeding in the mud.

I grit my teeth. I will not let Weiland win.

If we can make it to the sewer tunnel, we can get into the syndicate outpost without being spotted. Since our plan to take the train to the tower has been literally derailed, getting to the outpost is our best bet. From there, I'll crawl up the rusty elevator shaft on the side of the plateau if I have to. Once we get the metal out of Kiran's shoulder, nothing is going to stop me from saving Lyria and Sena.

I point to the barricade. "We need to get over that hill." Emeko nods, then grabs a large pack from the ground and slings it over her shoulder.

"Is that the pack of explosives?" I ask in bewilderment.

"What, you thought I wouldn't grab them before the train

crashed? We came here to blow corpo shit up, and I'm not leaving until we do."

I let out a shocked sort of laugh before leaning down to Kiran.

"You've got to stand up. We can't carry you and I need you to walk if you want us to make it out of here."

He nods, gritting his teeth, and Emeko and I help him stand. Then we're shuffling over a ramp and across a bridge, rushing as best we can. Just above our heads, I spy the tunnel that cuts through the barricade. I make Emeko climb up first, then she reaches down and we hoist Kiran into the tunnel. She holds on under his arms and I lift his feet as we crouch and inch through the passageway. Iska brings up the rear; her whines let me know that the commandos are coming in hot. Hopefully, the rain provided enough cover that they didn't see us disappear into the hole.

My leg protests with every step; my arms and back are still bleeding from the glass and shrapnel. Blood mixed with sweat trickles down into my eyes, stinging like a thousand needles straight into the sockets. But I don't drop Kiran's feet.

When we come out the other side, I can just make out the sewer entrance through the sheet of rain, not fifty feet up the hill. I point the way and Kiran manages to stand again with Emeko and me on either side.

Every step we take, mud slips under our boots as the rain pounds us. Debris comes loose and clatters down the hill. Somehow, we make it all the way to the grated sewer entrance without falling. Shouts follow us from the barricade. Blood oozes from Kiran's wound, mixing with the rainwater; his breathing is short and labored.

Must move faster.

Emeko moves the grating out of the way, and then we're in the sewer. The stench stabs up my nose, but I do my best to ignore it. I've got bigger problems than stink. After twenty minutes of labored movement, I spy the ladder that leads up to the restaurant, but Kiran stops me as I reach for the first rung.

"Keep going." His voice is still weak. "Arun . . ." He points farther down the tunnel. "Arun can help."

I press my lips together. Arun's den is on the other side of the outpost, which means more chances for us to get caught. Or further injured. A memory sparks suddenly; Alora mentioned the Vega tunnels that run from the old HQ building to the caves down here. If anyone knows about them, Arun would. Though I'm sure Arun's help will come with a price tag. But it's not like we really have much of a choice. With a frustrated sigh, I continue down the tunnel.

"Who's Arun?" Emeko asks. She helps me shift Kiran's weight as we pass through a narrow opening.

"He's a smaller Vega boss. Runs the biggest den down here in the outpost."

"That guy? I heard he was a real asshole."

"He is. But he's going to help us whether he likes it or not."

We spend the next forty minutes in the sewers. At some point I even stop noticing the smell. It takes us three different wrong turns to finally find the right tunnel that gets us close to the club. Fortunately, the exit isn't up a ladder but up a ramp that spits us out in the same alleyway where I first confronted Kiran.

Even in the alley, the beating of the bass inside the den pounds in my ears. The world is practically ending outside, but Arun won't stop the party.

The three of us and Iska push close to the building. I jiggle the handle of the side door, but it's locked tight. Then I realize what's wrong. The thump, thump, thump isn't from the pounding bass of club music.

Rather, it's the marching of commandos as they patrol the streets of the outpost.

We prop Kiran against the wall and inch to the end of the alley to get a better look.

"Damn," Emeko breathes as she peers around me into the street beyond. "Weiland must've taken over everything after she nabbed Lyria. This is not good." We quickly duck back into the alley as a troop of commandos turns onto the street. I head back to Kiran and bang on the side door.

No response.

"Open up, you chumps," I hiss, pounding again. Emeko shakes her head from her position at the street. No help coming from there.

I pound so hard on the door the vibrations reverberate up my arm, making my teeth rattle and my ribs smart.

"Shhh. Stop pounding!" Emeko darts back to us. "The commandos are almost here."

I scan the alley's nooks, looking in every corner. There must be a camera drone out here somewhere. Finally, I spot a tiny glare over the sewer entrance. They've already seen us and still haven't opened the door. Rage fills my veins and I clench my fists as I get close to the camera.

"Come on, Arun," I say to it, raising my voice just enough to be heard. "You know this isn't right." I point to Kiran bleeding on the ground. "You know we can fix it, but we need your help first."

The commandos' voices amplify as they near our alley. I growl at the camera again and turn to ready myself. I'll take them all on if I have to. I'll fight dirty and use whatever means I can.

But before I can flood my body with more adrenaline, the den door swings open, and two large men lift Kiran like he's a sack of grain. Arun stands in the shadows just beyond the light, an annoyed expression etched across his brown skin. Emeko darts inside after Kiran. I whistle softly for Iska to follow and we all file into the hallway. I catch a glimpse of the commandos turning into the alley just as the door snicks quietly shut.

"So, now I'm supposed to trust you to fix this mess?" Arun's deep voice rumbles in the darkened hallway. "It's your fault the world is broken in the first place."

I cross my arms. "We can argue about whose fault everything is after you patch Kiran up." A light flickers on somewhere in the empty club beyond, and I see that the two men have put Kiran on a stretcher. Relief floods my veins, replacing the rage.

Arun eyes the shrapnel protruding from Kiran's shoulder as they carry him toward the back rooms. "Well, that's going to have to come out." He turns back to me as I tear my eyes away from Kiran. "Let me guess. Weiland."

"Let me guess," I reply. "She's taken over the entire outpost."

The tall man growls in response. "TerraCo has been a menace for the last year, that bitch nothing but a thorn in my side. First they launch that obnoxious low-atmo satellite to spy on us all." My mind blinks, remembering the satellite Sena and I almost ran into before we crashed. "Then they cut off the train stations, killing our supplies. And ever since you waltzed into my club, things have only gotten worse. I'm not really sure who to blame. Weiland. Or you."

Something about his words tickle the back of my brain, but I don't have time to figure out what's off.

"You know this isn't my fault," I argue. "This has been Wei-land's plan all along. She wants to destroy all life on this world."

"Don't be so dramatic. It doesn't suit your nature, Remy." He rolls his eyes and walks toward the bar. Emeko and I trail behind him.

"She's telling the truth," Emeko says.

"What would you know about it, scavver?"

"Plenty," she snaps. "We're the ones who took out the substa-tions they hid in our jungle. Substations that spit out cloud seeders in an attempt to make the hellstorm unstoppable. If that's not try-ing to eradicate our lives, then you're right. I don't know anything about it, syndicate chump."

They glare at each other and then Arun reaches under the bar. I automatically assume he's going for a gun, but I've got no weap-ons to counter him. I lost my arken blade somewhere in the train crash. Instead, he pulls out a clean rag and tosses it to me.

"I'll get my boys to bring you some med-wipes so you can get cleaned up."

I catch the rag and hand it to Emeko. She looks at it with a wrin-kled nose, like it might be full of syndicate germs, but then starts wiping down her arms. I turn back to Arun.

"Kiran said you could help. I know he meant beyond his in-juries. You've been here longer than anyone. You have to know another way to get up to the plateau. Maybe through the old Vega tunnels?"

"Now why in the hell would I give away all my secrets to you?"

"Because without Kiran and me, you wouldn't even have this club. You were a low-level pit boss before Dekkard took over. You helped him and you were rewarded with this little empire down here. So, the way I see it, you owe me and Kiran everything. And you can pay us back by helping us out. Besides, we're the only ones capable of stopping Weiland."

He grumbles but doesn't protest outright.

"I don't know where you stand with Revas and Dekkard. But Dekkard left you to rot and Revas is trying to regain power here. So, you can help us do that or leave Weiland in charge and lose everything. Because if she isn't stopped, there won't be any patrons for you to entertain because this planet will be drowning in storms."

The syndicate glares at me. And then finally nods.

"I'll patch up your boy. And show you a way up. I'm not promising to support a full-on Revas revolution against Dekkard, though. I have my own people to think of. And I'm only doing this so we're even, got it?"

I smile as the first flames of hope flicker up my spine.

"Nothing taken, nothing given."

CHAPTER 31

One of Arun's people brings us a med kit a few minutes later. I strip off the ruined corpo armor, then grab painkillers and antiseptic foam to close up some of my worst cuts. Emeko takes a med-wipe and, to my utter surprise, kneels down to Iska. I open my mouth to warn her, but the wolf stands stock-still as the scavver slowly wipes mud and grime off her fur. She grabs some gauze and wraps it tight around Iska's injured leg while I stand there in slight shock.

Emeko eyes me, one eyebrow raised. "What? She likes me."

"I suppose so," I mutter, trying to wrap my head around the whole event.

"Don't act so surprised." The scavver stands. "I'm quite likable, you know."

I study her, again wondering what she and Sena got up to together while I was out in the jungle with Lyria and Kiran. The only way the wolf would trust her is if Sena showed trust in her. Interesting.

"I'm going to check on Kiran," I say. Emeko huffs in response, grabbing another med-wipe for her own arm.

I turn on my heel and head down a hallway made of stone, cut right into the plateau. I don't have to know my way around the den to find Kiran. I just follow my nose. The scent of his phero-mones is mixed with the iron tang of blood. I find him in a small room surrounded by Arun's people. The space is filled with cots and medical supplies. Arun's bar has an infirmary? That tells me a lot about the kind of trouble his patrons get up to.

What's left of the commando armor and Kiran's shirt lies in blood-soaked tatters on the floor. The shrapnel has been removed, and a man who I'm hoping is a doctor of some kind is stitching up Kiran's shoulder. He's finishing just as I step farther into the room. Kiran's face is still ashen, though I can hear his pulse, light but steady. He's going to be okay. The attendants clean up the gauze and blood before leaving. Finally, the doctor looks up at me.

"We've given him a sedative. He lost a lot of blood, but his heartbeat is strong."

I nod. His body will burn through the sedative as it works to heal his wound. At least the Nova hacks made sure we could repair most injuries without too much medical care. Our cells, bones, blood—it all regenerates, allowing us to heal much faster than even modified humans.

But we're not invincible. The osak bear on Tundar pretty much proved that when it broke three of my ribs and slashed my face. The snow and ice kept me from healing quickly, but once we were under the lake, once I felt warm again, my body recovered. Kiran will, too. Especially since there are no below-freezing temperatures here to slow him down.

When he wakes up, I know he won't stay cooped up. But for now, it's better he's stuck in this den. He'll be safe down here, away from Weiland's reach. One less person for me to worry about failing. Once I save Lyria and Sena, Kiran and I are going to finish our conversation from the train.

I track his breathing for a few minutes more, making sure that it's steady and not shaky. I also take a moment and swallow down a forgotten protein bar from my pocket. It's mostly smashed but I need the energy. My knee still twinges when I put all my weight on it, but the swelling in my ankle has gone down, thanks to the painkillers and my own blood working overtime. My ribs smart, but after Tundar, it's a familiar pain. One I can deal with until they stitch themselves back together.

After a final glance at Kiran, I head back to the bar.

Emeko has wrapped her injured arm with some gauze.

"Broken?" I ask.

She shakes her head. "Just bruised. I'll be fine. Unlike the others we left." There's a bite to her voice that's clearly directed at me. I clench my jaw.

"We can only help them by stopping Weiland. And getting caught by her commandos would've made that impossible."

She stares at me, her expression flat. "I know," she finally says. "But I'm still mad about leaving my people. I don't know if they're injured or taken . . . or worse. So, let's hurry this plan up so I can go find them again."

"Agreed."

A throat clears behind us. I turn and find Arun standing in a doorway, his arms crossed. Somehow, yet again, I didn't notice him. Sneaky chump.

"If you two are done bleeding all over my floor, I'd prefer you leave sooner rather than later in case Weiland sends troops in here looking for you." He turns without waiting to see if we follow.

Emeko shrugs and picks up the pack of sleeper mines. Together, the two of us and Iska follow the den boss. Arun leads us to an alcove of mirrors on the back wall and steps on a hidden latch. One of the mirrors clicks and opens a fraction. Dust coats the edges, and the smell of damp earth fills my nose as Arun opens it farther. Beyond is a short, dark hallway ending in a winding staircase. I raise my eyebrows in surprise.

"Access tunnel," Arun says with a sigh. "Built by Rixus Vega himself as an escape route from his headquarters above. One of the reasons he built up there and not down here. So he would always have a way out."

"That's handy," Emeko mumbles behind me.

I smirk. Alora's—Lyria's—secret passage. I knew it was here.

"How did you learn about it?" I ask, suddenly curious if there's even more Lyria never told me.

A smug smile stretches across his face. "There isn't much I don't know about on this planet. But how I earn these secrets is my own business. Now, are you going or not?" He holds out two chem-light sticks, then he passes me a handgun in a holster as well. I give him a surprised look as I take what appears to be a free weapon.

"What? You said you would take out Weiland, and even you can't take out that woman with your bare hands." He shrugs. "Get rid of her and that will make us even."

With a nod, I loop the holster around my leg and check that the gun is loaded. Just to be sure. Emeko grabs one of the chem-lights from me and nudges past us, Iska on her heels.

"You can thank us when the planet is saved, old man," she snaps.

Arun's eyes narrow after the scavver. With a growl, he pushes me farther into the passageway, then slams the mirrored door right on my ass.

"Nice going." I crack the chem-light and catch up to Emeko.

"What? He was annoying and pompous, and we really don't have time for his bullshit."

The words are ironic coming from her, but I don't entirely disagree, so I clamp my mouth shut and follow the scavver as she starts up the spiral staircase. My knee protests each step, but I ignore it. Emeko pants a few stairs above me. Iska continues to climb between us, not slowing for anything. I can hear the drip, drip, drip of water from somewhere above. The storm is seeping through even in here.

"How long have we been climbing already?" Emeko asks after a few more minutes, breaking our silence. "And just how many bloody stairs are there?"

My mind starts doing the calculations on autopilot. I factor in the height of the plateau along with the angle of the spiral and the size of the steps.

"Probably another twenty minutes more if we don't slow our pace. Longer if we do."

"I hate stairs," she says. "When I get up there, I plan on letting Weiland know that personally."

"Right before we blow her up?" I eye the pack full of sleeper mines on her back.

She grins wickedly as she glances at me over her shoulder. "Or right after. Doesn't matter to me."

I scoff, though her words spark the pieces of a new plan in my head.

"Give me the explosives," I say. "It will be nearly impossible to get out in time after planting them in the tower, but I can manage it. You go free the others in the old syndicate compound."

But Emeko halts dead on the stairs and turns to face me; I have to stop myself from bumping into her. Iska bounds a few steps up past her, then pauses and whines.

"No, Remy," the scavver says slowly. "I will be planting these explosives. You will be getting everyone else out."

"But you won't know your way around the tower, or the best place to put the sleeper mines—"

She holds up a hand. "Wrong. What, you think because you're some fancy genopath and I'm not that I don't know anything? That I don't have skills of my own? I've planned over a dozen attacks on that tower in the last two years. The council wouldn't approve any of them. Too risky. Too much loss of scavver life to infiltrate the city. Well, we're already here, and if you think you're going to take that away from me, think again. Too many scavvers have died already and I am going to avenge them today."

Her honey-brown eyes flash as she points a finger at my chest.

"I don't like you much. I know you know that," she continues. "I don't give two shits. But I am trusting that you'll do whatever it takes to get our friends safely out of that place. Because once the tower blows, I'll find my way back to the jungle, just like I always do. But I can't do that if they're not safe. So, you better get them all out of there, got it?"

I blink slowly. I should've noticed more about Emeko. Should've seen her pain and realized what lengths she'd go to. Kiran really is right about me. It's not my genes or instincts that have been forging my path this whole time. It's all me. My decisions, my needs. But I was so focused on my own problems, my own friends, that I failed to see what was right in front of my face.

My promise to Alora two years ago burns in the back of my brain. *Be better than what they made you for.*

But I need to be more than just better. I have to quit putting my needs above my friends'. I have to see the whole picture and make a difference for all of them, not just for me or Alora.

"I promise," I say to Emeko. "I'll get them all out."

I won't fail them again. My eyes jump to Iska. I won't let any of them down. Not Kiran. Not Sena or Lyria. None of them. I will keep my promises to be better.

I will.

"Good," Emeko says. "Because if you don't, I'm coming for you next."

I smile, a small laugh escaping my lips.

"I'm serious." She crosses her arms.

"I know you are," I reply. "Nothing taken, nothing given, right?"

She points a menacing finger at my face. "Exactly. Now, stop wasting time."

Before I can protest, she's already turned and bounded up three more steps, Iska barking and following on her heels. Another twenty or so minutes and we crawl through a grating into a tunnel that stretches out in two directions. This tunnel isn't carved out of hard stone but rather lined with metal grates and panels. Vega tunnels. Water flows in rivulets here and there down the walls, disappearing through the grating. The storm must be getting worse to cause leaks down here. Or Weiland didn't bother reinforcing this stretch of tunnel.

Iska sniffs the ground as I inhale and study each direction, relying on my internal compass to determine where the hell we are.
I catch a faint whiff of armor and gunpowder from one side. The
other way seems devoid of scents until a slight breeze blows, bringing the smell of burned engine oil with it. Which can only mean one
thing: transpos and flyers.

I point toward the smell of engines. "The hangar is that way.
You can get to the tower from there. There's an elevator that
goes right up to Weiland's suite. But I bet you can find some
lower offices to plant the mines in, or even in the elevator shaft
itself."

Emeko smiles. "Don't worry, I'll find exactly where to put these
to cause maximum damage." She jerks her chin in the other direction. "Hurry up and go save them already." And then she's gone,
running down the tunnel.

I blow out a long breath, mentally preparing myself for what's to
come. Halfway down the other tunnel, Iska suddenly howls. Then
she's off, a blur of red fur disappearing into darkness. I guess I know
which way Sena is.

I start a slow run, letting my knee adjust to the movement. Just
as I begin to pick up speed, Emeko's shout trails after me.

"Good luck, spy!"

Good luck to both of us indeed.

＞＜

The tunnel ends abruptly at a large panel, which has been
knocked out of place by one very determined wolf. I step
through the opening cautiously and find myself in a small closet
stocked with cleaning supplies. A large shelf is overturned in front

of the dislodged panel, and the closet door is slightly ajar. So much for a quiet surprise approach.

I peek my head out of the door briefly but see no movement. No commandos rushing this way. No Iska either. Pushing my senses further, I listen for any signs of life. Heartbeats finally reach my ears from a few corridors over. I try to pinpoint where I am in the old Vega headquarters, but Weiland's wiped away all traces of anything Vega, of anything familiar.

Where the halls were lined with warm lights, now they're cold, clinical. Like the Nova ship I grew up on. No personality. No markers. Nothing on the walls to indicate humanity or even a direction. Nothing but white and gray corridors with nameless doors. Even when Dekkard used these rooms for his own purposes, the space was not this menacing.

But Sena is somewhere down here. I inhale deeply, concentrating on the musk of Iska's fur, the hint of ice and snow. The lingering sting of the med-wipe that Emeko swiped across the wolf's body. And the jungle mud embedded in her paws.

My nose tells me the way to go. Ignoring all feelings of trepidation and oppressiveness, I slip out of the closet and head down the hall. Two turns and footsteps sound ahead of me. I dart to the nearest door and find it unlocked. I steal a glance inside to be sure the darkened room is empty before sneaking in.

Through a small frosted window, I watch the shapes of commandos pass by as I keep out of their line of sight just beyond the doorframe. They pause a few steps after passing the room. I can hear the murmur of voices talking about long shifts and the weather changes. While they talk, I glance around the office more carefully, looking for anything that might be useful.

One whole wall is a holoscreen of blinking feeds. Keeping an ear on the guards' position, I sneak over and activate a key on the command panel. Fortunately, nothing beeps as the screen switches to a view of the file lists. I scroll through them, looking for something familiar, for anything that might be important. I spy a file labeled *ARC1* and my memory snaps. I know that name. Where did I see it before?

After I select the file, the holofeed jumps to a camera view showing nothing but dark clouds. It's a wide-angle lens, the type usually used on drones and flyers. But what drone would be able to fly in this storm? Again, my mind tries to make sense of things, but nothing clicks into place. What is this office for?

The footsteps echo again as the commandos head farther down the hall. I click off the feed and go back to the door. I let the footage and the questions settle at the back of my mind. Whatever *ARC1* is, it can wait.

Back in the corridors, I weave my way farther into the lab. Or prison. I really can't tell what it's meant to be. Probably both. I gain ground, closing in on Iska's scent while dodging guards by sliding into offices or doubling back the way I came. I overhear some commandos searching for a "wild dog" that's gotten into the compound. They don't realize the threat the wolf truly is. And none of them seem to have caught her. Good girl.

Time ticks as I move; each minute that passes drives my adrenaline up.

I need to find my friends.

The longer they're here, the harder it will be for me to get them out safely. And when Emeko blows the tower, all hell will break loose, and this place will go into lockdown. And then there will be nowhere for any of us to hide.

I push the panic down. Panic and fear lead to mistakes, and

I can't afford to make any. I will find Sena and Lyria. I will not allow myself to be trapped in this place.

I'm about to turn a corner when a rough voice suddenly breaks the silence. More commandos. Shit.

I leap backward and try the nearest door. Locked.

The commandos are steps away from the corner.

I rush to another door. Locked.

I'm too far from the intersection to catch them by surprise and subdue them. They'll see me first and then they'll alert everyone. I don't want to use my gun either. I can't risk someone hearing the shots.

Last chance, a door across the hall. This one opens with a whoosh, and I scramble inside as the commandos round the corner. I jump away from the door as it closes. Did they see me? My heart pounds in my ears, but my movements are still silent, still controlled.

Until I see what room I've stepped into.

"I knew you'd come to me. So much easier this way."

And who is in it.

CHAPTER 32

I've stepped into a room from my nightmares.

Medical equipment hangs on the walls. Examination tables are lined up in a row with bright lights overhead and straps to hold subjects—people—down.

And standing directly in my path is Taggert.

He's in full-body combat armor, only the ruddy skin of his face showing. He holds a long arken blade beside his thigh. No sign of any guns, and that's enough to tell me he wants me to hurt before he throws me on one of those tables. His right arm, the arm Iska mangled, doesn't seem to be bothering him anymore. They must have accelerated his healing, wrapped the wounds up tight. No weakness for me to exploit. He stands not three feet in front of me, each of us still, waiting for the other to move. But I don't have time to wait.

I rip my gun out of the holster and fire two shots as I raise it, at his leg and then at his chest. The bullets bounce harmlessly off the armor. By the time I'm pointing the barrel at his face, he's already moving, already slinging the arken blade up at the gun. I'm not the only one with gene mods. I yank the gun upward, trying to avoid his swing, but the edge of the blade hits the barrel, and the third bullet goes wide as the gun flies out of my hand.

He didn't even activate the laser. Now I know he's going to try to draw this out; he wants me to run after the gun. Anything to waste my time or slow me down, to keep me from my friends.

I realize all this in the second it takes his blade to finish its arc. The only way for me to win is to make him think he already has.

His meaty fist comes faster than I expect. I jerk back, hitting the door, but I don't bother trying to escape. I'm sure he already disabled the lock somehow. Doesn't matter. I'm not going back outside until this is done. If this is the path to saving my friends, I'll take the pain that comes with it.

Taggert lunges again, this time with the blade, an evil smile twisted across his face. I dive under the sharp edge and roll across the room, trying to get distance between us while I figure out my plan of attack. The gun's somewhere in the opposite corner. I'll have to work my way back to it.

As I come out of the roll to standing, Taggert's leg kicks at me. I take the blow, his shin connecting with my lower rib cage. There's a crack as my ribs break further, and black spots blink in my vision. Breathing hurts, but at least my lungs are still intact. I throw a few wild punches to keep him at bay while my body tries to recover.

Taggert dances away from my fists easily with a grin on his face.

"Looks like you had a tough time on the train. I hope your injuries aren't too severe. How will you ever beat my ass?"

With a laugh, he sets the arken blade down on one of the tables and wiggles his fingers in my direction.

"Come on, then. Show me those fancy engineered skills of yours."

I breathe heavily, letting him think I'm winded. My ribs are killing me, but the sharp edge of the pain has already dulled. I can easily outpace him even though he's fresh with no injuries. But time is not on my side. I need this dance to end.

I need to get him close so I can finish this.

I rush forward with a shout and a wild haymaker to hide a fast left hook. My knuckles just glance off his cheek, but it's enough to enrage him. He rushes me, his arms going around my waist, lifting me off the ground and slamming me to the floor like I weigh nothing.

The air rushes out of my lungs, and I can barely brace myself as he kicks me in the gut. At least he missed my ribs this time. I curl up, protecting what I can. The bastard hauls back to kick me again, laughing. I whip my foot at his legs, but he bats my kick away and jerks me up by my shoulders. Pain rips down my chest like fire as he tosses me onto an examination table.

I let myself lie there, gasping and wheezing. Let my head roll to the side and my eyes unfocus as I attempt to weakly push myself up again.

Taggert slaps me hard across the face. It's a blow to exert his dominance rather than to cause pain. But I let him do it because now he thinks he's won and he's not thinking about using the restraining straps on me. I lift a feeble arm in his direction, but then let it collapse onto the table.

He sneers down at me, disgust and disappointment across his features, spelled out in his sharp green eyes.

He thinks I am too broken to fight back.

I attempt to lift myself up again, and this time, he slaps me harder, enough so that my head slams into the metal table. I blink past stars and the blackness, moaning, letting everything go completely limp.

"Pathetic," he says as he crosses the room to one of the glass shelves on the wall. "What a worthless attempt to save your little friends. I thought genopaths were supposed to be useful. What a disappointment you are."

I watch out of the corner of my eye as he pulls out a needle and fills it with liquid. A small but deadly weapon. One that doesn't care about body size or injuries or armor. He closes the distance between us and wraps his right hand around my throat. I gag and cough, clawing at his thick fingers.

"This won't hurt a bit."

He tests the needle in his other hand to make sure there's no air in the syringe. Liquid oozes out, slow and viscous.

"That's a lie. It's gonna burn like hellfire through your veins before it paralyzes you."

The tip of the needle dips closer to my skin. But I'm done pretending.

In a burst of speed, my legs fly up and wrap around the arm he's got on my throat. My fingers dig in, keeping his hand in place as I buck my hips up and straighten my legs to hyperextend his arm. The tendons in his elbow snap, the crack echoing off the walls, followed by his scream.

Then I throw all my weight down, slamming him into the table. The needle goes flying. He roars again, trying to pry my legs off his broken arm, but I buck and slam him down a second time. His weight buckles as his legs give out and he slips, pulling us both onto the floor.

I untangle my legs as we fall, then kick him hard in the throat with my heel. His hand flies to his neck as he chokes. I scramble past him, lunging for the needle just beyond the table.

My fingertips brush the handle, but a hand wraps around my weak ankle and yanks me backward. I look over my shoulder and kick the bastard square in the nose with my boot. I grasp once more at the needle, finally managing to grab it.

Taggert yanks on my leg again, except this time I let him.

Ignoring the pain, I twist around as he pulls and fling myself on top of him.

Not expecting me to attack, he's too shocked to stop my arm from plunging down. Too surprised to do anything but stare wide-eyed at the needle now protruding from the exposed skin of his bruised throat. Too late to stop me.

I ram my thumb onto the syringe and shoot all the liquid into his veins.

He screams as it spreads through his body, writhing as the pain hits him. Gradually, the squirming slows to a twitch and the screams die with a gurgle in his throat.

I sit there, staring at him as I breathe through my own pain.

Asshole.

I don't know what he put in the needle, but it clearly hurt like hell, just like he promised.

Blood trickles down my nose, the iron tang coating my lips. I can feel other places dripping with sweat and blood alike. The back of my neck. The gashes reopened on my arm.

But he's the one lying broken on the ground. Not me. So, even though I'm bleeding and my ribs are probably beyond broken, it was worth it.

I stand and hobble over to the corner, swipe up my gun, and

shove it back into the holster. I squint at the shelves and spot some painkillers. Perfect. After downing a few of those, I slip off my shirt, grab some gauze, and wrap my ribs up tight. It's not perfect, but at least now it doesn't feel like something is poking at my lungs when I breathe too deeply. I even manage to retie my hair into a ponytail without too much pain.

Patched up as well as I can be, I then pick up Taggert's giant arken blade from the table. It's practically a sword. The weight and grip feel good in my hand despite my aching body.

Now to find my friends.

I squat down to Taggert. He's still breathing. Mostly. I tug off his gloves and find the bump of the security chit chip in his right wrist. Using the edge of his arken blade, I cut a small incision in his skin and pull the chip out. The commando doesn't even flinch. I almost feel sorry for him, but he was going to inject that shit into me.

I stash the chit chip in my pocket and then reach for the comms piece in his ear. It was turned off. Either the bastard was really cocky or . . . I push away thoughts of my friends being dead. They're not. I quickly flip on the comms as I put it in my ear.

"Breach, breach in sector five. We've been overrun—" The voice cuts out. Then a distant pop, pop, pop of gunfire fills my ears, and I'm out the door before fully registering it. My senses expand past Taggert and the examination rooms, searching for any sign of Sena or Iska or Lyria.

The hallway is empty until I take a right and nearly run into two sprinting commandos. The arken blade moves without a thought, my instincts and training kicking in on high. The two drop, their armor shredded by the blade of light.

Then I'm running again, tracking the sounds and heartbeats,

scenting the blood as I rush down another hall and burst through a set of double doors.

A scene of finished chaos greets me. The large room is full of monitors and devices that I don't have time to place; another holoscreen takes up an entire wall. But most of the equipment is wrecked or damaged from a gunfight that's already moved on. I'm about to rush to the next set of doors, but a sudden quiet puts me on edge, prickling the hairs on the back of my neck. I carefully make my way across the room, stepping over broken glass, keeping an eye on the flickering holoscreen in my periphery.

Heartbeats are coming closer, but one of the images on the holo draws my attention; it's the same view as the other screen I saw, showing the storm raging. But this one has an even wider frame, revealing the entire structure where the camera is. And it isn't a drone like I thought.

ARC1. The name comes rushing out of the back of my mind. It's the low-orbit satellite that Sena and I nearly crashed into when we got pulled into Maraas's atmosphere. The same one Arun mentioned was spying on the syndicates. But the readouts across the bottom of the holoscreen are not about life-forms or human movement. They display power readings, energy meters. And then the puzzle pieces fall into place and Weiland's plan springs to life.

That's no satellite. It's a power station. It's the only explanation, given the energy readings and the positioning. TerraCo specializes in energy, in supplying power, in developing battery tech. And that's why the corpos have created a storm that won't stop. They've somehow managed to convert the storm's energy into stored power.

Their goal isn't to eradicate all life on Maraas. Instead, they're turning an entire planet into a giant battery, a new energy source, a new power plant. One that isn't reliant on other corpos or other resources. The profit margins will be massive, unheard of. And if they keep manipulating the storm, it'll be an energy source that will never end.

A crash sounds, ripping me from my thoughts, and the door on the far side of the room bursts open. My gun is pointed before I can register just who is standing in the doorway. But I lower it, smiling, as Sena storms into the room, her dark curls wild, Iska at her side and a group of scavvers and syndicates in her wake. Small cuts cross her ashen-pale face and there are blood stains on her layers, but she's otherwise unharmed.

"We've already been through here," she calls, and waves them forward. "We have to keep searching until we find the control room."

Then she spots me, standing in the glow of the holoscreen.

Sena grins before rushing over and throwing her arms around my neck. Everything hurts again, but it's beyond worth it.

"I was wondering when you'd show up," she says as she pulls away.

I shrug and then wince in pain. "I'm here to rescue you. But it looks like Iska beat me to it."

"Iska caused the distraction we needed to overrun the commandos." She looks me up and down. "Are you all right?"

"Got blown up along with the mag train. Dragged Kiran through the sewers. Walked up a bazillion stairs. Beat up Taggert. Now I'm here," I summarize while scanning the faces of the scavvers and syndicates as they fan out through the room. But my heart clenches when I don't spot one face.

"Where's Alora?"

Sena's eyebrows shoot up in confusion. "Alora?"

"I mean, Lyria." Sena's mouth drops. "Turns out they're one and the same," I clarify.

"That is . . . messed up." She shakes her head, a few black curls falling loose from her braid. "But I'll let you explain it later. Weiland has her in the tower, I think. She said something about Nova before separating us."

"Shit." I kick a piece of equipment hard enough to bruise my toe. Kiran mentioned that Nova wanted Alora because her alterations would make her a good agent. If Weiland gives her over to the Nova hacks, they'll try to recondition her, just like he said they would. My stomach drops at the thought, but fury and fire spread through my veins. I will not let that happen.

"Is it just you here?" Sena asks.

I shake my head. "Emeko's on her way to Weiland with a lot of sleeper mines."

Despite her worry, Sena smirks, her gray eyes sparking. "She's going to blow up that tower, isn't she?"

"Yes. But we need to get Lyria out first. I can go back and use the tunnels—"

"They've been blown," she interrupts. "We just came from there; the commandos blew them as they fled. There's an elevator a few yards back that way, but it only goes up." She gestures toward the door they burst through, but my mind is still trying to make sense of things.

"How did you overrun the commandos with so few people?"

She grins. "Oh, this is just the handful who came with me. There's over fifty other scavvers, syndicates, and even ex-corpos assailing the TerraCo troops across the compound. Some went above to chase them on the upper levels. Others are fanning out through the halls, looking for more captives. We're trying to find their control room to cut off their comms."

I blink in shock at the number of people Weiland had locked up in this place. Just days ago, I wandered the abandoned level above and didn't notice a soul. That bitch really needs to pay. My mind sifts through the moving parts as my gaze returns to the holoscreen. Stopping her means more than just blowing up the tower. We have to take down this entire operation. Kiran's not here to make a foolproof plan out of this mess, but maybe I never needed him to come up with the plans in the first place. Maybe I just do what I always do—create more fires, more explosions. Follow my impulses to push everything to the extreme.

Starting with that cursed power station.

"All right, forget the comms," I say, pointing to the structure on the holoscreen. "We need to find a way to destroy that thing. It's a power station up in atmo that Weiland made to absorb energy from the storms. That's why they had all those cloud seeders. That's why they tried to make the storm unstoppable. So they could siphon energy off it and sell it to the Assembly worlds."

"Bloody corpo chumps," Sena mutters, anger taking over her features. "Of course, profit is what they wanted the whole time." She eyes the power station on the holoscreen for a beat. "Some of the people down here said they used to work for Weiland. I'll find them and we'll figure out a way to bring that thing down. You go get Lyria and make sure Emeko doesn't blow up in her own blast."

Her words echo my exact thoughts. We may not be squadmates who have been together since birth, but without asking, she knows what I need, and without any hesitation, she'll do what needs to be done, too. She's a true friend, through and through. I grasp her hand.

"Be careful."

She squeezes back.

"Promise. But don't worry. This is a fight we're going to win." Then she and Iska are gone, off to tear a power station out of the sky. I trust that she'll find a way to end it somehow. Just like she trusts me to get to the tower in time. Steeling myself for the run, I push the pain racking my body down, down, down. The painkillers are starting to kick in. I'll feel it all later, when it's over, but right now, I need every ounce of strength, every facet of my senses, every single engineered cell.

It won't be an easy run across the city to the tower, not with the storm raging outside. But I won't let anything slow me down, not even myself.

This time, I will not fail.

CHAPTER 33

I'm soaked to the bone in seconds once I step outside some-where in the corpo district. My boots threaten to slip on the slick concrete wet with puddles and muck. Even up here in the city, Weiland can't keep the jungle mud from creeping in. The thought fuels me as I sprint across Verem's deserted streets. Every-one must be hiding away from the storm.

I whip around a corner and find myself running alongside a building with an overhang, giving me a short reprieve from the pelting rain. Static sounds in my ear on the comms I stole from Taggert.

"Hello, hello? Are there any scavvers on this damn channel?"

"Emeko!" I shout back as I turn another corner, not slowing down. She must've swiped some comms herself. "Where are you? What's your status?"

After a few seconds of static, her voice sounds again.

"Remy? I just set the timers on the sleeper mines and I'm on my way out. I've heard that Weiland's prisoners are free. Did you get Sena and Lyria?"

"Sena, yes. Lyria, no. She's with Weiland in the tower."

Her curse comes through loud and clear.

"How long until the mines go off?" I shout.

There's a pause as I hit the end of the overhang. I stop, waiting for Emeko's response before I dive back out into the storm.

"They're set for fifteen minutes, Remy." Now I'm cursing. "Are you going to make it?"

I crack my neck and flood more adrenaline into my veins to push away my aches and pains. It's time for speed and nothing else.

"I'm going to make it. Do you have a way out?"

"Oh, don't worry about me. I've got a way. See you on the other side."

"Emeko—" But there's nothing but static; her comms must be off already. Fifteen minutes until Weiland's ended, one way or another. I can make it. I will make it.

With another curse followed by a steadying breath, I set off into the storm again. The winds howl through intersections, pushing me every which way as I will my legs to move faster. Thunder cracks and rolls as the hellstorm beats down on the city, on the jungle, on Maraas.

Beats down on me.

Fourteen minutes.

There's a loud crack and a cord of lightning strikes the ground not three feet from me. The crackling electricity hums across my skin; the heat singes my layers even through the torrential rain.

Still, I don't stop running.

I hit the mag rail station without slowing down. I made it across the corpo district in three minutes. My body is protesting, but I've relegated the pain to background noise. I'll heal when this is done. I slide across the slick floor in the station, ignoring the pain in my knee, the ache in my ankle, the throbbing in my head from the fight with Taggert. Ignore my rain-drenched layers and mud-filled boots. The only thing I allow myself to see is the path in front of me and the countdown timer in my head.

Twelve minutes.

I slow as I make my way through the empty station and hallway to the elevator. There are no guards anywhere. Maybe because of the storm or maybe because Emeko took care of them already. Or it might be that Weiland suspected this move and has laid a trap. It doesn't matter, I'm going in anyway. I pull Taggert's chit chip out of my pocket and swipe it across the access panel. The elevator doors whoosh open, and with a smash of the top-level button and another chit chip scan, I'm heading up, up, up to the tower.

I stand poised at the door and draw the gun from my thigh. *Take out Weiland and any commandos. Save Lyria.* I repeat the words over and over as I pass the floors one by one. Nerves I'm not used to tingle down my limbs. All my training, all my genetics, none of it prepared me for this—for saving the people who matter to me.

Lives weren't supposed to matter; they didn't matter to Nova. Only the mission mattered. None of my relationships were ever supposed to be real connections. But this relationship, this friendship, is real. This life matters more than any other, more than my own. An entire world of syndicates are depending on Lyria. And I will not fail her this time.

The elevator stops.

Then the doors slide open.

My gun is ready, barrel raised, tight to my body, poised for the attack. As the room comes into view, my heart stutters in my chest.

Framed in the giant window with the storm raging outside are Weiland and two kneeling figures. The director's got her own gun pointed directly at the back of Lyria's head. I lock onto the outline of Lyria's figure. My mind still can't wrap itself around the fact that she's Alora. Gone is her wispy blond hair. Gone are the blue eyes that smiled and danced at me. Gone is the girl wishing for a different life.

Now all I see is the girl with flame-red hair and sharp hazel eyes who has embraced her fate as her father's heir. Who came to Maraas to take back what was hers. Whose fury and defiance are spelled out across her features even as she kneels in front of Weiland.

The doors finish opening and the director smiles at me from across the room. She shifts her gun to the other figure.

To Kiran, kneeling beside Lyria.

My heart stops completely.

"Come on in, Remy. We were just talking about you since one of my commandos found Kiran in the outpost below." She pushes Kiran's head forward with the barrel of the gun. His normally flushed bronze skin is still missing much of its color. "Time for a final family reunion."

I step out of the elevator, possible outcomes and scenarios running through my head. Commandos rush in from the deep alcoves of the room, but my eyes are now on Kiran. He must've grabbed layers from Arun's before coming after me. But now blood has soaked through his shirt where his wound is. His face is bruised even more, one eye swollen shut. The commandos shout at me, but

I don't focus on their orders; I only hear the anger burning like fire in my veins.

How dare they hit him. And how dare he leave Arun's. He couldn't just stay below where it was safe.

I let my gun slip from my fingers. I pull off Taggert's arken blade and drop it to the floor. Weiland's eyes follow the weapon, her own fury spelled out in their icy depths.

Good.

I raise my arms and a commando kicks my knees, collapsing me to the floor. They drag me closer to Weiland and I let my body go limp, let them toss me at her feet. I glance at Kiran, who's watching me with one eye from his spot in front of the windows. Next to him, Lyria, my Alora, struggles as a commando clamps a hand onto her shoulder.

"Remy," Lyria whispers, trying to move toward me, but the commando jerks her back. Her hands are bound behind her, and blood trickles down the side of her face. Her lip is swollen and bloody. I stare at her now-hazel eyes and finally notice my friend within their depths. How did I not see it before?

"Hi, friend," I whisper back. Then I glare at Kiran. "You were supposed to stay at Arun's."

He attempts a smile. "What? And leave all the fun for you two? You know I'm not good at letting go of control." He looks right at me before a commando smacks him across the head. Kiran pitches forward, chuckling to cover the moan escaping his lips. His words were meant to sound like he hasn't changed, like he's still playing all sides. But his eyes told me the truth. That he's trusting me to help him play Weiland, trusting me to get us all out of this mess. I watch him closely as they jerk him back to his knees.

Then one of the commandos holds up Taggert's arken blade,

showing Weiland, and she sneers in my face, dragging my attention away from Kiran.

"Where did you get this?"

I raise my eyes up to Weiland. "Why don't you ask the bastard who tried to kill me with it?"

She touches her comms with her free hand, the other still tight around the gun.

"Taggert, come in." Her voice echoes in my own ear. I hope she can hear it.

"He's going to have a hard time answering," I say when she repeats his name.

Weiland kicks me in the chest, knocking me flat on the floor. The pain barely registers.

"What did you do to him?" She spits out the words as she leans over me.

I push myself up and manage a shrug. "Shot him up with whatever he was going to inject me with."

A hand flies at my face, and my head rocks back from the force of her slap. I don't bother defending myself. Let her think she's in control, just like Taggert. I spit blood and use the moment to get a glimpse out the window. The mag rail tracks just beyond the tower are in ruins from the explosion earlier, but there's still a small portion down below the window that is intact. A plan clicks into place; it's messy but it will work. It has to. I glance at Kiran. He's looking right at me, ready. And then Weiland speaks.

"That was meant to freeze genopath cells, to keep the two of you pliant until Nova comes to retrieve your bodies." She leers at me. "Oh yes, I know exactly what you are."

Kiran grunts, low and full of rage at her words. He tries to move, but the commando shoves the butt of his machine gun into

Kiran's gut. I feel the blow deep in my own stomach as he collapses to the floor in front of me.

Weiland leans close to him but looks at me. "I guess they'll have to take you alive and aware instead." Then she straightens. "Your little coup is over. This planet is mine."

"Tell that to your ex-prisoners over at the old Vega compound," I say, keeping Emeko's countdown going in a corner of my head. "Your own employees joined up with the syndicates and scavvers to put a stop to you."

The director laughs as she stands beside me. "There's nothing they can do. Nothing you can do either. It's too late for any of you to change what happens next."

She raises the gun again, pointing it at Kiran, then moving it toward Lyria.

"I'm supposed to deliver these two to Nova. Dead or alive, they didn't specify." She pauses and I really don't like the look on her face.

"How long until the Nova convoy arrives?" she asks one of the commandos.

My heart freezes again in my chest. Nova. Coming here. Coming to see Weiland and the corpos triumph. This is the final part of their mission: absolute control of Maraas and the total destruction of other powers on this planet. Everything was building to this. And my instincts tell me they won't stop with just this Edge World.

"Fifteen or so minutes, ma'am," a commando answers. "They're navigating through atmo to avoid the worst of the storm."

Guess Weiland doesn't know about Emeko and the sleeper mines that are less than ten minutes from detonating. Those explosives are my lifeline and the only way to put a stop to Weiland, to Nova, to all the corpos who think they can take and take and take from us.

"Perfect. Let's make a wager, little genopath." She leans close enough for me to smell her breath. "I bet you will voluntarily switch sides and help me."

"Why the hell would I do that?" I growl.

She smiles and I know she's about to do something awful.

"Well, I could just shoot all three of you." She slowly moves her arm until the gun barrel is pointed at Kiran, and my breathing stops entirely. "But this is more fun, don't you think? As it turns out, Nova doesn't know you are here. Apparently, you've given them the slip even though they've been looking for you. And I haven't felt the need to inform them."

My eyes jump to Kiran. What other sacrifices did he have to make to ensure that Nova didn't track me from the Tundar jump station?

"So, it seems you're a bit of a ghost. You don't have to go back to them," Weiland continues. "You can volunteer to stay here and be my personal genopath, and I won't shoot this little con artist. What do you say to that choice, Remy? You stay with me, and Kiran and Revas can go with Nova together, in one piece. Or he'll go in a body bag, and I'll give both you and the syndicate over to Nova. I'm sure they'll be grateful that I recovered you for them. They'll probably reward me."

"Weiland, don't do this. I'll—" Lyria interrupts, but the director snaps at her.

"Shut up, stupid syndicate. This entire mess is your fault for being such a thorn in my side." She jerks her head and a commando grabs Lyria by the shoulder, pressing his gun barrel into her cheek. Lyria hisses, staring at me, worry and fear spelled out across her features. Weiland catches the look and laughs.

"Or maybe I'm threatening to shoot the wrong person." Her gun drifts from Kiran to Lyria and back again, my heart skipping a beat with each movement. "Maybe I should make you choose which one of them goes in a body bag instead."

I swallow past my rage and fear and lock eyes with Kiran. He dips his chin in the smallest movement. I can almost hear his words.

I see you.

He knows my thoughts like they're his own, and he's ready to act on them. Despite his injuries, despite the risk, he's ready. Weiland may think she's good at manipulating us, but Kiran and I have been playing this game together for much longer than she has.

The timer in my head blinks. Less than seven minutes until the building blows. Time to move. My eyes jump from Kiran to the window behind him, and then to Weiland's gun. Kiran blinks in confirmation, yielding the moves to me, letting me lead. I won't let him down.

Weiland taps her finger on the trigger. "Truthfully, I should just put him out of his misery. You know how Nova rehabilitates its lost property. The pain of reconditioning. They told me that not all genopaths survive it. Maybe it would be a mercy if I killed him."

Weiland's staring at me, waiting for me to beg or cry or break. But I smile slowly, keeping her focus on me while Kiran moves imperceptibly, scooting into position. Almost ready.

"I have a counteroffer," I say, distracting her further. The director cocks the gun dramatically as she waits for me to elaborate.

I'm about to move, but Kiran beats me to it. He lunges at

Weiland, purposefully overshooting it, making sure to get between her and the window.

Time slows as I hear Weiland's heart pulse, see the muscles of her arm flex. Kiran's body twists instinctively as he tries to avoid her shot, but his injuries have slowed him down. He's not going to dodge in time.

I move, throwing my weight forward, past the commandos around me, but I'm not fast enough either. The bullet slices through Kiran's already wounded shoulder and embeds itself in the window behind us, cracking the glass into a spiderweb, just like I planned. But Kiran collapses as I land beside him, his blood splattered everywhere, not at all like I planned.

I stare down at him, frozen in this moment. This isn't what I intended. He took the bullet before I could.

"You asshole," I whisper, but there's no bite in my words.

"Too slow, partner," he exhales, a ghost of a grin on his face. Somewhere behind me, Lyria's shouting my name. But all I see are Kiran's eyes closing. I flip my attention to the monster who did this. With the window now at my back, I push to my feet and rush toward the director with a scream, drawing her attention to me, only me.

Again, I hear her pulse skip. I move just before her finger squeezes the trigger, turning my body so the shot only grazes my arm before it connects with the window. The bullet smashes into the cobwebbed glass, shattering it into a thousand pieces.

And the storm rushes in.

Glass cuts into the exposed skin on my arms and shoulders and slices through my clothes. Wind and rain howl into the office as a gust pounds the tower. The commandos are blown backward while Lyria dives away from them.

I lunge, the tempest pushing me forward, and I grab Weiland's collar. The director swings the gun up, but I'm already dropping my weight down, yanking her as I roll backward, flipping her into the air. My foot pushes on her thigh as leverage and I fling her weight over my body, toward the gaping window.

But the bitch doesn't let go. She latches onto me like a spider vine, and together we tumble into the storm.

CHAPTER 34

Weiland and I free-fall into nothing. I lose my grip on her and flip myself into a better landing position as the tracks rush up to greet me. I slam into them feet first and then roll with the force, tumbling across the rails.

My lungs and chest scream in pain as I roll over and over. Finally, I find purchase on the metal, latching on tight and jerking to a stop. My legs are inches from the edge; I almost tumbled right off into the jungle below. I glance behind me, up at the broken window high above. I just fell two stories and didn't break anything. I'm really pushing Nova's engineering today.

Rain runs down my face, drenching my layers and skin. I push off my stomach, trying to get myself up, and a boot comes flying toward my face. I jerk back fast, the kick barely slipping past my nose as I scramble away. Guess I'm not the only one whose gene mods saved them.

Weiland stands over me, her pristine white layers now soaked and dirty, her face wild and unhinged. I push to my feet and stand toe-to-toe with her, wet hair loose and in my face, staring her down as she steps toward me.

"It doesn't matter what you do—you can't win," she shouts over the storm. I resist looking up over my shoulder, resist checking to see if Kiran still lies slumped on the floor or if Lyria's safe. My eyes don't leave the true monster, the threat right in front of me.

I still have six minutes before everything's on fire; six minutes to get back up there and help them.

"Don't you want to watch as your friends fall?" She points behind me at the window as thunder rolls around us. I ignore her until the rat-tat-tat of gunfire reaches my ears even over the pouring rain. I turn my head toward the sound instinctively and Weiland strikes, kicking me in the knee, dropping me to the tracks. She kicks again, but I jerk my body backward and her boot sails past my nose. I quickly get one foot under me, scrambling into a more defensive position.

"When Nova gets here, you will be locked up in a lab for the rest of your miserable life. You won't be able to save your syndicate friend." She pauses, listening as more guns go off. "Or Kiran, if he's even still alive."

A bullet ricochets past us and her focus jumps upward. I lash out and grab her boot behind the ankle. I slam my other palm on her knee, locking her leg and throwing off her balance. With a quick yank, I pull her feet out from under her, and she tumbles onto the tracks while I scramble on top of her. I reach into my boot for the serrated knife hidden there, unnoticed by the commandos earlier.

Weiland swings at me, but I block her fist with one arm and jerk the knife out with the other, then plunge it down toward her chest, stabbing her in the shoulder so hard my bones reverberate as the blade bites into the metal tracks below.

The director screams, and even with the storm, the sound gives me goose bumps. I stumble off, away from her, back toward the broken window. I have to save Kiran. I have to save Lyria. I have to save them before the building blows to nothing.

I reach up and find a ledge to grab on to. My arm screams where the bullet ripped through my flesh, but I push that away. My knee cracks, something ripping inside, but I ignore that, too. When everything is pain, it becomes easier to push through it. Only minutes left before this place goes and I don't have time to think about what hurts.

I keep moving, keep dumping adrenaline into my blood, and I manage to climb the distance back up to the broken window. I pull myself over the ledge, the shattered glass slicing more of my skin and layers.

But I'm already rolling onto the office floor, throwing myself in the path of a commando rushing at Lyria. He trips over my body, his foot landing somewhere in my broken ribs, and I see nothing but blackness and stars.

Then a bright red light slashes through the fog. Lyria stands over me, arken blade in her now freed hands, cutting down the last standing commando. The red light of the weapon glows against her freckled skin, casting her reddish hair in an even brighter shade. Then she drops the blade and shakes my shoulders, pulls at my weight.

"Remy! You have to get up!"

I blink, honing in on her face despite the stars swimming across my vision. She's pointing toward the jungle and shouting something. I turn my head and see a flyer hovering outside the window. I can just make out the shape of the pilot through the rain.

Emeko.

That bloody scavver didn't tell me she knew how to fly. I almost smile as she maneuvers the ship so the open cargo hold faces the window. She's barely keeping the flyer steady with the force of the winds outside; there's no way she can hold the position for long. Somewhere in the corner of my brain, the timeline continues to blink. A handful of minutes left until the sleeper mines detonate.

My senses rush back in, and I tighten my grip on Lyria's arm as I stand fully. "You first!" I shout, giving her a push. "I'll get Kiran." My eyes jump to his prone form, still breathing. Which is good because once we get out of here, I'm going to kill him myself for leaving the safety of Arun's den.

Lyria opens her mouth to protest, but I point at the flyer lurching in the storm. "I need you there to be sure we make it. You have to catch us!"

As I stagger to keep my balance, Lyria—my Alora—nods, then runs full speed at the flyer and leaps the distance to the cargo bay. She lands with ease, rolling to the side and flipping back around to face the window.

I lean down for Kiran, but a hand appears on the window ledge. I freeze in shock as Weiland pulls herself back into the office, my knife in her hand, blood dripping down her arm. She lunges at me with a bloodcurdling scream. I scoop up the arken blade, left but not forgotten, and slice at Weiland's torso. She jumps back, switching her grip on the knife, readying herself for another attack as wind pounds the office.

Two minutes and dropping.

I look beyond her silhouette to where Lyria stands on the edge of the cargo platform, waving at me to run to the flyer. She's safe, but she doesn't have a weapon to help us, to take out Weiland. And I will not leave Kiran here.

I will not let him die.

Not when I've only just begun to see him, see who he really is. He's looked out for me my entire life. It's time I return the favor. It's time I stop failing him and choose him, too.

I lash out again with the arken blade as the director flits closer. Sure, she's had some training, but it won't be enough to save her. If I weren't injured, I'd finish her in seconds. But even with my injuries, I'm better. She can't beat years of never-ending missions and training and the instincts hard-coded into my genes. I may be a screwup who doesn't know when to stop; I may have failed my friends before, but this, this is who I am.

A true friend who will do whatever it takes, no matter the limits I have to push — I'll do anything to save the people I love. The knowledge that Weiland can do nothing to stop her impending death makes me smile.

At my grin, the director screams maniacally and lunges at me, but then dances away as I swing the larger blade. I let her come close again before batting her back. Feint and circle, two steps forward, one step back.

Ninety-two seconds left.

I steer the fight closer to the window ledge, closer to the storm. And when Weiland slices the knife toward me again, I let her get even closer. I will take a blow to deliver a killing one. The knife in her hand flashes and I leave my side open, so obvious that even she won't miss. I brace for the icy grip of the pain.

But it never comes.

Something has gotten in the way.

No, not something. Someone.

A warm, familiar body is pressed up close to mine. Kiran. He moved too fast for even me to follow, blocking me from Weiland, and now the knife is buried in his upper chest.

Thunder cracks. Weiland's eyes flash in triumph as Kiran's body goes into shock, twitching; she digs the knife so deep it pierces through him into my own flesh. I feel his heartbeat stutter.

No.

Fifty-five seconds.

Rain pelts my face. A hand wraps around my fingers, the ones gripping the arken blade. Kiran lifts it up weakly. He knew what my plan was. He knew I needed her close, needed her guard to be down. Needed her to think she'd won.

So when I grip the blade tighter under his fingertips and we raise it together, she's not expecting it. And when we push it against her exposed throat, her wide eyes do nothing but reflect the red glow of the arc of light.

"Enjoy your jungle," Kiran hisses as lightning strikes the tracks below.

And in one movement, I shove her body away with my free arm while Kiran and I slice a line across her neck with the other. She stumbles backward in shock, blood spilling out of her exposed throat.

And steps into nothing but rain and air.

This time she does not hit the tracks. Her body is blown by the storm, down, down, down into the trees below.

Thirty seconds.

Kiran's knees buckle as he draws the knife out before I can stop him. I catch his weight while blood flows down his chest, his back, into the twin wound on my own chest. Only mine's on my right shoulder and his is over his heart.

"Why the fuck did you do that?" I scream, pulling him back up to his feet, pressing my hand over his wound.

"Couldn't let you take all the glory," he mumbles, and staggers toward the ledge and the ship beyond. "Time to go."

"Kiran!" I latch onto his arm to keep him from careening out the window. He slumps into me, letting me take all his weight. His pulse has slowed to a snail's pace. I put my hand over his wound, trying to apply pressure and stop the bleeding. But red still flows through my fingers and down my arms. He's taken too much damage in one day, and his body isn't recovering like it should.

"Why did you do that?" I whisper again, desperate for a reason to explain his actions. He manages to put some weight on his legs as he turns toward me. The building shudders deep underneath our feet as the sleeper mines detonate.

Time's up.

"I could never let her hurt you. There's nothing I won't do to protect you. Nothing." His eyes lock onto mine, our faces inches apart. "Because . . ." His hand reaches up, brushing the hair away from my face, and he whispers something too low for me to hear.

Then his hands grip my arms with strength I didn't know he still had and he's turning, throwing me off the ledge, out of the building.

For a second, I'm completely airborne, staring at him silhouetted in the window.

Then the world around him erupts into flames. Wind hits me and I slam into something hard.

And then there's nothing at all.

CHAPTER 35

Everything hurts.

I guess that means I'm not dead yet. Voices make noise somewhere, but I'm too tired to try and focus on them. Too tired to think about my injuries. Too tired to do anything but disappear again into the darkness. Images flash through my head. Weiland's open throat as she steps off the ledge. Sena, hugging me in the Vega compound with Iska. Lyria, leaping into the storm, catching me as I flew.

One final thought simmers to life as my consciousness slips away.

Kiran.

Is he alive? I can hear his voice in my head. From years ago, when we were still at Nova, still under their control, when he looked at me. Saw only me.

I'll always be okay.

When we were in the burned-out building in the sprawl.

I see you.

On the train, when he started to say something, started to tell me why he survived reconditioning over and over again.

I don't know what I would've done if they'd erased who you are.

Remy, the thing is, I—

And then somewhere, deep in the dark corners of my mind, I can finally hear what he told me before the world exploded.

I love you.

CHAPTER 36

The soft pitter-patter of rain drums out a beat along with the pounding in my head. Part of me knows it's time to wake up, but the rest wants to ignore the light growing at my edges, wants to stay suspended in the darkness.

Where it's safe.

Where no one else can get hurt.

"Remy, I know you're awake."

I sigh through my nose at the voice. Alora always knew somehow when I was faking sleep. I guess some things don't change. I don't know how I missed the familiar cadence of her words before. How I didn't notice the voice was still hers.

I crack open an eye and see her perched on a stool next to my bed. We're in a small room with a roof made of thatch and scrap metal. Must be a scavver building. But I'm not worried about where we are. Only who's sitting in front of me. Alora . . . Lyria. Her sharp features are a contrast to the face I knew before.

I guess some things do change.

"So, what?" I say in lieu of a greeting. "You got a nose job. Changed your cheekbones. Dyed your eyes and hair, got a lot more freckles . . ."

She raises an eyebrow. "That's what you want to talk about right now?"

"Did it hurt?" I ask, ignoring her question.

She sighs, studying me. "More than you know." And I know she's not talking about the physical pain. She erased everything that made her *her*. Every feature she inherited from her father. Every sign of the girl she was and wanted to be. Gone.

"Why didn't you just tell me?" My voice is a whisper, barely audible over the rain.

She stares at me, her hazel eyes, not blue, jumping down to my torso, where I can feel the bandages and bruises on my ribs and antiseptic and stitches over my right shoulder. Then she sighs again.

"I wanted to. So many times. But I—" She stops and swallows, tucking some of her short red hair behind her ear. "I had to make so many sacrifices these last few years. I had to let Alora die so Lyria could live. I had to make many hard choices to get here. Not telling you was the hardest one. I was so focused on my own goals that I pushed our friendship to the side. I put myself first."

A tear slides down her cheek as she looks away. "I've been a terrible friend."

Those eyes that always see through me, always. And now they look away as her thoughts mirror my own.

"It's my fault," I whisper. "How could you trust me after I failed you?"

Her eyes jump back to me. "No, Remy. You never failed me.

Not once. I was the one who made you question your entire existence and then expected you to do everything for me. I asked too much of you and I am sorry for that. You did the best you could to help me, to protect me. Every single time."

I move to squeeze her hand, but my body yells at me for the movement. I wince hard, shutting my eyes against the spots creeping in.

"Try not to move," she says. I slowly stretch my fingers out for hers. And after a moment, her hand finally crawls into mine. "I am so sorry, Remy," she repeats.

A sob hits me, racking my ribs with more pain as my lungs inflate.

"It doesn't matter," I finally manage to say. I give her fingertips the gentlest of squeezes. "Maybe we both screwed up. I broke the promise I made to you so many times. But I'm choosing to be better. To be the person you asked me to be. The person I want to be." Someone who uses her impulses and instincts to help her friends and not herself.

Lyria lays her other hand on top of mine. "You've always been that person to me. But, Remy, the promise that night in the jungle wasn't just for you."

I open my eyes. "What?"

"I was so mad at myself for the crash, and for making you come with me and getting you hurt, that I was making a promise to be better myself. That I wouldn't keep screwing around or putting us in harm's way every five minutes. That I would try to do something more than just dream and wish and sneak away from my responsibilities."

"But, no . . . you asked me to be better than what they made me for. . . ."

She squeezes my hand. "Better than what we were both made for. But I only asked for your promise because I made you one. It's why I decided to go after Dekkard. Why I led this whole take-back-Maraas revolution. I promised you I would be better."

I scoff and dull pain radiates at the movement of my muscles. "Wow, this whole time I thought you needed me to save you. Or that you'd hold me accountable. I didn't know what to think other than I'd broken my promise to you. That I let you down."

She laughs, though a tear slips out of the corner of her eye. "This whole time I was trying to keep my promise because you'd already saved me so many times."

I smile as silent tears fall down my cheeks. "I guess that makes us even, huh?"

Lyria nods. "I guess so."

"We were thinking of each other the whole time Kiran tried to keep us apart. He really underestimated how strong our friendship was."

Something falters in her expression. And suddenly I can't breathe. Suddenly, fear takes hold of my entire stomach, an iron grip on my gut.

"Kiran—" I can't even finish the question.

Lyria shakes her head as another tear slides down her cheek. "The tower exploded and collapsed. Nova's ship landed nearby and scoured the whole blast radius despite the storm. We sent scouts to search the wreckage after they left, when the storm finally died down." She swallows. "There wasn't any sign of Kiran."

The muscles in my stomach clinch at the idea of him no longer in my world.

"I think I'm going to throw up."

Lyria moves quickly, grabbing a wastebasket and holding it in front of me as I heave my nerves and the contents of my stomach out. I feel the stitches in my shoulder rip as my muscles spasm. When I finish, she hands me a glass of water. I sip slowly as I feel blood soak through the bandages, and I press a finger to the wound tentatively.

A mark left by Weiland. But one I share with Kiran. His blood mixed with mine when the knife sliced through both of us. A permanent reminder of him.

And what he would do to protect me.

The bastard. Why didn't he stay in the den? I wipe errant tears off my cheeks, not ready to think about it too closely. Instead, I focus on the other people I care about.

"What about everyone else?" I ask. "Sena . . ."

"Sena's fine. Iska's fine. Even Emeko. We all made it because of you."

I shake my head. "Sena saved herself. She always does."

"Maybe so. But you told her to bring the power station down from the sky and she did. It's a tangle of metal somewhere out in the far jungle now. You figured out what Weiland was doing with the storms. Over the last week, we destroyed what was left in all the substations. No more cloud seeders. It's still raining but it's lessening bit by bit."

A week has passed. A week of darkness and unconsciousness. A week without my friends. Without him.

"What about Nova?" I ask, keeping myself distracted from the mournful pull of those thoughts. "And their lab in the old mine?"

Lyria shakes her head. "They're gone. I took a scouting group down through the mines myself two days ago. Deserted. No more animals or people. It was like they were never there. I think they knew Maraas was no longer a place they could operate without constraint." She takes the empty glass from me and sets it on a side table. "You should rest."

"I've been out for a week," I protest.

She eyes the blood now seeping through the sheets. "You need the doctor."

"Where are we anyway?" I throw the question out, hoping it will keep her by my side for a bit longer.

"The scavver settlement where the council members are. They offered it as a safe haven while we clean up Verem and destroy all traces of Weiland in the city. It's far, but hey, we have all the ships now."

I smile. "You took your father's city back."

She nods, but instead of saying anything further about her father, she changes the subject. "I'm going to get the doctor to come and check on your stitches since you probably ripped them."

I shrug and wince again. "I need food—not stitches. I'm genetically engineered to heal without such things."

She rolls her eyes. "Probably those genetics are the only reason you're still alive. You got blown up, beat up, thrown down two stories, then stabbed, and then blown up again. It's truly a miracle you're not in worse shape."

"Nah, just corpo-made, top-of-the-line genetics. Nothing special."

Lyria shakes her head. "More special than you know. Now, don't go anywhere."

I roll my eyes at her. Like I can stumble around anywhere in this shape. My head is still pounding behind my ears. My leg below my knee is mostly numb, hopefully from anesthetics and not from damage. Tiny cuts cover my skin pretty much everywhere. My left hand is wrapped up from where I sliced it on the window glass. I can feel the bruises around my torso and my broken ribs smarting with every breath. Oh, and the knife wound is slowly oozing blood.

But somehow, I'm alive when others aren't. Thoughts of Kiran press again, but I push them away, thinking instead of Sena and Iska, even Emeko. Lyria. I didn't fail them all.

By the time Lyria comes back with the doc, my consciousness is fading fast. Thankfully, she lets me pretend to be asleep as the doctor fixes up my stitches. I try to stay awake after, to ask her to sit with me, but exhaustion pulls me under, pulls me into a sleep so deep, I can't sense a thing.

≫≪

Lyria returns the next day and the one after that, until I'm finally well enough to sit up on my own. She still won't let me leave the room; after two days I'm dying of boredom. I still won't let myself think about Kiran. Instead, I begrudgingly do some therapeutic exercises from the doctor and eat anacroc stew. At least the protein will help me heal even if I can't stand the smell anymore.

After three days of slurping stew and napping, I convince Lyria that I'm ready to get up and out of the small, stuffy room. The doctor gives me a crutch since my knee is still weak. I roll my eyes, but I use it to hobble outside.

The rain has stopped.

Well, not entirely stopped; it's turned into a light mist. But the sun peeks through the rolling clouds as I stand on the porch and let the moisture sink into my skin. It's still hot as hell, but somehow, I don't mind it as much. Scavvers run around the settlement, all busy with their daily lives, but I catch sight of some syndicates here and there. What a new world this is. Lyria went back to Verem earlier this morning, leaving me with no tasks or instructions. No mission for the first time in my whole life. Just me and the afterward I dreaded so much.

Rather than stay cooped up alone with my thoughts, I limp down the steps and set off to follow the hint of ice and snow. I want to check on my friends. I find Sena and Emeko with some others as they unload a flyer in a small clearing. I shuffle closer to the ship, careful of the soft, wet ground. Iska notices me before the girls do. The wolf bounds over and nudges my good leg with her nose. I slowly bend down and bury myself in her fur, whispering small thanks in her ears. She did save me, too, after all.

Sena rushes over and pulls me into a light embrace, her dark curls tickling my cheeks.

"You probably should be resting. But I know how hard it is to be still," she says, seeing my limp and how close I keep my arm to my injured ribs. She nods at the crutch with a smile. "Let me know if you need any pointers."

I laugh even though it still smarts. We've switched places. On Tundar, after the race, she was the one injured and hobbling around. I guess it's my turn now.

"What are you two doing?" I ask.

Her gray eyes glance over her shoulder toward the flyer. "We're rebuilding the scavver bases knocked out by the mudslide. Lyria's letting us use as many flyers as we want, and she's splitting resources between us and the syndicates working in Verem and in the sprawl."

I raise an eyebrow. "Us?"

She chuckles realizing she didn't even notice her choice of

words. "Yeah, since I'm not a syndicate, I guess I sort of lump my-self in with the scavvers. I might not be one of them exactly, but it's . . . nice, working with them. They remind me of my mothers. Living for themselves and not corpo greed."

I eye the scavver leader over by the cargo hold of the flyer as she pretends to be busy with a datapad. I know she's watching us, though.

"And Emeko?" I ask.

A slight blush spreads up Sena's slightly sunburned pale cheeks and she shrugs. "Well, Iska likes her."

"Oh, well, Iska is an excellent judge of character," I say with a smile. Sena's blush deepens and I laugh out loud.

My friend is saved from my teasing as another flyer appears over the treetops. I heard its hum a few minutes ago, but for once, it didn't set me on edge or send me sprinting away. The ship circles over the clearing, then slowly descends. This one must've flown through the storm because its external shielding is battered, and parts of the wings and tail have been haphazardly repaired.

With a start, I realize it's my ship.

Lyria waves from the cockpit and, seconds later, hops out the side door as I limp over to the flyer. Sena and Emeko follow while Iska rushes to the door to greet my friend.

"How's it looking?" Lyria asks, scratching Iska behind the ears with one hand and pointing to the flyer's wing with the other. "We're not quite done with repairs, obviously, but it got airborne and made it here."

Sena's smiling as she glances at me. "I can't believe Weiland didn't trash your ship, Remy."

I shake my head. "Probably couldn't be bothered." I glance around Lyria to see most of my crates and belongings still strewn about the common area and all the locked compartments undisturbed. "Looks like all our stuff is safe, too." I give Sena a knowing look. Her cloak is still there, still tucked away, waiting for her. True happiness lights up her face.

Lyria smacks me on the shoulder lightly and I wince. "Thanks for taking care of my ship, even if it is a little rough around the edges."

"Wait, your ship?" Sena asks in surprise.

"Yep," she says. "My ship, which Kiran and I left here so Remy would have a way to get off-world."

I laugh. I should've known. I can practically picture Lyria dragging Kiran out of Verem after she blackmailed him into helping her. They took another ship and left me this one and now I know why. I also know what Lyria had over him all this time. What Nova would never allow. What got him sent to reconditioning over and over again.

The way he felt about me.

No matter how many times he was tortured by Nova, he never stopped caring for me. Over the last few days in bed, I've slowly let his words sink in, let myself think about him here and there, stopping the thoughts when his loss makes my chest ache too much. Part of me is still mad at him. Mad that he left the safety of the den and got caught by Weiland's commandos. Mad that he stepped in the way of the knife.

Mad that he never told me the whole truth, never gave me a chance to figure out how I feel about him.

He loved me. I had my issues with the ways he chose to show it. But he was raised in a lab without any sort of guide or examples. I can't fully blame him for trying to protect me the only way he knew how. I'm still struggling to figure out my own impulses, my own feelings. Kiran deserved a chance to be better, too. I understand that now, even if he's . . .

I can't bring myself to think that he's gone. Lyria said there was no sign of him in the ruins of the tower, but she doesn't know him like I do. Doesn't know what he's capable of. If anyone could survive a blast like that, it's him. I eye Lyria standing next to my ship. I could hitch a ride back to Verem and look through the rubble myself. Even if Nova took him, he'd leave some sort of clue for me. I know he would.

"So." Sena's voice pulls me from my plotting. "We saved Maraas. What's our next move?" She looks to me, but it's not about what I need, not anymore. It's about how I can help. My eyes jump to Lyria.

"Maraas is just the beginning," she says, steel in her voice. "I'm going to finish what we started and take back my father's empire from the man who stole it all."

"Dekkard." I say his name with venom. Even if he is a murderer, he's still just Nova's pawn. And if there's any chance that Kiran survived, there's only one place he'll be. . . .

"Nova was behind all of Dekkard's moves," I say. "What do you say we pay them a visit, too?"

Lyria raises an eyebrow while Sena shakes her head.

"You did say you wanted to fight the corpos when we left Tundar."

Emeko crosses her arms, a smile in her brown eyes. "Oh, I see how it is. You're fighting more corpos and now shadowy organizations, too? Sounds like you'll need my help. You know you lot couldn't have gotten this far without me."

"It won't be easy," Lyria says to the scavver.

Emeko shrugs. "Nothing ever gets easier, syndicate princess.

You just have to get stronger." She locks eyes with Sena, and they share a smile.

I stare at the four of them. At my friends. At the wolf ready on our heels. At the world that broke me before but has somehow healed the wounds under my skin. My thoughts jump to Kiran. He's actually the catalyst that brought us all together, made everything possible.

He's out there still; I know he is. Like me, he's hard to kill. And I won't let Nova have him, even if I have to take apart every single one of its ships, piece by piece. I won't stop and I'll never yield because Kiran was never theirs to have in the first place.

Neither was I.

"Well, Remy? What do you think?" Sena asks as Iska barks, feeling our excitement.

"I think it's time to light a fire under some corpo asses." I grin, a plan beginning to form in the back of my mind. It's messy and impulsive and pushes limits to the extreme. But it will work. I'll make sure of it.

After all, I wasn't engineered to lose.

ACKNOWLEDGMENTS

Sequels and second books are often the hardest for debut authors to write and this book was no exception. Thankfully, I had the most amazing editor to hold my hand through the worst of it. The book you've just finished reading (or listening to) has been years in the making—many years and many, many drafts. It would not even remotely resemble a book if it hadn't been for my editor. She found the kernels of what I wanted to say, even when they were so buried I couldn't see them myself. Thank you, Eileen, for lighting my path and showing me the way through this process. It was a tangled, dense jungle itself, but we made it! Thank you, thank you, thank you.

To everyone who picked up *Cold the Night, Fast the Wolves* and loved it: the librarians and reading groups, the book box subscribers, my work colleagues, Kristi Tutt (a Long family super fan), the folks who bought it on a whim in an airport, every reader who wrote a review or told their friends to buy it—I cannot thank all of you enough for the kind words, for the fun fan art, for the excitement during every announcement, for every comment and small moment of support. Your messages on Instagram or surprise emails sustained me when I was in the hardest parts of drafting. You are why Remy's book exists. You are why I am still writing.

To everyone on my team: from my agent, Alexandra, for always championing me, to the Wednesday folks—you are all amazing to work with. Thank you for being so kind, so excited, and so supportive along every step. Whether it was organizing events or handling my many questions, you all had my back every time and didn't hesitate to figure out what was best for me and for this story. Lisa Bonvissuto, thank you for organizing literally all the things. I'd feel very lost if not for you! Special thanks also to Brant Janeway, Mary Moates, Sarah Bonamino, and Alexis Neuville for handling all the marketing and publicity for Remy's story. And to everyone I don't know by name (the copy editors, proofreaders, assistants, all of you), thank you for all of your endless help. This book is better because of you.

And especially to the Wednesday design team: this cover blew my mind. I didn't know how we were going to possibly match the cover for *CTNFTW*, but somehow Olga Grlic and Luisa Preissler went above and beyond what I could ever imagine. Working with all of you on both covers has been such a joy, and I know that's not something authors always get to say. So thank you for being so talented and amazing.

To the writers and friends who read (or suffered through) early, early versions of this draft and helped me through edits, I'd probably just wither and die without all of you. Special, special thanks to Lyssa Mia Smith, Rochelle Hassan, and Kate Dylan. Y'all are my ride or dies, and I'll never stop being thankful. Nor will I ever stop being obsessed with you and your books. To Claire Winn, Xiran Jay Zhao, and the many other sci-fi writers I've made friends with since debuting, thank you for welcoming me to the coolest club ever.

To Caitlin and Kendra, thank you for your never-ending words of wisdom and your constant support. I never would've made it this far without either of you. Thank you for being amazing writers along this crazy roller coaster with me.

· To all the Slackers, each one of you gives me life every day. Lyssa, Rochelle, Elvin, Mary, Jessica, Rachel, Marisa, Susan, Alexis, Chad, Ruby, Nanci, Jacki, Leslie, Meryl, Rosie, and Rowyn. I expect to be slacking with y'all about controversial food and monster picks when we're old and gray and even more melodramatic than now.

To all my friends. Remy's story is one of friendship and discovery, none of which I'd be able to write about with you. Lauren, Courtney, Cassie, the Megans, Emma, Katie, Wu, Nani, thank you for showing me what friendship means over and over again with your kindness and generosity. To Vanessa, this book is for you in case you missed it in the front. I hope I did better than Monica and actually made you cry. If not, I will have to try harder.

Of course, endless thanks to my family. To Mom and Dad, who taught me to love stories and who also push my books on all of their friends. To Tricia and JD, for reading everything I write at least seven times and for screaming at every milestone along with me. I couldn't ask for better siblings. To Paw Paw and the whole Rush and deVilliers clan, you all share books like food and make sure everyone you know has read mine. Love y'all.

To everyone at Tankhead, training with all of you is the light

ACKNOWLEDGMENTS

of my day. Thanks for all the elbows, knees, and sweeps. And for buying my books.

Finally, to Gallen. Thank you for forcing me to take breaks and for bringing me bubble tea. And all the other things you do every day.